The Naked Truth

'Remember, Callie,' Eldritch murmured, 'your Tarot reading said you had to question who was in control.'

Callie swallowed hard. 'I don't have to question that. I know who's in control.'

Her voice sounded unconvincing, even to herself.

'Are you sure about that?' Eldritch stood up, pushing his hands into his pockets. 'Or do you want to find out?'

Callie's courage suddenly faltered. It wasn't that she didn't trust Eldritch, but she'd never been with anyone like him in her life. Then an inner voice reminded her that sex didn't have to be all hearts and roses. Thoughts of being tied down and a dark, male voice had been invading her mind that past week. It was now or never.

The Naked Truth

NATASHA ROSTOVA

BLACK
lace

Black Lace novels contain sexual fantasies.
In real life, make sure you practise safe sex.

First published in 2000 by
Black Lace
Thames Wharf Studios,
Rainville Road, London W6 9HA

Typeset by SetSystems Ltd, Saffron Walden, Essex
Printed and bound by Mackays of Chatham PLC

ISBN 0 352 33497 5

Chapter One

'You look rather sluttish.'

Callie Waterford's head snapped up. She stared at her husband in shock. 'Excuse me?'

Logan's dark gaze skimmed over the figure-hugging silk dress Callie wore. 'Where did you get that dress? I certainly didn't buy it for you.'

Callie's fingers tightened on the bangle she was fastening around her wrist. 'No, you didn't. Gloria gave it to me a few months ago.'

'Ah, well, that explains it. Your sister wouldn't know decency if she took a bath in it. That dress is too short.'

Callie wondered briefly if he was joking, but she knew that Logan never joked. She glanced down at her sleeveless dress, which fell to mid-thigh in a clingy sheet of black silk. The scooped neckline revealed more than a hint of cleavage. Maybe it wasn't something Callie would have chosen for herself, but Gloria always knew what was fashionable.

'It's perfectly decent,' she retorted. 'Just because you didn't hand-pick it, it doesn't mean it makes me look like a slut.'

'Bend over.'

'What?'

'Bend over,' Logan repeated. 'I hope you're at least wearing a bra. Chances are anyone could see clear down that neckline.'

'Well, then, it's a lucky thing I usually stand upright and not bent over, isn't it?'

Logan's mouth tightened. 'Callie, you know that I expect you to present yourself accordingly to my business associates.'

Callie struggled not to be irritated by his pompous attitude, but failed miserably. 'Excuse me, Mr Prim, but the fact that I'm presenting myself at all to your stuffy associates is accordance enough for me.'

Logan sighed. 'Now what does that mean?'

'Your friends are more boring than a lecture on quantum mechanics. And it's a good thing I'm showing a little leg, or else Harold Winningham would put himself into a coma discussing his latest case.'

'There is no need to be melodramatic.' Logan turned to the mirror and began fastening his tie.

Callie let out a puff of pure indignation. 'Melodramatic? Me? You're the one who's acting as if I should be wearing a nun's habit.'

'I did not say that. I only expect you not to look like a streetwalker.'

'My God, Logan, I hope you're going in for surgery soon.'

'What are you talking about?'

'You need to get that stick removed. You know, the one up your arse.'

'Don't be childish, Callie.'

'Then don't criticise me so rudely,' Callie replied, disliking the sharp note in her voice. She had begun to hate showing her own emotions because any display of them always felt like surrender. In their stilted conversations, the unspoken prize went to the person who could restrain their emotions. Unfortunately, Logan always won. 'I'm your wife, not some little chippy you can order to your own specifications.'

Logan looked at her, his entire body perfectly still. Even the air around him seemed unmoving, as if he could command its very inertia. 'I'm aware of that. However, I also know that you come from quite a different background than mine.'

Callie's hands clenched into fists at her sides. She couldn't stand it when he reminded her that he came from silk ties, mahogany furniture, and country clubs, while she had been reared amidst secondhand clothes, TV dinners and state schools. It made her remember that she had been acceptable in Savannah society only through her association with her half-sister. Gloria was firmly ensconced in the upper echelons of society thanks to her mother's family, who could trace their money back to Civil War days. Callie's mother, on the other hand, had spent her life working as a clerk in a grocery store. The working-class association was one that never failed to rankle Callie, not because she was ashamed of her roots but because they gave Logan fodder for derision.

'Yes, Logan, you were rich, I was poor,' she snapped. 'What do you mean by bringing that up?'

'It means that I would have expected you to have learned by now.'

'Learned what? How to do everything according to how *you* want it done? Forgive me, but that's obviously a lesson I intend to have dropped from the curriculum.'

'I'm beginning to realise that.' Logan picked up a comb and ran it through his thick, dark hair. 'You know, I think it would be a good idea if you didn't see your sister quite as much.'

'This has nothing to do with Gloria!' Anger simmered through Callie's blood. 'Besides, she's the one who introduced us, or have you forgotten that? I never would have been accepted into society if it hadn't been for her.'

'Your sister rivals Meryl Streep when it comes to her acting ability,' Logan replied. 'I only wish that the ladies of Savannah could see past her proper facade. It would

3

be like turning over a rock to reveal the worms underneath.'

'Look, you knew both me and my family when you chose to marry me,' Callie reminded him. 'You had your pick of any number of pink-and-lace virgins from proper Savannah families so, if you regret your decision now, then don't you dare take it out on me.'

Turning her back on him, she plunked herself down at the dressing table and started applying mascara with a shaking hand. So he thought she looked like a hooker, did he? Fine, then, she'd give him plenty of hooker. The pompous ass.

Truth be told, as much as she hated admitting this to herself, she often wondered what Logan had seen in her when he asked her to marry him three years ago. They'd known each other for less than a month after Gloria first introduced them. While Callie had been rather infatuated with his powerful personality, he was ten years older than her and light years apart in social standing and bearing. She had hardly expected a relationship with him, let alone marriage.

Callie shook her head at the reflection that stared back at her from the mirror. She supposed now that all those differences should have given her a clue as to their chance at a successful future. Or lack thereof.

After putting on enough mascara to make her eyelashes look like Liza Minelli's, Callie stroked her cheeks with rouge and applied the reddest lipstick she could find. She enhanced the effect with dangly, silver earrings and the highest pair of black heels she owned.

Logan's eyes narrowed with disapproval when she turned back to face him. 'Callie, you know I dislike it when you behave this way.'

'Do you?' Callie gathered her shoulder-length brown hair into a twist and pinned it up. 'Well, I happen to dislike it when you treat me like a piece of trash.'

'I'm doing no such thing.' Logan turned and headed

4

for the door. 'Our guests will be here any minute now. I want you to change into something more acceptable.'

'This is as acceptable as I'm going to get,' Callie retorted.

'As you wish. Then this conversation is over.'

'The hell it is,' Callie muttered as she followed him down the carpeted stairs into the hall.

Elegance dominated the antebellum southern mansion, a luxurious display case for mahogany antiques and rich oil paintings designed to show just how far back her husband's heritage and money went. Callie appreciated the house on an intellectual level, the way one would appreciate a museum, but she had never felt at home here.

She cast Logan a sideways glance as they went into the sitting room to wait for their guests. He looked quite regal and autocratic in a dark suit and tie, his hair brushed away from his forehead to enhance the sharp planes of his features. He appeared perfectly suited to the immaculate decor of the mansion, reminding Callie of a museum sculpture: chiselled, cold, remote and utterly untouchable.

'Would you like a drink?' Logan asked cordially as he headed for the drinks cabinet.

The man could change moods like a chameleon changes colours, Callie thought. Only with Logan, it wasn't so much a change, but simply a variation of the same, constant mood.

'Just a glass of red wine, please.' She sat down on a leather chair, feeling like a stranger in her own home.

An intricate Oriental carpet covered the floor, and the chairs and chaise longues were covered with buttery silk. An oil painting of Logan's father hung over the fireplace mantel. Delicious scents of baked salmon and wild rice drifted from the kitchen, where the caterers were busy finishing their preparations for dinner.

Callie stared at the painting of Logan's father; she was uncomfortable now at the striking resemblance of father and son. Edward Waterford sat on a wing-backed, leather chair, looking at her with cold, varnished eyes. His features were strong, carved with the distinctive marks of time. He appeared very distinguished with his thick, grey hair and moustache, and yet totally remote. Callie wondered what kind of person he had been. She had never met her father-in-law, since he had died ten years ago, but she had always felt as if his presence hung like a dark, oppressive curtain over this house.

'Logan, what was your relationship with your father like?' she asked.

After the briefest hesitation, he glanced at her. 'My father?'

'Yes. You've never told me about him.'

Logan's shoulders lifted in a shrug. 'There's nothing to tell. He was my father.'

'Yes, but you must have had some kind of a relationship with him.'

'Not really.'

'Well, did he take you places?' Callie persisted. 'Fishing, sporting events, holidays?'

'Sometimes.'

'Did he teach you how to make sentences out of single words?'

He gave her a derisive look. Then the doorbell rang, and Callie stood to greet the six guests as they filed into the sitting room. The three couples were all associated with Logan's law firm and had long ago secured their positions as some of Savannah's most valued citizens.

'Callie, darling, you look lovely.' Anna Winningham's ice-blue gaze roved over Callie's figure, her lips curving into a plastic smile. 'What a beautiful dress.'

Her voice was edged with the slightest hint of disapproval, which made Callie smile. She glanced at Logan, noticing that he, too, hadn't missed Anna's undertone.

'Callie's sister purchased it for her,' he said by way of an explanation.

'I see. Gloria always did have her own style.'

6

'Evening, Callie.' Anna's husband Harold leant over to kiss Callie's cheek, making a point of wrapping his arm around her waist.

For the sole purpose of provoking Logan, Callie returned Harold's greeting with a bit more enthusiasm than was required.

'Harold, we're so pleased you could come,' she said, pressing her body full up against his. Then she winced when she felt his hips thrust against hers. 'What can we get you to drink?'

Logan gave Callie a mild glare, but turned and went back to the bar. After the guests had been secured with glasses in hand, Callie asked the caterers to start serving the hors d'oeuvres. She picked up her wineglass and sat down next to Stan Gerome, crossing her legs so that her skirt rode even further up her thighs.

'So, Stan,' she murmured, placing her hand on his arm. 'Logan tells me you just won a murder case. That must have been just fascinating.'

'Yes, it involved a robbery.' Stan blinked at her through his horn-rimmed glasses and tugged at the knot of his tie as if it were too tight.

'Really,' Callie drawled. 'Tell me about it.'

She stifled a yawn as Stan started going on about the case. She glanced in Logan's direction, not surprised to discover that he was watching her with more than a hint of contempt.

'Callie, some of our guests haven't had any hors d'oeuvres yet,' he said.

'I'm terribly sorry about that.' Callie turned to Stan and put her hand on his leg. 'Excuse me for a moment, would you, please? The master of the house requires my attention.'

She smiled, letting her breasts brush against his arm as she stood. She picked up a platter of hors d'oeuvres and walked over to Michael Richmond with another inviting smile. Her face was beginning to hurt, but she'd smile all evening if she had to.

7

'Michael, please, have some of this caviar. It's imported and quite delicious.' She leant down so that he could reach the platter, and the front of her dress gaped slightly, allowing him a full view of her small, lace-cupped breasts.

Callie almost chuckled at the way Michael's gaze darted quickly to ogle her breasts, as if she wouldn't notice. She didn't exactly possess huge mounds of over-flowing flesh, but apparently men would look at any-thing. Especially if they knew that the woman was off limits.

'And may I get you another drink?' She took his glass from him, brushing her fingers over his hand. 'Scotch on the rocks coming up.'

Logan strode over to meet her at the bar. His fingers wrapped around her arm. A quiver of alarm travelled through her as she realised she might be carrying this too far, but she'd be damned if she would let him talk to her as if she were a kept woman rather than his wife.

'Stop this behaviour right now,' Logan said, his voice low. 'You're acting like a perfect –'

Callie jerked around to glare at him. 'A perfect what?' she interrupted. 'A slut? Well, that's what I look like, apparently, so I might as well act the part.'

She yanked her arm out of his grasp and returned to Michael. She spent the remainder of the evening playing silly, flirting games with the men, aware all the while that she was irritating her husband. There was some-thing oddly arousing about this little game, knowing these other men were wanting her sexually. Warmth spread between her legs, making her press her thighs together underneath the dinner table and wish she had the kind of husband who didn't mind slipping away from a party to indulge in a quick fuck.

She looked at Logan and almost laughed. He didn't even indulge in furtive touching, either at dinner parties or anywhere else.

When they returned to the sitting room for coffee,

Callie made a point of sitting close to Stan again, so close that their thighs touched. Yet, as the evening drew to a close, she began to get a little nervous. There wasn't much Logan could do with guests around, but being alone with him was a whole other story.

He closed the door behind the Winninghams and turned to stride up the stairs. Callie went into the kitchen, where the caterers were finishing their cleaning.

'Send us the bill, please, Anita,' she told the head caterer, 'Thanks so much. Everything was just delicious.'

Anita smiled with pleasure. 'Thank you, Mrs Waterford. Please call us again for your next event.'

'I'll be sure to do that.' Callie saw them out and locked the door behind them.

She went slowly upstairs to the bedroom, irritated with herself for feeling nervous about facing her husband. It was just Logan, after all. Her inflexible, controlled, rigid husband who had a solid rod of steel in place of a spine.

She went into the bedroom, eyeing Logan cautiously. He had removed his jacket and tie and was standing near the armoire, his dark head bent as he unfastened his cuff links.

Callie gazed at him for a moment as an unexpected pang of regret coursed through her. He was a hardworking man, successful and handsome. Yes, he was far too set in his ways, but he had never been unfaithful or abusive to her. So why did it always feel as if she was living with a stranger?

With a sigh, she kicked off her heeled shoes and wriggled her aching toes in bliss. She went into the bathroom and took a shower, scrubbing off her heavy make-up. After slipping into her simple, cotton nightshirt, she went back into the bedroom.

Logan was already in bed, his attention focused on a new book. Callie's gaze skimmed over the muscled length of his body, which reminded her that he had a major physical advantage over her. An advantage he never chose to use, either for pleasure or pain.

She turned back the covers and slipped into bed beside him, somewhat irked by his lack of response to her behaviour.

'Aren't you going to yell at me?' she asked rhetorically. Logan never yelled.

He peered at her over the top of his reading glasses. 'Why? Because you chose to make a complete fool out of yourself?'

'Did I?' Callie replied. 'Funny, your associates didn't seem to think there was anything foolish about my behaviour. Quite the contrary, in fact.'

Only the clenching of Logan's jaw betrayed his irritation. 'My associates know quite well what kind of background you come from. All you did was confirm their worse suspicions about you.'

A wash of anger spread through Callie. She held up her hand to stop his words.

'Don't do it, Logan. Don't you dare use my past as an excuse. Yes, I grew up poor, but only because my father lied outright to my mother.'

Despite his lack of forcefulness, Logan did always seem to know exactly how to infuriate her, Callie thought reluctantly. She hated being reminded of the confusion and despair of her childhood. Not only had her father never told her mother that he already had a wife and daughter, but he wouldn't even acknowledge initially that Callie was his child.

'You might have been better off if your father had never told the truth,' Logan replied in a dry tone. 'Then you wouldn't have been mixed up with Gloria.'

'I didn't get "mixed up" with her! She's my sister. When her mother found out about me and my mother, she was the one who forced her husband to take responsibility. Gloria's mother is the only person I know who didn't give a damn what people thought. She knew that none of it was my fault. She welcomed me into her

10

home and wanted me to know my sister. I'll always be grateful to her, but I will never forget where I came from. And I certainly won't stand for your contempt!'

'Then don't earn it,' Logan said. He removed his glasses. 'Your behaviour was reprehensible. I hope you know I won't stand for it a second time.'

'What's making you stand for it the first time?' Callie taunted. She fairly ached to get a response from him. And something more than his damn, measured words.

'I'm hoping you'll realise how foolish you're being.'

Frustrated beyond all measure, Callie slid across the expanse of the bed towards him. She reached under the covers to slid her hand over his thigh, liking the sensation of hair-roughened muscle underneath her palm. She'd always appreciated Logan's body so much. Pity the man didn't use it more effectively in the bedroom.

'You mean you didn't like it?' she asked softly, rubbing her knuckles over the thin cotton of his boxer shorts and the bulge underneath them. 'Watching those men watching me, wondering what they were thinking, if they were imagining –'

'Callie, stop it.' Even as Logan said the words, Callie felt his penis swell underneath her fingertips.

Callie put her lips against his ear and reached out to tickle his earlobe with her tongue. Arousal quickened in her, spreading long fingers over her belly. She was still turned on from her flirtatious games at the party, and she hoped she could convince her husband to alleviate some of her tension.

'Come on, Logan,' she murmured huskily. 'Don't you want to fuck me now?'

'Don't talk like that.'

'Like what? Fuck me?' Callie eased her hand under the waistband of his shorts to grasp the hard warmth of his cock. The mere touch of him caused a pulse of responding need to dampen her pussy. 'But that's how a slut talks.'

She rubbed her other hand over the mat of dark hair

11

on his chest, gently tweaking his flat, male nipples into little points. His body never failed to fascinate and arouse her, but the man himself rarely followed up to the level she craved.

'Look, if you want to have sex, fine,' Logan said. 'But none of that kind of talk, do you hear me?'

Callie suddenly couldn't help grinning. 'You are such a pompous ass, did you know that?'

'I'll take that as a compliment.'

'You'd better, since it's the only one you'll get from me.'

Still thinking she could really get him going, Callie slid her leg between his and began pressing kisses over his neck and chest. He smelled perfectly delicious, all warm, male flesh with a hint of woody aftershave. Callie squeezed his cock and rubbed her fingers over the underside. A drop of moisture licked at her fingers, and she massaged it gently back into his skin. She sidled down to capture one of his nipples between her teeth, pressing her breasts against his abdomen. She licked and kissed a path down his belly to his groin, hungering to take his hard flesh in her mouth and suck him dry.

Logan's breathing had increased during her ministrations, but then his hand clamped around the back of her neck. 'What are you doing?'

Callie glanced up at him with a glint in her eye. 'I'm trying to give you a blow job, but you'll have to let go of me first.'

Logan frowned. 'Not now, Callie.'

She let out her breath in exasperation. 'What do you mean, not now? You've never let me do this.'

'So why start?'

With a groan of frustration, Callie pushed herself away from him and sat up. 'It's a perfectly normal act, Logan.'

'I'm aware of what it is.' Logan set his book on the bedside table and turned to grasp her shoulders, pulling her back towards him. His mouth met hers in a familiar,

12

comfortable kiss, his tongue sliding over her lower lip. He pressed her back against the pillows and grasped her nightshirt in his hands. Callie watched him as he pulled the shirt up over her hips, wondering if the man ever felt anything at all. His expression was virtually impassive. How flattering that she could inspire such lust in a man.

Callie sighed. Logan's hands slipped between her legs to push them apart, his fingers delving into the folds of her pussy.

'Well, I see you're already ready,' he observed.

'It turned me on, you know,' Callie replied, reaching out to slide her hands over his chest. 'Knowing those men wanted me.'

'I really wish you would find another way to get turned on. That was very indecent. You have my reputation to consider, too, you know.'

'Yes, I know,' Callie muttered. She squirmed underneath him, wishing he would take off her nightshirt completely and fondle her breasts. 'Logan –'

'Hush.'

Callie bit her lip in annoyance. He never spoke when they made love, never said a word, touching her in his quiet, restrained way as if she might break. He settled between her thighs, reaching down to guide his penis into her as if he were threading the eye of a needle. His breathing grew ragged, hot against her skin, as he pushed her open for his slow penetration.

Grasping the hem of her nightshirt, Callie pulled it over her head. She wrapped her arms around Logan's back, flexing her fingers against his smooth muscles. Her nipples brushed deliciously against his chest, stimulating her arousal all the more. She reached down to grip his hard buttocks, forcing him closer.

'Harder,' she whispered, her voice strained as he began thrusting into her with measured control. She longed to feel him really pound into her with a force that would shake her very soul; to feel him drive into her until he could go no further.

'Shh.' Logan slid his fingers down to rub her clit with deliberate concentration.

Callie nearly groaned in frustration over his lack of passion. Heaven forbid anything should make him actually enjoy the sexual act.

She wanted to plead with him, wanted to scream at him to fuck her, to squeal like a banshee and feel her breasts bounce with the force of his thrusts, but she knew, as she always did, that her pleas would be to no avail. She closed her eyes to block out the sight of her husband's dispassionate features and let her mind fill with images of a much rawer variety. An orgiastic feast, that's what she wanted; one in which she was the main course and the guests were all hulking men with pricks like tree trunks and no hesitations about fucking her to the edge of consciousness. Wine would flow freely at this bacchanalian celebration, lubricating their senses and eradicating their inhibitions. She'd be splayed out on a table, every orifice open for penetration, her skin damp with sweat and the air filled with the musky scent of sex. Gold jewellery would drip from her neck and silver rings encircle her fingers and toes, as if she were a sacrifice laid out for the pleasure of the gods.

The men would pour wine from their mouths into hers, then dribble it into her navel and lick it up with thirsty tongues. They would pour it into her pussy and drink as if she were their only oasis in the parched heat of a desert, their lips sucking her until she had to beg them to please stop. Then rough, callused hands would grab at her breasts and pinch her nipples, then push her thighs apart so that, one after another, the men could drive relentlessly into her. Grunting and panting, they would use her as if they hadn't had a woman in years, pumping into her cunt like oil drills and forcing her into every conceivable position.

She would then be on her hands and knees, her

buttocks thrust into the air as one man filled her from behind and another pushed his cock into her mouth, then on her back with her knees pushed clear up to her shoulders, then on her side with her leg over a man's shoulder. It would last for such a long time that she'd be sore from all the thrusting, her nipples swollen from bites, her jaw aching from sucking cock after cock, the bitter taste of come coating her tongue. And every man at the banquet would still be craving her, their appetites insatiable. They would let her rest and drink wine to cleanse her mouth. A lush, female servant with breasts spilling from her bodice would wipe Callie's tender pussy with a perfumed cloth before the men started getting restless and hard with the need to fuck her once more. And then it would start all over again as they made her straddle one of the men and ride him hard. Then she would bend forwards so that another man could probe at her arse, forcing her open until she was filled with two cocks in a delicious double penetration that left her gasping and exhausted.

'Wider.' Logan's whispered command broke through the haze of Callie's fantasy.

Reluctantly, she opened her eyes to look at him as she wrapped her legs around his back. Logan's hips pushed against her inner thighs, his chest pressing against her breasts as his cock slid in and out of her with gentle thrusts; so restrained that even his climax barely jerked his body against her. His low groan sounded as stifled as Callie's whimpers. Thanks to her fantasy, she came with a ripple of small shudders that vibrated pleasantly through her body but hardly satisfied her intense need. Logan held her against him and used his fingers to milk the last, sweet sensations from her. As soon as their breathing quietened, he moved away from her and lay back on his side of the bed.

Callie's chest tightened. She found her discarded nightshirt and slipped it on, suddenly disliking her nakedness. She looked at her husband for a moment, the shadows crawling over his hard, straight features – features that were so often completely inscrutable. His eyelashes lay like tiny feathers against his cheeks. She wanted to reach out and touch him, to let her fingertips wander over his face and into his thick, black hair, but then he spoke.

'Go to sleep, calla lily,' Logan said, his voice thick with impending slumber.

'Are you having an affair?'

Logan opened his eyes to look at her. 'Where in the hell did that come from?'

The knot in Callie's chest tightened. 'You've never been exactly passionate with me. I was wondering if you are with someone else.'

'Don't be ridiculous. I've never been unfaithful to you.'

'Then what's the matter?'

'The *matter* is that you're being foolish.' He closed his eyes again, his voice as flat and hard as a board. 'Callie, go to sleep.'

Without touching him, Callie turned her back on Logan and pulled the sheet over her body.

'Ladies, ladies!' Marcia Garrett stood up in front of the group of women and clapped her hands sharply. 'May I have your attention, please? This meeting must come to order.'

The fifty women settled down from their weekly gossip and turned their attention to Marcia, a tall, slender blonde dressed to the nines in a peach-coloured, linen suit with matching fingernail polish, a French twist and a strand of pearls around her neck.

'We've decided that this summer's charity project will be a Ladies' Guild cookbook,' Marcia announced. 'We'd like everyone to contribute their favourite recipes and menus.'

Sitting towards the back of the room, Callie brushed a piece of lint off her skirt and wondered just how long it took Marcia Garrett to prepare to present herself to the world every day.

'You know, her husband is fucking her niece,' said a low voice in Callie's ear.

Callie turned to stare at her sister in surprise. 'You're joking.'

Gloria Harper shook her head, a little smile playing about her perfectly lined lips. Her streaked, blonde hair was teased into a coif that resembled a large cream puff, and her face was enhanced by expensive cosmetics. Like most of the other women, she wore a designer suit, except hers revealed a substantial amount of abundant cleavage.

'I most certainly am not. The girl is nineteen, can you believe that? Her pussy must be as tight as a vise.'

Callie stifled a chuckle. It was always funny to hear coarse words in Gloria's honeyed, cloud-like voice. 'Does Marcia know?'

'She suspects, but of course she's not going to leave Roger,' Gloria whispered. 'She told me that last month. He has too much money, and he made her sign a prenuptial agreement. If she leaves him, she's finished in society.'

Callie's amusement drained quickly as she thought about Marcia's plight. Pity that so many women were in similar situations. At least Logan had never asked her to sign a prenuptial agreement, not that she wanted any of his money anyway.

'That's a bit sad,' she murmured.

'Don't bother feeling sorry for Marcia, sugar,' Gloria whispered. 'She has a few secrets herself, you know.'

'Callie and Gloria, will you volunteer to be in charge of collecting the recipes?' Marcia called.

'Yes, Marcia, we'd be most delighted,' Gloria replied in a cheery voice. 'What a wonderful idea this is.'

The women all applauded politely in agreement as Marcia beamed. She went on talking about other Ladies' Guild projects and charities before the meeting was adjourned. Then they gathered around the side table, where coffee and cakes had been laid out.

'Callie, thank you again for a lovely evening the other night.' A red-tipped hand grasped Callie's arm, and she turned to face Anna Winningham. 'Harold and I enjoyed ourselves.'

'Thank you for coming,' Callie replied, easing her arm out of the other woman's grip. 'You know my sister Gloria.'

'Of course.' The two women exchanged air kisses.

'Harold was saying what a lucky man Logan is to have a wife like you,' Anna went on, her voice dripping with such sweetness that Callie thought she would surely be plagued by cavities.

'That's very kind,' Callie replied.

'Such a nice figure and all, although of course you're not exactly a Playboy Bunny, are you?'

Callie sensed Gloria stiffen in indignation. At thirty-five, Gloria was eight years older than Callie and always got her feathers ruffled when someone insulted her younger sister.

'Well, Anna, isn't it interesting how that didn't seem to have bothered your husband?' Gloria retorted.

Anna's lips thinned into a tight line. 'How would you know, Gloria?'

'Oh, please.' Gloria waved her hand in the air dismissingly. 'Everyone knows that your husband has an eye for any woman in town. So long as she's not you, of course.'

'How dare you!' Anna gasped in outrage, two spots of colour appearing on her white cheeks. 'You weren't even there last night, although I should tell you that your sister was behaving like quite a little flirt.'

'Good for her,' Gloria said. 'It seems to have worked on your husband.'

Anna's eyes narrowed as she turned her attention to Callie. 'Are you sleeping with my husband? Because if you are, I'm going to drag your name through the mud so quickly your head will spin. And believe me, Callie, it wouldn't take much to do that.'

'Anna, I wouldn't sleep with your husband for all the orgasms in Italy.'

'Yes, and please refrain from insulting my sister,' Gloria chimed in. 'With a husband like Logan, you think she's going to go after Harold Winningham? Please, Anna. I thought even you could work out something as simple as that.'

'You didn't see her rubbing up against my husband.' Anna gave Callie a warning look. 'If I find out you've been sniffing around Harold, I warn you, you'll pay for it.'

'No need to worry,' Gloria replied. 'Tell Harold he's just going to have to continue fantasising about Callie while he's fucking you.'

A few heads turned in their direction. Anna's skin darkened to a deep red before she spun on her heel and stalked away.

'Bitch,' Gloria said cheerfully. She plucked a teacake off the table and popped it in her mouth. 'Was she right, though? You actually flirted? That's not like you, sugar.'

'Well, I'm not a demure Miss Muffet,' Callie replied. She was somewhat irked by Gloria's surprise, especially since she considered herself to be quite confident. More so than most women would be if they had been stifled in such a marriage, anyway.

Still, she had always known that she didn't fit into the upper stratum of society in which Logan and her sister moved with such fluid ease. No, Callie had always harboured a fear that she would say or do the wrong thing, that she would embarrass Logan somehow. Or that the polished women with their perfect fingernails and hair would see through her fragile veneer to the lower-class roots from which she had sprung.

'I never said you were,' Gloria said, 'But you've never been a flirt, either.'

'Well, Logan and I were arguing, and I guess I was

trying to prove a point,' Callie admitted. 'It was pretty stupid, but I wanted to see how he would react.'

'And how did he react?'

'In the same disapproving way he always does. I don't know why I expected anything different.'

Gloria glanced around and took Callie's arm. 'Let's get out of here. The walls not only have ears, but also very busy mouths. And I could use a drink.'

Callie suppressed the urge to comment on Gloria's need for a drink in the middle of the afternoon. She picked up her handbag and followed her sister outside. The air was damp and hot as the sun began burning through the river fog.

Callie took a deep breath as they walked, enjoying the air and the historic nature of this part of the city. The Old Savannah landscape was a mixture of crumbling Victorian mansions, townhouses embellished with pil-lared porches and wrought-iron balconies, and rows of shops and stores. Oak trees dripping with Spanish moss appeared like huge giants guarding their lair.

'Aren't we going to 45 South?' Callie asked, realising that her sister was leading her to a side street off Martin Luther King boulevard.

'I don't want to go there,' Gloria replied. 'I'm sick of the smell of perfume and hair spray. Come on.'

She curled her hand around Callie's arm and guided her towards a set of concrete steps that led to a dank, greasy pub with a flashing, neon beer sign in the win-dow. Callie blinked as they stepped inside, waiting for her eyes to adjust to the dim light. A long, scarred bar dominated the room, along with a few wooden tables and chairs. A few dockers in torn jeans and T-shirts stood around drinking beer and shooting pool. Several low whistles reverberated in the air as Callie and Gloria walked to the bar.

'What are we doing here?' Callie hissed, feeling more than a little out of place and conspicuous in her pale blue suit.

'Getting away from it all, sugar.' Gloria hitched herself up on to a barstool, letting her skirt ride up her thighs as she tossed a smile in the barman's direction. 'Hello, Roger. Vodka martini, no ice, two olives. Shaken, not stirred.'

'Good to see you again, Gloria.' Roger tore his gaze away from Gloria's cleavage long enough to look at Callie. 'And for you?'

'Just a glass of iced tea, please,' Callie requested.

'God, Callie, you're not at the Ladies' Guild meeting anymore,' Gloria said derisively. She looked at Roger. 'She'll have a martini as well.'

After the barman placed two glasses in front of them, Gloria glanced at her sister.

'I hope you and Logan are planning to attend my charity ball next month,' she said.

'I don't know, Gloria. Logan and I aren't getting on so well.'

'One little tiff is nothing.'

'It's not a little tiff. We're really not getting on.'

'What are you talking about? You and Logan get along perfectly well.'

'Sure, in public. Behind closed doors is another story.'

Gloria frowned. 'He doesn't slap you around, does he?'

'Heavens, no.' Callie took a sip of the potent martini. She was aware that most of the men in the room were watching them. 'That would require that he actually exhibit an emotion besides disapproval.'

'Well, it's not as if you're deprived,' Gloria remarked. She downed half her martini and gave a happy sigh. 'Married to one of the most respected men in town, not to mention one of the sexiest, living in a gorgeous mansion, free to come and go as you please. You must admit it's a life you never thought you'd have.'

'That's true,' Callie allowed. 'But that doesn't mean I necessarily like it.'

21

'For heaven's sake, Callie, you just have to get used to it.'

'I've had three years to get used to it.'

'So, what are you going to do? Leave him?' Gloria shook her head. 'Don't even think about that, my dear.'

'Why not?' Callie asked. 'Plenty of women leave their husbands.'

Gloria gave Callie a look of disbelief. 'Not husbands like Logan Waterford, they don't. Don't tell me you're actually considering it. I'd be furious with you.'

'I don't even really like Logan,' Callie admitted. 'How am I supposed to enjoy being married to him?'

Gloria fished the olive out of her martini and began sucking on it. 'You don't have to enjoy it,' she scoffed. 'You just have to realise that he gives you status and money. That's plenty enough for most women.'

'I'm not "most women",' Callie reminded her.

Gloria rolled her eyes. 'Tell me about it, sugar.'

'You come here often, darlin'?' asked a husky, male voice.

Callie and Gloria looked up to find a burly, bearded man standing next to Gloria's chair, making no effort to hide his appreciation of her cleavage. A cigarette dangled from the corner of his lip, and he held a beer bottle in his hand.

Gloria smiled at him. 'Not often enough, I do believe,' she replied pertly.

'Too bad for us, then.' He rested his hips against a barstool. Callie couldn't help staring at him. His muscles practically bulged beneath his T-shirt, and his body looked as if it would be as solid as a brick wall.

The man's eyes went to Gloria's bare legs and the hem of her skirt, which was hiked almost clear up to her crotch. 'Nice outfit.'

'We just came from our club meeting,' Gloria replied. 'Terribly stuffy, if I do say so myself.'

'You don't seem "terribly stuffy" to me,' he said. 'My name's Hank.'

'Hank.' Gloria rolled his name over her tongue as if she were tasting it. 'What a delicious name.'

'Not as delicious as you look.' He put his callused hands on her knees, rubbing his fingers over her skin.

'Gloria,' Callie hissed. She was well aware of her sister's underground antics, but she didn't appreciate being made to witness them.

Gloria threw her a lazy smile. 'Relax, Callie. Just enjoy yourself.'

Hank's fingers made their way halfway up her thighs, and Gloria didn't bother trying to stop him. In fact, she spread her legs wider. Hank gave her a leering smile.

'Wanna dance?' he asked.

'I'd love to.' Gloria downed the last of her martini and followed Hank out to the small, empty dance floor.

An Elvis Presley song was playing on the jukebox. Everyone in the bar watched as Gloria snuggled right up against Hank's big body as if she'd danced with him thousands of times before. Her breasts pressed against his chest as his hands massaged her arse. Callie was embarrassed on her sister's behalf, especially when Gloria and Hank began kissing with pornographic enthusiasm. Callie thought that if Gloria wasn't careful, she'd choke on Hank's tongue.

Roger the barman paused from wiping down the counter to look at Callie. 'You a friend of hers?'

'I'm her sister. Does she come her often?'

'Yeah, about once a week or so. She likes the back room.'

Callie took another swallow of her martini, not sure whether she wanted to know the answer to her next question. 'And what is the back room?'

'You know, where people go to fuck,' Roger explained bluntly.

'You have a room where people can fuck?'

'Sure, although it's not like we advertise it or anything. It's just there for customer use.'

'Do you want to dance?' a male voice suddenly asked.

Callie looked up to find herself staring at a skinny, pimple-faced boy holding a pool cue. 'No, thanks.'

He glanced towards Gloria and Hank. 'What, you don't put out like she does?'

'No, I don't.'

'Hey, Gary, back off,' Roger ordered.

With a scowl, Gary went back to the pool table with his tail between his legs. Callie gave Roger a grateful look before returning her attention to Gloria and Hank. She wasn't surprised to discover that Hank had started to feel her sister up, having stuffed one beefy hand into the top of Gloria's suit jacket. His hand roamed around brazenly underneath the material, his fingers pinching at her nipple while his other hand continued to massage her arse. For her part, Gloria appeared to be revelling in the indecent attention. Her skin was flushed a rosy pink, her eyes half closed in sensual abandon. She stood on tiptoe to whisper something in his ear. Amidst envious glances from the bar patrons, she and Hank slinked off the dance floor and went through an open doorway near the pool tables.

Callie shook her head and sighed. She had always known that Gloria was a back-room kind of woman, but suddenly she wasn't sure if her feelings about that were ones of disgust or envy.

Chapter Two

Callie woke when a stream of sunlight spilled through an opening in the curtains and touched her closed eyelids. She stretched, yawned and turned towards Logan's side of the bed. He was gone, his pillows and sheets pulled up neatly with every wrinkle smoothed. Callie shook her head and clambered out of bed. After brushing her teeth and hair, she wrapped a blue, silk robe around her body and went downstairs.

Logan was in the dining room, eating breakfast and reading the paper. He was fully dressed in a navy, pin-striped suit and tie, his dark hair combed to perfection. Callie often felt dishevelled and slightly frumpy around him, especially in the morning.

'Morning,' she mumbled.

'Good morning, calla lily.'

Callie poured herself a cup of coffee from the silver carafe on the sideboard and sat down next to him. The maid had laid the table with a basket of croissants, fruit and cheeses, but Logan had two pieces of toast, a hard-boiled egg and a black coffee in front of him. Callie had never known him to eat anything else in the morning.

She glanced at him as she spooned sugar into her coffee. 'So, what are you doing today?'

'I have a few meetings and a conference call in preparation for court on Thursday.'

'I see. Any interesting cases?'

'Not particularly.' He turned to the sports section of the paper. 'Assault and battery.'

Callie broke open a fresh croissant, her stomach rumbling in anticipation as the rich, buttery scent reached her nostrils. She let the flaky pastry melt on her tongue before she looked at Logan again.

'Logan?'

'Yes?'

'Why did you marry me?'

Logan glanced at her. 'Excuse me?'

'Why did you marry me?' Callie repeated. 'We'd only known each other for a month. That's not long enough to fall in love with someone.'

'I don't know, Callie.' A thread of irritation wove through Logan's voice. 'Do we have to start this now?'

Callie's eyebrows rose. 'You don't know why you married me?'

'I married you because I thought you would be a good wife.'

'Gee, thanks.' Callie sipped her coffee. 'Careful not to be too overwhelming in your response there.'

'I really don't have time for this.'

'No, I'm not surprised.'

'I have a long day ahead of me.'

'You wouldn't want to talk about this even if today were Saturday,' Callie pointed out.

'Talk about what? Why I married you? That's just a silly question.'

'For such a silly question, you certainly didn't answer it very thoroughly.'

Logan sighed. 'Callie, you know I dislike it when you become petulant. I've had quite enough of this after the other night.'

Tension tightened Callie's nerves. She forced herself to keep her voice calm and even. 'I'm not being petulant, and I wish you wouldn't speak to me as if I were a child.'

'When you act like one, I have little choice.'

'I asked you a question about our marriage,' Callie said. 'There's nothing more adult than that, is there?'

Logan didn't reply. He stood and went to the sideboard. 'If you're going out today, could you please pick up my shirts at the cleaners?'

Callie fought the urge to make a snappish retort. 'Yes.'

She remembered that she was scheduled to work at Nebula Arcana today, but she could pick up the shirts in her lunch hour. She hadn't told Logan about her part-time job, nor did she intend to. She'd started working at the City Market shop several months ago simply because she wanted some time away from the oppressive sphere of Logan's life.

She realised now that she had also wanted to earn extra money out of necessity. Logan never regulated her spending, but Callie no longer wanted to feel indebted to him. He knew nothing about her job. Callie suspected that he wouldn't disapprove of her working, but that he wouldn't be thrilled that Nebula Arcana was an alternative type of shop that sold funky candles, incense, tie-dyed clothing and handmade jewellery. Such an establishment was hardly in keeping with the Waterford image, and Logan certainly wouldn't have liked the fact that the clientele consisted mostly of ageing hippies, Goths, Wiccans and New Age followers.

'Could you bring me the cream, please?' she asked.

Logan poured himself another coffee. 'What are your plans for this week?'

Callie nibbled at her croissant. 'Nothing special. I have a museum fund raiser scheduled and lunch with my sister.'

Logan's mouth thinned slightly as he handed her the cream. Their fingers brushed, and he pulled away from her as if her touch somehow bothered him.

'And what is your sister doing with herself?'

'She's gotten involved with the Conservation League, a historical preservation society.' Callie poured cream into her coffee and stirred. 'She wants me to join, too.'

'What does this league do, raise money for the preservation of historical relics like Gloria?' A corner of his mouth rose in mild amusement as he reached over with his napkin to dab at a spilled drop of cream on the table.

Callie ignored his deprecating remark. 'No, it ensures that monuments and historic homes all around Georgia aren't torn down by greedy land developers.'

'Good. That should keep you busy.'

Callie's hand tightened on her cup. 'Logan, do you ever think something is wrong?'

'Wrong? Aren't you feeling well?'

'Yes, I'm fine.' Callie waved her hand in the air ineffectually. 'I mean, wrong with us. With this marriage.'

'What are you talking about? Nothing is wrong, Callie.'

'Are you sure about that?' She knew in advance what his answer would be. They had had this very conversation a number of times in the last three years, and the outcome was always the same.

'Of course.' Logan cracked his egg, giving her a mildly irritated look. Control collected around him like a suit: a suit perfectly tailored to his breadth and height. 'What's the matter with you lately? You've been very tense.'

'Maybe I'm *tense* because I can never get you to talk to me,' Callie said.

'We're talking now, aren't we?'

'Yes, I just ... oh, never mind.' Callie grabbed an apple from the basket and split it open with a knife.

'I'll be going to Boston next week for a couple of days,' Logan said. 'I think you scheduled a dinner with the Andersons, but I won't be able to make it.'

'I'll cancel, then.'

'There's no reason why you shouldn't go without me.'

'I said I'll cancel. I can't stand the Andersons anyway.'

28

'You've been rather disagreeable lately, haven't you?' Logan asked.

Anger suddenly seared through the ice inside Callie, overflowing with a sudden, tumultuous energy.

'Yes, well, have you given any thought to the reasons why I might be disagreeable?' she snapped. 'That maybe it has something to do with the fact that you never listen to me, or that you make love to me as if I were a goddamn statue?'

Logan levelled an even look at her. 'Well, this is new.'

'It's not new. It's been like this for three years, and I'm tired of it.'

'Callie, if you want something, all you have to do is ask.'

'Logan, the only thing I want is for you to – to express yourself.' As soon as the words were out of her mouth, Callie wished she could take them back. They hung in the air, sounding stupid and trite.

'Whatever your sister has told you, I wish you'd ignore her.'

'This has nothing to do with Gloria!' Callie cried. Her blood pulsed furiously, intensified by his sheer unwillingness to respond. 'Why do you always blame her? You can be such a fucking idiot sometimes, Logan. This has to do with you and me. No one else.'

'Callie, I don't like scenes. I wish you would compose yourself.'

'Dammit, maybe I don't want to,' Callie snapped. 'We are not the most communicative couple on the planet, in case you haven't realised that.'

'Is there something you want that you don't have?'

'I said no. I only want our marriage to work.'

'Are you unhappy?'

'You've given me everything I could possibly want except one thing.' Tension squeezed her so tightly she felt as if she might crack.

'What is that one thing, then?'

'You, Logan! Don't you get it?'

Logan's expression hardened. 'Callie, I don't appreci-ate these childish displays.'

Callie's frustration exploded. She slapped him as hard as she could, unable to prevent her emotions from taking a desperate, physical outlet. Logan's head jerked slightly before he stood and walked away from her, his eyes as cold as ever. The air thickened between them like acrid smoke. Callie knew then that she had to leave or suffocate.

As Callie closed and locked her suitcase, she couldn't believe she was actually doing this; that she was leaving Logan Waterford. At the same time, she knew it couldn't be any different. The tight, confined space of her hus-band's life was squeezing out her spirit like toothpaste from a tube.

She picked up the suitcase and descended the stairs, hating the tomblike stillness, the eerie shadows. She had no idea how Logan would react to her departure, but then she had never been able to read his emotions or predict his responses. She possessed no deeper knowl-edge of him now than she did when she first spoke her vows.

After calling a cab, she hurried outside. The night air was hot and slightly thick, laden with moisture from the Savannah river. Nerves clenched in Callie's stomach as she hurried outside the mansion gates to wait for the cab. Even though Logan was hundreds of kilometres away on business, she half expected him to come after her there and then.

'Where to, miss?'

Callie climbed into the car with her suitcase. 'Taylor, please,' she said.

The driver nodded and headed through the historic centre district in the direction of Gloria's home. Callie stared out of the window at the darkened streets, illu-minated by the ghostly yellow tinge of the streetlights.

The driver pulled up in front of Gloria's renovated

Edwardian home. Although it was past midnight, squares of light burned in the windows. Callie tensed at the thought of her sister's reaction, since Gloria had always considered herself to be responsible for Callie.

Callie paid the driver, then used her key to enter the house since she didn't want Gloria to cause a scene on the doorstep. And Callie suspected that a scene was imminent. She found her sister in the study, curled up on the couch in a ruffled silk robe with a box of Belgian chocolates by her side and a martini in her hand. As Gloria watched an old James Bond film playing on the television, her fingers eased up the filmy material of her gown and began stroking her inner thighs.

Callie cleared her throat. She really didn't want to know how far her sister's obsession for James Bond went. 'Hello, Gloria.'

Gloria blinked and quickly pushed her gown back over her legs. 'Callie! What are you doing here?'

'I've left Logan.' Callie put her suitcase by the door and approached her sister. Saying the words aloud suddenly made them seem real. 'I've actually left him.'

Gloria sat up, her perfectly plucked eyebrows shooting almost to her hairline. 'You must be joking.'

'No.' Callie sat down, twisting her hands in her lap. Adrenaline surged through her blood along with a sick feeling at the thought of what Logan would do when he discovered she had gone. 'He's out of town for a few days. I didn't leave during the day because I didn't want the help to know about it.'

'Well, this is so very modern!' Gloria's sprayed hair fairly quivered with shock. She reached for the martini shaker and poured herself a refill. 'I didn't think you were serious the other day. I mean, I knew you two weren't entirely compatible, but you can't possibly leave him.'

'Gloria, I already have,' Callie said. 'I can't live with him anymore.'

'Did you have a fight?'

31

'No. Logan never really fights. He just dictates.'

'What does that mean?' Gloria downed her martini and plucked out the olive with her long fingernails.

Callie gave an exasperated sigh. 'You know Logan, Gloria. He's so . . . so controlled. I never know what he's thinking.'

'And that's why you're leaving him?' Gloria chewed on the olive and began to pace the study, waving a hand in front of her face as if she were about to faint. 'Because you never fight?'

'No.' Callie didn't even know how to explain her reasons for wanting to leave her husband.

Gloria stopped and put her hands on her ample hips. Her lips curved upward. 'Don't tell me he's not passionate enough for you. I'll bet that man could make me come just by looking at me the right way.'

'Well, he certainly isn't very adventurous. Sex is always the same with him. He touches me as if I were made of glass.'

'Did you discuss this with him?'

'I tried, but it's not exactly the kind of thing you can discuss with Logan.'

'This is the most ridiculous thing I've ever heard,' Gloria said. 'You must be going through some sort of phase. You need a drink.'

'I don't need a drink.'

'You can't leave your husband, Callie! What will people say?'

'Probably "Thank God she finally left him so I can snatch him up for myself,"' Callie replied wryly.

She was only half joking. The ladies of Savannah society had never made a secret of their admiration for Logan Waterford, nor their surprise over the fact that he had deigned to marry Callie Bennis.

'And you're going to let them?' Gloria screeched, throwing her hands up. She reminded Callie of a rather plump, rather drunk bird flapping her wings with impotent fury.

'I don't care about them,' Callie replied. 'Besides, I was only acceptable by my association with you, and they never really thought I was appropriate for Logan. After all, he's one of Savannah's most reputable citizens.'

'That's my point!' Gloria went on. 'And he married *you*! You can't possibly walk away from him now.'

Callie leant her head against the back of the chair and let out her breath in a long sigh. 'I know I'm doing the right thing, Gloria. I know it.'

'The right thing according to whom?'

'According to me, who else?'

Gloria's lips tightened into a thin line. 'That's selfish of you, don't you think?'

'Gloria, I don't know the man I'm married to!' Callie said in exasperation. 'I don't even really like him.'

'Well, what about me?'

'What about you?'

'This doesn't bode well for my reputation, either, you know!' Gloria snapped. 'After all, I'm family, too. I even introduced you to Logan.'

'Good, now you can go and marry him,' Callie retorted. She scowled and plucked at a loose thread on her jumper.

'Well, now what are you going to do?'

'I don't know,' Callie admitted. 'I haven't given it much thought. I just knew I had to leave.'

'When did you make this momentous decision?'

'Last week. I've been thinking about it for some time, though. I swear, Gloria, I was stifling in that marriage.'

'Oh, don't be so dramatic, Callie,' Gloria said. 'You're just feeling sorry for yourself right now. You'll soon realise that you can't leave Logan. Your reputation will take a beating, but not his. Everyone will pity him, but they'll think you're either crazy or a tramp.'

'I don't care what people think. I need to think on my own for a change.'

Gloria shook her head, biting down on a lavender-tipped fingernail. 'I can't believe this.'

Fatigue settled like dust in Callie's bones. 'Gloria, can I stay here for the night?'

Gloria sighed. 'You can stay here until you come to your senses.'

'No, just for one night will be fine.' Callie had already made arrangements to live in the flat above Nebula Arcana. No one knew about her job there and certainly no one would find her. She didn't even want Gloria to know where she would be staying, since Logan would probably go to her sister first.

'Then where are you going to go?'

'I'm not sure yet.'

'Callie, I'm not going to let you leave if you don't have a place to stay!'

'Gloria, I'll explain everything tomorrow. I'm really tired.'

Gloria tugged the filmy robe of her gown over her large breasts. 'All right, come upstairs. You can sleep in the guest room. We'll discuss this tomorrow when you're feeling more like yourself.'

Callie didn't even bother to argue. She followed her sister upstairs and into the guest room. 'Where's Ted?'

'He's in our bedroom, sleeping.' Gloria turned down the eiderdown and went to open one of the windows. She shot Callie a sly smile. 'I wore him out.'

Callie wasn't surprised to hear that. Gloria had always possessed a voracious sexual appetite, and her recent marriage apparently hadn't curbed it. Against her better judgement, Callie asked, 'Doing what?'

Gloria laughed. 'Let's just say that I have a new, little toy I decided to try on him.'

Callie raised an eyebrow. 'A dildo? On Ted?'

'A dildo on Ted. Believe me, he loved it.'

'I thought men were squeamish about that kind of thing.'

'At the beginning he was a little nervous but, once he got used to the idea, he thoroughly enjoyed it. He even begged for more.'

'Really?'

'Mmm. Men are much more adventurous than you'd think.' Gloria put her hand on her hip and surveyed the room. 'I think you'll be comfortable here. There are clean towels in the bathroom.'

'Thanks. I appreciate this.'

'Well, I'm helping you out because you're my sister,' Gloria said. 'But I'm not happy about what you've done. I do hope you'll come to your senses soon.'

'Goodnight, Gloria.'

With a little sniff, Gloria turned and swept out of the room.

Callie went to the window and stared out at the moonlit night. A heavy, knotted oak tree stood in the garden; a tree that looked as if it were growing from the very centre of earth itself. Constant, immovable, dependable, unchanging. Just like someone she knew.

Gloria closed the door to her bedroom and flipped on the light, ignoring the sleepy protest of her husband. He shifted in bed amidst a tumble of pillows, lifting a hand to shield his eyes from the light.

'What's going on?'

'Callie is here.'

'Callie?' Ted yawned and rubbed his eyes, flopping back against the pillows. 'What's she doing here?'

'She's left Logan.' With a little grunt of indignation, Gloria sat down on the side of the bed. 'Honestly, Ted, that girl is so capricious sometimes.'

'Why did she leave Logan?'

Gloria waved her hand in the air. 'Who knows? Some nonsense about him being too domineering.' And not dominating enough, she thought, with a suppressed chuckle. 'It's ridiculous. She's married to one of the most upstanding men in Savannah, and she can't even come up with a decent reason for leaving him.'

'Well, I wouldn't say that Logan is the most upstanding man in Savannah,' Ted replied. 'At least, not at this very moment.'

Gloria turned to look at her husband, her eyebrows lifting as she saw the length of his cock tenting the sheet. 'My goodness. And I thought I'd exhausted you.'

She reached out to palm the hard bulge, giving Ted a smile as she did so. He was a nice-looking man, her husband. Tall and slender with light brown hair and blue eyes. The fact that he didn't resemble Sean Connery in his Bond days wasn't terribly distressing. After all, Gloria had a vivid enough imagination, and Ted had always been able to satisfy her in bed. She found that characteristic particularly attractive. He was a bit on the submissive side, as she had discovered recently, but she didn't mind catering to his needs that way.

She bent to press a kiss against his neck and slid the sheet over his hips to reveal his prick. Wrapping her fingers around the shaft, she slowly stroked him to a full erection. His skin was still scented with the fragrance of their mingled secretions from an earlier bout of love-making. Gloria took him in her mouth, sliding her lips over his shaft until he filled her mouth completely.

Ted gave a little moan of pleasure, spreading his legs apart to give her access to his testicles. Gloria's fingers stroked downwards to rub the crinkly sac, then further to the ring of his arsehole. She was surprised when he drew in a breath of pleasure.

'Yes, baby,' he whispered. 'Do that.'

'Even after the dildo?' Gloria asked.

Ted nodded. Gloria probed gently at the tight aperture, then lifted herself to remove her gown and then splay her body over his. She settled her breasts against his pelvis and parted her legs to give him access to her pussy. Her body jerked with pleasure when she felt his tongue start to explore the damp folds. He knew every inch of her, knew exactly where to put his tongue to stimulate her fully. With a moan, Gloria writhed against him, taking his penis in her mouth again as they simultaneously pleasured each other. Ted's hands spread over her buttocks, massaging and kneading her flesh as his mouth worked industriously between her thighs.

'Gloria?' he murmured, his voice muffled.

Gloria flicked her tongue into the little slit at the head of his cock. 'Hmm?'

'Ride me, would you?'

Gloria pulled her body up and turned to straddle him. She smiled down at him, pleased to note the flushed expression of his face and the beads of sweat forming on his forehead. With her around, Ted had no need to turn elsewhere for sexual satisfaction. Feeling the urge to indulge, Gloria rubbed Ted's knob over her cunt for lubrication, then shifted slightly so that he was pressing against the ring of her anus. The tight, delicious pleasure began to build as she slowly eased herself down on him. Ted closed his eyes, groaning as his hips bucked upwards in a sign of desperation.

'Don't!' Gloria snapped. 'I control you.'

Ted gasped, squeezing his eyes tight as he tried to regain control over himself. 'Yes ... God, yes, you magnificent woman ...'

Gloria pushed down harder, allowing him to move into her centimetre by careful centimetre. There was no feeling in the world like the sensation of being so utterly full. She drew in a sharp breath and leaned forward, grasping Ted's wrists and pinning them against the pillows. Slowly, she began moving up and down.

'Say it,' she whispered.

'Aw, Gloria.'

'Come on, baby. Just once.'

Ted cleared his throat. 'The name is Bond. James Bond.'

The mere sound of the words caused Gloria's sex to swell with moisture. She moaned and pressed her clit against him as she worked herself more fervently on his cock, imagining that it really was the British spy writhing underneath her. She threw her head back, thrilling in the thought as he filled her arse.

'You can fuck me now,' she gasped, feeling like her body had taken on a life of its own.

Desperate noises began to emerge from Ted's throat as he started to thrust his hips up. A coil of tension built around Gloria's lower body as she reacted to the intense stimulation. She rode him harder and faster, until they both broke through the wall of pressure and into a haze of pure ecstasy. Ted's come filled Gloria in creamy jets, allowing her to slip easily off him.

Ted drew in a heaving breath, his eyes glazed as he absorbed the final twinges of pleasure. 'Jesus, Gloria, no one fucks like you do.'

Gloria smiled and stroked her hand over his chest as her mind filled with images of spies, villains and lanky, big-breasted women. Such romance, such intrigue, such ... hot sex. With a happy sigh, Gloria settled against her husband. There was nothing like sexual satisfaction.

Her thoughts returned to Callie and especially to what Callie had said about her sex life with Logan. So, the reason she left the man was simply due to a lack of response on Logan's part? Maybe it wasn't Logan's fault at all. Maybe he just didn't know how to relax enough to give a woman a really good fuck.

A great wave of charitable feelings towards Logan rose in Gloria's heart. The poor man. With his looks and body, you'd think that fucking would come naturally to him, but apparently that wasn't the case. And Callie wasn't exactly one to help him out. No, Logan needed a wholly different kind of partner. Gloria stifled another chuckle as she realised that she was the perfect candidate for the job.

Chapter Three

'Where the hell is she?' Fury seethed through Logan Waterford like fiery lava, but his tone remained icy and even. His grip tightened on the telephone receiver until he thought the thick plastic would shatter in his fist.

'I don't know.' The voice on the other end sounded honeyed and utterly unperturbed, a fact that infuriated Logan all the more. Few things nettled him like nonchalance.

'Don't give me that shit,' he said coldly. 'You're her sister. If anyone knows where she is, then you do.'

'Well, Logan, I'm afraid I don't,' Gloria Harper replied. 'Of course, she came to see me, but she refused to stay with me and Ted.'

'Where did she go then?'

'I already told you. I don't know,' Gloria repeated. 'I pleaded with her to give me an address or phone number, but she kept it to herself. She did say she would contact me soon but, other than that, nothing.'

'Why in the love of God wouldn't she tell you?'

'Probably because she knew you would come to me first,' Gloria replied. 'I suspect that means she doesn't want you to find her.'

'That's ludicrous!' Logan couldn't comprehend the fact that Callie would willingly leave him. He'd thought she was nothing if not loyal. She would never betray him like this. 'She's my wife. Why wouldn't she want me to find her?'

'Logan, darling, she's left you,' Gloria said as if she were speaking to a child. 'Isn't that reason enough?'

'No, dammit, that isn't reason enough. She wouldn't just up and leave without an explanation.'

'Perhaps she already gave you an explanation.'

'No, she didn't.'

'Maybe you just weren't listening.'

Logan's teeth snapped together. 'What does that mean?'

'Look, I'm no happier about this than you are,' Gloria said. 'I told her she couldn't rationally do this. I mean, what about our reputations? For her to leave you is truly a travesty, but you know Callie. Once she sets her mind on something, it's nearly impossible to dissuade her. And, believe me, Logan, I tried to do just that.'

'Obviously, you didn't succeed.'

'I'm sure she'll come back soon,' Gloria assured him. 'She's going through a phase right now but, once she realises how idiotic she's being, she'll come back to you.'

'Yes, well, I'm not about to sit around waiting for that to happen.' Logan dropped the receiver back on to the telephone.

Jesus. Callie had left him. An explosion of fury rocketed through his body. He picked up a stone paperweight and hurled it against the wall. The stone narrowly missed an indecipherable landscape painting by a contemporary artist before falling with a thud to the floor. Spidery lines cracked through the plasterboard wall like the shell of a boiled egg.

Logan flexed the muscles of his hand. His blood went cold as he stared at the damage. If there was anything he hated more than being betrayed, then it was losing control, even for the briefest of moments.

'Mr Waterford?' A knock sounded at the door, and Logan's secretary peeked in. 'Is everything all right?'

'Yes, Violet, just indulging in a little aesthetic criticism, that's all.'

Violet glanced at the crooked painting before she nodded and slipped back out.

Logan dragged a hand through his hair and tried to think. So, maybe Callie had bitched and complained a little. He didn't think she was unhappy enough to walk out on him. God knew he'd given her everything she ever wanted. Why would any woman walk away from that? But regardless of the reasons, Callie obviously had. Now how in the hell could he find her?

'Logan.' Another knock sounded at the door.

'Come in.'

Adam Garabola, a thin, lanky man in his mid-twenties, poked his sandy blonde head in to the room. 'Um, Logan, I have those case reports that you wanted.'

'Well, don't just stand there, bring them here.'

Adam shoved his glasses back up the bridge of his nose and entered the room. He wore a wrinkled, linen suit that looked as if it had been purchased at a discount store, but his scruffed shoes were polished to a shine.

Through narrowed eyes, Logan watched the man approach him. He could have done without Adam's odd personality, but he knew that the younger man possessed a sharp intelligence that belied his eccentricity. That had been reason enough to hire him as a paralegal in the Waterford and Waterford law firm.

'Close the door.'

Adam complied, then approached Logan's desk. His gaze went to the large dent in the wall. 'Uh, are you angry about something?'

'You could say that.' Logan peered at Adam. 'What the hell is that in your eyebrow?'

Adam's hand went to the silver ring above his left eye. 'An earring. They're really cool right now.'

'Is that so? Well, I'm sure it will be really cool when it

41

gets infected or some angry con reaches across the defence table and rips it off you. Besides, it looks stupid.'

'You think so?' Adam looked crushed. 'I'll take it off if you want me to.'

'I couldn't care less what you do.'

'I got it done over the weekend at a science-fiction convention,' Adam explained. 'You should totally come with me to one of those. I bought a first edition Superman comic. Can you believe it?'

'Fascinating.'

'They'll be there next weekend, too,' Adam went on, looking at Logan hopefully. 'Why don't you come with me?'

'No, thanks. I have other things on my mind.'

'They have masquerade balls at night and everything,' Adam said. His gaze slid down to Logan's chest. 'We could dress up as partners, like Batman and Robin. You'd look so fantastic in a Batman costume.'

Logan eyed the young man suspiciously. 'Are you planning on growing up one of these days, or are you still going to be playing fantasy land when you're old and grey and living in a nursing home?'

Hurt flashed in Adam's eyes. 'I just thought it might be fun, and –'

'I said no,' Logan snapped. 'Now stop talking nonsense and sit down.'

Adam sighed and sat, clutching the folders to his chest. 'I've been trying to find information about that case way back in '76; you know, the one about the man who was prosecuted for hav –'

'Adam, be quiet,' Logan interrupted shortly as he turned over an idea in his mind. He still had to keep up with caseload and court appointments, but his priority was to find his wife. And, while he trusted very few people – if any – he did know that fear was a powerful method of obtaining a person's devout loyalty. Pity he apparently hadn't been able to instil that fear in Callie.

He reached for his Rolodex and flipped through it.

'We used a private detective for the Grossman case. What was his name?'

'Sam Houston, sir. He was very good.'

Logan found Houston's card in the file. 'All right, listen. I have a personal problem, but I don't want anyone either in or out of the office to know about it. I'm going to tell you because I need someone to keep track of this detective's activities. However, if I find out that you've told a soul, I'll kick your arse clear out of the state. Is that clear?'

Adam stared wide-eyed at him for a moment before nodding. 'Yes, sir. Crystal clear.'

'Good. Because I have to hire Sam Houston to find my wife.'

'Excuse me?'

'Are you sure they didn't pierce your brain along with your eyebrow?' Logan asked derisively. 'It seems that Callie has disappeared without a trace.'

'Wow, you mean, like, kidnapped? Did you call the police?'

'No. Callie left of her own accord, which is why I need a detective. The police won't be of any help.' Logan grabbed his suit jacket and slipped it on. 'I have an errand to run. Find me the records of Houston's cases. I want them on my desk by the time I'm back.'

Logan grabbed his car keys and strode outside to the car park. The heat lay like a wet blanket over the city. Logan drove to Gloria's house on Taylor Street and pulled into the driveway. If Callie were anywhere near her sister, he would find out about it.

He rapped hard on the door, forcing away a wave of frustration when no one responded. He turned the door-knob, found it unlocked, and let himself in. The muffled sounds of music emerged from the study.

Logan paused in the doorway, his gaze going to his sister-in-law. She lay sprawled on the leather couch, wearing a silk robe with a feathery boa that was fully open to reveal her tits. Her head was flung back in ecstasy, her fingers working frantically between her legs as the sounds of *For Your Eyes Only* jangled from the stereo speakers.

'Yes...' Gloria moaned, reaching up to twist her nipple between her pink, lacquered fingernails. 'Fuck me, fuck me, fuck me.'

Logan strode into the room and switched off the stereo before turning to face Gloria. She looked up in surprise, her eyes widening at the sight of him.

'Oh, shit,' she muttered.

'Sorry to interrupt.'

'Sure you are.' Gloria didn't bother pulling her robe closed. Instead, she ran a hand slowly down her body. She had a totally different figure than her slender, small-breasted sister. She was all rounded flesh and large tits, her thighs full and creamy.

Logan couldn't help wondering what it would feel like to fuck her. He winced as his prick hardened.

'I came to find Callie,' he said. 'Where is she?'

'How many times do I have to tell you? She's not here.' Gloria rubbed her fingers over her belly. Her skin was flushed with exertion and interrupted satisfaction. 'You don't mind if I finish myself off, do you?'

'You're a whore, Gloria,' Logan said in disgust. 'What did you say to Callie to make her leave?'

Gloria shrugged and spread her legs farther apart, giving him full view of her wet cunt. 'Not a thing, sugar. I told you, I was furious with her. Still am, but there's not much I can do.'

Logan headed towards the staircase as tension gripped his neck. 'I'm looking upstairs.'

'Really, Logan, I wouldn't be frigging myself in plain sight if my sister were upstairs,' Gloria said dryly. She pulled herself off the couch in a languid movement and approached him, her breasts swinging like large pillows. 'Maybe she left because you didn't fuck her often enough. Or hard enough.'

Logan's teeth clenched as the scent of Gloria's arousal billowed up around him. 'She told you that?'

'Not in so many words.'

'Then how?'

Gloria reached up to tug lightly at the knot of Logan's tie, her fingers still glistening with her own juices. 'Callie needs to be satisfied, darling. If you didn't do that, then maybe she's looking elsewhere.'

'You're telling me she's having an affair?'

'Heavens, no. I don't think she's wired for that.' Gloria sauntered over to the drinks cabinet and began mixing herself a vodka martini. 'Would you like a drink?'

'No. I would like to find my wife.'

'Give it up, sugar. She'll come back to you when she's ready.' She sipped her drink and looked at him with a glint in her blue eyes. 'My heavens. I've never seen you this worked up, Logan. It's quite attractive.'

Logan's hands tightened into fists as he turned and stalked out of the room. He went upstairs and threw open the doors of the bedrooms, certain he would find some evidence of Callie. But no, the guest bedrooms were pristine and perfect, and the library looked as if it hadn't been occupied for weeks. Logan slammed the door so hard it vibrated on its hinges.

'I told you.' Gloria's robe still hung open to reveal her abundant flesh when Logan stormed back into the study. 'You seem to be hard of hearing. Are you as hard in other ways, darling?'

'Don't call me darling, you lush – and would you cover yourself up?' Logan snapped. 'Jesus, you're indecent.'

Gloria gave a throaty laugh. 'And you're repressed.' She approached him, her breasts brushing suggestively against his arm. 'You know, I can help loosen you up.'

'For God's sake, Gloria, I'm your sister's husband.' Irritation grated his nerves, but he forced himself to keep his voice even. 'Have some respect for that, would you?'

Gloria blinked. 'I have the utmost respect for that.

However, I know that you and my sister don't exactly appreciate each other.'

'And that means I should fuck you?'

'Why not?' Gloria shrugged. 'Sometimes a fuck is just a fuck.'

With a mutter of exasperation, Logan turned and went back out to his car. It never ceased to surprise him how different Callie and Gloria were. For Gloria, fucking her sister's husband wouldn't even count as a betrayal, but simply an adventurous activity, like a weekend camping trip in the mountains. He had made a point of resisting her relentless advances up to this point but, now with his anger at Callie simmering like hot water in his blood, the idea of screwing Gloria suddenly seemed a just, if inefficient, revenge.

He got behind the wheel of his car and slammed the door. Now he was furious not only about Callie's leaving, but also over the fact that his cock was as hard as a piece of granite.

Callie pulled open the door of Nebula Arcana as the jingle of the bell heralded her entrance. The sweet scent of incense floated towards her, mingled with the light crispness of candle wax. The shop was filled with shelves of stones and crystals, home-made candles, New Age books, cotton and hemp clothing, and silver jewellery. An upstairs loft displayed Indian sheets and bedspreads, as well as a number of wall decorations. Callie loved the place. She took great pleasure in the quirky yet comforting atmosphere and found the clientele to be easy-going and honest, if a bit odd.

'Hey, Callie.'

'Hi, Tess.' Callie approached the young woman who stood behind the jewellery counter, arranging items in the glass case. 'Well, I did it.'

'Yeah? Good for you. How do you feel?' Tess flipped a lock of green-streaked hair out of her eyes and looked at Callie. Her silver nose ring glinted in the light, and she was wearing a new shade of sparkly purple eyeshadow.

Callie had always envied Tess her go-to-hell style of fashion. Dozens of silver bracelets and rings decorated Tess' arms and fingers, and she wore her traditional attire of torn, black jeans, a mesh shirt and leather vest.

'I feel OK,' she said. 'I thought I would be more relieved, but I'm not really. I guess I'm even a little sad.'

'At least you had the guts to do it,' Tess said. 'To leave him, I mean. Most women wouldn't.'

Callie nodded. 'Thanks for letting me stay upstairs. I hope I can pay you rent soon.'

Tess grinned and snapped her gum. 'Just open the shop at nine on weekends,' she said. 'Letting me sleep till eleven is plenty of compensation for me.'

'Speaking of which, how was your show last night?' Callie asked.

Tess sighed and shook her head. 'There were all of six people in the audience, and two of them walked out. I swear, no one appreciates art anymore.'

'Especially performance art,' Callie agreed sympathetically. 'What performance did you do?'

'It's a performance called *Paint*,' Tess explained. 'I'm trying to show how closely connected art is to the body, but it's just not daring enough. I need to revive a series called *Sexology*. I did it in LA and got a huge audience. Besides, I want to shake Savannah up a little.'

'That sounds provocative.'

Tess grinned. 'It is. And fun, too.'

'Let me know how I can help,' Callie said. 'I'll be right back. I just want to go and unpack.'

She went to the back of the shop and pulled open a door next to a shelf of home-made soaps. A narrow staircase led up to the small, one-room flat above Nebula Arcana. It wasn't much, simply a room with a kitchenette, a small table and a double bed, but it was more than enough for Callie. She would spruce it up with some things from the shop and make it her new home.

47

She unpacked her suitcase and hung her clothes in the wardrobe, then removed her vibrator from the bottom of the case.

She'd made frequent use of the toy during her three years with Logan, for no other reason than the fact that Logan couldn't give her the same intensity of orgasm. Hell, sometimes it had been more of a companion than he had been. And at least it didn't try to quieten her when she spoke her mind. With a rueful chuckle, Callie put the vibrator in the bedside-table drawer before going into the adjoining bathroom to freshen up.

When Callie returned to the shop, Tess was busy helping a woman pick out the right meditation cassette. Callie began working on her current project of categorising all the books and putting their details into the new computer system. As the morning passed, the tension began to seep from her neck and shoulders. She had left Logan. She had really done it. She had walked out of his closed, confined life and into a space that would finally allow her, after three long years, to take a deep breath.

'You want lunch, Cal?' Tess asked. 'I'm feeling the urge for a veggie burger.'

Callie placed *Mystical Memories* on her 'Done' pile. 'No, I'm not really hungry, thanks.'

Tess continued looking at her, arching a thick, black eyebrow. 'Are you going to keep dressing like that?'

Callie glanced down at her silk blouse and pressed trousers. 'Like what?'

'You look like a society matron on her way to a tea party,' Tess replied, then added, 'You know, one of those types with a large stick up her arse.'

Callie laughed. 'Tess, if society matrons have large sticks up their arses, then they are most assuredly not en route to a tea party.'

'Well, you really should loosen up a little,' Tess said. 'I mean, that's a nice outfit and all, but geez, do you ever look repressed.'

'I am not repressed,' Callie retorted, mildly offended.

'Just because my husband touched me as if I were a china doll doesn't make *me* the repressed one.'

'I didn't say you were repressed,' Tess replied. 'I said you look repressed.' She waved her hand towards the wall of loose, cotton clothing. 'Why don't you wear some of our clothes?'

'Tess, I can't afford to buy new clothes right now.'

'You don't have to buy them yet,' Tess said. 'It'll be good advertising for us, anyway, if we both wear the clothes. You'll pay me when you have the money.'

'I'll think about it,' Callie promised.

'I'm telling you, you don't know what you're missing. That hemp clothing is unbelievably soft. It's like wearing a second skin. Or nothing at all.' Tess leant her shoulder against the bookshelf and surveyed Callie. 'So, Logan was a lousy lay, huh?'

Callie picked up another book to enter into the computer. 'No, he wasn't. He just acted like the whole thing was so mechanical. A task rather than an act of love. Or even lust.'

Tess snorted. 'Sounds pretty lousy to me.'

'No, it wasn't, not really,' Callie insisted, somehow annoyed by the thought of anyone degrading Logan's sexuality. 'It was pleasant.'

'Pleasant? Ouch.'

'Yeah.' Callie sighed. 'Pleasant.'

'Did you ever try to be adventurous with him?' Tess asked.

'Adventurous with Logan?' Callie almost laughed. 'I could barely talk to the man, let alone be adventurous with him.'

'Hmm. Sounds to me like he was the one who had the intimate relationship with a stick.'

Callie couldn't help chuckling, even though something inside her was saddened by the thought that Tess was right. 'Yes, well, I guess it doesn't matter anymore.'

'You did the right thing, as far as I'm concerned. And it might do you good to go out somewhere other than tea parties and formal dinners. Listen, I'm going to get my veggie burger. Sure you don't want anything?'

'No, I'll get something later. Thanks.' Callie watched Tess saunter out of the shop, her slim hips swaying in an unconscious rhythm. She wondered what it would be like to feel so comfortable with her body, to feel as if she actually fit inside her skin, to be confident of every movement.

Callie thought well of herself, but she had never been able to cultivate Tess's brazenness. Even if she had tried harder to adopt such an attitude, she suspected that Logan wouldn't have let her get away with it. Her mild flirting games had been more than enough. And heaven knew that he would allow nothing to crack the perfect globe of his world. Especially not his wife.

'Excuse me?'

Callie started slightly and turned at the sound of the male voice. 'I'm sorry. I wasn't paying attention.'

Her gaze fell on a pale-skinned man wearing black trousers, scarlet shirt with ruffles down the front and a black trench coat. As if to match his ensemble, his close-cropped hair was dyed black and his lips were stained a deep maroon colour. The faint, spicy scent of incense rose from his clothing.

'You must have been paying attention to your thoughts, at least,' he said.

Callie smiled. 'Yes, a little too much attention to those, perhaps.'

'Is Tess around?'

'She's just gone to get some lunch. Can I help you with something?'

'I'm looking for some Tarot cards for my mother. She wants to learn how to read them.'

'We have several different kinds of Tarot card sets,' Callie replied. She went behind the front counter to the glass case in which the expensive sets were stored. 'Were you looking for something in particular?'

The Goth shrugged. 'Just a regular set, I guess.'

50

'Well, most of these have the same cards,' Callie explained. She removed several boxes and placed them on the counter top. 'So, often people choose the cards based on the style of the illustrations. This Russian set is one of my favourites.'

'Do you read them?'

'A little.'

Callie removed some of the thick, slippery cards so that he could see the illustrations. He leant forward to peer at them. 'Those are nice. I don't have a clue what she wants, though. I ought to just give her the money and let her buy them.'

'Oh, no, it's best if Tarot cards are a gift,' Callie told him. 'And it would be especially nice if you gave them to her in a silk scarf so that she can store them properly.'

'What's the deal with that?'

'The cards should be stored in silk or some sort of natural fibre,' Callie explained. 'It's a way of keeping the deck pure and treating it with respect.'

'Interesting. Hey, why don't you test them out for me? Give yourself a reading. An ex-girlfriend used to be into these, but I never learned how to read them.'

'OK.' Callie picked up the deck of cards and began shuffling them. She spread six cards out in a cross pattern and another four cards vertically along the side. She tapped her finger on the two overlapping cards in the centre of the cross. 'Each of these card positions means something different,' she explained. 'These two cards indicate what's most important to me now. This one is the six of Pentacles.'

He peered at the cards. 'Six of what?'

'The six of Pentacles,' Callie said. 'It's the card of having and not having, and of dominance and submission. See, there's a picture of a man giving coins to a beggar and holding the scales of justice. It's an ambiguous card, one that means I have to question what's truly going on in my life.'

'And who's in control?' the Goth murmured.

Callie gave him a startled look. 'That, too, I suppose.'

She looked quickly down at the second card. 'This one is the High Priestess, who represents the unconscious and the experience of the senses.'

'Meaning that you should examine your unconscious and experience your senses?'

Callie's eyebrows rose. 'You're sure you don't know more about Tarot readings than you're letting on?'

He gave her a disarming smile. 'No, I'm just brilliant. So what's in your future?'

Callie touched the card on the top of the cross. 'Well, this card represents what I'm worried about or what could come into being in the future.' She stared at the card for a moment, feeling her heart sink.

'Something wrong?' the Goth asked.

'No. I just . . .' She cleared her throat. 'This is the Devil. He represents darkness, of course, or bondage and loss of independence. The feeling of being tied down against your will.'

'Damn. That's it for you, then?'

'No. There's this card.' Callie tapped the card on the right of the cross. 'This one indicates possibilities for the future in terms of approaching influences or something unresolved that has to be dealt with. This is the Magician, the active male principle of the deck. He represents the force of creativity and tapping unknown resources inside yourself.'

'Well, that sounds more reasonable for a future.'

Callie thought she had just escaped the powerful male principle, not to mention lack of independence. She eyed her customer curiously.

'I thought all you Goths were into gloom and doom thinking.'

'Whoever said I was a Goth? And that's a royal misconception, as is the idea that all Goths think they're vampires and worship the devil.'

'What do you think you are, then?'

'I'm quite the opposite. I think I'm the devil and I worship vampires.'

There was a pause, and then the young man laughed. 'I'm kidding. I actually consider myself to be a romantic.'

Callie couldn't help smiling. She scooped up the cards and arranged them into a neat stack. 'I'm sure your mother can give you a good reading if need be. Would you like the Russian set?'

'Yes, I'll take it. And you'd better give me one of those silk scarves over there. Wouldn't want to screw with the order of the universe.'

'Good philosophy,' Callie approved. She rang up the purchases and placed them in a paper bag.

'You know, they're showing a revival of the film *Nosferatu* over at the Riverrun next weekend,' he said, handing her some bills. 'Interested?'

Callie looked at him in surprise. She thought he'd be far more interested in bloodless, white-skinned young women wearing black eyeshadow. 'You're asking me on a date?'

'No. I don't date. I'm asking you if you want to join me at the cinema.'

'OK,' Callie agreed before she could even process the request.

'I'll meet you here at six on Friday.'

He was out of the door before Callie could even collect her thoughts enough to reply. She stared after him, realising that she'd never even considered going out with another man in ages. Let alone a Goth.

Slowly she put the bills into the cash register. Technically, she was still married, of course, but heaven knew she'd been feeling little sense of loyalty towards Logan lately. She didn't think she even knew how to act around another man.

'Here, I got you a veggie burger anyway, since I don't want you eating mine.' A paper bag landed on the counter with a light thud.

Callie glanced absently at Tess. 'Thanks.'

53

Tess pulled herself up to sit the counter and began unwrapping her burger. 'What was Eldrich doing here?'

'Eldrich? That's his name?'

Tess shrugged. 'That's what he says his name is, anyway.'

'He was buying Tarot cards for his mother,' Callie explained. 'You know him, do you?'

'Yeah, we're cool.'

'I agreed to go to the cinema with him.'

'You did? Good for you. About time you got laid by someone who might actually know how to do it.' Tess glanced at Callie. 'Not that I've ever fucked him myself, you know.'

'I didn't say I agreed to fuck him!' Callie said. 'We're going to see *Nosferatu*.'

'Come on, Callie. Don't tell me it didn't even occur to you. Especially after your *pleasant* sex life with Logan.'

'Well, it may have crossed my mind,' Callie admitted.

'Eldrich is safe, Callie.' Tess bit into her burger. 'I can promise you that, so if you want to fool around a little, he's a good one to do it with.'

'He's a little odd.'

'And Logan isn't?'

'Point taken,' Callie muttered.

Eldrich the Goth who wasn't really a Goth remained on Callie's mind throughout the day as she finished cataloguing the books and helped customers. Tess headed home at five, and Callie locked the shop door before going upstairs to the loft. Rather nice to simply walk up a set of stairs and be at home, she thought. She opened the window to let in the balmy evening air and went to take a shower.

Feeling warm, clean and slightly tired, she stretched out on the bed in her cotton nightshirt and allowed herself to think about what it would be like to fuck another man. A man like Eldrich, totally different from Logan. Eldrich was probably in tune with his feelings and would delight in expressing them. Callie would put money on the fact that he even wrote poetry. She wondered what his lovemaking style was like. Candles and incense, no doubt, with some haunting church music in the background. Flickering shadows and deep, red wine.

Callie slipped her fingers to the hem of her nightshirt and touched her bare thigh. Her skin was warm and slightly damp, cooling swiftly from the evaporating droplets of water from her shower. Callie closed her eyes and pictured Eldrich in her mind, stripping him of his clothes to reveal a thin chest covered with a mat of light hair that narrowed down to his groin. His cock projected forth from a nest of curls, making Callie want to get down on her knees in front of him and take him in her mouth the way Logan never allowed.

Eldrich wouldn't respond like that. At least, not the Eldrich of her fantasy, the one standing before her with a heavy-lidded expression and a slender cock waiting to be sucked. Callie reached over to the bedside table and removed her vibrator, feeling her cunt swell at the thought of Eldrich and taking that length of hard flesh in her mouth. She imagined that his shaft would taste tangy and slightly salty against her tongue. And his hands, they would be buried in her hair, clutching her head so that he could thrust himself in and out of her mouth. She might even clutch his hips, or slide her palms around to grasp his buttocks. Maybe she would slip her fingers into the crack of his arse and explore there.

A shudder of sheer pleasure raced through her blood, intensified by the caress of night air against her damp skin. She pulled her nightshirt up above her breasts, pinching her hard nipples between her thumb and forefinger. Eldrich would love to touch her breasts, she knew that. Not like Logan, who usually just shoved her nightshirt up to her hips. Eldrich would rub her tits until her nipples pressed against his palms, and then he would take the stiff peaks between his lips until she writhed underneath him. He would worship her body.

55

Callie's skin warmed at the mere thought, as images flashed behind her closed eyelids. She rubbed the tip of the dildo around a nipple, letting the gentle vibrations flow into her skin. Slowly, she ran it along the length of her body. She was hardly surprised by how quickly she responded to the stimulation. The freedom of having left Logan, combined with the forbidden fantasy of another man, was a potent aphrodisiac.

With a little moan of pleasure, Callie slid the vibrator into her folds and began stroking gently. Her pussy reacted with a generous rush of moisture as a familiar ache began to tighten in her loins. And oh, how vivid were the pictures flashing in her mind: scenes of Eldrich stroking her sex with his fingers and murmuring husky phrases in her ear. 'Hungry, are you, precious? Do you want to feel my cock here, thrusting into you? Do you want me to really fuck you good and hard?'

God, yes, she did. She wanted a man to pound his penis into her until she begged for mercy. She pushed the dildo into her body as far as it would go, crying out as her muscles clamped around it. Grasping the base, Callie thrust the shaft back and forth. Pressure built, enveloping her like hot ribbons. Just as she felt her climax begin to climb to the edge, she took the dildo out and rubbed it lightly over her labia. Her heart raced as she forced herself to prolong her release.

'Fuck me, Eldrich. Fuck me hard.'

She imagined whispering those words to him as their sweat-dampened bodies writhed on the bed. And he would, too. He would slide his cock into her and pump with such strength that even the neighbours would hear the wet, slapping sounds of sex and their impassioned moans echoing through the walls. Maybe he would even take his cock out, slick with her juices, and tease the tight ring of her arsehole. And then he would slowly ease into her, filling her beyond belief in the most taboo of places.

Thrilled by the mere thought, Callie pressed the vibrator tip against that very hole. A shudder raced up her spine. Experimentally, she pushed it a little farther, stunned by how the vibrations reverberated through her entire body. With her other hand, she began to manipulate her clit. The double sensations were too much to take, and an explosive orgasm rocketed through her within seconds. Callie cried out with pleasure, thrusting the dildo in even more as she rode out her release.

Gasping, she let the vibrator fall to the floor as the last twinges pulsed through her body. Oh, yes. Who needed Logan Waterford now?

Chapter Four

'You think she's doing someone else?' Adam looked at the private investigator with a hint of eagerness. He thought it would be pretty cool if this case involved secret lust and betrayal. 'I mean, like, having a full-blown affair?'

'Probably.' Sam Houston lit a cigarette and blew a stream of smoke in Adam's direction. In his mid-fifties with a shock of greying, Albert Einstein-style hair and slouched shoulders, Sam appeared more suited to the role of mad scientist than sharp PI.

'So, how do we find out who it is?' Adam asked.

'Look, kid, this isn't as exciting a case as you want it to be,' Sam replied. 'Women leave their husbands all the time for thousands of reasons. Maybe Waterford was punching her around.'

Adam drew in a breath. 'How dare you?' he snapped. 'Logan would never do something like that! You can just cross that idea right off your list, detective.'

'Call me Sam, for Lord's sake. This isn't *Columbo*.'

The office door opened. Logan stepped in, his gaze going over Adam and Sam in one swoop. Adam sat up a little straighter, thinking that Logan looked rather magnificent in a charcoal-grey suit and tie. And how did he always manage to get his hair to look so perfect? Adam dragged a hand through his shaggy, blonde hair and tugged furtively at his eyebrow ring. He decided he'd get rid of it soon. If Logan thought it looked stupid, then what was the point?

'So, Mr Waterford, you want to tell me when you last saw your wife?' Sam asked.

'I saw Callie the night before I left for Boston,' Logan replied. 'I was gone for three days, and I returned around noon on Thursday. She wasn't at home, and I assumed she was off to one of her charitable society meetings. When I hadn't heard from her by nightfall, I began to wonder.'

'And you called all her friends?'

'Of course. Starting with her sister. No one had heard from her, or so they said.'

'I'll need lists of all her activities and friends,' Sam said. 'Phone numbers, addresses, that kind of thing.'

'Yes. Adam has been working on compiling such a list for you.' Logan nodded at Adam, who reached quickly into a folder on a nearby table.

'I hope I have everything,' he said. He'd been working on the list nonstop for the past three days. 'I have listings of friends going back to her school days, and also friends of her family. Her charity activities are substantial, so I've listed all the members of those organisations as well. There's also information about her brother-in-law's family and her sister's friends.'

'Did she work anywhere?' Sam asked.

Logan shook his head. 'Only for the charities that pricked her bleeding heart.'

Sam eyed him with a curious look. Logan returned it with an irritated one. 'What?'

'You're sure she wasn't involved in something you didn't know about?' Sam asked.

'Of course not,' Logan snapped.

Adam bit his lip and shifted in the chair. 'Uh, sir?'

Both Sam and Logan turned to look at him. He quailed

59

slightly under the combined authority of their gazes. When Logan alone looked at him like that, it was enough to make him feel like a kid from a village school.

'Well, Adam?' Logan said impatiently. 'What is it?'

'Sir, if she was involved in something you didn't know about, you . . . uh . . . well, you wouldn't know about it,' Adam said. He mentally kicked himself for contradicting Logan, but he was determined to examine all aspects of this case. 'So you wouldn't know if she was involved or not.'

Sam chuckled, then coughed to hide his amusement when Logan shot him a deathly glare.

'Well, the kid's right,' Sam pointed out. 'He must have studied philosophy at school.'

'Callie wouldn't run off and do something without my knowing about it,' Logan replied coldly. 'And I don't need Aristotle, Plato or Friedrich fucking Nietzsche to tell me that.'

'She ran off and left you,' Sam said. 'That's what I conclude, prima facie, as you lawyers like to say.'

'Look, enough with this damn logic.' Logan's eyes flashed as he looked from Sam to Adam and back again. 'I think we all know the situation here. Yes, Callie left me and, no, I don't know why. Do you think you can manage to find her or do I need to hire someone else?'

'I'll try my best, Mr Waterford,' Sam replied.

'Don't try,' Logan said, his voice flat and cold. 'Do it.'

A little quiver ran down Adam's spine. He wished he could issue dictates with the same kind of masterfulness that Logan did.

Sam cleared his throat. 'OK, we'll get to work, then,' he said. He headed towards the door. Adam grabbed his folder and stood up. He put his hand on Logan's arm, getting a thrill out of the fact that he could feel the other man's muscles clear through the suit jacket.

'Don't worry, Logan,' Adam said firmly, squeezing Logan's arm. 'We'll find her.' With that, he trotted after Sam and closed the door behind him.

'So where do we start?' Adam asked Sam as they walked out of the office.

Sam gave him a sideways glance. 'Kid, I don't exactly need your help with this. I'll find that woman within a week.'

'Logan said I was supposed to help you,' Adam retorted. 'So you're stuck with me. Should we start at the house?'

He'd never been to the Waterford mansion, but he couldn't wait to see where Logan lived, ate and slept when he wasn't at the office.

'We'll go there tomorrow,' Sam said. 'We'll check out these charities and her Ladies Guild association first.'

Adam shook his head. 'You suppose she was one of those stuck-up society matrons? That doesn't seem like the kind of woman Logan would want.'

Sam shrugged. 'I have some photos of her back at my office. And it doesn't make a rat's ass difference what kind of woman Logan wants. It just matters that we find her.'

'Well, it's just that he's so furious about this.' Adam kicked at a pebble on the street, suddenly wondering what Callie and Logan did in bed. Or didn't do. 'What's so great about her that he wants her back so badly?'

Sam chuckled. 'It probably has less to do with her and more to do with him and his ego.'

'What does that mean?'

'People don't betray Logan Waterford, kid. That's the bottom line.'

'Cinnamon or chocolate?'

'Chocolate, please.' Callie watched the young woman behind the counter sprinkle chocolate powder on her cappuccino. She accepted the cup with thanks and turned to find her date for the evening.

The coffee house on River Street was filled with people drawn in by the cosy, living-room atmosphere of worn, overstuffed chairs and couches. Eldrich had comman-

61

deered a small couch in the corner. Callie smiled at him as she sat down, balancing her cup and saucer on her lap. He looked quite unique this evening in a black, velvet coat and leather trousers, surrounded by a light haze of clove cigarette smoke. A large, silver cross dangled from his neck.

'Thanks, Eldrich. I enjoyed the movie.'

'No problem. *Nosferatu* is one of the greatest films ever made.'

'So, what do you do during the day?' Callie asked.

Eldrich sucked on his herbal cigarette and blew out a stream of smoke. 'I don't go out during the day much, but I'm a DJ most evenings for this Goth club just off of St Julian. It's called the Snake Pit. You should come sometime.'

'Maybe I will.' Callie sipped her coffee and considered her next words carefully. 'However, I think I should tell you something.'

'What's that?'

'Well, this isn't good news,' Callie admitted. 'I'm married. Separated, but married.' She glanced at him quickly, relived to see that he looked surprised, but not angry.

'Oh,' he said. 'Well, that's cool.'

Callie raised her eyebrows. 'It is?'

'Yeah. I don't want some dude attacking me with a knife but, philosophically, the idea of you being married doesn't bother me. Marriage is lame, anyway. Human beings aren't meant to be monogamous.'

'They aren't?'

'Hell, no. Look at how few other animal species mate for life. Humans are supposed to experience different people. It's called polyamory.'

Callie looked at him for a moment. A sudden recollection of her fantasy blow job flashed in her mind, causing a heated flush to rise to her cheeks.

'Well, I'm glad to know that,' she murmured.

Eldrich eyed her with a rather sly look. 'Why else

would you have left your husband? You know that you were just sick of him.'

Callie's flush deepened. 'Well, that's partly true,' she admitted.

'And your sex life?'

Callie figured that she should have been shocked by the question but, oddly enough, she wasn't. Must have something to do with the sequel to her fantasy, which was currently screening in her mind. 'That was . . . less than exciting.'

Eldrich sat there looking at her through his mascara-coated eyelashes until Callie shifted uncomfortably.

'What?' she muttered. 'Lots of people have less than exciting sex lives.'

'But not all of them want to do something about it.' Eldrich dragged on his cigarette again and continued watching her.

'Who said I wanted to do something about it?'

'You did.'

'Now you're a mind-reader?'

'No, I'm just perceptive.'

Callie shook her head at him. She was beginning to feel light-headed from the effects of smoke and the turn of this conversation. Eldrich leant forward and took her hand in his pale one, sliding his fingers over hers.

'Remember, Callie,' he murmured, 'your Tarot reading said you had to question who was in control.'

Callie swallowed hard. 'I don't have to question that. I know who's in control.'

Her voice sounded unconvincing even to herself. Eldrich put down his coffee mug and crushed out the cigarette.

'Are you sure about that?' He stood up, pushing his hands into the pockets of his jacket as he looked at her. 'Or do you want to find out?'

Callie's courage suddenly faltered. It wasn't that she didn't trust Eldrich, or at least Tess's opinion of him, but she'd never been with anyone like him in her life. Maybe that was the point, an inner voice reminded her. Sex didn't have to be all hearts and roses. Heaven knew it hadn't been with Logan. And Callie knew deep down inside that she wanted to have experiences with other men, if for no other reason than to reassure herself that the problem with her and Logan's sex life wasn't her fault; if only to reassure herself that sex didn't have to simply be *pleasant*.

'All right,' she finally said. 'But I'm not making you any promises.'

'That's cool,' Eldrich replied.

Callie's nerves tightened as she and Eldrich drove back to his flat. He lived on the top floor of a Tudor building complete with wrought-iron balconies and a tended garden. Dark colours dominated the interior, which was complete with Renaissance-style furniture, a canopied bed and an entire bookshelf full of CDs. The smell of incense and candle smoke clung to the air.

'Interesting place,' Callie observed, picking up a silver candleholder welded into the shape of a naked woman.

'So why did you separate from your husband?' Eldrich went into the kitchen and took a bottle of wine from a small wine rack.

'We just weren't compatible,' Callie replied dismissingly. She picked up a box of matches and began to light the candles. 'We're quite different in personality.'

'Any chance of reconciliation?'

'No.' A tinge of regret appeared in Callie as she said the word. 'I don't think there's any chance of that.'

'You don't think?' Eldrich asked.

Callie shrugged and didn't reply. She hated the notion of giving up completely on her marriage, but how on earth could she convince Logan of the need for change?

Eldrich poured the wine and handed Callie a glass. 'Cheers, then.'

They clinked glasses. Callie took a long swallow of the velvety, red wine. The alcohol flowed into her nerves, loosening them and making her feel more relaxed. She sat down in a chair near the doors that led to the balcony, slowly processing the thought of actually fucking another man.

'So, what do you do when you're not working at the club?' she asked.

'I write poetry, and I'm working on a novel,' Eldrich replied. 'Or I go to Renaissance fairs and shit like that.'

Callie smiled. 'I had a feeling you wrote poetry. Would you read me something?'

To her amusement, Eldrich flushed. 'I don't know.'

'Come on,' Callie urged. 'I'd love to hear something.'

'Maybe later.' He went to slip a CD into the stereo. 'This is a band called the Sisters of Mercy.'

Callie listened to the thumping sound and the singer's wails about his contempt for the social order, before coming to the conclusion that she would probably never be a Goth. Probably, hell. Never.

'I meant to ask you how your mother was enjoying her Tarot cards,' she said.

'She loves them.' He lit a stick of incense, and the spicy scent filled the air. 'She's doing readings for all her friends and she's thinking of charging people now.' He stretched out on the bed, crossing his legs at the ankle, and regarded Callie with a curious look. 'And what about that reading you did for yourself?'

Callie glanced at him. 'What about it?'

'Pretty dark reading with the Devil and all.'

'I'm not worried about it,' Callie lied. She wished he hadn't brought it up. Thoughts of being tied down and a dark, male force had been invading her thoughts quite frequently for the past week. The kind of thoughts her sister was supposed to think. 'My husband doesn't even know where I am.'

'Secrecy is often what the soul is seeking.' Eldrich stroked his hand over the bed next to him. 'Come here. I'll read to you.'

Callie approached him cautiously and sat down next to him, leaning against the pillows. Eldrich reached into the bedside-table drawer and pulled out a notebook. 'This is a poem called "The Worm".' He read the poem in a low, haunting voice.

> I am the worm, burrowing down,
> wriggling in her heaven, to drown
> her hair, soil rich and black.
> Dirt beneath her nails,
> her fingers blazing red trails
> down the desert of my back:
> Hunger for the flesh, erotic fright
> at my warm, wet snack.
> The worm must bite,
> his appetite never fails:
> Ah, with ecstasy she wails.

Eldrich set the notebook aside and looked at Callie. A portentous silence filled the air. Callie cleared her throat.

'Well, that's very . . . interesting,' she said.

'My poetry is an acquired taste.'

'So am I.'

They looked at each other for a moment, and then Eldrich bent his head to kiss her. Callie stiffened slightly at first, unaccustomed to the sensation of another man's lips, but then she forced herself to relax. As she did, she began to enjoy the dry movement of Eldrich's mouth against hers and even the waxy taste of his scarlet lipstick. This was certainly the first time a man had smeared his lipstick on her, rather than the other way around.

Eldrich's hand slipped around to the back of her neck, drawing her closer as his tongue moved to part her lips. Callie opened her mouth to let him in. A shock of delight raced through her at the feeling of their tongues moving together. The scent of his incense-tinged clothes filled her nostrils.

Part of Callie was surprised by the swiftness with which her body reacted. Her pussy dampened quickly, her skin becoming so warm that beads of perspiration broke out on her chest. She drove her fingers into Eldrich's spiky, black hair. His breath brushed her lips as he pulled away from her, his eyes darkening.

'So, Callie? What now?'

'Now you fuck me, I hope.'

Eldrich shook his head. 'Now you wait.'

Callie watched as he leant over and picked up one of the flickering candles. A thrill of trepidation raced through her.

'What are you doing?' she asked.

'You'll see.' He handed her the candle, wrapping her fingers around the smooth shaft. 'Hold this.'

He kissed her cheek in a tender gesture, then moved lower to the pulse on her neck. Callie shuddered when he bit gently at the throbbing vein. With adept fingers, he unbuttoned her shirt and exposed her small breasts hugged by a dark blue camisole. Callie shrugged the shirt off her shoulders, letting Eldrich's lips move even lower. He pushed the thin material of her camisole aside. Callie was almost embarrassed by how hard her nipples already were, but Eldrich gazed at them with such lust that her modesty quickly evaporated. He took the hard peaks into his mouth, drawing and sucking at them until a moan escaped Callie's throat. She arched her back to give him better access to her flesh, signalling her readiness.

Eldrich lifted himself slightly to remove his own clothes. Callie watched with unhidden curiosity as he bared his body. He didn't exactly look the way he had in her fantasy. His body was bony and pale, his nipples pastel pink beneath a layer of sparse chest hair. A sudden image of Logan's beefier build came to Callie's mind, and she forced it away with irritation. She let her gaze move lower to Eldrich's slender penis, wondering how it would feel thrusting inside her.

'Give me that.'

'What?' Callie tore her gaze from his prick and looked up at him.

He took the candle from her. 'Take off the rest of your clothes.'

Hooking her fingers underneath the waistband of her skirt, Callie slowly pulled it down over her hips. She hadn't worn tights due to the warm weather, and Eldrich took the opportunity to run his palm up and down her bare legs. Then he slipped his hands between her thighs, pushing them apart so that he could rub her moist cunt through her underwear. Callie drew in a sharp breath, stunned by how utterly delicious the light, teasing touch of his finger felt.

She stretched out on her back as Eldrich tugged her underwear off. She loved this spread naked feeling, and the knowledge that a man really desired her. She wanted to touch Eldrich, to grasp his penis in her hand and feel every inch of his skin, but there would be time for that later. Right now, she would revel in what he was doing to her. Callie stretched her arms above her head and spread her legs as wide as she could. Eldrich dipped his fingers into her cunt, stroking the slippery folds with a precision that almost surprised her.

'Oh, Eldrich,' she gasped, wanting desperately to feel him inside of her. 'Please.'

'Close your eyes.' His hand came up to cover her eyes, blocking out even the flickering glow of the candles.

Callie's breath caught in her throat as she felt the heat of the candle flame close to her skin. Her entire body jerked in reaction when a sizzling drop of melted wax fell on her nipple, startling and thrilling her at the same time.

'Eldrich –'

'It's supposed to hurt a little,' he murmured. 'Think about how it feels.'

Another drop fell on her breast; a pool of hot wax that burned her skin and then hardened into a small coin. Sweat broke out on Callie's forehead as Eldrich dripped a path of wax over her chest, the fiery trickle cooling so quickly that her brain barely had time to register between pain and relief. Eldrich kept his hand over her eyes, forcing her to experience the heightened sensation of not knowing when the next drop of wax would fall. Callie's nerves tensed with anticipation and unease as Eldrich dripped a small puddle into her navel. Where was he going with this?

Wax drizzled in a line towards her pussy until Callie clamped her legs together. The mingled scent of lust and candles filled her throat.

'Don't do it,' she gasped. Every inch of her skin seemed to burn from the viscous path.

'Open your legs.' Eldrich's mellow voice contained a commanding note.

Heart thudding, Callie spread her legs and clenched a fistful of the bedcover as she waited for what would surely be intense pain. But, instead of hot wax scorching her tender flesh, she felt the base of the candle probing into her. With a moan, she pushed her hips upward and tried to impale herself on the thick shaft. Eldrich gave a low chuckle as he pushed the candle further into her and began fucking her with it. Callie whimpered with pleasure, every one of her senses heightened to extremes. The wax shaft slid deliciously in and out of her, and Eldrich used his other hand to massage her clit. Pleasure tightened Callie's nerves, her pussy swelling with moisture as she strained for release. Just as she was about to come, Eldrich removed the candle.

'Eldrich, please!' Callie begged, unable to stand the exquisite torture any longer.

And then a drop of melted wax fell on her swollen clit, causing her to cry out with a mixture of pain and pleasure. An intense relief followed the swift, scorching pain. It was Callie's final undoing, as her hips bucked and she came with a force that left her gasping for air.

Callie opened her eyes and stared at Eldrich in shock. His painted lips curved into a slow smile.

'And now,' he murmured. 'I'm going to fuck you.'

Moving over her, he grasped his cock in his hand as he guided it easily into her wet cunt. He pushed forth slowly to prolong the lushness of his penetration. Callie gasped, clutching his shoulders as she felt the differing sensation of his penis versus the candle. Eldrich drew back from her a little, as if he were trying to continue the slow invasion, but then he surrendered. With a low groan, he plunged into her with one long stroke.

Callie cried out as his cock filled her. The combination of humidity and hard flesh sent her into a fog of pure sensation, and then Eldrich hooked his hands underneath her thighs so that he could thrust inside her. Callie revelled in this blatant, carnal fucking. She wrapped her calves around Eldrich's legs, spurring him on with her throaty moans.

'Yeah, spread them wide . . .' Eldrich moaned, burying his head between the fleshy mounds of her breasts.

'Harder,' Callie gasped, digging her fingernails into his back. 'Fuck me really hard.'

He did, his slim hips working with increasing force, driving towards the imminent release. Callie reached up to grip the headboard. She had craved this kind of possession for so long. Eldrich gave a hoarse shout when his body exploded and he collapsed on top of her with one final thrust. Callie squirmed underneath him, her own aching need unsatisfied. Panting, she ground her lower body against him, wanting more.

'Eldrich . . .' She tried to reach between their sweaty bodies to relieve herself of the tightness, but Eldrich got there first.

His fingers stroked her sore clit, rubbing and manipulating it. Callie's entire body jerked and shuddered underneath him as she gripped his back and rode out her pleasure for the second time.

Gasping, Eldrich moved off her and on to the bed. Callie closed her eyes and tried to catch her breath, stunned by the multitude of sensations to which Eldrich had introduced her. Another infuriating image of Logan appeared behind her eyelids; one of cold, disapproving eyes and a twisted mouth. Callie gave a muffled groan and turned to bury her face in the pillow. *Damn you, Logan Waterford. Leave me the hell alone.*

Chapter Five

'So, how was your weekend?' Tess leant over the counter and gave Callie a leering look. 'Did you and Eldrich enjoy *Nosferatu*, among other things?'

Callie favoured her friend with a mild glare and popped another chocolate mint into her mouth. 'If you want details, you're not getting them.'

Tess grinned. 'Now that has to mean that you let Eldrich lure you into his clutches, doesn't it? Good for you, Callie. Just tell me one thing. Was it better than pleasant?'

Callie let her thoughts drift back to the night of candles, incense and hot wax. She smiled and nodded.

'Definitely better than pleasant. We don't have much in common, but he's an interesting man.'

'Are you going to see him again?' Tess asked.

'I don't know. I certainly don't want a serious relationship with him, or with anyone else for that matter.'

'Well, Eldrich isn't exactly a commitment kind of man, you know. That doesn't mean you two can't have a bit of fun.' Tess's eyes narrowed slightly. 'Don't tell me you're feeling guilty.'

Callie sprayed the glass counter top with cleaner and

began wiping it down. 'I'm not feeling guilty,' she said. 'But I am still married.'

Tess groaned and thunked her head on the counter for emphasis. 'Callie, for God's sake, you're married to a plank of wood! What loyalty do you owe to that man?'

'You don't know Logan,' Callie said defensively. 'Believe me, I'm well aware that he was hardly demonstrative, but that doesn't make him a horrible person.'

'Then why did you bother leaving him?' Tess retorted.

'Because you don't stay with a man just because he's not a horrible person,' Callie said. 'You know that there has to be more than that. And it's true, I did feel like I was starting to stifle in that marriage.'

Tess lifted her head. 'So why feel guilty about Eldrich?'

'I said I don't feel guilty.' Callie crossed her arms and shook her head. 'OK, maybe I feel a little regretful, but certainly not guilty.'

'Then you're definitely not ready to end things with Logan,' Tess observed.

'Yes, I am. I wouldn't have left him if I wasn't.' Callie debated about whether or not to tell Tess about her Tarot card reading, but maybe her friend could put things into perspective. 'OK, listen. I did a Tarot reading for myself the day that Eldrich came in.'

'So?'

'So it wasn't a very positive outcome,' Callie explained. 'My card for the future was the Devil. I mean, I thought that leaving Logan would *give* me independence, not take it from me.'

'It doesn't necessarily mean that,' Tess replied. 'Sometimes it's all in the interpretation.'

'I know.' Callie couldn't get rid of the nagging feeling that her own interpretation would prove to be the correct one. 'But then Logan kept popping into my head when I was with Eldrich. Do you have any idea how annoying that is?'

Tess snapped her gum and grinned. 'Actually, Logan

73

has popped into my head a few times, too, when I'm between the sheets. I didn't find it at all annoying.'

'I'm serious, Tess. Besides, you've never met the man.'

'I've seen him, though,' Tess reminded her. 'That's usually enough for me.'

'Well, I hope he was more satisfying in your fantasy life than he was in my real life,' Callie said.

Tess chuckled. 'So do you think he's looking for you?'

'Are you kidding? Of course he's looking for me. He's not one to give up.'

'Well, he'll be hard pressed to find you,' Tess pointed out. 'I'm the only one who knows you're living here.' She propped her head on her hand and narrowed her eyes. 'You know, if you really want to get him out of your head, there are ways of going about that.'

'What ways?'

'I know a woman from Haiti who performs voodoo,' Tess explained. 'She could probably perform a spell or ritual to protect you from Logan.'

Callie shook her head in disbelief. 'Tess, get real. I'm not resorting to voodoo, of all things.'

'I am being real!' Tess replied, her eyes widening with offence. 'Callie, just because you belong to the goddamn Ladies Guild doesn't mean you have the right to knock something you know nothing about.'

Callie was surprised by Tess's rather vehement response. 'OK, OK, I'm sorry. I'm not knocking voodoo. I just doubt it could do anything for me.'

'You do, huh? Why's that?'

'Well, I don't believe in it, for one thing,' Callie said.

'That's because you've never experienced it,' Tess said earnestly. 'I'm telling you, Callie, Abiona is a true mambo.'

'I thought a mambo was a dance.'

Tess rolled her eyes. 'A mambo is an ordained voodoo priestess. About a year ago, I was having trouble with this woman who thought she was in love with me. When I told her I wasn't interested, she went berserk

74

and started stalking me to the point where I got really scared. She'd leave flowers covered in blood on my doorstep and spooky shit like that. The police weren't much help, so I went to Abiona. She invoked what's called a *djab*, or a devil. Next thing I knew, my wacko stalker was in a car accident. The cops found drugs in her car, and she's been in prison ever since.'

Callie stared at her. 'Good Lord.'

Tess nodded emphatically. 'Eerie, huh?'

'I don't want Logan in a car accident!'

'Oh, no, that was because Abiona performed a black magic spell,' Tess said quickly. 'Really, Callie, I was so freaked out that I asked for the darkest ritual she could conjure up, and it worked. She usually doesn't do that. She's more interested in white magic.'

'No way, Tess. I'm not going to a mimbo.'

'A mambo,' Tess corrected. 'And why not? It couldn't hurt.'

'It hurt your stalker.'

'She deserved it,' Tess sighed. 'Look, Abiona can perform a protection spell of some kind for you. Logan doesn't even have to be involved. She can help you banish Logan from your mind so he's not haunting you all the time. And so that you can resolve whatever it is you're trying to resolve about your relationship with him.'

'Tess, I just left Logan a week ago,' Callie reminded her. 'I think it's only normal that I'm still thinking about him.'

'Ah, but remember the Tarot reading,' Tess replied. 'Abiona can also help you protect yourself from Logan in the future.'

'Look, it just seems like a bunch of nonsense to me,' Callie admitted.

'Then why do you believe the Tarot prediction?' Triumph flashed in Tess's expression when Callie didn't respond. 'You don't know, do you? So why not give voodoo a chance?'

'Because it's weird, Tess, that's why,' Callie retorted. 'I may have been willing to fuck my first Goth, but I'm hardly about to jump right into black magic, spells and sacrificing chickens. Tarot cards are a little more benign, don't you think? Voodoo is absurd foolishness.'

Tess's mouth turned down at the corners as she moved away from the counter. 'I pity you, Callie.'

'You do, do you?'

'Yes. You left Logan because you wanted freedom, and yet you're still trapped in his Euro-centric, WASP, logical way of thinking.'

Callie looked at Tess. 'What on earth does that mean?'

'Think about it. Wouldn't Logan say the exact same thing about voodoo? That it was absurd and foolish and nonsense? Wouldn't he look down his nose at something he's only experienced through rumour?'

A slight feeling of shame trickled through Callie. She rubbed her finger over a crack in the counter.

'He might say that,' she allowed.

'Then why are you saying the same thing?' Tess asked. 'That's not going to get you very far in trying to distance yourself from him.'

Callie bit her lip as her friend's words hit a bit too close to home. But voodoo? What in the world would Logan have to say if he ever discovered she'd gone to a voodoo priestess? He probably wouldn't say anything. He'd be too busy going ballistic. Callie had to smile slightly at the thought. She pushed her hair away from her forehead and sighed.

'All right, point well taken,' she said. 'I'll think about it, OK? I'm not promising anything, but I will think about it.'

'Awesome.' Tess smiled and ambled towards the back of the store. 'I'll be right here when you're finished thinking.'

'I don't doubt it,' Callie muttered.

* * *

The envelope bore no return address, but the postmark read 'Hilton Head, South Carolina'. Logan turned the envelope over and slipped the blade of his silver letter opener underneath the flap. He pulled out a sheet of plain white paper and unfolded it. As he scanned the spidery handwriting, his heart plummeted.

Logan swore and crushed the paper in his fist. A sudden assault of memories pushed at the back of his mind. He forced them away, blocking them off with mental walls as thick as the Great Wall of China. He'd be damned to hell if he would let the mistakes of his past return to haunt him. Especially not after he'd spent fifteen years covering them up.

'Logan?' A knock sounded at the door, and Adam poked his head into the room.

'What is it, Adam?' Logan tossed the crumpled letter into the bin and told himself to forget about it.

Adam entered the room, carrying a notepad. 'I thought you might want an update about your wife's situation.'

'Have you found her yet?'

'No, but –'

'Then I'm not interested.'

Adam looked hurt. 'You'll be interested in this, I think,' he suggested.

Logan sat down and levelled a look at the younger man. 'What is it, then?'

Adam arranged himself in one of the leather chairs in front of the desk. He cleared his throat and consulted his notepad.

'First of all, did you know that Callie has a bank account in her name?'

Logan's eyebrows lifted. 'We have a joint account.'

'Yes, but apparently she has one on her own, too,' Adam reported. 'With the Wachovia Bank on York Avenue.'

'How much money is in it?'

'About two thousand dollars.'

'And where did she get this money?' Logan asked. 'Not from me, I hope.'

Adam scratched his head and examined his notes again. 'I'm not sure, to be honest with you. Her records show that she has been making deposits twice a month. The same amount of money each time.'

Logan tried to think. He'd never been particularly concerned about money where Callie was concerned. She didn't have extravagant tastes like her sister, so he had never bothered to keep track of her purchases unless he was straightening out their finances. Now he wondered if she'd been taking money from their account and putting it into her own.

He opened a drawer of his filing cabinet and pulled out a folder of bank statements. 'When were these deposits made?'

'Around the first and fifteenth of every month.'

Logan frowned. 'That's when pay cheques are usually issued.'

He shuffled through the bank paperwork of the last few months. As far as he could tell, there had been no withdrawals or transfers that corresponded to Callie's deposits into her account.

'She made a withdrawal yesterday of forty dollars,' Adam said. 'So obviously she's still alive.'

'Well, of course she's alive,' Logan said, suddenly realising that he hadn't even considered the alternative. What if something sinister had happened to Callie? He shook his head to clear the thought from his mind and reached for the telephone. No way. She'd left him of her own free will.

'Go and find out where those deposits came from,' he told Adam. 'And do it quickly.'

'Yes, sir.' Adam closed his notebook and hurried from the office, closing the door behind him.

Logan stabbed out a series of numbers on the telephone keypad and waited as the phone rang at the other end.

'Hello?' Gloria Harper's voice flowed breathlessly over the line.

'Gloria, it's Logan. Do you know if Callie has been working somewhere without my knowledge?'

'Hello, sugar,' Gloria said delightedly. 'I'm fine, thank you. How are you?'

Logan's fingers tightened on the receiver. 'Don't fuck with me, Gloria. Has Callie been working?'

Gloria laughed. 'Oh, I'd love to fuck with you, darling, you know that.'

'Never mind then.' Logan almost slammed the telephone down, but then Gloria's voice came over the receiver again.

'All right, all right,' she said. 'But you know, Logan, there's nothing wrong with basic pleasantries.'

'I never said that there was. Now would you please answer my question?'

'No, as far as I know, Callie was not working anywhere,' Gloria said. 'Why do you ask?'

'It appears that she had a separate bank account that I didn't know about,' Logan replied. 'I'm wondering where she got the money to deposit.'

'You poor dear,' Gloria murmured. 'I'm so sorry that Callie is putting you through such nonsense.'

'Have you heard from her yet?'

'No, but I'm sure that she's fine.'

'Of course she's fine. She's probably holed up somewhere in the city, laughing about this whole situation.'

'Well, she wasn't exactly gleeful about it when she came to see me,' Gloria said. 'Look, I hate to think of you rambling all alone in that big house of yours. Why don't you come over for dinner tonight?'

'No, thanks. I have work to do at home this evening. If you hear from Callie, I'd appreciate it if you would let me know immediately.'

'You know I will, sugar. Good luck.'

Logan hung up the telephone and glanced at his watch. He had to be in court tomorrow, which meant an evening of preparation. With a sigh, he packed up his briefcase and headed out to the car park. He admitted to himself that he'd been hoping Callie would at least call by now to let him know that she was all right. Of course, she probably assumed that he'd had tracers put on his telephones. And that would be an accurate assumption.

When he got home, Logan took a quick shower and tried not to think about either his wife or the letter he'd received earlier that day. When was the last time he'd thought about his experiences fifteen years ago? The answer was fifteen years ago. He'd effectively blocked that all from his mind and had no intentions of reliving it now.

He stepped out of the shower, his gaze falling on the small array of bottles and creams that belonged to Callie. She appeared to have taken very few of her personal belongings with her. Logan uncapped a bottle of lotion and took a whiff. Vanilla and lemons. He remembered that Callie always smelled that way in the morning.

With a mutter of frustration, he replaced the cap and went back into the bedroom. As he dressed in jeans and a T-shirt, he realised that many of Callie's things were still around: the silver vanity set he'd given her for an anniversary present, her jewellery box, the photos of her mother, even a ragged stuffed animal she'd kept for years.

One month, Logan decided. If he didn't hear from her within a month, then he'd throw away all this stuff. There was no sense in keeping any of it if Callie wasn't here.

Logan went downstairs, aware of a nagging feeling of regret inside. He tried to shove it away. He was just used to Callie being around, he told himself. He was accustomed to sitting with her at breakfast, to her presence when he got home from work, to watching her get ready for dinner parties and listening to her latest activities. It was no wonder the place seemed empty without her. After three years, the absence of another person became glaringly apparent.

He went into the kitchen and poured himself a drink, then sat down at the kitchen table to read the evening newspaper. Before he finished even the first article, the doorbell rang.

Gloria Harper stood on the doorstep, bearing a foil-wrapped package. She smiled and held it up for his inspection.

'Hi, sugar! I brought you some fresh lasagne.'

Logan eyed her sceptically. 'You made lasagne?'

Gloria giggled. 'Don't be silly, honey. My cook made it this afternoon. I just thought you might enjoy it. What with Callie gone and all, I suspect you aren't doing much cooking. I'll just pop this in the oven for you.'

She brushed past him and marched into the kitchen as if she belonged there. With a mutter of irritation, Logan closed the door and followed her. He leaned against the kitchen doorjamb and crossed his arms over his chest.

'Make me a vodka martini, would you?' Gloria flashed him a pert smile and began prancing around the kitchen as she checked the oven temperature, added Parmesan cheese to the lasagne and laid the table.

For a moment, Logan watched her. She was wearing a tight, little suit jacket cut low enough to reveal a considerable amount of her fleshy cleavage and a skirt that showed off the full length of her rounded legs. Her blonde hair was perfectly teased, her face made up to perfection. She had a flagrant, overt sexuality that was the exact opposite of Callie's unpretentious nature. Overt sexuality always had an effect on a man's prick.

'Gloria, I have court tomorrow,' Logan said. 'I have a lot of work to do this evening.'

'Well, you can't do it on an empty stomach, now, can you?' Gloria reached out to pat his stomach as she sailed past him. Then she paused and lifted her eyebrows, letting her fingertips trail over his abdomen. 'My goodness, Logan. You have quite a washboard stomach there, don't you?'

Logan moved away from her and opened the drinks cabinet. 'One drink and then you're leaving.'

Gloria's lower lip jutted outwards in a mild sulk. 'Really, Logan. Here I bring you dinner and you don't even invite me to stay?'

Logan sighed. 'I said I have work to do tonight.'

'And plenty of time to do it in.' Gloria looked into the bread bin and removed half a baguette.

'So, how's Ted, Gloria?' Logan asked dryly. He handed her the martini and watched her slice the bread.

She threw him another smile. 'Fabulous, sugar, just fabulous. Come now, sit down.'

She downed half her martini and filled two plates with bread and lasagne. Logan's stomach rumbled at the smell of the rich tomato sauce and cheese. Figuring he could throw Gloria out after they ate, he sat down across from her and picked up his silverware.

'There, see, isn't this nice?' Gloria asked. 'I really can't stand the thought of you alone here every night.'

'Believe me, I'm fine.' Logan was in no mood to engage in idle chatter, least of all with Gloria Harper.

She nibbled a piece of lasagne and looked at him. 'Callie said you were too controlled.'

'What?'

'That's what she said when she came to see me after she left. Something about the fact that she didn't feel like she knew you at all. She also mentioned that your sex life wasn't exactly satisfying.'

'Jesus.' Logan shoved his plate away and reached for his scotch. 'What are you, her psychotherapist?'

'I'm her sister,' Gloria said earnestly. 'She trusts me with these things. And really, Logan, I'm sure she tried to talk to you about them as well.'

'I don't even know what that means,' Logan snapped. 'She doesn't know me? Is that some sort of code or something? And I'm too controlled because I happen to believe in dignity?' He downed his scotch and wiped his mouth, glowering at Gloria. 'And there is nothing wrong with our sex life.'

Gloria blinked. 'I wasn't the one who said that, sugar. But then, I also wasn't the one who had a sex life with you.'

'Thank heavens for that,' Logan muttered. He ripped apart a piece of bread. What nerve Callie had, discussing the intimate details of their relationship with Gloria, of all people.

'Now, Logan, there's no need to be rude to me simply because you couldn't satisfy your wife.' Gloria stood up and took her plate to the sink, her hips swaying.

Logan sighed, well aware that she was trying to needle him. 'Thanks for the lasagne, Gloria. Now goodnight.'

'Or maybe it was the other way around.' Gloria reached over to take his plate, letting her full breasts press against his shoulder. 'Maybe Callie couldn't satisfy you.'

'I am not about to discuss this with you.'

'Pity. A little discussion might change things.'

Logan glared at her. 'There are no "things" that need to be changed.'

Gloria laughed and swallowed the last of her martini. She hitched herself up on to the table next to him and crossed her legs.

'Darling, if that were the case, then Callie wouldn't have left you,' she said. 'Women want men who really know how to *take* them. Like James Bond, for instance. You never saw him being wishy-washy about going after a woman, did you? Of course not. That's because he knew how to make them really feel like women.' She pursed her lips and began swinging one leg thoughtfully. 'That's what you have to do, sugar. Make a woman feel like a woman.'

'Gloria, if you're trying to seduce me again, it's not working.' Even as Logan said the words, his prick

83

hardened in his jeans. It wasn't an odd result, given that his eyes were on a level with Gloria's cleavage. The woman's chest could rival that of any porn star.

She laughed again. 'I'm not trying to seduce you, Logan. I'm trying to make you seduce me.'

'That's not working either.' He glared at her, but refused to move away. He'd be damned if this woman would get the better of him.

Gloria heaved a sigh. 'Oh, sugar, don't make me think that Callie was right about you. I didn't believe her, you know. In fact, I told her that you could probably make me come just by looking at me the right way.' She smiled. 'Who do you want to prove right? Me or her?'

'Neither one of you.' Logan pushed his chair away from the table, which proved to be his first mistake.

Gloria quickly slipped her high-heeled shoe off and placed her foot on Logan's thigh. He groaned inwardly. Sure, he had wondered what it would be like to fuck Gloria, but he'd never had any intention of actually finding out. He'd thought that his sex life with Callie was enough. Apparently, she didn't feel the same way. A growing sense of bitterness filled the back of Logan's throat. Who did Callie think she was, anyway? She came from a lower-class background, and she'd only ever been able to dream of living the kind of life he'd given her. Walking out on him and mouthing off about their sex life is the way she'd chosen to repay him? He didn't need that kind of gratitude.

His eyes narrowed as he looked at Gloria. Her foot moved closer to his crotch as her toes brushed against the bulge in his jeans.

'Come on, Logan,' she purred. 'Just once, OK? You know I've wanted this ever since you married Callie. And she never has to know. I wouldn't want to hurt her in any way.'

She scooted her arse up to the edge of the table and placed her other foot on his thigh. Then her fingers went to the buttons of her suit jacket. She winked at him with a false eyelash and began unfastening the buttons. Logan watched without expression as the full curves of Gloria's breasts came into view. She wore a pastel-pink teddy that barely covered her nipples, which jutted forward like a couple of bullets. Definitely nothing like her sister.

Gloria smiled and began circling her nipples with her fingernails. 'Nice, huh? Men have always loved my tits.'

She reached behind her to unzip her skirt and wriggled out of it, leaving herself clad only in the skimpy lingerie. She had a creamy, fleshy body that looked as if it were designed for the sole purpose of carnal pleasure. Logan's prick strained against the button fly of his jeans as Gloria slid off the table and approached him. Her fingers quickly worked his fly, then she grasped the waistband of his jeans and pulled them down over his hips. Logan didn't bother trying to stop her. She murmured a little cooing noise in her throat as she grasped his penis and started to kneel.

Logan grabbed her arms to stop her. 'No.'

She gave him quizzical look. 'No?'

'You said you wanted to fuck me, so fuck.' Damn, her fist was tight around his cock.

'Well, aren't you impatient?' Gloria giggled and thrust her hips forward. 'Undo me then, would you?'

Logan reached between her legs and yanked at the poppers of the teddy. He rubbed one finger over her pussy and felt the viscous heat of her dampening his hand. Gloria gave a moan and twisted her nipples between her fingers.

'Mmm, nice touch, sugar. A little higher ... yeah, right there.'

Logan reached up to pull the cups of her bra down, exposing her large nipples to his gaze. Without thinking, he captured one of her nipples between his lips and rolled it over his tongue. Gloria gasped and moved closer, planting her legs on either side of him as she straddled his lap. The warmth and scent of her body surged up between them. Logan clutched her hips and pulled her forward, settling her over his cock. With a wriggle, a giggle and a slide, Gloria sank down on to him and began to ride. She was a full-blown expert at this, her inner muscles squeezing and releasing as her body bounced up and down. Her hot breath brushed against his jaw.

'Take off your shirt,' she gasped. 'I love feeling a man's chest against my nipples.'

Logan pulled his shirt off, thinking that this woman was going to milk him dry with those muscles. She was working herself into quite a frenzy, her head thrown back and her skin flushed pink. She sidled forward and rubbed her tits against his chest in time with her undulations.

'Oh, yes,' she groaned, wrapping her arms around his neck. 'God, sugar, I knew you'd have a cock like a rod of fucking steel. Filling me to the brim, you are. Ah, that feels so, so incredible.'

She pulled back slightly and rubbed her hands over his damp chest, giving a happy sigh as she traced every muscle. 'Logan, you could be another Bond if you tried.'

'I don't know about that, but you do put Pussy Galore to shame.'

Gloria giggled with delight and began accelerating her springy movements. The slick moistness of her seemed to spread through Logan's body. But as much as he liked being snugly ensconced in Gloria's pussy, Logan disliked more the passive position she'd put him in. He grabbed her around the waist and stood in one swift movement. Gloria gave a little yelp and tightened her arms around his neck.

'Logan!'

He spread her out on the table, reaching down to push her thighs apart as he descended upon her. She stared up at him with both shock and exhilaration. With a grunt, Logan pushed into her and braced his hands on either side of her head. He slammed into her repeatedly, making Gloria squeal her pleasure in short, loud bursts, her breasts bouncing with every thrust. Logan tugged at her nipples with his lips as she wrapped her legs around his waist and forced him in even deeper. Logan gritted his teeth and reined in his control as long as he could, feeling Gloria's pussy convulse tightly around him. Then, he pulled out and stroked his cock until a wave coursed through his body and his come spilled on to the pastel-pink lingerie still covering Gloria's belly.

'Oh, honey.' She opened her eyes and stared at him, reaching up to wipe a trickle of sweat off her forehead. 'That was amazing. Callie is obviously out of her mind.'

Logan pulled away from her and reached for his jeans. After putting them on, he handed her a teatowel. Gloria sat up slowly, still looking rather dazed.

'Sugar, make me another martini, would you?'

Logan was tempted to refuse, but he realised it would be callous to throw her out immediately. He poured another martini and handed it to her. She swallowed half of it and patted her neck with the teatowel.

'You can get dressed now,' Logan said evenly.

Gloria blinked at him. 'Darling, don't tell me you're upset with me. Come on, we both wanted to try this, didn't we? I wanted to find out for myself what you were really like, and you ... well, you wanted to find out what it was like to fuck me. All men want that, you know.'

Logan shook his head. 'I'm not upset with you, Gloria. It was great, but it's not going to happen again. And I do have a lot of work to do this evening.'

Gloria's lip thrust forward in another pout, but she bent to retrieve her skirt and slip it on. 'So why did Callie say those things about you?'

Logan felt his muscles tense with irritation. 'I don't know. Frankly, I don't even know if she said them at all.'

Gloria's eyes widened. 'Of course she did. I wouldn't lie to you.'

'No? You won't lie to me, but you'll lie to your husband and sister?'

'I'm not lying to Ted or Callie,' Gloria retorted. 'I'm just not telling them certain things. There's nothing wrong with that.'

Logan dragged a hand down his face and sighed. He suddenly felt very weary. 'I'm going to call you a cab.'

'Don't be silly. I can drive.'

Logan ignored her protest and called for a cab. After he made sure she was heading safely home, he cleaned up the kitchen and tried to ignore the hollow feeling inside. Given that his wife had left him without the briefest explanation, Logan didn't think it was necessary to feel guilty about screwing Gloria. Still, he went upstairs and took another scorching hot shower.

Chapter Six

'*I*s that her?' Adam grabbed the binoculars and peered through the side window of the van at the woman walking out of Nebula Arcana. The shop was located in trendy City Market, sandwiched between a bookstore and an art gallery. 'Wow, she has green hair. What's that about? Logan's wife can have green hair, but my eyebrow ring looks stupid?'

Sam gave the younger man a strange look. 'What the hell are you talking about?'

'Nothing,' Adam muttered.

'Does she look anything like this photograph?' He handed Adam one of several photographs of Callie Waterford that Logan had given them.

Adam tore his gaze away from the binoculars and glanced at the photos of the dark-haired woman. Callie Waterford was nice looking enough, although hardly the kind of bombshell Adam would have expected Logan to marry. He looked back at Green Hair again.

'Well, no,' he admitted. 'Who is that, then?'

'Probably another worker or the owner.' Sam picked up the folder and looked through it at Callie's banking statements. 'The deposits Callie made to her private account came from this place. The owner is Tess Zimmerman. I don't have a photo of her.'

'I can't believe Logan would let his wife work in a place like this. She belongs to the Ladies' Guild, and she works at a hippie joint?'

'He didn't know,' Sam replied. 'I asked him.'

Adam looked at Sam. 'You talked to him without me? When?'

'Relax, kid. I called him last night.'

'You could've let me know,' Adam retorted. He put down the binoculars and grabbed a doughnut from a box on the floor. He and Sam had been stuck in this van nearly all day without a single Callie Waterford spotting. Adam was getting bored stiff. 'What did he say?'

'He was annoyed, of course, what did you think? He had no idea his wife was working here.'

'Why didn't she tell him?'

'I have no idea. Maybe he didn't want her to work.'

Adam chewed on the sugary doughnut and peered out of the window again. 'So, what's Logan going to do? You think he's going to show up here?'

'He wants us to find out where she's living first.'

'Wait, someone's coming out!' Adam grabbed the binoculars and looked at the woman who opened the shop door. She was carrying a watering can, and she began watering the flower boxes outside the shop. Adam adjusted the binoculars and focused them on the woman's face. 'I think that's her!'

'Mission accomplished,' Sam said dryly.

Adam watched as Callie Waterford continued watering the plants. She wore loose, linen trousers and a baggy cotton shirt that made her look casual and unsophisticated; a far cry from the manicured society women who frequented Savannah's upper crust. What in the hell had Logan seen in her? And why did he want her back so badly? She must be a dynamo in bed.

Uncomfortable with the thought, Adam put down the binoculars. 'So, now what do we do?'

'We wait until she leaves, then we follow her home.' Sam squinted and looked out of the window. 'Now, who's this?'

A pale, lanky man wearing a black coat ambled down the street towards Callie. He stopped and said something to her, then put his arm around her and kissed her cheek.

'Hah!' Sam said. 'She must be fucking him.'

'Him?' Adam stared at the punk fellow. 'You've got to be kidding me. She'd pick him over Logan?'

'Maybe she's slumming.'

Callie and the punk went back into Nebula Arcana and closed the door. Callie put the CLOSED sign in the window, but neither one of them emerged again.

'Why isn't she leaving?' Adam asked.

'Maybe they've gone out of the back door.' Sam pulled open the van door and hopped on to the street. 'Wait here. I'm going to check it out.'

Adam waited impatiently for Sam to return. An image of Callie Waterford and the punk fucking each other appeared in his mind, then was swiftly followed by an image of Callie and Logan doing the same thing. The first image disgusted Adam; the second made his penis harden.

'I think they're staying there.' Sam came back into the van. 'I saw a light go on upstairs. Give me the binoculars.'

He peered up at the room above the shop. Adam followed his gaze. The curtains were open, and he could clearly see the silhouettes of Callie and the man moving around.

'Must be a flat up there.' Sam put down the binoculars and yawned. 'So, that's that. I'll call Waterford tonight.'

'Why don't we stop by his house?' Adam suggested. He was a bit disappointed that they had found Callie so quickly, since it meant Logan wouldn't need them anymore. 'I'm sure he's home.'

'Yeah, OK. Might as well get paid now, too.' Sam pulled the van back on to the street and headed towards the Waterford home.

Adam gaped at the ivy-covered brick mansion as Sam paused at the wrought-iron gate surrounding the property. This? Callie Waterford had left this house *and* Logan for a job at a hippie joint and a punk bastard? She must be a bit strange in the head.

Sam spoke into the intercom system, and the gates slid open in front of them.

'I can't believe it,' Adam said. 'Why would she leave this?'

'Kid, we don't care about her motive,' Sam said. 'Our job was just to find her.'

Adam jumped out of the van, his heart pounding as he and Sam walked up the steps to the front of the house and rang the doorbell. So, this was where Logan lived! It was like visiting a Savannah Mecca.

The door opened, and the god himself stood there dressed in jeans and a dark-blue shirt with a newspaper under his arm. His black hair was ruffled, giving him a slightly dishevelled look.

Adam swallowed hard. 'We have some news, Logan,' he said importantly.

'Yeah? What is it?'

'How about a drink first?' Sam asked. 'I've been trapped in a van all afternoon with this dweeb.' He jerked a thumb towards Adam.

Logan's mouth quirked slightly before he pushed open the door further to let them in.

Adam drank in the sights of the polished floors, mahogany furniture and oil paintings as Logan led them into a sitting room. Everything was so crisp and clean, reeking of good taste and money.

'What'll you have?' Logan asked.

'Gin and tonic,' Sam replied.

'Adam?'

'Um, I'll have the same, sir.' Adam sat down on the

edge of a chair and watched Logan mix the drinks. He noticed that Logan was barefoot. He couldn't help staring at the other man's feet, which were long and beautifully shaped. Even his toenails were perfect, clipped into half-moons. Adam wondered if it was possible to have a foot fetish for men's feet rather than women's.

'Adam.'

Adam's head jerked up as he realised that Logan was holding out a glass.

'Thanks.' Adam took a long draught of the drink and tried to force his mind away from Logan's feet.

'So, as I told you, we found Callie working at this New Age shop in City Market,' Sam said. 'She seems to be living there as well.'

Logan frowned. 'Living there?'

'Yes, in a room above the shop.'

'This is the stupidest thing I've ever heard. Why didn't she tell me she was working there?'

'Probably because she knew you'd make her stop,' Sam suggested.

'There's something else, Logan,' Adam said.

'What?'

Adam paused for effect before delivering the news. 'There was a man with her.'

'What man?' Logan snapped.

'Some idiot who looked like a corpse,' Adam snorted.

'I think he's called a Gothic,' Sam said. 'You know, those kids that worship Satan and crap.'

'What in the hell was Callie doing with someone like that?'

Sam downed his gin and tonic. 'Well, we don't know that they were actually *doing* anything.'

'Least of all with each other,' Adam piped in. He cringed when Logan shot him a deadly glare.

Sam sighed. 'What the dweeb means is that we saw the Gothic chap go up to Callie's room, but we can't confirm that they're romantically involved.'

'They'd better not be,' Logan said, his voice as cold and hard as ice. 'Both of you, get out of here. I'm going down to this place myself.'

'Can I come with you?' Adam couldn't stand the thought of missing all the action.

'No.' Logan stalked towards the staircase. 'Get out.'

Callie stifled a yawn and shifted in her seat. The theatre held only a hundred people, but the seats were crammed so closely together that leg room was a distant fantasy. A spotlight shone on to the stage, illuminating Tess in all her naked glory. She had a slim, tomboy figure and skin that glowed paper white underneath the lights. The large nipples that crowned her small breasts gave her a very erotic sensibility. Two attendants moved around her, using brushes to cover her body with multicoloured paints. The metallic sounds of industrial music drifted from hidden speakers.

After Tess's body was covered in gloppy paint, she moved slowly over to a series of blank canvases that had been hung behind her. In time to the music, she started twisting and writhing against the canvas in a sort of dance.

'Magnificent,' a man in the seat behind Callie murmured. 'It's like she's paying homage to the muses of creativity, much as ancient women did in temples dedicated to the gods.'

Callie bit her lip to keep from smiling at the man's pompous intellectuality. Next to her, Eldrich slouched in his chair and chewed on a piece of red licorice. Amidst the rumble of music, Tess continued her writhings until all of the canvases had been smeared with paint. Then she plunged her hands into two buckets and began flinging paint at the canvases, all the while swivelling her hips in a frenzy. At the end of the hour-long performance, her chest heaved as she tried to catch her breath and take her bows to uncertain applause.

'Well, that was different,' Eldrich observed as the

theatre lights came on. 'Should we stay and congratulate her?'

'No, she told me not to bother. She needs to shower, and then she's going to try and sell the paintings. I'll see her tomorrow.'

Callie and Eldrich exited the theatre and drove back to City Market. He parked on St Julian, and they began walking back to the shop.

'Has Tess ever asked you to be in one of her shows?' Eldrich asked, lighting a herbal cigarette.

'No. Why, has she asked you?'

'Yeah, she wanted to know if I'd be in her *Sexology* show, whatever that is.'

'Did you agree?' Callie asked.

'I told her I'd consider it as long as I don't have to strip.'

Callie chuckled. As she and Eldrich rounded the corner towards Nebula Arcana, she noticed a man standing in front of the shop. She stopped in her tracks. Even though he was wrapped in dark shadows, she would have known that figure anywhere. Her heart plummeted.

'Callie?' Eldrich turned to glance at her. 'What's the matter?'

Callie pressed a hand against her chest. She should have known she could never escape him. 'It's Logan.'

'Logan?'

She gestured towards the shop. 'My husband.'

'Oh, shit.' Eldrich backed away a few steps. 'This can't be good.'

'No, it's not good.'

'You want me to call 911?'

'No, that won't be necessary.' Callie wondered if she could flee without Logan seeing her, but she knew that would be another futile effort. They would have to have it out once and for all.

'He's not dangerous,' she said. 'At least, I don't think he is.'

Eldrich had suddenly turned even paler, which made him look ghostly. 'Well, um, I guess you'd want to talk to him alone, then, huh?'

'Don't worry,' Callie replied. 'He won't hurt you.'

'No? He looks pretty big.' Eldrich dropped the cigarette and ground it out with his heel. 'Look, Callie, I don't want to get messed up in this.'

Callie looked at him. 'You knew I was married, Eldrich. I didn't try and hide that from you.'

'Yeah, but your husband doesn't look like the very understanding type,' Eldrich muttered. He backed away, holding up his hands. 'Look, I'll give you a call sometime, OK? In the meantime, I think I should stay out of this.'

With that, he spun on his heel and began walking quickly in the opposite direction. Callie watched him go, then turned back to Logan. The muscles at the back of her neck tightened as she started towards him. She should have known this would happen sooner or later. She only wished it had been later. Her heels clicked on the sidewalk and adrenaline began to surge in her blood.

Logan glanced in her direction. The entire line of his body tensed as he saw her.

'Hello, Logan.' Callie fought both the tremble in her voice and the urge to turn and run.

'Callie.' His expression looked as if it had been carved from stone, but his eyes flashed with intense displeasure.

Callie paused some distance away from him. 'How did you find me?'

'I have my ways. Do you want to tell me what you think you're doing?'

A couple of passers-by glanced in their direction as the angry undertone of Logan's words floated on the hot air. Callie debated the wisdom of telling him to come into the store, but decided she didn't want the rest of the world knowing her business.

'Come inside,' she said, reaching for her keys. 'I've

been trying to explain things to you for weeks now, only you never listen to me.'

'Don't start this shit with me again,' Logan snapped. 'I give you everything you want.'

A responding anger ignited inside Callie. Who was he to tell her what she wanted? She suppressed the urge to snap at him and instead unlocked the door. She didn't bother turning the lights on, preferring the cloak of semi-darkness. Logan followed her inside, taking in the tie-dyed atmosphere of the shop in one glance.

'This is where you chose to work?' he said, his voice dripping with contempt. 'Christ, it looks like Jerry Garcia threw up in here.'

Callie locked the door behind her and gave Logan a derisive look. 'There is no need to be condescending.'

'There is every need to be condescending,' Logan retorted. 'Why didn't you tell me you were working here? How long has this been going on?'

'For several months,' Callie said. 'And I didn't tell you because I knew you wouldn't approve.'

'And is that why you didn't tell me you were leaving me?' Logan snapped. 'Because you knew I wouldn't approve?'

'No, I thought you'd try and stop me.'

'And you thought I wouldn't find you anyway? You should know by now that I have more than enough resources at my disposal.'

'Yes, I do know that.' Callie's hands clenched into fists as she struggled against an increasing anger. 'I know that you're the great and powerful Logan who sees everything and always gets what he wants.'

'Damn right.' Logan picked up a crystal ball that sat on a nearby shelf. 'Get your things. You're coming home.'

'I am not,' Callie said. 'I didn't leave you only to have you drag me back again.'

'What is this all about, Callie?' Logan asked. His fingers tightened on the crystal ball, but his voice didn't rise a single octave. 'You're trying to prove something, is that it?'

'Maybe I am,' Callie replied. 'Maybe I'm trying to prove that I'm sick of the life we've been leading.'

'You mean the life of expensive furnishings, gourmet food, designer clothing and everything you could possible want? Is that the life you're talking about?'

'No,' Callie snapped. 'I'm talking about the life of stilted conversations and a black hole of emotional warmth. A life based on our image rather than our relationship. A life devoid of any kind of connection to my own husband.'

Logan rolled his eyes. 'This kind of *Cosmopolitan* magazine drama is a bit overdone. If you want to continue working at this ridiculous place, then fine. But I want you to pack your belongings and come home right now.'

A wave of sheer fury rose in Callie like an overflowing pot of water.

'Fuck you, Logan,' she bit out. 'I'm not a child, and you sure as hell can't treat me like one. If you can't even understand why I left you, then what makes you think I'm coming back?'

'The fact that you can't possibly expect to continue living like this.'

'I can continue living like this! I have my own money and my own place to stay. More importantly, I have some freedom. I can wear a black dress somewhere without my own husband telling me I look like a slut.'

Logan's eyes narrowed. 'And do you also have someone to take that dress off you?'

Startled, Callie took a step back. How on earth did the man know everything? 'What are you talking about?'

'I'm talking about this punk kid you've been seeing. Are you fucking him?'

'That is none of your business!'

'The hell it's not.' Anger darkened Logan's eyes as he strode towards her in three long steps. 'You're still my wife, or have you conveniently forgotten that?'

Callie clenched her fists and battled the urge to step away from him. 'I most certainly have not forgotten that. My status as your wife is what got me here in the first place!'

'And it's what's bringing you back home right now.' A vein throbbed in Logan's neck as he grabbed her arm, his fingers tightening around her so hard that his grip almost hurt.

Alarm fluttered in Callie. Logan had never physically hurt her, but then she had never left him before.

'No,' she said firmly. 'I'm not coming back.'

His grip tightened. 'You want a divorce? Is that what this is all about?'

'I want to be away from you.' A divorce? Was that what she wanted? It sounded so painfully final. Callie twisted her arm in a vain effort to free herself. 'Logan, let go! You're hurting me.'

'I'm getting very tired of this, Callie. I don't have time for it.'

'That's the problem!' Callie cried. 'You don't have time for our relationship when it should be the most important thing in the world to you.'

'Where do you get the stupid idea that it isn't important?'

'From you! You treat me like a stranger or a child or a sister. Anything but what I am. Your wife. You don't even fuck me right!'

Callie knew she had pushed him too far when his jaw clenched with fury. He yanked her against him so swiftly that she almost fell.

'So that's it, is it?' he said, his voice low and icy. 'You want to be fucked right? What's your definition of "right", then?'

'Doing it with anyone but you,' Callie retorted. 'Now, let me go, you bastard!'

She pressed her hand against his chest and tried to shove him away. He didn't budge. His body was so

99

tense with anger that he felt like a stone wall. Fear and an odd excitement began to swirl inside her.

'Why should I let you go?' He grabbed her other hand and pressed it against his crotch. 'Don't you want to be fucked right for a change?'

'By you?' Callie sneered, even as her body quickened like an electrical wire when she felt his growing erection. 'The day you do that is the day that hell freezes over.'

'Did you or didn't you fuck that punk bastard?' Logan asked, his hands tightening on her painfully. 'Was that "right" for you?'

'What if it was? What are you going to do about it? Punish me?' The instant she looked up at him, Callie knew she had pushed him over the edge. 'Logan –'

His eyes burnt. 'Is that what you want? Now that I think about it, a punishment would be very deserving. After all, you owed me at least an explanation before you walked out on me.'

'You wouldn't dare.' Suddenly nervous, Callie tried to pull away from him. His grip was steadfast.

'Wouldn't I?' he asked.

'No.' Her eyes flashed a challenge at him, and before she knew it, Logan gripped her around the waist and pulled her towards a chair. He sat down and hauled her over his lap as if she weighed no more than a feather.

'Logan!' Callie's heart thudded almost painfully as she fought to get away from him. His thighs were like tree trunks underneath her belly. 'Don't you dare!'

He ignored her as he flipped up her skirt to reveal the cotton of her underpants stretched over her buttocks. Hooking his fingers into the waistband, he yanked her knickers over her legs and left them to dangle around her thighs. Callie gasped as she felt the air on her naked bottom. He was really going to do this. Logan's hand caressed the twin mounds briefly before he landed the first loud slap on her backside. Callie yelped more from shock than actual pain, but she squirmed forwards to try to escape the inevitability of a second blow.

'Logan!'

Logan's hand came down again; the accompanying smack of flesh against flesh resounded through the air with a sharp tone of finality. Callie cried out as prickles of discomfort coated her skin, her hips squirming against his legs. Logan's other arm clamped around her waist, holding her weight down effortlessly as he spanked her again and again. Callie writhed in discomfort, feeling her flesh scorched from the sting of Logan's hand and the embarrassment of her position. He landed another smack and another, and then Callie realised that the sensation of his hand slapping her tender flesh was spreading heat through her lower body. Even as she writhed to escape his blows, she was aware of an increasing swell centring in her pussy. And even more distinctly aware of Logan's hard cock pressing into her belly. The knowledge that this aroused him only served to intensify her own excitement.

'Ow! Logan, you're hurting,' Callie panted. The pain spread through her blood, firing it with pure sensation.

'Isn't that the point of punishment?' Logan replied, his voice both husky and edged with steel.

Another hot sting landed on her bottom, building into a staccato pattern. Callie moaned and twisted, rubbing her belly against the increasing stiffness of his prick, her legs kicking behind her. Her hands scrabbled at the carpet as she searched vainly for something to grasp on to pull herself away, but Logan's grip was inexorable. Her bottom flared with scorched heat. Then the rhythm of Logan's hand paused briefly, and his fingers smoothed gently over her reddened arse before dipping into her sex. He chuckled low in his throat as he touched the certain dampness.

'Oh.' A moan escaped Callie's parted lips as her entire body went limp with relief. Her movements shifted subtly into luscious wriggles as Logan's fingers began to manipulate her folds with an unmatched expertise.

Callie bit her lip on a groan, unable to prevent the

thrusts of her hips as she started to work her body against Logan's fingers. Her mind swam in sensations evoked by his hard palm slapping against her buttocks, his fingers sliding into the humid warmth of her pussy, his erection pressing obscenely against her belly. Poised on the brink, she closed her eyes, her breath coming in rapid gasps as she struggled to impale herself on his fingers. Then, the movements of his fingers stopped abruptly.

Callie groaned. 'Logan, please –'

His palm skimmed over her buttocks again before his hands clutched her waist and pulled her upright. Callie grasped his arm to steady herself as her head cleared. A pool of unfulfilled desire expanded within her. She drew in a breath.

'You bastard,' she gasped, her hand going automatically to the tender flesh of her bottom. 'Can't stand the thought of me with another man, can you?'

Logan stood. His face was a mask, his jaw clenched tightly. He looked at her for a moment, and then his eyes darkened to black the instant before his mouth descended on hers. Callie's heart leaped as the sheer power of his body sank into her. Anger rolled off him in waves. Her fingers clenched a fistful of his shirt. As his lips pushed hers apart, Logan's hand slipped around to the small of Callie's back, forcing their lower bodies together. His cock pushed against her belly with lewd insistence.

Summoning every ounce of energy she had, Callie yanked her head away from him. Her heart pounded wildly, her skin aflame.

'Now what?' she snapped, well aware that she was goading him to the point of no return. And also well aware that she was incredibly aroused. 'You're trying to prove me wrong so I'll come home?'

'Suddenly, I couldn't give a rat's ass if you come home,' Logan rasped. 'But wouldn't you like to come right here?'

He clutched the back of her neck and dragged her mouth back to his. His tongue thrust into her mouth so swiftly that Callie was shocked by the potent eroticism of his anger. Heat bloomed inside her, swelling her cunt and firing her blood. She gripped Logan's shirt with her other hand and was seized by a sudden desire to rip it off him and feel every tight muscle in his body. She drew in a sharp breath when he pushed her against the front counter, grinding his hips against hers. Callie twisted her head away from him as his mouth moved down to her neck, his teeth biting down on the vein pulsing ferociously at her throat. His breath scorched her skin.

Thoughts spun out of control in Callie's mind, blurring and mixing together so fast that she couldn't grasp on to anything rational. Buttons popped off her blouse, scattering to the floor like marbles. Logan yanked the front clasp of her bra open so quickly that the flimsy material ripped. A sudden feeling of blatant exposure came over Callie, even as her arousal intensified. And then Logan's lips were on her breasts, tugging at her nipples, his tongue laving them with painful strokes. Callie groaned and felt her body weakening, responding to every touch of his hands and mouth. His dark hair brushed against her skin in a delicious, feather-light contrast to the roughness of his touch. She grabbed his shirt and pulled him towards her, fumbling to unfasten the buttons, hungry to feel the warmth of his skin. His body heat burnt through the material.

Logan suddenly grasped her hips and turned her around, pushing her down over the counter. Callie gasped when she felt him yank her skirt up again, his hand moving over her sore bottom.

'See?' Logan thrust one finger into her dripping pussy. 'If you weren't a slut before, then you're becoming one, aren't you?'

Callie closed her eyes and gripped the edge of the counter, leaning her forehead against the cool glass.

God, one flick of his finger on her clit and she'd burst into flames. Logan pushed her legs apart with his knee, spreading her fully open. A rush of air brushed against her pussy with delicate fingertips. Through a haze of need, Callie heard Logan unzip his jeans. Then, he pushed inside her so swiftly that her body jerked forward.

'There,' Logan hissed as her buttocks slammed against his belly. 'Is that what you want?'

Callie couldn't respond beyond a whimper of pained pleasure. Sweat broke out on her forehead as Logan began thrusting into her. His fingers dug tightly into her hips, his body pumping against hers. He leaned fully over her, his breath rasping against her neck. Callie moaned and pushed her hips back against his as her body began to tighten with pleasure. His belly smacked against her buttocks, irritating the sore skin, but she no longer cared. Contrasting sensations filled Callie's entire being: the heat of Logan's skin and the coolness of the glass, the hard ridge of the counter pressing against her belly and the hot slickness of Logan's cock; the uninhibited abandon of her position and the oppressive weight of his body on hers.

'Hurry,' Callie gasped, her fingers frantic as she tried to reach between her legs.

Logan pushed her hand aside, slipping his fingers around to rub her clit, his touch rough and quick on her sensitive flesh. Callie cried out as a wave of intense vibrations shuddered through her body. Her hands tightened on the edge of the counter as she absorbed every last sensation, relishing the feeling of Logan's repeated thrusts until he gave a hoarse shout and came with a force unlike any Callie had felt before.

Silence descended, broken only by the ragged, harsh sound of their breath. Then Logan lifted himself away from her. Callie felt oddly bereft without the weight of him against her. She turned slowly, letting her skirt fall back over her hips to cover herself. Her bottom continued to burn. As she struggled to catch her breath, she pushed her damp hair away from her forehead and eyed her husband warily.

A sheen of sweat glistened on Logan's skin, but his eyes looked as if they had been shuttered closed. He hiked his jeans over his hips and buttoned them. The air between them thickened with unease.

Callie leaned against the counter for support. She was totally uncertain about what she should be feeling right now, but she was aware of an increasing sense of dread. How could he have such an effect on her now when he never had before?

'Did that meet your definition of "right"?' he asked coldly.

Callie's chest tightened. She forced herself to keep her tone as detached as his. 'One time means nothing. Coming from you, it's merely an aberration.'

Logan picked up his car keys and turned away, his eyes as cold as his voice. 'So, I'm to assume that you're refusing to come home?'

'There's no assuming about it.' Callie struggled against a wave of sudden confusion. 'I'm not coming home.'

Logan nodded shortly. 'If you think this is over, then you are dead wrong.'

'That's perfectly all right because I've been wrong before.' Callie tried to prevent her voice from shaking. 'I was wrong about you, wasn't I? And I was certainly wrong about our marriage.'

Logan's eyes hardened with contempt. He began walking towards the door. 'I'll be in touch, Callie.'

'It won't do you any good.'

He paused at the door and turned to look at her. 'We'll see about that.'

Then he was gone.

Chapter Seven

The air in Savannah was always bloated with heat and moisture. Adam tugged at his tie and wished he'd worn shorts and a T-shirt. He hoped he hadn't missed something exciting. He took another sip of iced coffee and sat down on a nearby bench. Logan and Callie had gone into Nebula Arcana an hour ago, and neither one of them had emerged yet. Adam sighed. Maybe he shouldn't have taken a break to get an iced mocha. What if they'd both left already? What if they were already cosily ensconced back in *La Maison du Waterford*?

With a scowl, Adam fixed his gaze on the door of the shop and willed one of them, preferably Logan, to emerge. Nothing. He glanced up at the window above the shop. His heart leaped as he saw Callie flick on the light and move towards the window. Was Logan with her? Adam couldn't tell. And then she closed the blinds and the curtains, effectively blocking the room from Adam's sight.

Why, oh why had he gone for that coffee, Adam berated himself. He should have remained vigilant at his post. Not that anyone would scold him for having taken a break. He'd sneaked back here after Logan's magnificent departure from the mansion in the hopes of seeing a scene play out before him. Instead, Logan and Callie had disappeared into the store and appeared to have stayed there. A deep quickening started in Adam's stomach at the thought of what Logan was doing to his wife right at this very instant. If he was up there with her, of course. Or maybe Callie was giving him a foot massage. Logan did have marvellous feet, after all. Who wouldn't want to massage them?

Adam squinted and peered up at the flat. He suspected unhappily that Callie wouldn't open the blinds again until the following morning. Well, fine. He would just have to sit here and wait because, if Logan was still in there, then Adam damn well wanted to be there when he left. If Logan left within an hour, then maybe he and Callie just had a quick fuck that didn't mean anything. On the other hand, if Logan didn't leave until the following morning, then maybe they were actually working things out.

Adam sighed and looked at his watch. He didn't move from his post for the next few hours, lapsing into a few of his favourite daydreams. The next thing he knew, someone was shaking his shoulder. He sat upright, rubbing the sleep from his eyes as he realised that darkness had given way to the threads of morning.

'What? What happened?' he mumbled.

A burly police officer stood near him. 'You been drinking, son?'

'Yeah, I had an iced coffee.' Disoriented, Adam fumbled to hold up his empty plastic cup as proof.

'So is there a reason you're sleeping out here?'

Adam's mind slowly began to clear as he looked across the way at Nebula Arcana. Confound it! Had he missed Logan?

'Sorry, officer, I was just waiting for that shop to open.'

The officer hesitated for a moment before he nodded

and began walking away. 'All right, well, see that you stay awake next time.'

'Yes, sir.' Adam stood up and stretched, feeling his bones crack as they straightened out from their cramped position. He glanced at his watch. The store would in fact be open soon, which meant that Logan must have already left.

Adam sighed. Maybe he should stop at the Waterford mansion and see if Logan was there. He probably needed someone to talk to after what happened last night. Whatever that might be.

Adam did a couple more stretches and noticed a woman walking towards Nebula Arcana. She wore torn, faded jeans, a big leather belt and a lacy, black top that showed off her bare midriff. Her arms and fingers were decorated with dozens of silver bracelets and rings, and her hair bore a thick, green streak. Adam couldn't remember her name, but he recognised her immediately.

'Excuse me? Hello?' He almost tripped on a loose shoelace as he hurried over to greet the woman.

She paused and watched him through eyes embellished with heavy silver and black make-up. 'Yes?'

'Are you ... I mean, do you work here?' Adam gestured towards the shop.

'Yes, I'm the owner.' She glanced at her watch. 'We open in half an hour.'

'Can I just come in and look around?' Adam pleaded. If Logan was still with Callie, then there was no way that Adam could miss him if he was actually inside the shop. 'I'm ... um, I'm looking for some candles.'

The woman's gaze skimmed over his wrinkled suit and tie and unshaven features. She snapped her gum and shrugged. 'Yeah, OK. But you can't buy anything until I get the cash set up.'

'That's okay. I just want to look first.'

She shrugged again and turned to unlock the door. After flicking on the lights and turning off the alarm system, she tilted her head towards the interior. 'Well, come in, then.'

Adam entered the store, impressed by the array of interesting items. Still, he couldn't help but wonder what Logan thought of the multicoloured candles, incense, decorative wind chimes and Indian print fabrics. Talk about being at the opposite end of the spectrum from the Waterford mansion.

Adam giggled at the thought and sniffed a blueberry-scented candle. He felt the owner watching him from behind the counter.

'So, you looking for any candles in particular?' she asked.

Adam held up the candle. 'Yeah, this is nice. I like blueberry pie.'

She rested her elbows on the counter and continued looking at him. Adam couldn't help shifting uncomfortably under that razor-sharp gaze. He turned his attention to a set of raspberry-scented tapers.

'Do you work around here?' she asked.

'No, not really,' Adam replied vaguely. He sniffed another squat candle. Vanilla this time. Geez, too much more of this candle sniffing and he was going to start getting hungry.

'What's your name?' the owner asked.

'Adam.'

'I see. I'm Tess.'

Adam gave her a little wave from across the room. 'Hi, Tess.'

Her mouth turned upward slightly. 'Hi, Adam.'

Adam peered at her for a moment, then moved closer. 'Do you have a tongue piercing?'

'Sure do.' She stuck her tongue out to let him see the steel ball and rod that impaled it. 'Like it?'

'Yeah, it's really cool,' Adam said with admiration. He touched his bare eyebrow forlornly. 'I used to have my eyebrow pierced, but my boss thought it looked stupid, so I took it out.'

'So who cares what your boss thinks?' Tess asked. 'I think you'd look righteous with a pierced eyebrow.'

'Oh, you don't know my boss,' Adam replied quickly. 'He's very ... well, refined. And he has exquisite taste, but he's also incredibly masculine.' Adam shook his head. 'I don't know how he does that.'

'Refined, exquisite and masculine, huh?'

Adam nodded. 'Yes. Besides, I don't want him thinking I look stupid.'

Tess grinned. 'No? Why's that?'

'Well, because I work for him, that's why. I want him to respect me.'

'Sounds like you want him to do something else to you, too.'

Adam stared at her for a moment before her words sank in. He blushed hotly. 'I most certainly do not! I just admire him very deeply, that's all.'

She shrugged. 'Whatever you say, pal.'

'It's the truth!'

'I said OK,' Tess replied. She drummed her black-tipped fingernails on the counter. 'So, what's his name?'

Adam almost blurted out Logan's name before he remembered where he was. 'Uh, Tony. Tony Manicotti.'

Tess grinned again. 'Tony Manicotti? Sounds Italian.'

'Oh, very Italian. He's one of those dark, hunky types.' Adam began warming to his lie. 'He's originally from Rome, and his family has ties to the Vatican. They also have their own private collection of Renaissance art. Lo ... I mean, Tony has even taken me with him when he goes back to visit. Of course, we always go in his private jet.'

'Sounds fascinating.'

'So, I thought I'd buy him a little thank-you gift.' Adam held up the candle. Then he realised how absurd it sounded that he would purchase a scented candle as a thank-you gift for a trip to Rome. He cleared his throat. 'Well, this among other things as well, like ... potpourri and ... and soap.'

'Well, Adam, it sounds to me like you have a little crush on Mr Manicotti,' Tess observed.

Adam scowled at her. 'Look, just because I admire my boss doesn't mean I have a crush on him.'

Then he thought of Logan's gorgeous feet and wondered if he was deluding himself.

'Hey, don't get upset,' Tess said. 'Nothing wrong with having a crush on your boss. God knows I've done that a few times in my day. So, what kind of work does Mr Manicotti do? Is he a chef?'

She seemed to find the question particularly funny. Adam frowned.

'No, he's an art dealer. He deals in Renaissance art.'

'Cool. I'm an artist myself, you know.'

'Really?'

'Yes, a performance artist,' Tess explained. 'I create paintings, though. I'm just finishing up a show called *Paint*, where I brush paint all over my naked body and writhe against life-sized canvases.'

Adam stared at her in shocked awe. 'Really? You do that on stage in front of an audience?'

'Sure. It's very liberating.' Her gaze slid up and down his body. 'You've never been to a performance art show?'

'No.'

'My last show is tonight, if you want to come,' Tess said. 'After that, I'll be starting a revival performance next weekend of a show called *Sexology*.'

Adam's eyes widened. 'And what do you do in that?'

Tess chuckled. 'I'm not into false advertising, Adam. There are a lot of sexual things that go on in that series. Mostly BDSM related. Whippings, canings, spankings, wrappings, that kind of thing. But I also want to start incorporating some vanilla acts so that it expresses the range of human sexual activity.' She spread her hands in the air as if she were creating a rainbow.

Adam scratched his nose and wondered if Tess was

111

slightly whacked in the head. 'And you're in this show?' he asked.

'Of course. I'm in everything. One year I even invited members of the audience to join me on stage, although I didn't allow them to have actual sex with me.'

'So what did they do?'

'They can do the spankings or whatever they like. The catch is that they have to let me do whatever I want to them, too.'

'Wow.' Adam shook his head in disbelief as he pictured Tess being spanked. The mere thought made his dick twitch. 'That sounds amazing.'

'You mean you've never been involved in anything like that?'

'No, but I've heard about it.'

'I'm surprised that Mr Manicotti never wanted to give you ten lashes with a wet noodle,' Tess said in amusement.

Adam experienced a sudden, vivid image of Logan fully decked out in leather and chains, wielding a bullwhip. A shiver of both fear and delight ran down his spine. His dick twitched a little more fiercely.

'I'd love to see your show,' he said.

'Great.' Tess picked up a business card and wrote down an address and telephone number on the back. 'This is the theatre where I perform. By the way, I'm also looking for a few people to help me out with *Sexology*. Would you be interested?'

'You mean be in the show?'

'Yeah. As a matter of fact, I was thinking of doing a piercing segment. We could pierce a part of your body on stage.'

'Uh, no, I don't think I'd be into that.'

Tess shrugged. 'Whatever. Think about it, though.'

'OK.' Adam realised he was still holding the blueberry candle. He glanced towards the back of the store. 'Um, are you the only one who works here?'

'No, I have another full-time employee.'

'She's not working today?'

'She might be in soon.'

'I see.' Disappointed, Adam reached into his pocket for his wallet. Either Logan and Callie were still cosily holed up in bed, or Logan had already gone.

Tess pushed the candle towards him. 'On the house,' she said generously. 'Just make sure you show up for my swan-song *Paint* performance tonight, OK? Eight o'clock sharp. And be sure to come backstage afterwards.'

Adam nodded. 'I will.' He hesitated, then edged towards the door. 'Well, thanks again, Tess. Nice meeting you.'

'You too, Adam. Give my regards to Tony Manicotti.'

Adam blushed again and ducked out of the door, clutching the candle in his hand. Well, not only had he missed Logan completely, but he'd just made friends with a complete kook. An attractive kook, but a kook nonetheless.

Tess watched the peculiar fellow leave the store and chuckled to herself. Tony Manicotti! If Adam didn't work for Logan, then Tess would exchange her leather vests for buttoned-up lace dresses. Rome and ties to the Vatican, my arse, she thought.

But Adam was a cute one, there was no doubt about that. Sandy blonde hair and clear, blue eyes that seemed so amusingly innocent. She hoped he'd come and see her tonight. More importantly, she hoped he'd agree to get involved in *Sexology*. She could use a sweet oddball like him.

'Sorry I'm late.'

Tess glanced up as Callie came down the stairs, looking exhausted and pale with dark circles standing out starkly underneath her eyes. She carried a big mug of coffee and didn't look as if she'd even bothered to brush her hair.

113

'I'd say you look like hell, but hell can't be that bad,' Tess remarked.

Callie groaned and sank down into a chair near the counter. 'I feel worse than that. Well, part of me does, at least. Other parts feel pretty good.'

Tess put her hand on Callie's forehead, which felt cool and smooth. 'What's the matter? Don't you feel well?'

'I didn't get any sleep last night.' Callie leant her head on the back of the chair and closed her eyes.

'You don't feel like you have a fever.'

'No, it's not that.' Callie waved her hand limply in the air. 'It's Logan. He was waiting for me last night when I got back.'

'Here?' Alarm fluttered through Tess. She didn't like this whole situation with Logan to begin with, and she especially didn't like the thought that he now knew where Callie was.

Callie opened her eyes suddenly. 'Oh, Tess, I'm so sorry. I really enjoyed your performance last night.'

'Thanks, but enough about me. Logan was here?'

Callie nodded. 'He was waiting outside. He must have hired someone to find me.'

'Was Eldrich with you?'

'Yes, but he ran at the first sight of Logan,' Callie said. She sighed. 'I guess I can't blame him. Even I didn't want to have to confront Logan.'

'What happened?' Tess's body tightened as she thought of what might have occurred. She liked the look of Logan, but he was also a powerful man who seemed as if he could easily do damage to someone. She wondered if that was the reason that Adam was here. 'Did he hurt you?'

'No. We got into a huge argument and then we had sex.'

Tess's eyebrows lifted. 'You did, huh? Was it good?'

'Oh God, it really was.' Callie covered her eyes with her hand and took a long swallow of coffee. 'That's the bad part.'

114

Tess blinked. 'Good sex is bad?'

'No, I mean that all it did was confuse me,' Callie explained. 'I've been up all night thinking about it. I know it only happened because he was angry, but really, Tess, I didn't even know he was capable of that kind of thing.'

Tess's mouth quirked at the corners. 'What kind of thing is that, Callie?'

'You know, like ... well, like an animalistic thing.' Her voice was husky.

Despite her animosity towards Logan, a shiver prickled Tess's skin. 'Mmm. Sounds nice.'

'It was more than nice. It was beyond belief. I've never seen Logan like that before. Ever.'

Tess wondered exactly what had happened. She suspected it was more than just amazing sex, especially considering that Callie looked as if she had been utterly ravished.

'Wow. So does this mean you're back together?'

'No, no, it doesn't mean that at all.' Callie groaned and shook her head. 'He doesn't even understand why I left him! How can I go back to him when we're still at such opposite ends of the pole?'

Tess tried to think of a way to phrase her next words tactfully. She saw absolutely nothing wrong with a bout of animalistic sex for herself, but she knew that Callie didn't think quite the same way.

'Well,' she said carefully. 'Maybe you shouldn't have let him shag you if you still need some time apart from him.'

Callie groaned again. 'I know that, Tess. It was a huge mistake. Such a huge mistake. I don't know what came over me. I just got all caught up in the moment. And I've never been caught up in the moment with Logan. Logan doesn't even *have* moments! But, my God, he had one last night.'

'Sounds like you did, too,' Tess observed. 'Hey, listen. Does a bloke named Adam work for Logan?'

'Adam? Yes, I think so. Why?'

'Just curious.' Tess stroked Callie's hair soothingly. 'Look, maybe this fuck was a good thing. Maybe you just needed to get him out of your system.'

'No, that's not it,' Callie said. 'It was like injecting a serum directly into my bloodstream. I couldn't stop thinking about it all night. And then I started wondering if I made a mistake in leaving him, which of course I didn't.'

Tess didn't bother agreeing or disagreeing. It was pretty clear to her that Callie was a wreck over this. A rush of sudden anger towards Logan Waterford swept over her. What kind of a bastard was he, messing with her friend like this?

'What happened afterwards?' she asked.

'He just left. Of course, he was trying to convince me to come home, which is what started everything in the first place.' Callie removed her hand from her eyes and looked at Tess. 'Okay, Tess. Take me to your mimbo.'

'Mambo,' Tess said automatically before she processed the meaning of Callie's words. 'You're serious?'

Callie nodded emphatically. 'Yes. Yes, I am. I'm doing a lousy job of getting Logan out of my life by myself. I could use a little help.'

'Callie, that's great! Abiona really will help you, I promise. I'm going to call her right now.' Tess scurried behind the counter and picked up her address book. 'I swear, this situation with Logan is getting dangerous. I'll make an appointment for tomorrow.'

'Won't you be too tired after your performance tonight?'

'Nah, I'll be fine.' Tess thumbed through the book and picked up the telephone. 'Pemba, it's Tess Zimmerman.'

'Tess, child, how are you?' The deep, throaty voice on the other end was salted with a Haitian accent.

'I'm fine, but a close friend of mine is in a bit of trouble with her estranged husband,' Tess explained.

116

'Her name is Callie Waterford. Can we come and see you and Abiona sometime tomorrow?'

'Yes, of course. Come at noon, yes?'

'Can we come in the evening? We both have to work tomorrow.'

'How about eight o'clock?'

'Perfect. Thanks, Pemba.' Tess hung up the phone and smiled at Callie. 'They'll see us at eight tomorrow. You're really not going to regret this, Callie.'

Callie downed the last of her coffee and stood up. 'I'd better not. And I don't want Logan in any car crashes or accidents of any kind, for that matter.'

'Don't worry. Maybe we can just give him a bad rash or something.'

Callie glowered at her. 'No rashes. I don't want the man to suffer.'

Tess was disappointed. 'Not even a little wart or something?'

'No. I just want him out of my life. He can go on living his own as freely as he pleases.' Callie gave Tess a pointed look. 'I'm serious about this. No warts or mosquito bites or even spots, OK?'

'OK, OK. You just tell Abiona what you want and she'll deliver.' Tess pushed Callie towards the back of the store. 'Look, go and take a nap at least so that you're not falling asleep all over my hand-woven pillows.'

'But Saturdays are so busy. You'll be swamped.'

'I'll wake you if it gets really bad. You're supposed to sleep off the effects of animalistic coitus, you know.'

Callie appeared too tired to argue and went back upstairs. Tess busied herself for the next few hours with restocking some clothing and helping customers.

Callie came back down after lunch, looking slightly more alert, but still weary. 'Hey, Tess?'

Tess finished folding a Nehru jacket and placed it on a shelf. 'Yes?'

'How did you know about Adam?'

Tess gave Callie a surprised look. 'Adam?'

'Yes, you asked me if Logan worked with a man named Adam. How did you know that?'

Knowledge was power, Tess thought. Callie might not be happy about hearing this, but it was better than being in the dark.

'He stopped by this morning,' Tess admitted. 'Seemed a little weird, but very cute. He didn't tell me outright that he worked for Logan, but it wasn't difficult to figure out.'

'Dammit,' Callie muttered. 'Maybe he's the one Logan sent to find me.'

Tess considered the idea. 'I can find out, if you want.'

'Really? How?'

'He promised to come and see *Paint* tonight,' Tess explained. 'I was thinking about inviting him over to my place afterwards, so maybe I can get him to do a little talking.'

'I don't know what good it would do, anyway.'

'It would give you some ammunition against Logan,' Tess pointed out. 'Look, he thinks he can control what you do and has the balls to send people after you. But if you know more about his manoeuvres, then you'll be empowered.'

'True, I suppose,' Callie admitted. 'Well, don't torture the poor fellow or anything.'

'I wouldn't hurt him. Have you met him? He's like a dandelion.'

'You mean you just want to pluck him and blow him?' Callie gave her a half-hearted grin.

Tess laughed. 'Yeah, something like that.'

She let Callie take over at the store for the rest of the afternoon while she went home to get ready for her final performance. She was surprised at how much she hoped that Adam would be there. Tess had had her share of lovers, but she'd never been the type of woman who waited on edge for the men to call the following day. As far as she was concerned, sex could be a blast when

118

emotions weren't involved. She wondered if Adam felt the same way.

When she got to the theatre, she peered out between the curtains as the audience began arriving. The house was only half full, but Adam arrived early and took a seat in the front row. Tess grinned. He'd changed into a freshly pressed suit and tie, and he sat there looking all around him as if he suddenly found himself in a new universe. What an adorable fellow he was.

'Five minutes, Tess,' the stage manager said.

Tess pulled the diaphanous folds of her gown over her naked body and took her position in the centre of the stage. Her assistants positioned themselves on either side of her. As the lights came on and the curtains parted, Tess lost herself in the movements of her performance. Her assistants slowly tore the gown from her body as she spun and writhed in time to the piped music. She loved the sensation of being naked in front of an audience, knowing that all eyes were on her body. There was something both liberating and vulnerable about it at the same time. And the paint! Slathering her body with paint, rubbing against the canvases, stimulating her nipples ... by the time the performance was over, she was always highly aroused.

She danced and painted for over and hour and a half before taking her bows. Due to the blinding lights, she could only see the people in the first few rows of the theatre. Adam was watching her with a wide-eyed expression as he applauded along with the rest of the crowd. In fact, he even gave her a one-man standing ovation. Tess smiled and winked at him before going back to her dressing room to shower. She was going to miss doing the *Paint* performance, but she was also greatly looking forward to reviving *Sexology*.

'Tess?' A knock sounded at the door.

'Yeah, come in.' Tess slipped into a robe and scrubbed her wet hair with a towel.

One of her assistants poked his head in to the room.

119

'There's a fellow here to see you. Said you invited him backstage. Name's Adam.'

'Sure, let him in.'

Adam appeared in the doorway, clutching his programme. 'Wow, Tess. That was amazing.'

Tess smiled. 'Thanks, Adam. I'm glad you liked it.'

He gestured towards the stage. 'I just bought one of the paintings. The blue one.'

Tess was delighted that he'd actually purchased one of her final paintings. 'Really? Thank you.'

'Yeah, I thought it would go with the blueberry candle.' He smiled weakly. 'You know, blue colours and . . . and everything.'

Tess chuckled. She wanted to hug him, even though she'd never considered herself to be a particularly hug-oriented type of person. She picked up a bottle of champagne from her dressing table and held it up.

'Would you like some? The theatre owner sent it to me this evening.'

'Sure.'

'Sit down.' Tess gestured to the couch and began unwrapping the foil of the bottle. She popped the cork and poured two glasses, then went to lock the door before settling down next to Adam. 'So, have you given any further thought to participating in *Sexology*?'

Adam sipped his champagne and rubbed his nose. 'Um, I don't know.'

'You wouldn't have to do anything you didn't want to do,' Tess assured him. She reached out and touched a few strands of his sandy hair, brushing them between her fingers. Adam blushed. God, he was cute. She wanted to ravish him.

'I'll . . . I'll t-think about it,' Adam stammered. He glanced at her with both wariness and fascination in those blue eyes. 'You were really amazing tonight.'

'Being on stage is such a high for me,' Tess explained. 'Getting naked in front of all those people and letting the music get into my blood. And all that paint really feels incredibly sexy.'

'You still have some there.' Adam pointed to Tess's neck.

Tess touched the hollow of her throat, rubbing off a bit of red paint. She smiled wryly. 'That's the trouble, though. I never seem to be able to scrub it all off.'

They looked at each other for a moment. Tess eased her fingers a little more deeply into Adam's hair. She didn't want to scare him away, since he seemed as skittish as a kitten. His throat worked as he swallowed hard, but he didn't move.

'So, um, what kind of things would you want me to do in the *Sexology* show?' Adam asked, then quickly added, 'provided I agree to participate, of course.'

'Of course,' Tess replied. 'Whatever you want, Adam. If you don't want to be pierced, then maybe we can get you involved with a caning or bondage of some sort.'

A deep flush coloured Adam's cheeks. 'I don't know.'

'If you've never done it before, then we can always have a practice session.' Tess was so fascinated by the young man's shyness, not to mention turned on by her performance, that she felt her pussy start to quiver and dampen. She eased a little closer to Adam. 'I won't hurt you. I promise.'

He swallowed again and reached up to tug his tie away from his throat as if it were choking him. 'I know.'

Tess frowned slightly. 'You're not a virgin, are you, Adam?'

'Oh no,' he assured her hastily. 'I've been with . . . with a woman.'

'*A* woman?' Tess asked. 'And men?'

'Yeah, and a man, too. Not at the same time, of course.'

'Of course,' Tess murmured. She reached up to work the knot of his tie, watching him closely for signs of freaking out. He seemed nervous, but not about to bolt out of the room. Slowly, Tess pulled off his tie and pushed his jacket over his shoulders. Adam didn't protest. His breathing became slightly erratic as Tess began unbuttoning his starched shirt. She couldn't wait to touch him.

Flashing him a smile, she knelt on the couch and helped him off with his shirt. He had a lovely chest, pale and covered with a light mat of blonde hair. His little nipples poked forward. Adam blanched a bit when Tess stroked her hand over his chest, but there was no way she was letting him go now. She captured his earlobe between her teeth. He smelled like soap and shaving cream. Her pussy was starting to throb.

'It's OK, Adam,' she breathed. 'I just find you very attractive.'

Her hand slipped down to his bulging penis. She squeezed it lightly, smiling as he drew in a breath.

'So, was the man Tony Manicotti?' Tess asked. She unzipped his trousers and tugged them over his hips.

'The . . . the man?'

'The man you slept with.'

'Oh! Oh, no. That was a chap in college.' Adam watched as Tess bent to take his penis in her mouth. His hips jerked forward.

Tess slid her lips over his shaft, enjoying the taste and scent of him. He was already fully erect, and she reached between his legs to fondle his balls. Little gasps began to emerge from Adam's throat as she worked her lips and tongue on him. She pulled away and glanced up at him. He was an endearing sight with his head leaning against the wall, his eyes half-closed as he watched her sucking his prick. She laved his shaft with her tongue and pressed a wet kiss on the engorged tip before pulling away.

Tess sat up and shrugged herself out of her robe. Adam stared at her for a moment, then reached up tentatively to touch one of her breasts. His odd innocence aroused her like few things had before. She imagined herself teaching him all sorts of kinky acts that he probably didn't even know existed. She let Adam palm her breasts, plucking at her nipples as if he'd never seen such tantalising things before in his life. Then Tess reached into the drawer of the side-table and pulled out two pairs of leather handcuffs. She climbed off the couch.

'Lie down,' she instructed.

'But, I want –'

'Lie down,' Tess commanded, a bit more forcefully.

Adam gaped at her before he stretched out on the couch, his penis twitching. Tess admired the lean, pale length of his body before she straddled his waist and grasped his wrists. With a few expert manoeuvres, she cuffed each of his hands above his head, lashing him to the legs of a nearby table. Adam's eyes were wide with excitement and a hint of trepidation.

Tess smiled and rocked back and forth to let her cunt rub against his belly, enjoying the sensation of his hairs brushing her damp folds. She bent to kiss him, stroking her tongue over his luscious lips. Ah, he tasted like sweet champagne and naiveté.

'So, tell me this,' she murmured. 'There isn't really a Tony Manicotti, is there?'

'Uh . . . Tony?' Adam blushed.

'You were lying to me, weren't you?' Tess asked, instilling a scolding note in her voice. She kissed her way over his neck to his chest and began sucking on one of his nipples. Adam gave a moan of pleasure as his body tensed.

'No, I –'

Tess bit down hard on his nipple. Adam yelped and bucked up off the couch as much as he could with his hands cuffed.

'Hey, that hurt!'

Tess narrowed her eyes as she looked at him. 'It was supposed to. I don't like it when people lie to me.'

'I . . . OK, OK. There is no Tony Manicotti.'

Tess clambered off him and went to her dressing table.

She removed a switch from a drawer and returned to Adam. His mouth dropped open as she flicked the tip over one of his nipples.

'Are you going to . . . ow!'

Tess brought the switch down lightly over his abdomen. 'Just a little reminder that you're not to lie to me again.'

She patterned a series of criss cross red lines over his chest and stomach. Tess made certain that she wasn't hitting him too hard, but Adam was such a cream puff that he yelped and squirmed with every lash. His prick bobbed and trembled as Tess slapped his thighs, leaving delicious marks that she would soon soothe with her tongue. Her blood surged at the thought.

'Ow, ow, ow!' Sweat broke out on Adam's forehead, his hips bucking every which way like popcorn kernels in hot oil.

Tess realised that she would have to teach him how to take a mild whipping. More severe ones would come later. She put the switch aside and bent to lick the thin, hot welts. Whimpers emerged from Adam's throat as Tess stroked her tongue over his belly and thighs to cool the heated flesh. She loved the feeling of his hot skin underneath her tongue, knowing she had the power to soothe the same pain she had created.

She tossed her hair away from her face and levelled a look on him. His face was red and splotchy, his chest heaving.

'Understand?' Tess asked quietly.

Adam gulped and nodded.

'You work for Logan Waterford, don't you? Callie's husband.'

He stared at her with a stunned expression. 'H-how did you know?'

Tess's mouth twisted in amusement. 'Considering Callie works for me, it wasn't difficult to figure out. Did he hire you to find him?'

'No ... I ... he hired a private detective. I was supposed to h-help, that's all.'

Tess braced her hands on either side of his head, leaning over him and gazing down into his eyes.

'So, Adam,' she murmured. 'Were you talking about Logan? Is he the refined, sexy, masculine boss you think so highly of?'

Adam closed his eyes and swallowed hard. Sweat dripped from his temples. 'I just ... he's just so ...'

'What would you like him to do to you?' Tess whispered.

Adam's eyes flew open. 'Do to me?'

'Don't you want him to fuck you with his big cock?' Tess's lips curved. 'I imagine he has one, you know. Not just a cock, but a nice, thick, long one. Don't you think?'

Adam's skin darkened to a deep red. 'P-probably.'

'Mmm. I'd love to feel that pumping into my pussy. Wouldn't you like to feel it easing in your arse? Nice and slow, filling you up.'

Adam gasped. His prick fairly leapt underneath her, making her smile. The poor dear, Tess thought. Unrequited lust for the man he worked for. She rubbed her pussy against him again and slid backwards a bit, lowering her breasts to his level.

'Go on,' she whispered. 'Suck.'

Adam opened his eyes and stared at her jutting nipple before taking it between his lips. Quivers of pleasure slipped through Tess's body. Adam sucked her nipple with growing enthusiasm, running his tongue around the areola. Tess let him suckle her other breast before reaching over to pick up the switch again.

Adam moaned. 'Not again, Tess, please.'

'Don't worry, darling.' A wave of tenderness rose in Tess as she looked at Adam's helpless, panting form. What a dear boy he was. She scooted down to spread Adam's legs apart. He watched her with growing trepidation.

'What are you doing?'

'Helping you live out a fantasy.' Tess positioned the handle of the switch at the ring of his cute, little anus. 'Close your eyes and pretend this is Logan's cock.'

'What?' Adam's body strained as he fought to sit upright. 'What are you doing?'

'Relax,' Tess murmured. 'I promise this will feel good.'

Once she had the handle positioned correctly, she straddled his cock and eased it into her moist pussy. He filled her deliciously, his own juices easing the path of his penetration. Adam groaned as his hips strained upward. Tess smiled and began to ride him, working herself up and down with increasing force. As she did so, she reached behind her to thrust the handle slowly into Adam's arse. He sucked in a gasp of air, then grunts of exhilaration started coming from his throat as the handle slipped in. He came within seconds, his body jerking as he cried out and spilled into her. Tess reached down to rub her clit, bringing herself to her own orgasm before Adam went limp. She threw her head back and bucked her hips, absorbing the fierce sensations that ripped through her body.

She opened her eyes and looked at Adam, then began easing the handle out of him. He was lying there panting, his eyes closed and his hands still lashed above his head. Tess smiled and deposited a kiss on his damp forehead.

'You precious dear,' she murmured. 'I have so much to teach you.'

Chapter Eight

*L*ogan shoved aside a pile of papers and stood up. He had a splitting headache. He was supposed to attend a Sunday brunch at the home of one of his partners, but he'd called to cancel. Not only did he not feel like socialising, but he especially didn't feel like answering questions about Callie's whereabouts. He suspected that several people thought he had something to do with her disappearance and not in a pleasant manner.

He downed two aspirin and went into the kitchen to pour himself another coffee. What a mess this was turning out to be. And what the hell was Callie's problem? He'd never seen her as worked up as she was on Friday night. And he had definitely never seen her as wildly unrestrained. He winced as his jeans tightened. He didn't even know how all that had happened. All he remembered was fury oozing from every pore, a blind rage at the thought of his wife with another man. And the way she'd been standing there, her dark eyes flashing and chest heaving as she swore at him and told him to go to hell.

Logan dragged a hand through his hair and sighed. He hadn't known that Callie had the potential to lose control so completely. Moreover, he disliked the reminder that he, too, possessed that same potential. Jesus, he'd actually spanked her. And then he'd wanted to fuck her like an animal. He frowned as a wave of self-disgust rose in him. He'd spent far too many years cultivating control to lose it now, even with his wife. It had felt good, though, he had to admit. Damn good.

The telephone in his study rang. Logan left the kitchen and picked up the receiver on the fourth ring.

'Logan Waterford.'

After a moment's silence, a woman's voice came over the line. 'Well, well, well. I knew I'd track you down sooner or later.'

Dread like a thousand icy fingers clutched suddenly at the back of Logan's neck. He sat down and reminded himself that he was the one with the advantage now.

'Elenore.'

'Why, yes. I'm surprised you remember me.'

'How could I forget you?' Logan muttered. The image of a tall, slender woman with jet-black hair and a sophisticated bearing appeared like a ghost in his mind.

'Did you get my letter?' Elenore Lawrence asked. 'I sent it to your law firm. Congratulations, by the way. I hear that you're one of the best lawyers in the state, if not the country.'

'I got your letter,' Logan replied. 'As you must have realised, I ignored your request to contact you.'

'And as you must have realised, I don't give up that easily,' Elenore replied smoothly.

'What do you want?' Logan's voice tightened.

'I want to speak with you,' she said. 'I have a business proposal to discuss.'

'I'm not interested.'

'You haven't even heard it yet.'

'I don't care. I'm still not interested.'

Elenore was quiet for a moment. 'Well, Logan, you've certainly become disagreeable over the years.'

'No, just smarter.'

'Really? I've got smarter, too, you know.'

'If there's nothing else, I have a lot of work to do,' Logan said. He hated the sound of Elenore's voice in his ear.

'I'm coming to Savannah on Wednesday for a few weeks,' she explained, as if he hadn't spoken. 'I'm in the process of refurbishing a nineteenth-century riverboat so that I can turn it into a floating hotel and gambling casino.'

'Good for you.'

'Heavens, Logan, don't be so unpleasant,' Elenore said. 'We're old friends, remember? You might at least show a little interest.'

'I'm *not* interested, Elenore, all right?'

'It would be a good investment for you.'

Logan knew well about Elenore and Gerald Lawrence's 'investments', which were usually financed by black-market money laundering and insider trading. He didn't have the slightest intention of getting involved with that kind of thing.

'I'm not interested in bankrolling your enterprises. And I am especially not interested in resuming contact with you. Don't call me again.' He was about to hang up when Elenore's voice came over the line once more.

'I wouldn't dismiss this quite so easily, Logan.'

Logan frowned. 'What does that mean?'

'Nothing in particular,' Elenore replied airily. 'By the way, are you still moonlighting, or have you dedicated yourself solely to your law firm?'

Logan's blood went cold. The tone of her words was too insidious for his liking. 'I'm a lawyer, not that it's any of your business.'

'Of course not. I was simply wondering if you were for hire.'

'Not to you.'

'Well, perhaps we can set up an appointment to discuss this.'

Logan suspected that Elenore wouldn't leave him alone until he agreed to meet with her. The thought made him sick to his stomach, but he knew that Elenore and Gerald Lawrence were capable of anything. Including blackmail and extortion.

'Logan, I dislike being ignored,' Elenore continued. 'I think you know that already.'

Logan rubbed the back of his neck and closed his eyes. Why did his world seem to be unravelling all at once? Only a couple of weeks ago, everything had been secure and intact. Now, his life was threaded with cracks threatening to break it all apart. First Callie and now this bitch.

'One meeting,' he said. 'But I'll tell you right now that I'm not giving you a penny.'

'All I'm asking is that you hear me out,' Elenore replied. 'I doubt you'll regret at least doing that.'

'I regret even picking up the telephone,' Logan said curtly.

Elenore chuckled. 'You have become ill-tempered, haven't you? I have a few appointments Wednesday morning, so why don't we meet in the afternoon? Say around three? We sold the house a few years ago, but I'll be staying in our penthouse.'

'Fine. Goodbye, Elenore.' Logan hung up the phone before she could respond.

He sat there for a moment with a disgusted feeling in his gut and unpleasant memories pushing at the back of his head. Fifteen years ago, he'd wanted to be free from the Lawrences so badly that he'd even vaguely considered the idea of black magic before dismissing the idea as ridiculous. He had known deep down that nothing could get the Lawrences out of his life. Apparently, he'd been right. His thoughts returned to Callie. He didn't want her to know anything about Elenore Lawrence. Things were tenuous enough without his own wife giving him trouble. It was as if he'd spent years building a solid sand castle, and now wave after wave was washing up on shore to erode all he'd worked for.

* * *

Callie looked at the scarred doorway that rested at the base of some cement steps. A faded, wooden sign hung from a chain. Tess grabbed Callie's elbow and urged her down the steps.

'Come on, Callie, it'll be fine.'

'Tess, I wasn't exactly lucid when I made this decision,' Callie reminded her. Come to think if it, she still hadn't regained all of her cognitive abilities after her confrontation with Logan.

Tess sighed and shook her head. 'Callie, I know you haven't been able to stop thinking about Logan. If you want him to continue torturing you, then we can turn around and go home right now. But if you want him out of your life, then Abiona can help you. Personally, I think Logan is a right bastard who could use a good black magic spell, but Abiona won't do that.'

'She's not going to sacrifice a goat or anything, is she?'

'No, that kind of thing only happens at the group ceremonies.'

Callie chuckled, assuming that it was a joke. One look at her friend told her that Tess was completely serious.

'Oh, Tess –'

Tess grabbed Callie's hand firmly and knocked on the door. 'Now, come on. Keep an open mind.'

The door opened to reveal a large, attractive black woman dressed in an extraordinarily colourful robe and turban. She had a deep twinkle in her brown eyes and a smile that caused dimples to form in her cheeks. Callie relaxed a bit, taking immediate comfort in the woman's amiable, calm demeanour.

'Hello, Pemba. It's wonderful to see you again.' Tess reached out to hug the other woman.

'Come in, children, come in.' Pemba stepped aside and ushered them inside. Her home was decorated with African masks hanging on the walls and shelves full of books and relics. Brightly coloured, woven rugs lay on the floor with matching cushions scattered over the furniture. The strong scent of incense lingered in the air.

'You must be Callie.' Pemba turned to clasp Callie's hands in hers. She had a marvellous voice, throaty and rich with a lilting accent. 'I am so happy to meet you.'

Callie smiled. 'Thank you. I'm happy to meet you, too.'

'May I offer you some tea?' Pemba gestured for them to sit down as she poured two cups of milky tea. She settled her large frame into a chair across from them and looked at Callie. 'My daughter will be joining us shortly. Tess tells me you have some trouble.'

'Yes, a little bit,' Callie admitted. 'I left my husband about a fortnight ago, but I seem to be getting somewhat obsessed with him. And he with me,' she added.

'Logan hired someone to find her,' Tess said. 'He's refusing to let her go. I think he might even be psychotic. What if he hurts her?'

'He's not psychotic and he's not going to hurt me,' Callie said, then wondered why she always felt the need to defend Logan.

'I see.' Pemba leaned forward slightly and began to gesture gracefully with her hands. 'Let me explain something about voodoo, Callie. It is not only a religion, but also a form of philosophy and a way of life. Devotees of voodoo serve what are called *loas*. These are spiritual beings, and forms of the *Bon Dieu*. These *loas* must be properly honoured to maintain our well-being. That is what we do; we serve the spirits.'

Callie glanced at Tess. 'I've heard that it can also harm people.'

Pemba spread her hands. 'Yes, of course. If one is confronted with evil, sometimes one must fight back with black magic. After all, we must know evil in order to fight it. The *loa* is . . . how shall we say, the mediating force between good and evil magic.'

'I don't want evil magic,' Callie said. 'Logan isn't evil by any stretch of the imagination. I simply want him to leave me alone, both in my mind and in my life.'

'If his presence so disturbs your harmony, then you

must take action,' Pemba replied. 'And remember that, while there are invisible forces in the world designed to harm people, for every one of those forces there is a *garde*, which serves to protect the individual.'

She stood in a fluid movement. She was surprisingly graceful despite her bulk. 'Come into my other room. I will help you banish this man.'

Callie glanced towards the other room. A beaded curtain hung in the doorway between the two rooms. Then the beads clicked together as a young woman came into the room. Callie couldn't help staring at her. She was incredibly beautiful; tall and curvaceous with smooth skin the colour of mocha and thick, curly hair. She wore a simple white shift that reached her knees and flowed in graceful lines over her body.

'Hello.' She smiled, revealing even, white teeth. 'I'm sorry I'm late.'

'This is my daughter, Abiona,' Pemba said. 'Abiona, you remember Tess, of course. This is her friend, Callie Waterford.'

'A pleasure.' Callie shook the other woman's hand. Her skin was smooth and dry.

'For me as well. Please forgive me, but I must take care of something first.' She glanced at her mother. '*Maman*, could you come, please? This is about Lucia's *lave-tet*.'

'Will you please excuse me for a moment?' Pemba asked.

'Of course,' Tess said. 'We'll finish our tea.'

Callie looked at Tess after the two women had left the room. 'Abiona is beautiful.'

'Isn't she? I'd ask her to get involved in *Sexology* if I wasn't worried about offending her.'

'Are they both mim ... I mean, mambos?' Callie asked.

Tess nodded. 'Abiona does most of the work now. Her mother is more of an advisor, but she often helps at rituals and ceremonies.'

'What did she say she had questions about?'

'It's called a *lave-tet*, a cleaning of the head. It's supposed to get rid of impurities and junk so that a spirit can possess a person.'

Callie gave Tess a derisive look. 'You don't really believe all this, do you?'

'Of course I do.' Tess frowned. 'You know, you are so uptight. Can't you give a little credit to these people? I've been to voodoo ceremonies, Callie. The people truly are possessed by other spirits.'

'I'm sorry, but it just seems far fetched to me sometimes,' Callie said. 'Now, why does Lucia have to clean her head?'

'The head is the container for two invisible elements,' Tess explained. 'The *gros bon ange* is basically the intelligence and memory of a person. It defines who a person is. Then there's the *ti bon ange*, which is the conscience of a person. If the head is clean, then those two elements can separate and allow room for the spirit to enter.'

'How do you know all this about voodoo?'

Tess shrugged. 'I'm just learning as I go along. I was so impressed by what Abiona did for me that I wanted to learn more about it. I'm even thinking of somehow incorporating voodoo into my next performance series.'

'I am so sorry.' The beads clicked again as Pemba reentered the room. 'Please, come inside.'

Callie and Tess put down their teacups and followed the priestess into what appeared to be her sanctuary. A round, wooden table dominated the room. Abiona sat in one of the chairs. Icons of Catholic saints hung on the walls, alongside images of wooden African idols and dozens of votive candles. Several of the idols had dishes of food, cigarettes and small bottles of alcohol arranged in front of their shrines. A glass cabinet contained numerous vials and bags of herbs and powders.

'Sit,' Pemba said.

Callie sat, uncertain of what she should be expecting.

She hoped that Pemba wasn't going to be possessed by a spirit right now. Callie wasn't quite ready for that.

'First, you will wear this around your neck.' Pemba produced a small pouch on a leather string and slipped it over Callie's head. 'This *mojo* bag will protect you from your husband.'

Abiona blinked her lovely eyes at Callie. 'Why do you need this protection?'

'My husband is very . . .' Callie's voice faltered. How could she even explain the situation? 'He's very controlling,' she finally said.

'He hits you?'

'No, never.'

'Yet you wish to be protected from him?' Abiona asked, exchanging glances with her mother.

'Yes.'

'Do you have a picture of him?'

'Yes, in my wallet.' Callie took out the picture of Logan and handed it to Abiona.

She examined it for a moment. 'He is very handsome.'

'That doesn't make him easy to live with.'

Abiona smiled and handed the photo to her mother. 'No, I imagine it doesn't. We will provide you with a *garde* spell. This will put you under the protection of a certain *loa*.'

Pemba lit several candles and took a blackened pot from a cupboard. She tossed the photo of Logan inside, along with a number of herbs. She lit the whole concoction with a match and began chanting in an unintelligible Haitian Creole. Abiona rose and moved to stand behind Callie.

'Please,' she said. 'Remove your blouse.'

'Excuse me?'

'We will give you a protection tattoo,' Abiona explained. 'This is usually done by cutting and scarring the flesh, but I suspect you don't want that.'

'God, no.' Callie was beginning to feel extremely warm. She unbuttoned her blouse and slipped it off her shoulders. Abiona's long fingers slipped one of Callie's bra straps off and picked up a small bowl of dark paste.

'What is that?' Callie asked.

'Henna,' Abiona explained. 'I am placing the auspicious mark over your heart.'

She leant in close and began applying the henna with a pointed applicator just above Callie's left breast. Callie's head filled with the delicious, clean scent of the other woman. She could feel Abiona's breath brushing against her skin. A bead of sweat trickled into the hollow of Callie's throat. All too quickly, Abiona finished the tattoo and moved away. Callie looked down at the tattoo, which bore the form of two Xs surrounded by five dots. Callie returned her gaze to Pemba, who was still chanting over the smoky embers burning in the pot. She took a wooden rattle and waved it over the pot, stirring the smoke in Callie's direction before she ended the ritual.

'Now, you must rub this in your skin every night before you sleep.' Abiona handed Callie a bag of herbs. 'This will help banish him from your consciousness as you sleep.'

Callie nodded and took the bag. 'All right. Thank you.'

Abiona gave Callie a curious look. 'You are sceptical, I think.'

'A little bit,' Callie admitted.

'Do not dismiss the power of the *loas*, Callie,' Abiona said. 'They can be very powerful. We are having a ceremony in honour of them on Saturday night. You are most welcome to come.'

Callie glanced at Tess, who nodded. 'They're quite amazing, Callie. I'm going to go.'

'I'll think about it,' Callie promised. She was intrigued by the possibility of attending an actual voodoo ceremony. Heaven knows that she would never have been able to do that if she were still with Logan. She buttoned her blouse and picked up her bag.

'I'll be there,' she corrected. 'Thank you for inviting me.'

Pemba and Abiona smiled widely. Abiona really was stunning with that creamy, dark skin and deep eyes. Callie suddenly wondered what she would look like naked, all slender limbs and smooth skin. Surprised by the daring of her thought, she pushed her chair away and stood up. After paying the two women and thanking them again, Callie and Tess left the house and walked back to the street. Although the outside air was muggy, it felt refreshing after the confinement of the room.

'So, how do you feel?' Tess asked.

Callie shrugged and touched the small packet around her neck. 'The same so far, I guess. Am I supposed to feel any different?'

'Probably not.' Tess slung her bag over her shoulder. 'Speaking of different, I had a little event with Adam last night.'

'Really? Did he come to your performance?'

'He not only came to my performance, he also came *after* my performance,' Tess replied with a grin.

Callie chuckled. 'Tess, you're shameless. I thought you weren't going to scare the poor kid.'

'I didn't scare him, are you kidding me? He loved it. He even agreed to be in *Sexology*. He's so cute, Callie. I just want to squeeze his cheeks and make him do all sorts of nasty things.'

'Which cheeks?' Callie asked in amusement. A thought suddenly occurred to her. 'What if he tells Logan that he's seeing you?'

Tess shrugged. 'I doubt he will and, even if he does, it's none of Master Waterford's business, anyway. Besides, Adam seems to be both simultaneously in love with Logan and afraid of him.'

Callie stared at her. 'In love with Logan? Adam?'

'Yep. He's always rambling about how masculine and

137

sexy and exquisite Logan is. Definitely has a crush on him.'

'Wow. I wonder if Logan knows.'

Tess snorted. 'Please. If Logan doesn't even know what's wrong with his marriage, he's not going to know that an assistant has a crush on him.'

Callie grinned. 'True enough.'

'Have you met Adam yet?'

'No, I never have. We socialised a lot with Logan's partners, but I don't ever remember meeting Adam.' She glanced absently across the street to the row of parked cars in front of the buildings. A tall figure stood leaning in a deceptively casual position against one of the cars. Callie stopped in her tracks as her heart sank like a brick.

'Callie?' Tess paused and turned. 'What's wrong?' She followed the line of Callie's gaze. 'Shit! Is that Logan?'

'Tess –' Callie stepped forward to prevent her friend's next action, but Tess was too quick for her. In all her green-hair, leather-vested glory, Tess stormed across the street towards Logan and stopped right in front of him. She began gesturing wildly and snapping at him like a rabid pitbull.

Callie ran to catch up with her. 'Tess!'

'You stupid fuck,' Tess barked at Logan. 'What are you, obsessed or something? She doesn't want you around, so you'd better damn well stay away from her because if I ever see you around my store again, I'm calling the cops to haul your arse into prison!'

Logan didn't even seem to see Tess. He simply stood there with that impassive look on his face, ignoring her as he watched Callie approach.

'Tess!' Callie grabbed Tess's arm and pulled her a short distance away from Logan so that she wouldn't lash out and hit the man. 'Tess, please. Calm down.'

'Bastard,' Tess snarled. 'Stay away from her, do you hear me?'

Callie grabbed Tess's shoulders and gave her a hard shake. 'Stop it! I can handle this, all right?'

Muttering and scowling, Tess backed off a few feet, but didn't leave. Callie sighed and pressed her fingers against her temples. So much for voodoo protection spells, she thought. She walked back towards Logan, who hadn't moved. Her entire body quickened suddenly as an image of their ferocious lovemaking appeared in her mind. She groaned inwardly and tried to suppress the memory.

Logan looked at her soberly. 'Callie.'

'Logan, what are you doing here?' Callie asked, her voice edged with weariness. 'Are you following me?'

'Are you sleeping with that deranged woman?'

Callie stared at him in shock. 'No! She's just a good friend of mine. She's worried about me. And answer my question. What are you doing here?'

He shrugged. 'I followed you here.'

'Now you're following me? Logan, I want to be left alone!'

His expression hardened. 'You should know by now that's not going to happen,' he replied coldly. 'You belong with me.'

'I do not,' Callie retorted. She tried to force herself to remain calm, even though she felt like railing at him like Tess had. 'I don't *belong* with anyone except myself, OK?'

Logan pulled open the car door. 'Get in, Callie. You're coming home.'

Callie backed off a step, unable to believe his nerve. 'I am not. You can't just barge around, ordering me to do things, Logan. You can't even figure out why I left you in the first place.'

'What I dislike about you leaving me is the way you chose to do it,' Logan replied curtly. 'I didn't and I still don't have time for games.'

Callie sighed. 'It's not a game, Logan. It's never been a game.'

'What are you doing here anyway?' Logan asked.

Callie decided to tell him just to irritated him. 'I came to see a voodoo priestess, if you must know.'

His eyebrows rose in disbelief. 'Callie –'

'Don't start, Logan. What I do is none of your business.'

Let him chew on the idea of voodoo for awhile, she thought.

'In my experience, the occult is not necessarily helpful,' Logan replied.

Callie frowned at his remark, as she had been expecting immediate ridicule. 'What experience is that?'

'If you think voodoo can keep me away from you, you're wrong,' Logan said. 'Nothing other-worldly can interfere with your own decisions.'

'You don't know anything about it,' Callie snapped. 'And you *will* leave me alone or I'll get a restraining order against you.'

She turned away, realising that she was never going to get through to him. Trying to talk to Logan was like pounding one's head against a wall. She started back towards Tess when she suddenly felt Logan's hand grip her arm. Alarm fluttered through Callie as she realised that he could easily force her into the car. She spun around, yanking her arm out of his grasp with a speed she hadn't known she possessed.

'Don't touch me,' she said coldly. 'I don't like it.'

His eyes darkened. 'Funny. You seemed to like it the other night.'

A hot flush coloured Callie's skin. She backed away from him, realising that her heart was pounding wildly.

'I mean it, Logan. Next time you bother me, I'm calling the police. And don't think I won't.'

'And don't think you'll win, either,' Logan replied.

His voice was so hard and certain that Callie almost shuddered. How could she go up against this man? Did she really think she could walk out one night and be free from him?

'Win?' she retorted. 'What is there to win? I thought you didn't want this to be a game.'

'You know exactly what I mean, Callie,' Logan said. 'I reached the end of my tether a week ago. I would suggest that you don't try and push me any further.'

'And I would suggest that you leave me the hell alone.' Callie continued backing away, watching him warily until she felt Tess's hand on her shoulder.

'Let's go the other way,' Tess said. 'I know a short cut we can take.'

Only when they were a good distance away from Logan did the two women turn and begin walking quickly back home. Tess wrapped her arm through Callie's.

'Sorry,' she muttered. 'I just went ballistic when I saw him, after everything he's done to you.'

Callie gave her a slight smile. 'Actually, you were quite a magnificent sight. I'm just sorry it was like railing at a statue.'

Tess chuckled and squeezed Callie's arm. 'Don't worry. The spell will take effect. It just might take a little time. Obviously, we can't expect immediate results.'

'Obviously,' Callie agreed. She sent up a silent prayer to whatever *loa* might be watching over her to hurry up and start doing his or her job.

Chapter Nine

*L*ord, but it was hot under these lights. Like being on a planet with a dozen blazing suns. Perspiration trickled down Adam's back. He squinted at the faces of the audience, hoping that no one he knew was out there. How had he got into this position? Well, he knew how he'd got into *this* particular position, since Tess had tied him into it, but what in the world was he doing on stage?

Oh, they were about to twirl him again. Adam closed his eyes and hoped he wouldn't puke as one of Tess's beefy assistants spun the large wheel. Adam felt his entire body spinning, his stomach ending up where his head should be and vice versa. No wonder he hadn't liked carnival rides as a kid. His constitution was clearly not made for being twirled around on a huge wheel. In front of several dozen people, no less.

The wheel came to a slow halt, leaving Adam hanging upside down. He squirmed slightly. Prior to the show, Tess had helped him into a pair of leather trousers with an open crotch that left his penis hanging in the breeze. He couldn't believe he was doing this, but he wasn't surprised that Tess had managed to talk him into it. He saw her moving towards him, and he gazed adoringly at her legs. She was so magnificent.

The thumping sound of German industrial music filled the theatre through hidden speakers, increasing the intense density of the air. Two other people, a woman and a man, lay lashed to boards, each decked out in some form of leather or chains. Adam squirmed again, hoping that Tess would take pity on his aching penis. Instead she smiled at him and removed a cat-o-nine-tails from her belt, letting him suck on the handle before she nodded at the assistant to spin the wheel again. Around and around Adam went as Tess began slapping him with the leather straps. Adam moaned and yelped and writhed around, both with real pain and with awareness of the audience. Hell, he was getting dizzy. Thankfully, the wheel landed upright this time, and he had a chance to clear his head. He also liked being upright, since he could watch Tess strutting around, having her way with the other two participants.

She was dressed in thigh-high boots and a leather apron that left her rounded buttocks bare. Lace gloves reached her elbows. Her hair was teased into spiky points, and she wore gobs of silver and black make-up. She looked incredible as she performed strange manoeuvres in time with the music, dancing like a ballerina one minute and break dancer the next. Wielding various implements of leather and metal, she whipped her three slaves into a frenzy of arousal, fucking the two men and masturbating the woman until they were all torturously poised on the brink of rapture. Tess refused to let anyone come, however, making them lick her boots and kiss her nipples for her own pleasure.

The audience appeared to be enraptured with the performance. Almost every seat had been filled, and not a single person walked out. Finally, as the music crescendoed into the sound of crushing metal, Tess approached two of the slaves, ignoring Adam, and brought them both to orgasm, fucking the woman with the handle of a whip and masturbating the man with an industrial rubber glove. The audience sat in stunned silence for a

143

moment as the music crashed to a halt, and then burst into applause. Tess smiled happily, her skin damp with sweat as she took her bows and gestured towards her loyal slaves.

As the hot, aroused audience filtered out, Tess and her assistants removed the slaves from their wheels. With relief, Adam saw one of the assistants move towards him. Finally he would be freed from this contraption.

'Wait!' Tess held up her hand. 'Not him.'

The assistant shrugged and went backstage. Adam squirmed. His arm and leg muscles were killing him from being in a spread-eagle position for so long.

'Tess, please,' he whined. 'This is starting to hurt.'

'I know, precious.' Tess paused in front of him and smiled, reaching out to pat his cheek with her hand. The lace of her glove rasped against his damp skin in a rather erotic friction.

Adam was aware of the other people leaving the stage. He wondered what Tess was going to do to him. His body quivered at the thought. She was always so full of surprises. Then, to his utter surprise, she leant forward to kiss him.

'You were so marvellous, do you know that?' she murmured against his lips. 'I'm so proud of you.'

Happiness swelled in Adam's heart. 'You are? Really?'

'I am,' Tess said. 'Sean and Anna have both done this before, but this was your very first performance. You're a natural, Adam. A pure natural.'

Adam beamed. 'Thanks. I enjoyed it, too.'

His prick was still throbbing, his arms ached, and he was hotter than a daisy in the desert, but he no longer cared. Tess's praise was like a salve to all his discomfort. She placed her hands on his bare chest, rubbing them over his skin. Her lace gloves were surprisingly rough. She tweaked his nipples and then grasped his cock in her fist. Adam gasped at the sensation of the lace against his pained flesh.

'Oh, fuck, Tess, that hurts.'

'Not for long,' Tess murmured. She flashed him a smile and began stroking him up and down, moving her hand faster and faster until her lace glove chaffed his skin and aroused him to untold heights. 'I want you to come like a fucking rocket.'

Adam whimpered as pressure built in his prick, augmenting the ache that he'd been suffering for the last hour. Tess slipped her other hand underneath him and began to caress his tender balls. Adam closed his eyes and tried to absorb the painful, wonderful combination of Tess's touch and the lace glove. He bucked his hips forward and let out a cry of both pain and delight as he spurted all over Tess's hand and the front of her leather apron. Tess scraped her thumb over his sensitive glans, sending a wave of shocked pain up Adam's spine. He groaned. She smiled and stepped away.

'I'm becoming quite fond of you, Adam.'

He opened his eyes to look at her. 'You are?'

'Are you going to help me out with all my performances?' she asked, stripping off her gloves.

Adam nodded, his chest heaving. 'Yes. Do I have to be on this wheel all the time?'

'No. This is a series, meaning that I do something a little different for every performance.' She reached up to unstrap his hands, giving his sore muscles a quick massage.

The relief was so great that Adam could have cried. Tess unstrapped his legs and helped him off the wheel, grasping his arm to steady him as he wobbled and tried to regain his balance.

'You know, I'll bet they used something like that during the Inquisition,' Adam said.

Tess lifted her eyebrows. 'Now there's an interesting idea.'

'The Inquisition?'

'Yes. We could do a performance with a Spanish Inquisition setting. We could wear red robes and strap people to wooden torture devices. And the music could be very haunting – church chants or choral music. Wouldn't that be fantastic?'

Adam rubbed his now-limp penis and winced slightly. 'Yes, but do I have to be on one of the torture devices?'

Tess chuckled. 'We'll see. Perhaps you can have a different role for that.' She kissed him again. 'Really, Adam, it's a wonderful idea.'

'You thought of it,' Adam reminded her, even as his heart lightened at her compliment.

'We'll work on the logistics together,' Tess said. She settled down on a folding chair and spread her legs. 'But before we think about that, you can do a little something for me.'

Adam didn't even have to question what. He went down on his knees in front of her, pushing up her apron as he plunged his tongue into her cunt. God, she smelled like heaven. She was wet and dripping with both arousal and exertion. Tess cried out with pleasure and tightened her thighs around his head. Adam licked up salty droplets as he circled her pussy with his tongue and sucked on her clit. He thought that he could quite happily live in this position for years to come.

'Stick it in me,' Tess gasped.

Adam shoved his tongue into her slit, not bothering to take his time or make this gentle. He knew that she was pumped up on adrenaline after a performance, wanting everything rough and immediate. Her flesh enclosed him like a fist, her scent filling his head with the most potent of perfumes. Reaching underneath her, he grasped her buttocks and began kneading them, dipping his fingertips into the crack. Then he pushed his forefinger into her tight arsehole. Tess moaned and crossed her booted legs over his back. A stiletto heel dug into Adam's spine, but he couldn't have cared less. All that mattered was the pleasure of this magnificent woman before him. Tess came ferociously, her buttocks lurching off the chair as she squealed her excitement and a rush of moisture bathed Adam's tongue.

Panting, he eased out from underneath her apron, adoring the flushed, sated expression on Tess's face. She smiled slowly and bent to kiss him again, licking her dampness from his lips.

'I think we'd better go backstage,' she murmured. 'People are going to wonder what's become of us. A few friends are meeting me in the dressing room.'

Adam would much rather have hung around for another private performance, but he stood up slowly.

'Do I have to go like this?' he asked worriedly, staring down at his leather trousers and flaccid penis. It was one thing to appear like this in front of an audience and quite another to appear with only a few people in a small room.

'Wait here. I'll get you a robe.' Tess hurried backstage and returned with a white bathrobe.

Adam slipped it on and followed Tess to her dressing room. He blushed at the sight of Callie Waterford sitting on the couch, remembering all the things he'd thought of her and Logan. Another fellow was with her, the pale Gothic man with scarlet lipstick, and a couple more of Tess's friends.

'Tess, that was incredible.' Callie stood up and hugged her friend. 'Strange, but incredible.'

Tess smiled with delight. 'Thanks. This is Adam, one of my new friends.'

'Adam.' Callie reached out to shake his hand, her gaze going over him curiously. 'Nice job.'

'Thanks.' Adam scratched his nose and wondered if Tess had told Callie that he worked for Logan. Oh my God, he thought, what if it somehow got back to Logan that he was in this performance? The mere thought made his entire body blush.

Tess meandered over to greet her other well-wishers. Adam sat down in a chair near Callie and stared at her. She was prettier than she appeared in the photographs, with shoulder-length brown hair and nice, dark eyes. She was no bombshell, but that didn't mean she wasn't a whirlwind in the bedroom. That had to be the reason Logan wanted her back, hadn't it?

Adam's gaze went to the Gothic, punk, whatever-he-was. 'I'm Adam.'

'Eldrich.' The bloke was sucking on a herbal cigarette and looking bored. 'Why didn't Tess let you come?'

'She did,' Adam assured him. He looked from Eldrich to Callie, remembering what he and the detective had initially thought. 'Are you two . . . you know, together?'

'No, we're just friends,' Callie said. She settled back in her seat and eyed Adam curiously. 'So, Tess tells me you work for Logan.'

Adam swallowed hard and glanced down to make sure his penis wasn't poking out of his robe. 'Um, yeah. I'm a paralegal in the firm. I've been working for him for about a year. I haven't passed the bar yet, though. Logan says I have to pass it the next time around or I'm fired.'

'And does Logan know you're studying to become a performance artist in your spare time?' Callie asked in amusement.

'N-no,' Adam stammered, suddenly very worried. He didn't even want to consider what Logan might think of his nocturnal activities. 'You're not going to tell him, are you? He gets annoyed enough when I tell him about my science-fiction conventions.'

'Why would he get annoyed about that?'

'He thinks they're stupid and childish,' Adam explained.

Callie's mouth twisted slightly. 'That sounds like Logan,' she muttered. 'Don't worry, Adam. What you do is your business, and I'm not going to tell Logan anything. However, I would like to know how he found me.'

Relieved, Adam relaxed a bit. 'Oh, that. He hired a private detective and told me to help the chap out. It wasn't too difficult. We found out about your private bank account and traced your deposits here.'

Callie's expression tensed. 'You mean you went to those lengths? You found my bank-account details?'

'Well, the detective did,' Adam corrected hastily. 'I'm sorry. It was his idea.'

Callie shook her head in disbelief. 'It's not your fault. I should have suspected that Logan would do something extreme.'

'I really think he was very worried about you,' Adam explained, leaning forward to look at her. 'I mean, he was flat-out furious when he found out you'd gone. I know he was really concerned for your safety.'

A hint of guilt flashed in Callie's eyes. 'I know, I suppose I should have told him something,' she muttered. 'But you don't know Logan.'

'Yes I do!' Adam said emphatically. 'He wouldn't let me keep my eyebrow ring.'

'Your eyebrow ring?'

Adam waved his hand in the air. 'It's just an example. I meant that I know how very domineering and aggressive he can be.'

'Yes, well, until he figures some things out, our relationship doesn't stand a chance.' Callie looked saddened by the thought.

'What is it he needs to figure out?' Adam had already decided that he liked Callie Waterford a great deal. Even after this one conversation, he could see how she and Logan would argue about any number of things. But as kind as Callie appeared to be, Adam knew she would meet Logan head on if she had to.

'He needs to understand what makes a marriage work, for starters,' Callie said.

'How long have you been married to him?'

'Three years. I'm not even sure why we got married in the first place. We're completely different in personality. He's ... well, you know how he is.'

'And how are you?' Adam asked.

Callie considered the question. 'I don't know,' she finally said. 'I'm more relaxed and certainly more tolerant. I grew up in very working-class household, though, so I've learned to appreciate everything. Well, almost everything.'

'Maybe the problem was that Logan didn't appreciate you,' Adam said gently.

Callie looked at him and smiled. She had a perfectly lovely smile that made her eyes light up and her features relax. 'Thanks, Adam. But given Logan's recent behaviour, I suspect he has no intentions of even thinking about our relationship, let alone appreciating me.'

'I'm sorry.'

She nodded. 'So am I. I just wish he knew how . . .' Her voice trailed off and she shrugged.

'How to do what?' Adam prompted.

'How to feel. How to unbend a little.' She smiled slightly. 'Or, in his case, how to unbend a lot. I think that's the main reason our marriage is in such trouble. He never even wanted to talk about things.'

'Well,' Adam said, coming to a realisation of his own. 'It seems to me that if things don't work out, then it would be his loss.'

Chapter Ten

*L*ogan picked up the ringing telephone. 'Logan Waterford.'

'Sugar, it's Gloria.'

'Gloria.' Logan sighed and clicked off his computer. He'd completely forgotten to call her about Callie.

'I'm sorry I haven't been in touch, but I went to New York for awhile,' Gloria said. 'Bloomingdale's was having the most marvellous sale. Although I was a bit disappointed to discover that you hadn't tried to contact me at all during my absence.'

'I'm sorry, Gloria,' Logan replied. 'I've been swamped with a court case and other things. I meant to call and tell you that I found Callie.'

'You did? Where is she?'

'She's living and working at a shop in City Market,' Logan said. 'It's called Nebula Arcana.'

'You're joking. She's living in a shop?'

'In a flat above the shop.'

'Have you seen her?'

'Yes, a couple of times.'

'And she's coming back to you, I hope.'

Logan's fist tightened on the receiver. 'I haven't been able to convince her to, no.'

'This is completely absurd!' Gloria said in outrage. 'I'm going to talk to her myself, Logan. This has gone far enough. It's about time she came to her senses.'

'Her senses appear to have deserted her completely,' Logan replied dryly. He remembered seeing her outside of the home of the voodoo priestess. The whole concept of voodoo didn't shock him so much as the knowledge that Callie was becoming involved with it, since that meant she must be getting very desperate. Logan himself had even gone so far as to consult a psychic years ago when he'd been entrenched so deeply in a black hole that he hadn't foreseen any way out. Unfortunately, neither had the psychic.

'Isn't she thinking about our reputations?' Gloria snapped, breaking Logan out of his thoughts. 'The women at the Ladies Guild are already talking. Heaven only knows what kind of rumours they're starting.'

Logan glanced at his watch and stood up. 'Gloria, I have to go. I have an appointment in half an hour.'

'All right. Can I bring you dinner tonight?'

'No, I won't be here.'

'I'm going to talk to Callie myself tomorrow,' Gloria assured him. 'Don't fret, sugar. She'll come home soon.'

Damn right she will, Logan thought. He hung up the telephone and pulled on his suit jacket. He was dreading this meeting with the Lawrences. He wanted to get it over with as quickly as possible.

After parking on River Street, Logan pressed the entry buzzer of the five-storey building. The oak-and-glass door opened automatically. He stepped into the elegant, lobby. Two chandeliers cast moving patterns of light on the forest-green carpet. A chubby, uniformed man was sitting at a carved, wooden desk near a row of pigeon-holes. He looked up from his newspaper at the sound of Logan's entry.

'May I help you, sir?'

'Yes. I'm here to see the Lawrences. They should be expecting me. Logan Waterford.'

'One moment, please, Mr Waterford.' He picked up the receiver of a telephone and punched in several numbers, then spoke in a low whisper. After placing the receiver back into the cradle, he nodded at Logan. 'Mrs Lawrence says you may go up.'

'Thank you.' Tightening his hand on his briefcase, Logan walked to the lift and pressed the button.

'Top floor,' the doorman called out unnecessarily. 'Penthouse suite.'

Nerves knotted in Logan's stomach as the lift began its ascent. Every single muscle in his body felt tight, but he refused to betray the slightest sense of anxiety. Not with Elenore and Gerald Lawrence. Not with anyone. He rang the bell of the penthouse and waited.

'Mr Waterford?' A young woman in a maid's outfit opened the door. 'Please come in.'

'Thank you.'

She ushered him inside. The marbled hall led to a sunken drawing room appointed with Victorian elegance. Floral prints hung on the walls, and fresh flowers bloomed from crystal vases. Sepia-toned photographs rested on the tables and the marble mantel of the fireplace. Logan walked to the windows, which opened to a magnificent view of the Savannah River and surrounding wetlands.

'May I bring you some coffee or tea?' the maid asked.

'No, thank you. I won't be staying long.'

'Mrs Lawrence will be with you shortly.'

Wasn't that just like Elenore, Logan thought. Making him wait gave her some sort of advantage.

'Logan, darling.'

To Logan's ears, the silky, southern voice sounded like fingernails raking across a blackboard. He turned and watched her enter the room, assessing the changes that fifteen years had wrought. She was a tall woman, clothed in a filmy, white garment that consisted of a gown and a transparent robe that billowed behind her like a cloud. Her dark hair was pulled into a chignon, emphasising the aristocratic lines of her face and her kohl-lined, dark eyes. Two silver streaks of grey hair swept back from her temples. Lines radiated from the corners of her eyes and bracketed her reddened lips, but her skin was smooth and supple. She looked older, of course, but she was still a striking woman. Logan calculated that she was almost sixty now.

She smiled. 'Well, my goodness, look at you. Don't you look wonderful? The boy has become quite a man. The years have done you great justice.'

She approached him and reached up to kiss his cheek. A waft of her sweet perfume made Logan feel sick.

'Hello, Elenore,' he said. 'Where's Gerald?'

Elenore pulled away from him as her lavender-tipped hand went to her chest. 'You didn't hear? He died five years ago of a heart attack. I still miss him rather desperately.'

Logan's first reaction was one of relief that he wouldn't have the old bastard to deal with, but he forced himself to say that he was sorry.

'Thank you.' Elenore waved towards a chair. 'Please, sit down. I asked Julie to bring us some tea.'

'I don't have time for tea,' Logan replied shortly. 'What is it you want, Elenore?'

'Still getting right to the point, I see,' Elenore replied. She sat down, arranging her gown over her legs as she crossed them. 'Very well. As I told you, I'm starting a new venture that involves renovating my riverboat. I think it will be quite a success, especially where tourists are concerned. However, I'm running low on funds.'

'I'm not giving you money, Elenore.'

She looked at him. 'You might at least hear me out first. I have several investors, but they've only agreed to set amounts. And, since I want the boat to be decorated entirely in authentic nineteenth-century furnishings, I'm refusing to skimp on expenses.'

Logan glanced around the suite. 'Seems to me you

should have enough money to finance it yourself,' he said dryly.

'Yes, you'd think so, wouldn't you?' Elenore rose and approached him, padding lightly across the carpet. 'Unfortunately, that's not the case. Gerald purchased this penthouse, but I've had to liquidate many of our assets since his death. You see, he left behind a substantial number of creditors when he passed away, and one thing creditors don't have is patience.'

Logan laughed humourlessly. 'And that surprises you? If I recall correctly, and I know I do, you two were always sticking your fingers into illegal businesses. It's no wonder you have to pay off now.'

Elenore's expression hardened. 'There is no need to gloat.'

Logan shrugged. 'You mess with sharks, you get your arse bitten. It's a simple fact. And I can't help you, Elenore. I don't loan money.'

Her mouth twisted. 'You mean, you don't loan money to *me*.'

'That, too.'

She crossed her arms over her ample breasts and narrowed her eyes. 'I've heard that you're married, Logan.'

'You heard right.' Logan's fists clenched as he thought of Callie. He'd been watching her sporadically for the past week, but he hadn't had a confrontation with her since he saw her on the street. Right now, keeping track of Callie's whereabouts seemed to be the only thing he had control over.

He levelled a hard look at Elenore. She wouldn't dare do anything to hurt Callie, not if he could stop her. 'What does that have to do with anything?'

'Does she know of your little escapades of the past?' Elenore asked.

A rock sank into Logan's gut. He'd known that Elenore was fully capable of playing dirty pool, but he realised now that he had also hoped that age would have mellowed her. So much for hopes.

'What are you getting at?' he asked tightly.

She reached out to straighten his already-straight tie with her long fingers, pursing her lips thoughtfully.

'Well, I'm sure you would hate it if Savannah society found out the truth about you.'

Logan's blood turned to ice. 'You wouldn't dare.'

'Wouldn't I?' Elenore shot back, her dark eyes flashing at him. 'I want this business to succeed, Logan. I'll do anything to make that happen, even ruin you if I have to.'

'Trying to ruin me won't get you the money,' Logan said coldly. 'I know the kind of people you deal with, Elenore. I'm not about to put my money into your schemes.'

'Why, because you think it'll damage your sterling reputation?' Elenore laughed. 'And you don't think I can do equal amounts of damage?'

'You bitch,' Logan snapped, unable to help himself from letting his anger show. He was ready to strangle her. 'You can't blackmail me into investing in a god-damn casino. I know you. You're not going to play straight either with your so-called investors or your customers. Forget it.'

Elenore's expression turned ugly. 'You have the nerve to criticise my business practices after what you did fifteen years ago?'

'My situation was completely different.'

'Was it, Logan?' Elenore taunted. 'I don't think so. You needed something and you went after it however you could. But I'll bet you never thought it could all come back to wreck your life so many years later.'

Logan dragged a hand through his hair and tried to think. He felt sick, unable to think of even a single way this could work out without ruining him. If he gave Elenore the money, he knew the entire thing would explode into scandal when people discovered Elenore's illegal finances. And his name would be right up there with hers. But if he didn't give her the money, she'd yank the past into the present and destroy him in a whole other way.

Shit. Logan sank down on to a chair and rested his forehead in his hand. For the first time in fifteen years, a horrible sensation of defeat coursed through him. She would not ruin him. No matter what he had to do.

'Elenore, right now I could strangle you with my bare hands.'

'I don't doubt that you would succeed, too,' Elenore replied coldly. She paused in front of him and put her hands on her hips. 'You want me to keep my mouth shut? Fine. You know what you have to do. I want two million dollars. You have until next Saturday to think about your answer.'

'Two million dollars? What are you planning to fuel that goddamn boat with? Dom Perignon and beluga caviar?

'I said that I wanted the most authentic decor I could find,' Elenore said. 'I have a team of people around the world attending auctions and sales to find certified items. I'm collecting as many original pieces of furniture, rugs and paintings as I can.'

'Jesus Christ. And you think you can recoup all that money? You're a lousy businesswoman, Elenore.'

'On the contrary,' she said. 'I have you over a barrel, don't I? Anyone that can best Logan Waterford has to be good.'

'Yeah, blackmail is right up there with creating the computer superchip,' Logan retorted acidly. 'You've sunk lower than your bastard husband, did you know that?'

'Actually, I think Gerald would be quite proud of me,' she replied.

'Well, he always was an idiot.'

Elenore chuckled. 'All right, Logan, enough with the

insults. As I said, you can take some time to think about this or you can give me your answer now.'

She reached to cup his chin in her hand, forcing him to look up at her. Bile rose in Logan's throat at the sight of the expression in her eyes. Her mouth had an ugly, downward curve.

'You disgust me,' he said tightly.

Her eyes froze into chips of ice. 'Do I? You mean you haven't been thinking about what it would be like to fuck me again?'

'Yeah, sure. The thought made my skin crawl.'

Elenore shook her head and walked to a nearby table. She removed a length of thick rope and a knife, then held them both up. 'Oh, Logan. You're just sinking deeper and deeper into the quicksand. You forget that I *know* you. I know exactly what you like.'

She approached him with a cold glint in her eye. Logan watched her dispassionately.

'You still want to fuck me even though you know I despise you?' he asked.

Elenore chuckled. 'Honey, sometimes hate can fuel the best fucks, didn't you know that?' She set the rope and knife down. 'By the way, I'd suggest you don't spurn me this time. As you know, I have plenty of ammunition to use against you.'

Logan shook his head. 'Now you're threatening me if I don't fuck you? Jesus, are you that desperate, you old hag?'

Anger tightened her jaw. 'Nice, Logan. That's exactly the way to treat the woman who could destroy everything you have.'

She began unbuttoning her gown with sharp movements. There was nothing coquettish or coy about Elenore Lawrence. There never had been. She knew what she wanted and went after it with a vengeance. She stripped off her skirt until she stood before him, wearing a black bra, matching knickers and her high-heels. Her figure had thickened over the years, her breasts sagging slightly, but she carried herself like a queen. She put her hands on her hips and gave him a challenging glare.

'Well, Logan? You up for it or not?'

Logan looked at her for an extended moment. Something clicked in his mind. There was one way that he could regain some form of control over Elenore Lawrence. Without a word, he picked up the knife.

'I see you still have the same tastes, Elenore.'

Elenore's gaze went to the rope. Her mouth twitched. She held out her hand. 'Give me the knife.'

'The hell I will.' Logan approached her. Desire burnt in his blood, but it wasn't desire for the woman in front of him. It was desire for control. He reached out and placed the tip of the knife at the base of Elenore's throat. She gasped, her hand curling around the back of the couch.

Logan slowly lowered the knife, trailing it over her skin before flicking at the front of her bra. With one slash, the cups fell open to reveal her weighty breasts. Elenore let out a moan as a flare of excitement appeared in her eyes. Logan dragged the point of the knife over the curve of her belly and into the elastic waistband of her knickers. He drew it down quickly, ripping them into shreds. Elenore stared at him, her body trembling just slightly.

Logan pointed the knife at the floor. 'Get down there, you bitch.'

She went down on her hands and knees. Logan almost laughed. She still got herself worked up over the most perverse sex games, and probably even the dangerous ones. He picked up the rope and cut off a long length, then bent to grasp Elenore's wrists. For a split second, he stared into her cold eyes.

'You know, I could kill you,' he said.

'You don't have the balls.'

'Don't tempt me.' He lashed the rope tightly around her wrists and tied the other end to the leg of the couch. He moved behind her and tied her ankles together, securing them to a table leg. Then he stepped back to admire his handiwork. Her fleshy arse stuck into the air, her breasts hanging down like overripe fruits. Logan chuckled. This was definitely how he preferred to see Elenore Lawrence.

Elenore flipped her hair back and lifted her head to look at him. 'You've got me right where you want me for a change, haven't you, Logan?' she asked tauntingly.

Logan walked to the drinks cabinet and removed a bottle of wine. He returned to Elenore and pushed her legs apart, then pressed the bottleneck against her cunt. She gasped and jerked forward.

'You wish this was my prick, don't you, Elenore?' Logan eased the bottle further into her. She gave a moan and thrust her buttocks backwards as she tried to impale herself on the cold glass. Logan let her work herself back and forth on the bottle a few times before he tossed it aside.

'Bastard,' Elenore muttered, straining against the tightly bound ropes.

'Uh huh.'

Her body quivered with excitement. He knew she loved this, this lack of knowledge about what he would do next and the added danger of his intense dislike. In her life, she'd tried everything, and she constantly needed to take things up a notch in order to keep herself on the edge. His cock hardened at the sight of her lashed to the furniture, even as nothing but disgust filled his mind.

Elenore tossed her head as he returned to stand in front of her. Her eyes flashed at him. 'You want to get revenge on me? Whip me, then, why don't you?'

'You'd love it if I did, wouldn't you?' Logan leaned his hips against the back of a chair and observed his Nemesis. Even in her bound, helpless state, Elenore radiated a kind of power. He might even have found it oddly erotic if he didn't hate her so much.

Elenore's mouth curved into a slow smile. 'Does your

wife let you do this kind of thing to her?' she asked. 'What's her name? Oh, yes. Callie.'

Logan tensed. 'How do you know her name?'

'I find out things.'

A wave of anger swept over Logan. He grabbed Elenore's hair suddenly, forcing her head up. 'Did you talk to her, you bitch?'

She laughed. 'Heavens, I didn't expect such a reaction. Does she let you do perverse things to her, lover? Or do you let her do them to you?'

The thought of Callie knowing anything about this mess inflamed Logan like a hot poker. God, he loathed Elenore Lawrence. Even worse, he loathed everything she stood for and everything she reminded him of.

'What do you know about Callie?' he snapped.

'I know that she's a pretty little thing who recently left you.'

'Where did you find this out?' A red mist descended in front of Logan's eyes. He cursed the very thought that the sordidness of his relationship with Elenore would somehow reach Callie. He'd do anything to keep that from happening.

'Why did she leave you, Logan?' Elenore asked coldly. 'Or did you kick her out? Couldn't she satisfy all your dark desires?'

Logan's hand tightened on Elenore's hair. 'Did you talk to her or not?'

Something dark appeared in Elenore's eyes. 'Fuck me, Logan. Or I pay a visit to your sweet wife.'

Images of Callie flashed across Logan's mind; dozens of them in a constant, moving picture. Her silky hair and skin, her wide smile and brown eyes. The gestures of her hands when she was angry with at him, the look on her face after they made love, how she always stood up against him the way no one else ever dared.

He unzipped his trousers and moved behind Elenore, plunging his cock into her with a fierceness borne of rage. She let out a squeal of both pleasure and pain, pumping her hips back to match his increasing thrusts. Logan's mind separated from the baseness of this particular physical act, latching on to everything that was good in his life, everything that had to do with Callie. He suddenly couldn't stand the thought that he might have been treating her the way that others once treated him. Self-disgust rose in his throat.

'Fuck, yes, pound me hard,' Elenore gasped, twisting against the ropes as her body jerked and swayed with the force of his thrusts. 'Jesus, Logan, you fuck like a goddamn stallion. Put your finger in my arse.'

Logan grabbed a length of the thick rope and pushed a frayed end into the quivering ring of her anus. Elenore wriggled her hips, pushing the rope in even deeper.

'That's it, honey, force it in there,' she panted. 'Come on, hurt me if you hate me so much.'

Logan shoved the rope into her arse and slammed into her, wanting to hurt her and knowing she was loving every minute of it. He reached around her to grab her breasts as they jiggled underneath her, pinching her nipples hard. She squealed again. Logan's own body reacted to the heat of her cunt as she clenched around him and milked his cock for all she was worth. He gritted his teeth and shot into her just as she convulsed around him with a loud howl. As soon as he felt her come, Logan pulled out of her and hitched up his trousers. She was the woman he'd thought was out of his life, and here he was fucking her again.

Elenore's head was hanging down, her chest heaving as she caught her breath. She lifted her head to look at him. Her eyes gleamed.

'You have an incredible tool there, darling. Even better, you know how to use it.'

Logan picked up the knife and slashed it through the rope binding one of her wrists. Then he tossed the knife on to the floor.

'Cut yourself free and leave me the fuck alone.'

He turned and stalked out of the room, his body tight with tension.

'A week from Saturday!' Elenore called after him. 'That's my final offer.'

Logan ignored her and slammed the front door closed. He tried to draw air into his tight chest as he descended to the first floor. He should have known that Elenore wouldn't forget about him. She was a leech, latching on to whoever might give her an advantage.

He stepped on to the street and took a deep breath. His mind worked almost mechanically, clicking and whirring as it sought vainly for some kind of solution. It came up empty. For the first time in his life, Logan didn't know what to do. Everything he had was lined up like ducks in a shooting gallery for Elenore's disposal. His finances, his business, his reputation, his status. His wife. An image of Callie's face appeared in his mind. No, he wasn't in danger of losing her because of Elenore. He was in danger of losing her because of himself.

Not wanting to go back to work, Logan returned home. He went upstairs and stripped off his clothes, feeling grimy and soiled. He turned on the shower full blast and stepped inside. He hated not knowing what to do about Elenore Lawrence. The woman would haunt his life like the devil if he didn't come up with a way to break her hold over him. Christ, what if she wanted him to fuck her regularly? The thought nauseated him. He ran the soap over his body, working up a thick lather. It was true that, if Callie came home, there was more chance of her finding out about Elenore, but that was one risk Logan was willing to take. Maybe he'd be able to think more clearly if she were here.

He stepped out of the shower and dried off, then changed into a pair of clean jeans and a T-shirt. He picked up his car keys and went outside. He had usually shunned the mere idea of the occult, but he was running out of options. He drove to a street off Bay, where he

163

had first seen Callie and Tess leaving the home of the voodoo priestess. He parked and went towards the house, feeling more than a little foolish. He was going to a voodoo priestess about his trouble with Elenore. Brilliant.

Logan paused outside the door. What the hell was he doing? He'd always been able to handle his own problems. What was the difference now? Just as he was about to turn away, the door opened.

'May I help you?'

The smooth voice made him pause. He looked at the stunning woman who held the door open. She wore a long, multicoloured robe and a matching headband that enhanced the richness of her mocha-coloured skin. The questioning look in her eyes was replacing by dawning recognition.

'I know you,' she said.

Logan's eyebrows lifted. 'You do?'

She tapped her temple. 'Yes. I recognise you from a photograph. You are Callie's husband.'

Logan frowned. 'How did you get a photograph of me?'

'Callie had one, of course.'

'Why did she show it to you?'

'Ah, you are sceptic.' She lifted her finger and shook her head, her dark eyes twinkling. 'You and Callie both. I suspect you are more alike than either one of you wishes to believe.'

'Callie and I are completely different.'

She shrugged and held out her hand gracefully. 'I am Abiona. Would you like to come in for a moment?'

Logan hesitated, but figured he had very few things left to lose. He shook her hand and followed her inside, glancing around at the bold colours, African masks and fetish items. Abiona watched him for a moment, then shook her head.

'Your harmony is in complete disarray, Logan.'

'My harmony?'

164

'Your inner self.'

Logan almost muttered something about 'New Age crap', but stopped himself just in time.

'Please, sit.' Abiona waved towards a chair. 'May I ask why you came to see me?'

'It's a mistake,' Logan replied. 'I'm sorry to have taken up your time.'

'Sit, sit.' Abiona draped herself over a chair and looked him up and down. 'People don't come to me in error, Logan.'

'Maybe not, but I did.'

'Well, then, a fortuitous error it must be,' Abiona said lightly. 'At least have some tea before you go. You can tell me about Callie. I like her very much.'

Logan sat down. He had the odd sensation that Abiona's creamy voice and the strange spirituality of her home could wipe away the sordidness of his encounter with Elenore.

Abiona rose and left the room for a moment before returning with a pot of tea. After handing him a cup, she curled up in her chair and eyed him curiously. 'Who is damaging your harmony so badly?'

Logan gave her a startled look. He'd always prided himself on being difficult to read. 'How do you know that anyone is?'

'I suspect you wouldn't have come to me for another reason,' Abiona replied. 'Unless you wish a love spell to return Callie to you?'

'I don't need a spell for that.'

'No, I imagine you don't.' She sipped her tea and continued looking at him with a penetratingly perceptive gaze. 'So, what is it then?'

Logan cleared his throat. 'What was Callie doing here?'

'If she wants you to know, she will tell you herself,' Abiona said. 'You cannot expect to know everything about her. I doubt she knows everything about you.'

'There are some things she doesn't need to know.'

'Perhaps that's part of the reason she left you,' Abiona replied. She glanced at the clock on the wall and stood up. 'I'm afraid I have an appointment in fifteen minutes. I do hope you will come back to see me again. Perhaps a ritual or a spell will be in order.'

'I'm sorry, but I don't believe in this sort of thing.'

'Never dismiss worlds outside your own, Logan.' Abiona placed her hand on his back and walked him to the door. 'We are having a voodoo ceremony this Saturday night on Tybee Island. You are most welcome to attend. Perhaps it will provide you with more insight into our religion.'

'I'll think about it. Thank you for your time.'

As he left the priestess's home, Logan caught himself wondering if Callie would be at this so-called ceremony.

Chapter Eleven

Callie slipped a full, white skirt over her hips and buttoned a loose, cotton blouse. Abiona had told her to wear light colours but, other than that, Callie had no idea what the proper attire was for a voodoo ceremony. Still, she suspected that formal dress wasn't required. She brushed her hair and looked in the mirror. The henna tattoo Abiona painted on her breast had faded, but Callie had been wearing the *mojo* bag around her neck all week.

Considering she hadn't seen Logan for the last week, she thought the protective spell had, indeed, started to work. That aspect of it, at least. But she couldn't help wondering if Logan had simply given up on her after their last encounter. And why on earth did she feel somewhat disappointed at the thought? Wasn't that what she wanted?

'Ready, Callie?' Tess called up the stairs.

'Yes.' Callie hurried down to meet Tess. 'I didn't know what to wear.'

'You look great,' Tess assured her. Adam stood next to her, dressed in beige trousers and a T-shirt.

'Hey, Callie,' he greeted. 'Hope you don't mind if I go along.'

'Of course not. Nice to see you again.' Callie gave the young man a warm smile. She couldn't help liking him, despite his connection to her husband. She was certain, however, that Adam wasn't reporting back to Logan about her activities. He was too afraid that Logan would find out about his own latest hobbies.

The three of them went out to Tess's car and climbed inside. The voodoo ceremony site was located on a remote corner of Tybee Island that hadn't yet been overrun by development. Right near an isolated spot of beach, a large roof made of wood and palm leaves was held up by five posts, one in the centre and four at each corner. There were no walls, leaving the space open on all sides to the breeze and the scent of the beach. At least ten drums sat around the perimeter of the structure, and five intricately painted altars dedicated to the *loas* rested along one side. Numerous flowers, candles, food items, and bottles of perfume and alcohol had been placed before the altars.

'It's called the peristyle,' Tess explained as they walked towards the structure. 'That's where the sacred dances take place.'

Next to the peristyle, a group of women were busy setting out massive amounts of food and drink. Several dozen people wandered around the area, some dressed in what appeared to be ritual costumes of colourful sarongs and shell jewellery, and others wearing simple jeans or skirts. As the thickness of darkness began to descend, three men began lighting torches and lanterns.

Pemba waved and approached them with a wide smile on her face. She was elaborately dressed in a flowing black-and-white robe, with a matching turban and chunky, white jewellery.

'Hello, children,' she said. 'I am so pleased you came.'

Tess introduced Adam, and Pemba kissed them all on the cheek.

'Abiona has been waiting for you as well,' Pemba said. 'We will begin shortly. Come and eat something first.'

She led them towards the food, which consisted of everything from coconut cake to an entire roasted pig. Abiona came towards them, looking stunning in a white sarong with a cloth band wrapped around her head. She smiled and greeted them, then took Callie's arm and pulled her aside.

'The spell, Callie,' she said. 'It is working?'

'I think so,' Callie admitted. 'My husband was waiting for me after I left your house last Sunday, but I haven't seen or heard from him since then.'

'And your thoughts?'

Callie flushed and glanced away from Abiona's penetrating gaze. How could she explain that she couldn't seem to get Logan out of her thoughts? He appeared in her mind so frequently – usually memories of him when his guard had been down. He had so seldom been unguarded, but sometimes Callie would look at him when he was reading or planting new shrubs in the garden, or unfurling the sail on his boat, or even working at his desk. And every now and then, she would catch him with his features relaxed, his dark hair falling over his forehead, the lines of his body eased from tension. Those were the moments that haunted her now. Those and the memory of that one night of angry passion.

'Callie?' Abiona's long fingers touched Callie's chin, urging their eyes to meet again. 'He is still with you, yes?'

Callie nodded. 'I'm not surprised, though. It's been almost a month since I left him, but I lived with him for three years. I can't expect to stop thinking about him so soon.'

Abiona nodded. 'That is true.' She pursed her lips thoughtfully and touched Callie's hair. 'You miss him then, yes?'

The question startled Callie. 'Well, I don't miss the restrictions of being with him, but I guess sometimes I . . . I might miss *him*.'

Abiona smiled her beautiful smile and patted Callie's cheek. 'Your harmony will be returned soon.'

'I hope so.'

The crowd of people began moving towards the peristyle, signalling the beginning of the ceremony. Abiona kissed Callie's cheek and hurried off to join the other devotees. Callie found Tess and Adam, who were sitting cross-legged around the edge of the structure. She slipped her shoes off and sat down next to Tess, arranging her full skirt over her legs. A nervous excitement stirred in her belly. She had no idea what to expect from this ceremony.

The drummers took their positions and began to beat a slow, steady rhythm with their hands. Flames from the torches and lanterns flickered over the scene, creating an eerie, reddish glow. A tall man wearing white trousers and a loose shirt approached the centre of the peristyle, holding a bowl of water. He had striking features with high cheekbones and large eyes. His white clothing highlighted the smooth darkness of his skin. He began chanting words that Callie couldn't understand, but they carried a musical intonation that rose and fell with the drumbeat.

'That's Kadja,' Tess whispered to Callie. 'He's one of the priests. Now he'll draw what's called a *vever* in order to invoke the *loa*.'

Kadja lifted the bowl towards all four corners of the peristyle, then poured water at each entrance. Then he passed the bowl to Pemba, who repeated the actions. Several other participants had begun chanting, their words a strange twisting of French, English and West African dialects. Kadja took another bowl of flour and cornmeal, picking a small amount between his thumb and forefinger as he trickled it around the centre post. His body shifted with each step he took around the peristyle, creating an elaborate pattern on the floor. His movements were so graceful and hypnotic that Callie was entranced.

The drumbeat continued and began to resound in Callie's head. The deep, rich sound of chanting filled the air. Two other men approached the centre of the peristyle and circled round the centre post, before kneeling and kissing the ground. Moving rhythmically, they scattered bits of food over the intricate *vever* design to feed the *loa*. Kadja continued his singular incantation as Pemba approached, carrying a live, squawking chicken by its legs. The sound of prayer began to rise from the crowd.

Callie winced. She'd heard the rumours about voodoo sacrifice, but she had been hoping they were just that: rumours. Tess touched her arm and leant close to whisper in her ear.

'I know it seems weird, but it's an important part of honouring the *loa*.'

Callie tried not to cringe as she watched Kadja walk around the peristyle with the chicken, passing it over the heads of the participants. His dark skin began to glow with a sheen of sweat. Slowly, he lowered the bird towards the food on the *vever*, and the chicken pecked at a piece of grain.

'There, now the chicken is identified with the spirit,' Tess explained. 'Now it can be sacrificed because the *loa* will accept it.'

The voices began to rise, reaching a crescendo of growing excitement along with the pounding drums. The air vibrated with anticipation and uncertainty. Callie's mouth went dry as she watched Kadja, his body in constant, fluid motion, hold up the chicken. He took a knife and slit the bird's throat, letting the blood drip into a bowl of water. Callie wanted to look away, but she was completely mesmerised by the gracefulness of Kadja's movements and the increasing reverence of the participants. Most of them stood around the peristyle, clapping and chanting in time to the drumbeat. As Kadja laid the bird on the *vever*, the others began sprinkling it with flour, coffee grains and water.

171

'That's the final offering,' Tess said. 'Now they'll take it away to be cleaned and cooked, and wait for the *loa* to mount someone.'

'Mount?'

'Possess.'

Callie swallowed hard. Echoes of the drumbeat began to pulse in her blood, recalling some deep, primitive instinct. She watched as people began to stand and move around the peristyle and the *vever*, stamping the ground with their feet and clapping wildly. Voices hovered in the air. Bodies shifted and writhed, hips twisting as they shook wooden rattles and danced around the centre post. Callie's gaze went to Abiona, who joined in the ritual. Her body was so loose and pliant that she seemed almost other-worldly as she moved in exultation to honour the spirits. The dancers were totally unselfconscious, shedding their egos to give themselves over to ritual. The sound of clanging iron split through the air to accompany the drums. Energy stirred in Callie's blood, intensified by the heady, thick beat.

Abiona stopped in front of her. Callie stared up at the other woman, unable to process her thoughts in the face of Abiona's exquisite beauty. Abiona's body vibrated with exertion, her skin glowing with sweat. Without a word, she reached down and took Callie's hands, pulling her into the ritualistic dance. Sound filled Callie's ears; an intensity without pause or relief. Body heat from the other dancers coated the air around her. She grasped Abiona's hand and began to move, letting the electric atmosphere into her soul. Bodies undulated like waves of the ocean around the centre post, voices rising.

Callie didn't stop to think; she flowed with the movement, entranced by the dynamism around her and the rhythm of Abiona's body so close to hers. Faces and bodies blurred and whipped together, firelight crackling over sweat-dampened skin. A tornado of movement as even the air lit with eroticism and the spirit of possession.

The drums ceased so quickly that Callie barely had time to react. She felt Abiona's hand steady her by the elbow. Callie stared at the other woman, her breathing harsh and her mind spinning.

'Rest for a moment, Callie.'

Callie nodded and returned to Tess and Adam, sinking down into her place as she fought to catch her breath. Adam leaned across Tess to hand Callie a white handkerchief.

'Thanks, Adam.' Sweat dripped from Callie's forehead, and she patted her skin with the handkerchief.

'You were ... wow, you were good,' Adam said admiringly.

'Do you feel OK?' Tess asked.

Callie's heart thudded like the beating of a hummingbird's wings and her blood felt like fire. She couldn't seem to grasp a coherent thought. Shakily, she stood and stepped out of the peristyle on to the sand of the beach.

'Yes ... I just ... I need water.'

'I'll get it for you,' Tess said quickly.

'No. I want some air.' Callie took a breath and made her way over to the food area. She found a bottle of water in an ice-filled bucket and twisted off the cap. After drinking half the bottle in three large gulps, she started to feel a bit better. Slowly, she walked down to the edge of the ocean and drew in a deep breath of salty air. Away from the hot torches and the noise, her body and mind began to calm somewhat, but a flickering energy continued to stir in her. She turned and looked back towards the peristyle as the drumbeat started up again. How incredible that these people could lose themselves to a force much greater than themselves.

Callie made her way back to the peristyle, her feet sinking into the cool sand. She was oddly reluctant to return to the intensity of the ritual, so she paused near a tree and leant her shoulder against the trunk. She could see the dancing begin again, but it was a relief to watch from a distance. Amidst the newly energised, writhing bodies, Abiona suddenly leapt out from the crowd and began a fierce undulation, her hips twisting and breasts swaying. Callie knew instinctively that the *loa* had come down to mount the beautiful woman. Abiona reached out to touch several of the other participants, her eyes so wide that the entire whites were visible. She lurched wildly from one to the other like a spinning top, her body in a symphony of constant movement.

Callie wrapped one arm around the tree branch as she watched the whirling, impassioned bodies. She was intensely aware of her own being, the rapid beating of her heart, the sound of her breath and the damp heat of her skin. Never before had she been so painfully alive and human.

Suddenly, a male hand slipped around her waist with such swiftness that Callie had no time to react. She started in surprise for an instant before she recognised the touch as belonging to her husband.

Callie drew in a breath as Logan's body came up behind her. His hand splayed flat across her abdomen, but he didn't force her back against him.

'You're not . . .' Callie's voice faltered. She swallowed and tried again. 'You didn't follow me here?'

'What do you think?' His deep voice sounded ghostly on the undulating night air.

Callie closed her eyes. She experienced an insane desire to ask him where he had been for the last week, which was ridiculous, considering she wasn't supposed to care. Logan's hand slipped a bit lower to the gentle swell of her stomach. His thighs pressed against her buttocks. She could feel his breath stirring her hair. Images of that night a few weeks ago swam behind her eyelids: her splayed over the counter, him pounding into her from behind, gasps and whimpers, cold glass and hot flesh.

'Why?' she asked.

'Curiosity.'

Callie waited for Logan to tell her in a voice edged with disapproval exactly what he thought of her attending a voodoo ceremony. To her surprise, he didn't chastise her. Instead, his next question was low and merely curious.

'Why this?' he asked. His other hand snaked around her waist.

'I-I was trying to get you out of my life.'

'It didn't work.' Logan's fingertips slid into the elastic waistband of Callie's skirt.

'I've discovered that.' Callie opened her eyes and stared at the scene at the peristyle. Abiona was still dancing in wild, frenzied movements, urged on by the beat of the drums and the rhythmic sound of clapping and chanting. Her movements were overtly sexual, her hips thrusting back and forth and her breasts swaying.

Logan's head lifted from Callie's neck as he looked towards the peristyle. 'She's your priestess, isn't she?'

'Her name is Abiona. Right now, she's possessed by a *loa*, which is a spirit.'

'She's quite striking.'

'I know.'

Logan's fingers moved further down. Some dim part of Callie's mind told her she shouldn't let him do this, but she couldn't find it in her to push him away. Quite the contrary, in fact. She welcomed the heat of his body against hers, the touch of his fingers on her moist skin. She closed her eyes again and took another drink of water. Christ, it was hot. Not even the ocean breeze cooled her. The tempo of the dance continued to pound in her blood.

Logan splayed his hand over the soft skin of her belly, edging downwards to her pussy. His other hand pushed her hair away from her neck. Callie shivered when his lips touched the nape of her neck. He had never kissed her there before now. She eased herself back slightly and felt his erection pushing against her. Arousal spread through her like a skein of unravelling yarn. Logan's

175

fingers reached her clit, massaging the creamy button with an increasing roughness. Callie moaned and pressed his hand even harder against her. Her sex was already wet from arousal and exertion, so Logan easily stimulated the sensitive nerves even further. Just as Callie's excitement began to augment, he pulled his hand away from her and reached up to cup her breasts.

'No bra, hmm?' he murmured. His fingers circled her nipples, plucking and pulling them until a waterfall of shivers rained down Callie's spine. She tensed slightly as she waited for him to tell her she was being indecent, but he didn't. Instead, he seemed to take great pleasure in fondling her unfettered breasts. He touched the small bag around her neck.

'What's this?' he asked.

Callie couldn't help chuckling. 'It's called a *mojo* bag. It's supposed to protect me from you.'

'Hmm. It's not working either.'

'I noticed that, too.'

'I saw you dancing,' Logan said. His tongue flicked out to touch her neck.

'Did you?'

'You reminded me of a whirling dervish.'

Callie could hardly believe he wasn't criticising her actions. 'It was amazing. I didn't even feel like myself.'

'You looked pretty incredible, calla lily.'

His use of the endearment went straight to her heart. It had been one of his few displays of affection for her. Slowly, she opened her eyes and turned to look at him. His features were mapped with firelight and shadows, his expression the same stoic one she had seen so often before. But this time, there was something different in his eyes, something Callie didn't even recognise. Was it pain? Or desperation? For what? For *her*?

She reached up and put her trembling fingers against his mouth. It was on the tip of her tongue to tell him that he couldn't do this, that she still wasn't coming home, but then he took one of her fingertips between his lips. Callie stared at him, stunned by the teasingly erotic touch. She pressed her thighs together as her pussy quivered in response. The beat of the ritual drums sounded endless, running together in a never-ending throb that echoed inside her head.

She knew that Logan felt it, too. His muscles were rigid, his cock straining against the front of his jeans. He gazed at her, the burnt darkness of his eyes seeing right through her. Callie shed any pretence of resistance as every last one of her senses demanded that she wanted him. With a moan of surrender, she dropped her hands to the fly of his jeans as his mouth descended on hers. Oh God, he had never kissed her like this before. His lips were rough and demanding, his tongue driving into her mouth as if he were claiming some part of her. Callie's gasp was lost in the depths of his mouth. Her fingers worked frantically to unfasten his jeans as the world of drums and chanting faded into the distance, leaving only the pounding of hearts and the rhythm of breath.

Working quickly, Logan undid the buttons of her blouse and bared her breasts to the sea air. To Callie's further surprise, he went down on his knees in front of her to pull her skirt over her hips. She hadn't bothered with knickers, either. Logan pressed his hands between her thighs to spread them apart. Callie gave a choked gasp when he plunged his tongue into her pussy. Where had he learned to do this so expertly? She'd only ever experienced his brand of restraint when it came to sex. Her hands tightened on his hair as he worked her to orgasm, sucking and licking until Callie could stand it no longer. Tension exploded in her body, causing her to cry out and grasp on to the tree trunk for support. Logan wrapped his arm around her thighs to steady her, his tongue flickering over her clit before he pulled away.

Shaken, Callie stared down at him. The burn in his eyes scorched her. She sank to her knees next to him, desperate to get his clothes off and take his warm flesh

177

in her hand. She tore at his shirt and jeans until she could touch his body, sliding her palms over every muscle, stroking his cock, feeling the roughness of his hair and the heat of his skin. It was like learning about her own husband for the first time.

Logan gripped her around the waist, his breath hard against her forehead as he lowered her to the ground and took her. Callie parted her legs and reached for him, her blood simmering with heat and a new-found awe at the man in front of her. Sweat glistened on his forehead and his jaw clenched as his cock pressed against her. He bent his head to suck on her nipples, creating little paths of electricity directly to her pussy. She drove her hands into his hair. She was wholly submerged in the friction of their bodies and the weight of him on top of her. With a groan, Logan thrust into her creamy slit. Callie gave a cry as he plunged into her, wrapping her legs around his thighs, her hips bucking upwards to match his movements.

Now the drumbeats were the echo – the echo of carnal thrusting and guttural noises. The slick slide of Logan's body against hers filled Callie's senses. His harsh breaths mingled with her own and then, right as she stood poised on the edge of the cliff, his mouth came down on hers, his tongue invading her. Full of him, surrounded by him, Callie clutched Logan against her and came with a furious series of shudders. He thrust into her violently, groaning against her mouth as he collapsed on top of her.

Callie drew in a long breath as their bodies began to relax. She stroked her hands over Logan's back. He eased away from her slowly, rolling on to his back beside her. After a moment, Callie turned on her side and propped her head on her hand. She looked at her husband, examining the austere planes of his face and the coarse texture of his dark hair. He had always been such a mystery to her. People weren't born with disapproval and rigid self-control. So what was it that made

Logan the type of man he had become? Or used to be? For a moment, she found it difficult to recognise the Logan she thought she knew.

He opened his eyes and met her curious gaze. For a long minute, they laid there staring at each other as if they had never even met before now. Callie reached out a tentative hand and placed it on his chest. Previously, Logan would always brush her touches aside, never seeming to want too much intimacy. This time, he didn't. He merely lay there looking at her as Callie twined her fingers through his damp chest hair and rubbed the muscles of his abdomen.

'I'm still not coming home, Logan,' Callie whispered. An odd pain began to take the place of her exhilaration.

His mouth tightened. 'I didn't fuck you just to convince you to come home.'

'I know.'

'However, if you would bother thinking about it, you might realise that coming home might change things.'

'How can it change things when you don't even realise what was wrong in the first place?'

'And you think being apart will help?'

'I don't know.'

Logan sat up, and Callie's hand fell away from him. She knew that somehow he had just shut himself off from her again. He pulled his jeans over his hips. Callie reached for her skirt and blouse. She wanted to say something more to him, but what was there to say? If anything had changed between them, she didn't know what it was.

'Logan –' Callie reached out and put her hand on his arm.

He dragged a hand through his rumpled hair and looked at her. 'Forget it, Callie. By the way, if you want any more of your things, you'd better come and get them soon. You also have some stuff on the boat.'

Callie bit her lip and nodded. The knowledge that he was giving up hurt her with a surprising force. Yes, she had wanted him to leave her alone, but she had also been hoping that he would take the time to think about their relationship. Apparently, he wasn't even willing to do that. An incredible sadness filled her.

'OK. I'll collect my things from the boat on Thursday. That's my day off. I'll send some people to the house this weekend.'

'Fine.' Logan hesitated for a minute, as if he wanted to say something more, and then he turned away.

Callie watched him walk down the beach until he disappeared into the darkness. Then she slowly made her way back to the peristyle. She hadn't even heard the drums stop pounding, but it looked as if the main ritual was over. People milled around the beach, feasting on the wide array of foods and indulging in drink. Callie found Tess and Adam, who were busy piling their plates with desserts.

Adam waved with one hand while balancing a paper plate and a soft drink with the other. 'Hey, Callie, are you OK? You disappeared.'

'Yes, I'm sorry. I just needed a break.'

Tess flipped her hair back and chewed on a chicken leg. 'I know, it's a little overwhelming the first time. Don't worry, though. You'll get used to it.'

Callie glanced around the crowd. 'Is Abiona here? I'd like to speak with her for a moment.'

'Yes, she's resting over in the peristyle,' Tess said. 'She had quite a night.'

'Thanks.' Callie went back to the peristyle, where Abiona was stretched out on a lawn chair. Two empty plates and a cup rested beside her, and her mother hovered nearby. Both women smiled at Callie.

'Callie, you enjoyed our ceremony?' Pemba asked.

'I did. It was incredible. Thank you for inviting me.' Suddenly feeling a bit nervous, Callie smoothed down her skirt. 'Abiona, can I speak to you for a moment?'

'Of course, child, come and sit beside me.' Abiona waved to a nearby chair. She looked tired from the events of the evening, but she radiated with an inner light that didn't seem as if it would ever dim.

Callie sat down, unable to take her eyes off the other woman. 'How do you feel?' she asked.

'Weary, but very alive,' Abiona said. 'It was Ghede, the god of both death and eroticism, who chose to mount me tonight. He can be very demanding, but he is one of the most powerful *loas*.'

Callie couldn't bring herself to lie to this stunning woman. 'I'm sorry, but I didn't see the entire ceremony,' she admitted. 'I loved the dancing, but I got so hot that I had to take a short walk. I found . . . I mean, I met my husband a short distance away.'

To Callie's surprise, the priestess smiled slightly. 'I suspected he would come tonight. He came to see me a few days ago.'

Callie looked up. 'He did?'

'Yes. He appeared to be quite disturbed.'

'Disturbed? Or was he just angry?'

'No, he was disturbed. He didn't show it, but I could sense it within him. Something bothers him very deeply.'

'Yes, maybe the fact that I'm not obeying his orders,' Callie muttered.

Abiona shook her head. 'No, this is something beyond you. He is upset about you, of that there is no question. But there are dark forces in his life.'

Callie shrugged. 'Maybe he has a difficult court case.'

'I must tell you to think of your husband with compassion,' Abiona said. 'I believe he is a good man. Difficult to understand, perhaps, but innately good.'

'It can be difficult to treat him with compassion when that's a quality he doesn't even seem to possess himself.'

'Of course he does, Callie. He's as human as you are. Besides, do you always treat people according to the qualities they possess? If someone is full of hate, do you in turn hate them? Or if someone shows no mercy towards others, do you show no mercy towards them?'

181

'Well, no,' Callie murmured. 'But maybe I should. An eye for an eye.'

Abiona shook her head and pressed her lips together. 'And then what happens if everyone thinks like that? The world goes blind.'

'I'm sorry.' Callie let out her breath and tried to clear her head. 'I'm just confused. I don't know what's going to happen with Logan. Moreover, I don't even know what I want.'

'You will know,' Abiona assured her. 'Answers can come in the strangest of ways. And at the strangest of times. For me, it is through the *loas*.'

'I don't have any answers,' Callie admitted. 'Only questions about why my husband wants to keep track of me.'

'He follows you everywhere?'

'No, I don't think so. He's a very busy lawyer, and I know he would never sacrifice his job just to keep track of me. But he's shown up twice where I haven't expected him. He followed me to your house last weekend, and then tonight he followed me here.'

'I told him about the ceremony. Perhaps he suspected you would be here.' Abiona eyed Callie curiously. 'You had sex with him, yes?'

Callie flushed. 'Look, I realise that's not the most productive way of getting rid of him, but –'

Abiona laughed so suddenly that Callie was startled. She clutched her hands together as a sense of shame trickled through her.

'My child.' Abiona reached out and took one of Callie's hands in hers. 'I'm sorry, I'm not laughing at you. I'm laughing because I believe Ghede had a bit of an influence over you tonight. He has a vast amount of power, and he often uses it to confuse others.'

'Well, it worked,' Callie muttered. She sighed and rubbed her forehead. Everything had seemed quite clear after she left Logan, but now all of her rationalisations

182

were muddled up in her head like a foggy windscreen. 'But the ritual doesn't appear to have done much good.'

'Come back to our home on Tuesday, yes? I will give you another protection charm.'

'Thank you, but I doubt it'll work either.'

Abiona looked thoughtful. 'Callie, you must remember that everyone has *loas* watching over them. If your husband has spirits around him who are quite powerful, then there is always a chance that they can divert any spells placed upon him.'

Callie thought of Logan's commanding presence and shook her head. 'If Logan has *loas* protecting him, then my *loa* doesn't stand a chance of succeeding.'

'Perhaps the problem does not even lie with the spirit world,' Abiona suggested. 'Perhaps it lies within you. May I ask why you married this man?'

'Well, because I ... because I thought he was very intriguing. And my sister kept telling me that marriage to him would be good for my status in society.'

'And that is all?'

Confusion gripped Callie. She remembered once asking Logan why he married her, but she had never given much thought as to why she had married him. 'No, that's not all. I suppose I loved him.'

Abiona frowned. 'You suppose? Child, if you don't even know your own mind and heart, then you can't possibly expect to salvage your relationship with your husband.'

'I know,' Callie said in a low voice, suddenly not sure if she knew anything at all.

'Were you honestly so concerned about your status that you would marry for it?' Abiona asked gently.

Callie shook her head. 'No, I really wasn't. I've never cared about that kind of thing. I must have loved him, or been infatuated with him at the very least.'

'And now?'

'I don't know,' Callie admitted. 'I haven't even

thought of love with Logan. He's been so unreachable that it just didn't occur to me.'

'Perhaps you need to start thinking about it,' Abiona suggested. 'That could be the source of your difficulties.'

Callie shrugged. 'Maybe I thought I could change him. Obviously, that didn't work.'

Abiona squeezed Callie's hand. 'Or maybe you recognised something in him that no one else did.'

Chapter Twelve

*L*ogan stepped out of the French windows that led to the terrace and gardens of the house. Twilight was just beginning to descend. He took a deep breath of humid air scented with magnolias and grass. Over the past few weeks, weeds had started to choke the flower-beds since Callie wasn't here to tend to them as she usually did. She had often spent her weekends out here, digging her hands into the dirt and planting new flowers.

Now, crabgrass pushed up between the cracks of the flagstone pathways, and cones of fire-ant hills appeared in various places. It seemed as if everywhere Logan turned lately, there was some evidence of Callie's absence. A humourless smile twisted his mouth as he bent to pluck a few weeds. It was hardly a stretch to view the encroaching weeds as a metaphor for what was happening in his own life.

Except for last night. His entire body responded as an image of Callie stretched out naked before him appeared in his mind. And then another image of her swirling and dancing, her hair flying around her shoulders and her body undulating. Damn, he'd never realised before how incredible she could be. He was beginning to understand that there were quite a few things he hadn't realised about his wife. And yet she was still refusing to come home.

He pulled a cluster of weeds from a flowerbed just as the doorbell rang. Wiping his hands on his jeans, he went into the hall and opened the door. His muscles tightened.

'Elenore.'

'Hello, Logan.' She was dressed in her Sunday best, a navy-blue suit tailored perfectly to her figure, with matching gloves and a hat. 'May I come in?'

Logan's fist clenched on the doorknob. 'No. What do you want?'

'I'm not happy about the way we parted last week,' Elenore explained.

'And so you're here to make amends?' Logan shook his head. 'Sorry. Not interested.'

Elenore's lips thinned. 'I really don't appreciate the way you've been treating me. Your past is not my fault. You made the decisions, Logan, not me.'

'You made plenty of decisions,' Logan replied dryly. 'Believe me, I haven't forgotten them.'

'Good, then surely you also remember that I am the one in control right now, just as I was back then.'

Something ugly coiled in Logan's gut, but he pulled the door open to let Elenore in. She glanced around approvingly as they walked to the sitting room.

'My goodness, Logan, you really have done well for yourself. Your home is simply beautiful. Where did you find these antiques?'

'Around,' Logan replied vaguely. He didn't bother offering her a drink or even a cup of coffee. Instead, he sat down on the arm of the couch and gave her a hard look.

'Well, it seems to me that investing in my little riverboat wouldn't cause a dent in your fortune,' Elenore observed as she settled into a plush chair.

'That's hardly the point.'

She looked at him. 'You know, even Gerald would be proud of you.'

'I couldn't really give a shit about your husband.'

'Honestly, Logan, I can't understand why you're so hostile towards us. I can perhaps understand why you continue to berate yourself, but us?'

'You're a manipulative bitch,' Logan replied. 'Now, what do you want? You gave me a week. It's been four days.'

Her lips curved into a smile. 'What do you think I want?'

Logan went cold. 'Forget it, Elenore. I'm not fucking you again.'

'You know, I'm not happy with this uncooperative attitude of yours,' she said.

'Yeah? Well, I'm not happy with the manipulative attitude of yours,' Logan snapped.

Elenore glanced around the room before walking to table and picking up a slender, patterned vase. 'Who did the decorating here? Was it your wife?'

'Don't bother using Callie to get at me,' Logan said. 'It won't work.'

'Why not? Has she come back to you?'

'What the fuck business is it of yours?' Logan retorted. 'Get out, Elenore. I don't have time for this.'

'You'd better start having time for it, Logan,' Elenore replied curtly. 'I'm a woman of my word, and so I'll give you until Saturday. After that, I'm going to reopen our negotiations.'

'What does that mean?'

'Exactly what it means. I so enjoyed our little *tête-à-tête* the other day that it gave me a craving for more.'

'You mean you want fucking thrown into the deal, no matter what.' Logan's fists clenched as he fought the urge to go after her physically. 'Get out, you psychotic bitch.'

He stalked up the stairs and into his bedroom. He was relieved when he heard the front door slam. Jesus. She'd make good on her threat, he knew that much. Elenore Lawrence had never been one to let anything stand in her way. Nausea gripped him at the thought of being reduced to fucking her again on a regular basis. He'd kill her first.

Without thinking, he grabbed his car keys and drove to Abiona's house off Bay Street. As sceptical as he was about voodoo, he wanted to see her again. He knocked on the door and waited impatiently.

'Logan.' Abiona opened the door and ushered him inside. 'I have been expecting you.'

'You have?'

She nodded. 'I had a dream about you the other night. You were in the middle of a desert and you were walking and walking to try to find your way out. The sun was blazingly hot, and you had no water, but you continued walking as if you could have gone on for days.'

'Did I manage to get out?'

Her eyebrows drew together. She shook her head. 'No. The desert has pockets of quicksand. You stepped into one and disappeared for ever.'

She looked so concerned that Logan almost felt guilty.

'I'm sorry,' he said. 'If that dream means anything, then it has to do with my workload.'

Abiona shook her head. 'No. It has to do with this dark force in your life. You must tell me what is wrong, Logan. I am worried for both you and Callie.'

Logan reminded himself that he was the one who had come here. Abiona hadn't sought him out to tell him about her dream.

'There's a woman,' he admitted. 'She wants me to invest in some racket of hers and has threatened to ruin me if I don't.'

'And can she do that?'

'Yes, she probably can.'

'I see.' Abiona went to a cabinet and removed several

candles, a clay pot and two small dolls. 'Does Callie know?'

'No. I don't want her to.'

She gave him a curious look. 'No? Why not?'

Logan shrugged even as a rush of shame rose in him. 'She doesn't need to know.'

'She's your wife. Knowing Callie, I'm sure she would want to know.'

'It really doesn't concern her,' Logan said. 'I knew this woman fifteen years ago. I'd thought she was out of my life.'

'Ah, but she is back now, yes?' Abiona nodded. 'Dark forces do not go gently into the night. What is her name?'

'Elenore Lawrence.'

She handed him a piece of lined paper and a pencil. 'Please write her name ten times on one side of this paper and eleven times on the other.'

Logan reminded himself he had nothing to lose. And he sure as hell hadn't come up with any of his own ideas on how to handle Elenore. He sat down and began writing her name, disliking even the sight of the words on paper.

'Has this woman blackmailed you before?' Abiona asked.

'No.'

'But you had a relationship in the past. Not a good one, either.'

'No, not a good one.'

'Did she blackmail you then?'

'No.' Logan turned the paper over and tried to think of how to put his and Elenore's past relationship into words. 'She did have control, though.'

'Yes, I understand,' Abiona murmured. She placed the items in a basket and took the paper from him. 'Come. We will go to the cemetery.'

'The cemetery,' Logan repeated.

She nodded, her expression very serious. 'There are

different levels on which others can harm you,' she explained. 'For example, if you are suffering from 'eyes', this means that too many people are thinking about you and this attention throws you off balance. With you, it is more serious. People have done work against you, Logan, and I don't mean Callie. She wanted to be protected from you, but she would never harm you wilfully. Others, however, are deliberately trying to hurt you. This could conceivably harm Callie as well.'

'I can't deny that,' Logan admitted. 'But why the cemetery?'

Abiona stood and walked to the door. 'The cemetery is where Baron Samdi resides. He is the most powerful of all the gods. We will call upon him for help.'

Logan shook his head. 'Look, I appreciate this, but you should know that I really don't believe any of this can help.'

As they stepped on to the street, Abiona looked at him with her liquid brown eyes. 'You are not a weak man, Logan. And you must put forth much strength in order for the *loas* to assist you. How badly do you want this woman out of your life?'

'With everything I have.'

'Then use that.' She squeezed his arm. 'Please, help me. I am terribly worried for both you and Callie.'

She appeared so sincere that Logan was ashamed of his scepticism. Abiona was such a lovely woman. Moreover, she had an incredibly honest, kind soul that made her the exact opposite of Elenore Lawrence. He nodded.

'All right. I'll do what I can.'

Abiona gave him a warm smile that went straight to his blood. He'd never met a woman who was a combination of such elegance and goodness. He'd known plenty of elegant woman, but they all had a hard edge to them that made them mildly unpleasant. By contrast, Abiona was all softness and gentle curves.

She kept her hand on his arm as they entered the gates of Laurel Grove Cemetery. Tombstones lay in symmetrical rows like a chessboard, some of them so old that the lettering had started to fade. Flowers in various stages of life sprouted on some of the graves. Logan's gaze went towards one corner of the cemetery.

'You have a loved one buried here?' Abiona asked.

Damn, she was perceptive. 'My father,' he admitted.

'Would you like to visit him first?' She stopped to fill her clay pot with water from a tap.

'Not particularly. I haven't visited his grave in years.'

A flash of unhappiness appeared in her eyes. 'No? Why not?'

Logan shrugged. Truth be told, he'd never been able to get rid of the bitterness towards his father, nor to stop blaming him for everything that had happened.

'You did not have a good relationship with him?' Abiona asked. She paused underneath an oak tree and knelt on the grass. With slow movements that drew Logan's gaze to her, she began setting out the items in her basket.

'No, not really.'

Abiona shook her head. She looked incredibly sad. 'Logan, I am very sorry for you. Your relationships are filled with unhappiness.'

'Not all of them,' Logan amended. 'Well, I used to think my marriage wasn't.'

She blinked at him. 'You must realise now that Callie was unhappy. If one partner in a marriage is unhappy, then how can the relationship be a good one?'

Logan struggled against a rush of irritation. 'And how can a relationship get repaired when one partner isn't even around?'

'Perhaps you must learn to listen first.' She struck a match and lit the votive candles, then placed the two dolls in front of them. She glanced up at the stratified sky, the layers of red and orange that darkened with each passing second. 'This is a good night. The spirit of Papa Ghede lives in the cemetery as well. It is the place

191

where the living world intersects with the world of the dead. The crossroads.'

'So, how can this help me?'

'By invoking the most powerful of spirits.' She pointed to an old, dilapidated tombstone. 'According to the dates, that is the grave of the first male buried in this cemetery. We will ask of Baron Samdi that he send a *mò* to protect you. A *mò* is a very strong spirit of the dead.'

A thought suddenly occurred to Logan. 'Did you bring Callie here for a protection spirit?'

Abiona's eyes widened. 'Heavens, no, Logan. You cannot use cemetery rituals to engage family members against each other. Baron Samdi does not look upon that kindly. As it stands, he might not be willing to help you now since he believes that families should remain united.'

Not wanting to disrespect her, Logan merely nodded and continued watching. Abiona placed her hands on each doll and began murmuring incantations, then she bound the dolls back-to-back. She made the sign of the cross and lit a candle, then picked up the paper with Elenore's name written on it and the clay pot. She stood and closed her eyes, her lips moving with words of prayer as she lifted both items towards all four corners of the cemetery. Logan couldn't help being mildly captivated by the sincerity and utter grace in each gesture. Her entire body flowed with her movements, almost as if she were being guided by a force beyond herself.

Abiona saluted each of the four corners again before she put the pot down and ripped the paper in half twice. She handed the torn pieces to Logan.

'Tear them again three times and tell Baron Samdi what you want.'

She looked so completely earnest that Logan didn't have the heart to let her down. Feeling slightly foolish, he tore the papers again. 'I want Elenore Lawrence out of my life.'

'Say it again and mean it.'

'I want Elenore Lawrence out of my life for ever.' He ripped the papers and handed them back to her.

Abiona picked up another pot and placed the papers at the bottom. She then put a penny in, along with several different herbs and powders. She lit another candle and dropped it into the pot. The paper and herbs burst into flames. She handed the pot to Logan.

'You must salute the four directions of the crossroads. Come. I will do it with you.' She stood and slipped her arm around his waist, guiding him towards each of the four corners again. Words spilled from her lips in a never-ending stream; Haitian Creole prayers that sounded both musical and haunting. Once they were finished, she knelt and took a small spade from her basket.

She held it out to Logan. 'Dig a small hole underneath the tree, then smash the pot with your foot.'

Logan dug the hole and stamped on the pot, crushing it underneath his heel. At Abiona's instruction, he buried the remnants of the pot and the ashes underneath the tree. She watched him, her eyes glowing.

'Good. When we return to my home, I will give you a lamp to hang outside your house. This will help prevent evil from entering.' She collected her basket and made the sign of the cross again. 'There is a cemetery in Port-au-Prince where a large cross dedicated to Baron Samdi resides. Many people visit to make offerings and prayers. I am visiting Haiti next month, and I will make another prayer for you and Callie.'

'I appreciate that. Thank you.'

They fell silent as they watched the remaining candles burn underneath the oak. Logan turned his gaze to Abiona. In the last embers of day, he realised again just how beautiful she was. Candlelight glowed on her skin, making it look like burnished teak. She smiled at him and held out her hand. Logan took it. Long, tapered fingers and a touch that was whisper-gentle. He remembered watching her dance at the voodoo ceremony the night before. Her body had moved with such sensual, frenzied undulations that even he had been half convinced that she was actually possessed by a spirit.

He helped her to her feet, then bent to collect the remaining candles.

'No, leave them,' she said. 'We will return.'

'I don't think –'

She took his arm. 'Come. We are going to visit your father.'

Logan stilled. 'I'd rather not.'

'You must honour your ancestors, Logan. They and the spirits are the ones who can help us with our problems.'

'Actually, I handle my own problems.'

Her eyebrows lifted. 'Do you now? Then why do you have so many of them at the moment?'

'Good question,' Logan muttered. He walked with her to his father's grave.

Abiona paused and looked at the grey marble tombstone carved in strong, block letters with the name EDWARD WATERFORD and the dates of his birth and death. The grave itself was also covered with a slab of grey marble. Two small, metal pots rested on each side of the tombstone. Someone had placed flowers in them, although they were beginning to turn brown.

Logan shoved his hands into his pockets and stared at his father's grave. A hint of resentment nudged at him, but for the most part he felt empty inside. Abiona shifted beside him and removed a bottle of water from her basket. Murmuring in Creole, she walked around the grave and poured water around the perimeter, then knocked three times at the head of the grave. She looked at Logan.

'You must speak to him.'

He shook his head. He'd only go so far with this business. 'I have nothing to say to him.'

She looked so sad that Logan almost changed his mind for her sake, but speaking to his dead father was beyond his limits.

'Logan, perhaps your father can help you now.'

'I doubt it.'

'He might believe that he owes you for whatever wrongs he has committed.'

'He can believe whatever he wants. I have nothing to say to him. He's dead.'

'Then I will speak to him for you.' Abiona knocked again at the grave and began murmuring a prayer for Edward to assist Logan in his current crisis. When she had finished, she looked at him again. 'Does Callie visit him?'

'Not that I know of. She never knew him.'

Abiona pointed to the withering flowers. 'Who leaves offerings, then?'

Logan shrugged. He glanced at the sky, which had become covered with a layer of black dotted with silver stars. 'It's getting late. I've taken up enough of your time.'

Abiona still looked sad, but they returned to the oak tree, where the votive candle continued to burn.

'I am sorry for you, Logan,' she said. 'If you cannot make peace with the dead, then how are you to live?'

Logan didn't even know how to respond to her question. They looked at each other for a moment before she lifted her hand and placed it against his cheek. Her touch was like cotton. His gaze slipped down to her full lips as an increasing desire for her invaded his blood. He didn't buy the whole concept of voodoo or spells, but he was entranced by the sincerity and purity of Abiona's devotion. He wondered what it was like to believe in something so wholly that there was no room for questioning.

He lifted his hand to her dark, curly hair. She didn't move, only continued watching him with those chocolate-coloured eyes. Logan slipped his palm to the back of her neck. He'd always loved the nape of a woman's neck, the smooth warmth hidden under a cascade of hair. Abiona's hand went to his chest as he drew her closer to him, their lips meeting in a sudden crush of heat. She gave a little moan against his mouth. She tasted like sweetness and spices. Her body melted against his as if she were boneless.

Her body. Logan's hands skimmed over her cotton caftan, touching her soft, round curves with increasing urgency. His penis hardened within seconds as he felt her heavy breasts, her nipples already hard against his fingertips. Damn how he wanted her in all her mystical, haunting glory. No one had ever looked at him with the same, acute perception. It was as if Abiona knew so much more than he realised. A charge of lust coursed through his nerves. He felt it in her, too, in the increasing tension of her muscles and the sway of her hips.

She twined her arms around his neck and drew him closer, plunging her tongue into his mouth. Logan grasped the material of her caftan in his fists and drew it slowly over her legs and hips. Thoughts spun through his mind. What was she doing to him? He, Logan Waterford, suddenly didn't care that they were in the middle of a cemetery, that anyone could walk by. Shaded by the darkness and the oak tree, he wanted nothing more than to sink into this incredible woman.

He trailed his fingers up the soft skin of her inner thigh, then thrust them gently into the moist warmth of her pussy. Abiona gasped, her eyes glowing with excitement and lust as she leaned back against the tree and spread her long legs apart for him. She murmured something in Creole that Logan didn't understand, but the sound went into his blood. He reached down and quickly worked the buttons of his jeans. Abiona's breathing grew hard as she pushed his hands aside and grasped his penis. Her long fingers stroked him with a surprising intuition, as if she knew exactly what motions would be the most effective. Logan closed his eyes and pressed his forehead against hers as he pushed a forefinger into her slit. She moaned, all silky wetness and malleability. He slid his hands up the curves of her hips

196

to her breasts, rolling her stiff nipples between his fingers. Then he hooked his hands underneath her thighs, lifting her against the tree as she guided his prick towards her.

In one swift movement, he was buried in her humid warmth. Abiona gasped and wrapped her arms around his shoulders, her body totally open to his penetration. She felt like heaven. Her inner muscles clenched around him as he began thrusting inside her. His blood felt like fire, his every nerve concentrated on the woman before him. Whimpers emerged from Abiona's throat in an unending stream, her hips working against him to increase the depth of his immersion. Logan fought to retain control of himself. He had been so taken by this woman from the beginning that he wanted her utter rapture. His fingers sank into her thighs as he pumped inside her, his engorged prick stimulated by the intermittent sensations of her heat and the cool air. Holding her with his body, Logan moved one hand down to her swollen clit and began rubbing.

'Oh, yes,' Abiona moaned. 'Harder, please.'

He rubbed harder as her pussy tightened around him and she let out a squeal. She worked herself almost frantically on his cock as she came, riding out every last shudder of pleasure. The feeling of her flesh vibrating around his cock was too much to stand. Logan thrust deep inside her with a groan as he spilled into her with wave after wave of sensation.

Gasping, Abiona sank back against the tree. Logan lowered her legs gently to the ground as he struggled to catch his breath. Abiona opened her eyes to look at him, her lips curving into a smile.

'You know, Logan, they say that Ghede is also a great spirit of sex,' she murmured.

He wiped his forehead with the back of his hand. 'Now that's something I can believe.'

Her laughter sounded like bells. She drew her caftan

back over her body and stood on tiptoe to kiss him. 'Thank you.'

Logan fastened his jeans and shook his head. He'd never imagined that he would be capable of something like this, let alone with a voodoo priestess. Oddly enough, he felt a strange calmness inside. 'No. Thank you.'

She smiled again and bent to blow out the candles before placing them in her basket. She slipped her arm through his as they walked out of the cemetery.

'I believe this will help you, Logan,' Abiona said. 'The ritual, I mean. But you must also make amends with your father.'

The calm feeling evaporated. 'I don't think so.'

She gave him a quizzical look. 'Why are you so hostile to him?'

'He was irresponsible.'

Abiona chuckled. 'Ah, now there is the Logan Waterford Callie left.'

'What does that mean?'

'Simply that I know you are much more complex than this image you project to the world.' She glanced at him from beneath her dark eyelashes. 'And I believe Elenore Lawrence knows that, too. I only wish your wife did as well.'

Chapter Thirteen

'Sir?' Adam's heart pounded as he knocked on Logan's office door and peeped around the corner. They'd both been working late, and everyone else had left for the day. 'You wanted to see me?'

Logan glanced up from his computer. 'Yes. Close the door and sit down.'

Adam smoothed down his hair and entered the room. Logan returned his attention to the computer, effectively ignoring Adam for the next couple of minutes. Adam glanced furtively at his watch. It was past eight and he had to be at the theatre that evening. He stared at Logan for a moment, drinking in the strong line of his jaw and the way his reading glasses rested on the bridge of his nose. He adored it when Logan wore his glasses; they gave him a certain vulnerability.

Logan finally pushed his chair away from the computer and turned to Adam. His eyes narrowed slightly.

'I thought you were going to get rid of that earring.'

Adam touched his eyebrow. Tess had given him a gorgeous ring to wear and he wasn't about to remove it, not even for Logan. 'I was. I just . . . I mean, I kind of like it. Is there a company policy against it?'

Logan shrugged. 'I have no idea. But if you want to look like a fool, that's fine by me.'

Adam squirmed. 'OK. Um, thanks.'

'I want you to do some research into a married couple,' Logan said. 'Elenore and Gerald Lawrence. They lived in Charleston for five years before moving to Savannah about twenty years ago. Gerald is dead now, and Elenore lives in Hilton Head. She's purchased a riverboat and wants to turn it into a floating hotel and gambling casino.'

'That's a great idea, sir!' Adam said eagerly as he scribbled down all the information. 'Those are really big with tourists, especially on the Mississippi.'

'I didn't ask for your opinion,' Logan reminded him dryly. 'Get as much information as you can about their legal activities. You can call Sam Houston again if you need his help.'

'Are they clients?' Adam asked. 'The Lawrences, I mean.'

'No. I'd also like to know about their finances. Keep this quiet.'

Adam nodded and looked at his boss. He wondered why Logan had so many hush-hush things going on lately.

'Sir, um, can I ask you about your wife?'

Logan's expression tightened. 'No.'

Adam debated about just how much he should tell Logan. 'Um, because, you know . . . I've talked to her.'

Logan looked up abruptly. 'What? When?'

'Once after a show I went to,' Adam explained. He quailed slightly under that razor-sharp gaze, but forced himself to go on for Callie's sake. 'She's really nice. She seems to really love you, too.'

For the first time since he had known Logan, Adam saw the other man look startled. Adam almost dropped his pen. He'd actually shocked Logan Waterford?

'How do you know that?' Logan asked sharply.

Adam's throat convulsed. Maybe he should learn how

to keep his big mouth shut. 'W-when I was talking to her, she mentioned you. She . . . she just seemed as if she m-missed you.'

'What did she say?'

'That she was sorry your relationship didn't look as if it would work out.' Adam shifted in his chair and wondered about the wisdom of trying to help Callie out here. 'She seems like a great lady. Too bad you let her go.'

He winced when Logan glowered at him.

'I didn't "let her go",' Logan snapped. 'She walked out on me.'

'Oh. Well, she probably had a good reason, then. She didn't strike me as the kind of woman who does things without thinking.'

Logan's gaze narrowed. 'How did you discover all this about her?'

'It was just one conversation,' Adam replied quickly. 'I swear, Logan, that was all.'

He glanced at his watch and saw with relief that it was nearing nine o'clock. 'I'm sorry, but I have to go. I have a thing to attend this evening.'

'What thing?'

Adam stood, aware of an increasing blush. 'Just a . . . well, a theatre event.'

'What show?'

'You probably haven't heard of it. It's kind of an experimental performance art show.'

'And will my wife be there?' Logan asked.

'I don't think so.'

Logan stood and shrugged into his suit jacket. 'Well, why don't I go with you and find out for myself?'

Oh shit. 'L-logan, I don't think you want to do that,' Adam stammered.

'And why is that?'

A trickle of sweat ran down Adam's back. 'It's kind of a sex show.'

Logan frowned. 'Kind of?'

'Y-yes.' Adam began backing towards the door, sending up a silent prayer that Logan wouldn't follow. 'You really don't want to see it.'

'On the contrary. I think I do.' Logan picked up his briefcase and strode towards the door. 'I'll drive.'

Oh man, oh man, oh man. Adam's knees fairly knocked together as he followed Logan out to his car. He couldn't just leave Tess in the lurch by attempting to flee, but how could he possibly get on stage with Logan in the audience? Even worse, how could he do what he was supposed to do? His face flamed.

As he directed Logan to the theatre, Adam tried frantically to think of a way out of this situation.

'You know, Logan, I think Callie might be working this evening. The owner of Nebula Arcana is the star of the show. Maybe you should go to the shop instead.'

Logan glanced at him. 'I don't think so.'

'I'm telling you, Logan. Callie won't be here.'

'Why are you so eager to get rid of me?'

Adam squirmed. 'Logan, uh ... I should t-tell you something.'

'What?'

'I'm sort of in the show.'

Logan's head whipped around to fix him with a piercing look. 'You're *in* the show?'

'Y-yes.'

'As what?'

'A performer.' Maybe it would be better if Logan knew up front what to expect.

'What the hell do you perform?'

'Well, it is a pretty explicit sex show.' Adam saw all his hours of hard work and overtime spinning down the drain. His fist curled around his seat belt as he watched the mask of disapproval descend over Logan's features. 'Am I fired?'

'Not yet.' Logan pulled into the car park next to the theatre and got out.

Adam couldn't believe this was happening. His mind

spun back over their conversation. How had Logan ended up here with him? Lord, Tess was going to have a fit about this.

'The performance starts at ten,' he said. 'I have to get ready.'

'Good, you get ready.' Logan looked at the dilapidated theatre and broken marquee and shook his head. 'This is brilliant.'

Adam grabbed his bag and hurried towards the theatre. His stomach churned. Logan was going to be in the audience! He went backstage and found Tess applying her make-up in her dressing room.

'Tess, I have terrible news,' Adam gasped.

She glanced at his reflection in the mirror. 'Adam, you're all flushed. What's wrong?'

Adam sank down on to the couch and put his head in his hands. 'I'm ruined. I made the mistake of telling Logan that I had a performance to attend, and he got it in to his head that Callie would be here. He insisted on coming with me.'

Tess's eyes widened as she swivelled around to look at him. 'Callie *will* be here, Adam! It's the first night of the Spanish Inquisition set, and she promised she'd come.'

Adam groaned. 'Oh man. We are in such a crisis.'

'Let me see if I can reach her at the shop.' Tess picked up the telephone, then sat there chewing on a silver fingernail as the phone rang. She shook her head and hung up. 'She's not there. She and Eldrich were going to grab some supper before coming over. They must have left already.'

Adam gaped at her. 'She's coming with Eldrich?'

'They're not dating,' Tess assured him. 'They're just friends.'

'But Logan doesn't know that!'

'Shit, he doesn't, does he?' Tess stood up and walked to the closet. 'Why in the hell did he decide to come with you, anyway?'

'I don't know,' Adam moaned. 'I was telling him that I thought Callie missed him, and then I saw that it was time to go. Next thing I knew, he was driving us both here. This is a total disaster.'

'Adam, hurry and get dressed,' Tess urged as she slipped out of her robe and into her leather apron. 'Don't worry. Callie knows how to handle that fascist.'

Adam gasped. 'Don't call him that!'

Tess rolled her eyes. 'Sorry, precious, sorry.'

'I know he's demanding, but there is no need to insult him.'

Tess smiled and approached him, reaching out to run her hand over his head. 'You really do have a torch for Logan Waterford, don't you?'

Adam flushed hotly. 'I do not.'

Tess pulled his head against her breasts, letting him feel the slickness of the leather and the warmth of her skin.

'Don't you?' she murmured. 'You mean it doesn't excite you the tiniest bit to know that he's going to be out there in the audience watching you?'

A quiver travelled through Adam. His dick twitched. Tess knew him better than he knew himself. He groaned and shook his head.

'This is a catastrophe.'

'Catastrophe or not, we have a show to perform,' Tess reminded him. She tugged him off the couch and slapped his arse. 'Now get dressed. I'm expecting you to be on top form tonight.'

With a heavy heart, Adam went into the second dressing room and took his outfit from the wardrobe. The other four performers bustled about, decking themselves out in leather, chains and lace. Adam caught the gaze of Peter, who had previously been one of Tess's assistants. Tonight, he was to have a completely different role. He was a good-looking young man with auburn hair and a meaty build.

Peter approached him with a slow smile. 'So, Adam. You ready for me?'

Adam blushed and tried not to look down to gauge the size of Peter's cock. 'I hope so.'

'Just remember to relax.'

Yeah, right, Adam thought. With Logan in the audience? He sighed and stripped off his clothes, then put on a leather G-string. Tess had told him that was all he was allowed to wear for this series. A pot of black greasepaint rested on the dressing table, and he smeared it all over his face as per Tess's instructions. The four heathens were wearing only leather undergarments and black paint underneath their red robes. Adam hoped that maybe Logan wouldn't recognise him with black paint smeared all over his face. It was a futile hope, considering Logan could probably identify a marshmallow in a cloud, but a hope nonetheless.

The chatter of the audience began to build as the theatre filled. Nerves clenched in Adam's stomach. He hoped he wasn't about to be sick. He took his position with the other heathens behind the curtain. Several wooden torture devices had been set up around them. A low, haunting music began to drift from the speakers as the lights dimmed. Monks chanted in deep, resonant voices like other-worldly beings. Adam took a few deep breaths and tried to think calming thoughts. A deep, fragrant meadow, the sun on the beach, the first flower of spring, Tess's big nipples. Adam's penis tightened. At least he didn't have to worry about getting it up for the performance.

The curtain parted. The audience grew hushed. Adam's face burnt with embarrassment underneath the black greasepaint as Peter came forward to lead him to centre stage. Adam could practically feel Logan's disgusted presence as Peter stripped off Adam's robe in one quick movement. The lights blasted on to his naked skin and his bulging penis in its leather encasing. The audience murmured slightly as Tess stripped the other heathens amidst one of her slow, sinuous dances. Adam squinted and peered out into the audience, hoping he could at least figure out where Logan was sitting. He couldn't see a darned thing because of the blinding lights.

Suddenly, Tess whipped him across the buttocks with her switch. Adam gasped as pain flared through him. He gave her a pleading look, but she would show no mercy. She pointed to a pillory. Peter grasped Adam's neck and forced his head through the wooden device, then put each hand beside him before clamping the frame over his head. Adam groaned. He was on his knees, his head and wrists imprisoned like a slave's, his arse sticking up for all to see. He cried out as the whip lashed across his buttocks again. The pain spread, blocking out the murmurs of the audience. Breath whooshed out of his lungs as he watched his majestic Tess strut around him, lashing him with the whip and demanding his obedience. The sound of chanting filled Adam's ears. His penis ached. He couldn't even move his neck.

He felt a man's big hands grab on to his hips. Peter. Sweat broke out on Adam's forehead. He tried to relax. Impossible. His anus clenched. Peter's hands moved to his arse cheeks. Adam yelped. The entire surface of his buttocks ached from the bite of the whip. Peter spread his cheeks. Adam winced as he felt the head of Peter's cock pushing against his hole. Shit, this was going to hurt. He squeezed his eyes shut. He could feel the audience's collective gaze burning into him. Pressure collected in his body. Peter was really forcing it there. He tore off Adam's G-string, letting his penis flop out. The audience drew in a breath. Adam opened one eye to look at them. They seemed to be enjoying his little performance. He wriggled his hips slightly, stimulated by the pain and the exhibitionism. His blood grew hot from the lights and the tension of another man's cock.

To his eternal gratitude, Peter reached down and began to massage Adam's cock as he continued easing into his anus. Adam gasped and tried to take all of the other man in. He closed his eyes again and imagined that it was Logan. Oh, yeah. His sphincter relaxed, allowing Peter to begin thrusting into him. Grunts filled the air. Adam was painfully full of the other man's thick stalk. He pictured Logan's muscular, naked body behind him, his big hands on Adam's hips. Excitement prickled his spine. Peter's hand worked frantically on Adam's shaft until his entire body became submerged in sensation. Pressure built at the base of his penis. He moaned, unable to stand it any longer. He suspected that Tess would be unhappy, but he couldn't hold on. He came with a guttural cry, spurting all over Peter's hand and the floor. Peter continued grunting and thrusting, before he shouted and submitted to his own orgasm.

Adam's head spun. He drew in choked gasps of air, trying to collect his senses and his thoughts. He was dimly aware of the performance continuing around him, of Tess leaping about, torturing the other heathens, fucking them with her switch, lashing them with her whip. Adam's mind closed in on Logan again. Was he still out there, or had he stormed out in disgust? A hot flush covered Adam's entire body. He could only imagine how he must look, stark naked and dripping in sweat, his buttocks covered with red marks. He was definitely going to get fired after tonight.

Much to Adam's relief, Tess seemed to realise that he was intensely uncomfortable, because she made Peter release him from the pillory and allowed him to go backstage. Adam returned to his dressing room, where he downed a glass of water and wiped off the sweat with a towel. The pain began to ease a bit into a rather pleasurable ache. He slipped on a robe and decided to wait for Tess in her dressing room, where her well-wishers would congregate.

As he approached her room, he realised that the door was slightly ajar. Adam frowned. Tess always locked her room during a performance. He went a little closer and nearly leapt out of his skin when he heard Logan's raised voice. Was the older man waiting to burn him alive and then fire him? No, there was another voice. Callie's. Adam's heart began to pound. Uh oh.

'Do you get off on it? Is that why your life suddenly seems packed with perversity?' Logan wasn't yelling, but he was definitely angry.

'The point is that it's my life,' Callie retorted. 'I am not discussing this with you. Tess is a good friend of mine, and I'm here to support her. I frankly couldn't care less what she does on or off stage. And maybe you should be a little less concerned with what other people are doing and a little more concerned with your own life.'

Adam peeked through the crack in the door. Logan stood there with his hands on his hips and his body lined with tension. Callie crossed her arms and glared at him.

'Besides,' she continued. 'I'm getting a little sick of you following me around.'

'I didn't follow you,' Logan snapped. 'I came with Adam.'

Callie's eyebrows lifted. 'Adam?'

'Yes. He said he was in a performance.'

'And you wanted to see it?' Callie asked in disbelief.

'No. I suspected that you might be here. Of course, I was right.'

'So, what did you want to do, Logan?' Callie asked tightly. 'Do you want to fuck me again? Was that why you came to the voodoo ceremony?'

Adam's eyes widened. Logan had been at the voodoo ceremony? Even from a short distance, Adam could see a muscle begin to tick on Logan's jaw. Oh, he was mad now.

'I came to talk some sense into you,' Logan replied curtly.

'Are you sure about that? Because every time we see each other, we seem to end up fucking. You know, maybe if that had happened a little more often during our marriage, I might not have left you.'

Adam clapped a hand over his mouth to keep from gasping aloud. Or from giving Callie a great big cheer.

Logan's hands clenched into fists. 'That's what this all comes down to, then? You needed a good fuck?'

Callie sighed, her shoulders slumping. 'No, Logan, of course not.'

'Callie, I want you to come home.'

She looked at him. 'Why?'

Logan appeared almost startled. Adam tried not to cackle. Twice in one evening something had surprised the man. It must be a record.

'Why?' Logan repeated. 'Because you're my wife, that's why.'

'And because it's not good for your reputation that I've left you.'

'I couldn't care less about what people are saying. I want you home because that's where you belong.'

'Where I *belong*? You know, that kind of ownership vocabulary doesn't work with me.'

Logan gave a frustrated sigh. 'I'm not saying that I own you, Callie, I'm saying I want you home because that's the way things should be. Part of a marriage is living together.'

'There are other aspects to a marriage,' Callie replied. 'I wish you would understand that.'

'And how in the hell is your living in a flat above a hippie shop supposed to make any of that better?' Logan asked. 'You belong at home.'

'And that's your reason,' Callie said. Her voice sounded defeated.

Tell her you love her, you ass! Adam wanted to shout at Logan, but the sound of applause broke him out of his fascination with the scene before him. He backed away from the door and tried to pretend that he was just approaching.

'Tess, are you in here?' he called loudly, knocking on

the door before pushing it open. 'Tess? Um, sorry, I didn't realise anyone was here.'

Logan glared at him. 'Adam, you're fired.'

Adam winced. 'Yeah, I thought so.'

'Callie, I'm tired of rehashing this,' Logan said, turning back to his wife. 'Think about what I've said. You won't have many more chances.'

'What does that mean?'

'It means I've had enough.' He stalked out of the room.

Callie sighed and gave Adam an apologetic look.

'I'm sorry.'

He shrugged and scratched his head. The thought of not seeing Logan on a daily basis pained him deeply, but maybe it was better this way. 'That's OK. I guess I'm not exactly lawyer material anyway. I didn't mean to interrupt you.'

'I'm glad you did. I didn't realise Logan would be here.'

'I thought you came with Eldrich.'

'I did,' Callie said. 'He scurried out of the side door when he saw Logan approaching. Can't say I blame him.' She smiled faintly. 'You were really good tonight. It looked . . . um, difficult.'

'Yeah, it was. I think I should train for this kind of thing. You know, like an athlete.'

They exchanged smiles. Adam thought that Logan was a damn fool.

'So, are you going to go back to him?' he asked.

Callie lifted her shoulders in a shrug. 'I don't see why. He doesn't seem to have changed at all.'

Adam remembered Logan's reaction to his words earlier that evening. 'Excuse me for asking, but does he know you love him?'

She gave him a startled look that was almost identical to the one Logan had given him. Adam was beginning to realise what part of the problem was with this couple.

'That I love him?' Callie repeated. 'Why do you ask that?'

'I just thought that you did, that's all. Does he know?'

Such sadness filled Callie's eyes that Adam's heart nearly broke.

'Adam, I don't even know if I do love him.'

Chapter Fourteen

'*C*allie, I am so furious with you!'
   Callie nearly groaned at the sound of her sister's steel-and-honey voice. Gloria was the last person she wanted to deal with. She finished stocking the last few packets of incense and turned to face Gloria.

'Gloria, I'm sorry.'

'As well you should be!' Gloria stood there dressed in a tight, pale green suit and matching shoes, her hands planted firmly on her hips. From the over-bright expression in her eyes, Callie could tell that Gloria had downed one too many martinis that afternoon. Shaken, not stirred, of course.

'Look, come upstairs, and we'll talk.' Callie glanced at Tess, who stood behind the counter with a grin on her face as she examined Gloria's puffy, blonde hair, inch-long fingernails and too-tight clothing. 'Tess, I'm sorry, but I'll be back shortly.'

Gloria's head whipped around to fix Tess with a piercing look. 'Tess? Are you responsible for enslaving my sister in this place?'

Tess laughed. Callie grabbed Gloria by the arm and forced her to walk up the stairs to her flat.

'Stop making a scene,' she ordered. 'Didn't you get my messages?'

Gloria held up two fingers and stumbled on the stairs. 'Two messages!' she sniffed. 'Almost a month you've been gone and you have the balls to leave me two lousy phone messages. Have you forgotten I'm your sister? I accepted you even though your mother was a grocery clerk! I introduced you to Logan! I got you involved in the Ladies Guild and the historical –'

'Gloria, be quiet!' Callie snapped. She yanked her sister into her flat and closed the door. She pushed Gloria down on to the bed and put on a pot of coffee. 'Now, if you just calm down, I can explain everything.'

Gloria drew herself up with dignity and patted her hair. 'Well, you don't have to manhandle me, you know.' She glanced around the room and wrinkled her nose. 'This is where you live? This is a shoe box, for God's sake. And not even Gucci!'

She screeched with laughter at her own joke. Callie muttered a curse and sat down at the narrow desk. A headache began to throb at her temples.

'Are you going to calm down?'

'Why should I be calm?' Gloria retorted. 'I'm your sister! How could you leave me in the dark like that?' Her blue eyes suddenly filled with tears and her lower lip quivered. 'I was so worried about you, Callie. I thought you'd been murdered and left to die in a gutter with old cigarette butts and empty vodka bottles!' She made a great show of sniffling and dabbing at her eyes with a lace handkerchief. 'Speaking of vodka, do you have any around here?'

'We're not speaking of vodka and no, I don't.' Callie poured a cup of strong, black coffee and handed it to Gloria. 'Drink this.'

Gloria sniffed at the brew distastefully. 'Ugh. I don't drink coffee. It's so bad for your health.'

'Start drinking it now,' Callie suggested, pushing the mug towards her. 'Now, listen. I said I'm sorry I didn't contact you more often, but I've really needed some time alone.'

Gloria rolled her eyes and sipped daintily at the coffee. 'God, Callie, who are you, Greta Garbo? A husband like Logan and you need time *alone*?'

'I don't expect you to understand.'

Gloria's lower lip quivered again. 'You never want me to understand. I try and try to understand you, but you're an ... an enigma to me, Callie, that's what you are.'

'Look, Logan and I are figuring things out between ourselves,' Callie said. She didn't think this was the best time to tell Gloria that it looked as if her relationship with her husband was drawing to a close. Nor how much the thought pained her. 'I promise I'll tell you if there are any major developments.'

'Callie, you must go back to him!' Gloria wailed. 'This is so terrible for him. Everyone is gossiping about you two, and of course that means my name is being tossed about like a beachball.'

'And what a pity that is,' Callie muttered. She bent to remove her sister's shoes and eased Gloria's legs up on the bed. 'I think you need to take a nap.'

Gloria put the back of her hand against her forehead as if she were about to collapse. 'Yes, perhaps that would be best. I'm so overcome by all this. It's just devastating for me, you understand.'

'I understand,' Callie assured her. 'I'll come back to check on you.'

'Go to see Logan!' Gloria called as Callie opened the door. 'We mustn't continue with this nonsense, Callie, because what if Ted decides to run for mayor? Well, then we'll just be in all sorts of scandalous –'

Callie shut the door, effectively blocking out the sounds of Gloria's voice, and went back downstairs.

'Wow, that was your sister?' Tess asked.

'Half-sister,' Callie admitted. 'Sorry again. She has a thing for James Bond and vodka martinis.'

214

Tess chuckled. 'She's a riot. Do you think she'd want to be in my *Sexology* show?'

'I suspect she's in her own *Sexology* show,' Callie replied dryly. She glanced at her watch. 'Listen, I have an appointment with Abiona at noon, so I might be back late.'

'You can take the afternoon off if you work for me tomorrow morning,' Tess suggested.

'Great, thanks.' Callie picked up her bag and fished around for her keys.

'Why are you going to see Abiona again?' Tess asked.

Callie didn't want to lie to her friend, but she also wasn't willing to tell her about her experience with Logan at the voodoo ceremony.

'She's going to give me another spell,' Callie said vaguely.

'I thought the one you had was working.'

'Yes, but I don't think it's strong enough.'

Tess's eyes widened with excitement. 'Callie! You're not going to give Logan a rash, are you?'

'No, no. I would never do anything that might hurt him. I have to go, Tess. I'll let you know what happens.'

She hurried outside and walked to Abiona's house, shoving thoughts of her sister out of her mind. Summer had really started to heat up the air, and tourists were beginning to meander around the streets, entranced by the mixture of architecture and aura of the Old South that pervaded the city. Callie glanced around automatically for Logan, relieved when she didn't see him or his car anywhere nearby. She knew that he would never hide from her; if he were following her, she would most certainly know about it.

Callie knocked on the priestess's door and smiled when Abiona opened it. As always, the woman looked stunning in a multicoloured cotton robe and matching headband.

'Callie, come in, precious.' She bent to kiss Callie's

cheek. The musky, clean scent of sandalwood rose from her skin.

Callie entered the house, leaving her bag near the door. She followed Abiona into the sanctuary and sat down at the table. The scent of incense hung heavily in the air.

'Is your mother here?'

'No, she is not at home.' Abiona lit a few candles and placed them on the table. 'May I offer you some tea?'

'I'd love some, thank you.' Callie stood and examined one of the small altars. A carved, wooden figure rested inside, and a plank of wood in front of the altar was covered with flowers, nuts, perfume bottles, soap, golden rings, and even a few cosmetics and a mirror. Despite attending the voodoo ceremony, Callie still found herself fascinated by the mysterious religion. 'Abiona?'

'Yes?' Abiona set out two teacups and began to pour.

'Why do you make these kinds of offerings to the spirits?'

'The *loas* have very human aspects,' Abiona explained. 'In fact, many of them actually used to be humans. They love to eat and drink just as we do. So, we offer them different goods depending on their preferences. For example, the *loa* you are looking at is Erzulie. She is the goddess of love and beauty, so she requires things that will be of use to her vanity.'

Callie sat back down and sipped at the sweet tea. 'Have you been . . . um, mounted by her?'

Abiona nodded. 'She is very coquettish, not extreme like Ghede. Grace, beauty and luxury are her trade-marks, which is why she is the goddess of love.'

'Love is a luxury?'

Abiona's shoulders lifted in a delicate shrug. 'Anything one does not require to survive is a luxury, I think. One does not physically need love.'

'Then why do people die of broken hearts?'

Abiona's face broke into a smile. 'Perhaps one needs

love emotionally, yes? I have never heard of anyone dying from lack of sex.'

Callie's mouth turned upward. 'True.'

'So, tell me, Callie.' Abiona placed her elbows on the table and leant forward. 'Do you need love to survive?'

The question startled Callie. 'I guess so.'

'And do you love your husband?'

Callie sighed, remembering Adam asking her that very question. As much as she disliked some of Logan's qualities, she also had deep affection for him that wasn't easily diminished. 'I think I ... I love the person he could be if he tried.'

'But not the person he is now?'

Callie thought of her last confrontation with Logan and shivered. She disliked that cold steel in him. If she knew for certain that the man during the night of the voodoo ceremony, the one with warmth and curiosity, was really her husband, then she could admit that she loved him. As things stood, she didn't know that at all. Logan's temperament had been so constant over the past three years, and now it seemed suddenly mercurial and changing. Callie no longer knew which person he truly was.

'I don't know,' she admitted. 'I want to love the person he is now, but I'm not even sure who that is.'

'He came to see me again on Sunday.'

Callie's eyebrows lifted. 'He did? That's not like Logan.'

'I suspected it wasn't. I am not at liberty to divulge what he told me, but suffice it to say there is darkness in his life.'

'Tell me about it,' Callie muttered.

'He is a good man, Callie. I hope you know that.'

Callie nodded, wondering about the look in Abiona's eyes as she talked about Logan. Had something more gone on between them than the priestess was letting on? Callie was mildly surprised to discover that she wasn't terribly upset by the thought. Abiona was so full of

beauty and compassion that Callie could easily understand it if Logan had been taken by her. After all, she
herself was enchanted by the other woman.

'I know he's a good man,' she said. 'I just don't know
who that good man truly is.'

'You will find out,' Abiona assured her. 'Sometimes a
loa is not the force that mounts a person in order to help
resolve issues.'

Callie hesitated to ask her next question, but she felt
so extraordinarily comfortable with this woman that she
couldn't resist. 'Will you tell me what it feels like to be
mounted by a *loa*?'

Abiona's expression grew thoughtful. 'How can I
explain? In the first few moments, it is quite terrifying,
because you are aware that you will lose complete
control of your own senses. It is a very helpless feeling.
You become totally vulnerable, unable to move your
own body. The *loa* is moving within you. Spasms can
shake and torture you. It is a trace, a psychic leaving of
oneself and entrance of another.'

'Do you remember it?'

'No. I always have a great feeling of both happiness
and exhaustion afterwards, but little memory of the
actual experience.'

'Doesn't that scare you?' Callie asked.

'No, of course not. It is the supreme honour, and I
always know that my people will protect me should
anything happen.'

She smiled and stood, reaching for a small bowl of
henna. 'For a sceptic, you are very curious about voodoo,
yes?'

'I guess so,' Callie replied sheepishly. 'I admit I was
sceptical at first, but the ceremony was incredibly
powerful.'

'Yes. You must have felt it when you were dancing.'

'Felt what?'

'The losing of yourself to another force.' Abiona
moved to Callie's side of the table and reached out to

218

unbutton her blouse. 'I don't mean a *loa*, but to the rhythms of the dance and the drums.'

Callie nodded, aware of the light brush of Abiona's fingertips on her skin. 'Yes, I did feel that.'

Abiona smiled again. 'I know.'

She was so exquisite when she smiled. Callie felt her heartbeat increase slightly when Abiona leaned in to begin working on the tattoo.

'Do all voodoo practitioners use henna?' she asked.

Abiona chuckled, her warm breath brushing Callie's skin. 'No. As I said, one of the more traditional methods is cutting and scarring. Some people still do that. Others get real tattoos, but for non-practitioners, we use temporary henna unless someone requests otherwise. Voodoo in the south has changed quite a bit from what it is in Haiti and Africa. We still retain many of the customs, but we have had to adapt to the needs of a new land.'

She began applying the henna to the curve of Callie's breast. Callie watched her careful, delicate movements and wished that she could reach out and touch Abiona's gorgeous, curly hair. In fact, she wished she could touch her anywhere. The thought didn't startle Callie nearly as much as it should have. She'd been fascinated by Abiona at first sight, and she certainly thought highly of her as a person. She had never before thought about a woman sexually, but Abiona was different. So different.

Abiona finished the tattoo and lifted her eyes to meet Callie's. 'There. We will see what that does.'

Callie stared at her for a moment, thinking that any woman could lose herself in the depth of those incredible eyes.

'I can understand why Erzulie would want to possess you,' she murmured.

The voodoo priestess smiled. 'And I can understand why your husband wants the same of you.'

A flutter of surprise went through Callie. 'You can?'

Abiona smiled. 'You are lovely. You have a great

sense of self and courage. And you have harmony and peace within you. It is a most attractive quality.'

'I . . . I do?'

'Callie,' Abiona said. 'May I kiss you?'

The question was so charmingly direct that Callie smiled. She couldn't attribute her feelings to the effects of drums or chanting or anything except her own desires. She was entirely clear minded, and all she wanted was one chance to touch this lovely woman. She nodded.

Abiona rose and brushed her lips lightly across Callie's in a movement so delicate it was like the brush of a bird's wing. Warmth filled Callie's body. Abiona's fingers trailed lightly over lace-covered breasts, her long, brown fingers providing a striking visual contrast to Callie's pale skin. It was as if she had struck a chord, leaving Callie's body vibrating with increasing arousal and curiosity. Callie slipped out of her blouse and reached behind her to unclasp her bra. Abiona's eyes grew even darker as she gazed at the hard-tipped mounds of Callie's breasts. She straightened and grasped the folds of her own robe, lifting it over her head.

Callie drew in a breath. She had known that Abiona possessed a beautiful body, but she hadn't expected such perfection. Her shapely legs and curved hips inclined upwards to a narrow waist and large, rounded breasts. All over, her skin was a perfect, even tone: the colour of coffee and cream. She was succulent.

'Come.' Abiona took Callie's hands and urged her to stand. Then she unfastened Callie's skirt and let it fall to the ground. 'There. Now I can properly kiss you.'

And she did. Callie was enchanted. Abiona's full lips moved over hers with a striking degree of tenderness, her hands skimming down to caress Callie's breasts. After a brief hesitation, Callie let herself touch the other woman. Abiona's skin felt as smooth as satin underneath her palms. She let her hands wander, tracing the curved lines of Abiona's body in a fascinated exploration. Her buttocks were perfectly rounded and pliable, her breasts deliciously touchable.

As they sank to the floor, Callie told herself to remember everything about this. This was not a trance, not a leaving of herself after which her mind would be wiped clean. No, this was two warm, living bodies; an experience she had never had and one that she wanted to remember. She lowered her body over Abiona's so that they were fully pressed together. Abiona stroked her hands over Callie's back, nibbling at her lower lip.

'You know, we should not be doing this in a room with the *loas*,' she said.

'You said they used to be human,' Callie reminded her, squirming lower to press kisses over her breasts. 'I'm sure they'll understand.'

Abiona giggled, then gasped as Callie took one of her nipples between her teeth. Callie's pussy was already swollen and moist, but she wasn't ready for this to end just yet. She took her time making her way down Abiona's body, drinking in the scent of her skin and licking a path with her tongue. When she reached the crisp hairs of Abiona's cunt, Callie glanced up. Abiona's breathing had become erratic, her eyes hot as she nodded her assent.

'Yes, Callie, lick me.'

Moving on instinct, Callie parted the other woman's thighs and gazed in uninhibited fascination at her sex. Then she drove her tongue inside and sucked up the droplets of moisture coating Abiona's folds. Callie had never tasted another woman's juices before, and the flavour and scent filled her head like an aphrodisiac. She spread her hands over Abiona's belly, feeling the woman's body twisting and tensing as moans came from her throat. Abiona's long legs wrapped over Callie's back as her hips thrust upward, encouraging the sweeping strokes of her tongue. And then Abiona's entire body jerked rhythmically as she came, her hands gripping Callie's head.

Panting, Callie pulled away and smiled at the sight of Abiona spread out before her, looking both sated and lovely. Abiona reached out to pull Callie beside her, easing her knee between Callie's thighs.

'Ah, Callie, I found you intriguing from the very beginning,' she murmured.

Her fingers slipped between Callie's legs to manipulate the folds of her pussy. Callie gave herself up to the sensual ministrations of the other woman, letting her body relax.

'You did?' she murmured, rolling one of Abiona's dark nipples between her fingers. 'I thought the same of you.'

She buried her face in Abiona's delicious neck, her breathing increasing as arousal climbed in her body. Abiona's long finger slipped inside her, working back and forth as her thumb circled Callie's clit. Callie cried out and clamped her thighs together as her body vibrated forcefully against Abiona's hand. She writhed against her, letting Abiona ease the final sensations from her body before they sank against each other.

Abiona kissed Callie again. 'I think we must redo your henna, yes?'

Callie glanced down at the tattoo, which was smudged beyond recognition. She chuckled. 'Yes, I think so.'

They stood slowly. Callie watched Abiona's graceful movements as she dampened a cloth with water and prepared a fresh henna paste. She was simply mesmerised by the totality of Abiona's self-assurance and the singularity of her beauty.

'I wish I could be more like you,' she confessed.

Abiona's eyebrows lifted as she reached out to wipe away the smudged tattoo. 'Why is that?'

'You're so beautiful and confident.'

'And you're not?'

'I've never thought I was.'

Abiona lifted Callie's chin and looked into her eyes.

'Callie, precious, you can't wish to be like someone else. If you do not like who you are, then how can you be happy?'

'I like who I am,' Callie assured her quickly. 'But you seem to know exactly what you want, while I don't.'

'Yes, you do. You simply haven't realised it yet.'

Chapter Fifteen

Callie shaded her eyes from the sun and looked across the Turner Creek marina at the gleaming white lines of Logan's yacht. If there was one thing she had loved about her life with him, then it had been the days when they took the boat out on to the river. For a few brief hours, he would relax and even seem to enjoy himself as they skimmed over the water and drank in the warm sun. Six months after they married, he had renamed the boat *The Calla Lily*. The name was still painted on the side of the hull.

Callie took her keys out of her handbag and went down the ramp to the docks. She had some good memories of her marriage. Maybe she didn't realise that a month ago, but there had been islands of happiness and fun. But they were just that: warm islands amidst a cold sea of control and disapproval. With a sigh, Callie climbed on to the boat and unlocked the door of the cabin. The interior was decorated in gorgeous, polished teak and antiques that had always made Callie feel warmly comfortable and secure. She sat down on the bed and looked around, remembering several nights when they had simply drifted off to sleep rocked by the movement of the water.

Regret nudged at her soul. She tried to push it aside as she opened the wardrobe and began to remove her clothes. It was better this way, she told herself sternly. Logan wouldn't change, and she certainly couldn't go back to the same kind of life with him. She supposed that some things just weren't meant to happen.

Her heart suddenly leaped as she heard footsteps on the deck. Who had followed her here? She hurried to the door just as Logan's tall figure appeared in the doorway. Callie closed her eyes and pressed her hand against her chest.

'Logan! Why didn't you tell me you would be here?'

'I didn't think it was necessary,' he replied. He was dressed in shorts and a T-shirt, which was odd, considering it was Thursday morning and he should be at the office. He rested his hands on his hips and levelled her with an even look. 'Find everything?'

'Yes, of course.' Callie looked at him curiously. A strange kind of tension emanated from him. She put down the pile of clothes she was holding and ran her hands over her thighs. She was suddenly nervous. 'I thought you'd be at the office this morning.'

'I took the day off.'

'I see. Why?'

He shrugged. 'I figured I was due for a day off.'

'Well, then, I can just come back another time if that would be easier for you,' Callie suggested. She didn't know why, but she had the odd feeling that she should get off this boat sooner rather than later.

Logan shook his head and reached for the doorknob. 'That won't be necessary.'

'I don't have to –'

'Just stay here, Callie. I want to talk to you.'

'I thought we'd done all the talking we needed to do,' Callie retorted. She picked up her bag and moved towards the door, but he blocked her exit. Alarm fluttered in Callie's stomach. 'Logan, I said I'll come back later.'

His mouth tightened as he shook his head. 'No. You'll stay here now.'

With that, he stepped outside and closed the door behind him. The lock clicked. Callie stared at the door in shock, unable to process what was happened. Within moments, she heard the coughing and sputtering of the engine, which gradually gave way to an even hum.

'Logan!' Callie ran to the door and yanked furiously at the handle. It didn't budge. He had really locked her into the cabin. 'Logan, open the door! What the fuck are you doing?'

No response, except the gentle bump of the boat as it passed over ripples in the water. Heart pounding, Callie hurried to the porthole. Sure enough, they were leaving the marina and heading for the open expanse of the river. Callie pressed her fingers against her temples and tried to think. Her own husband had tricked her into getting on the boat so that he could abduct her. My God, was he deranged?

Callie went to the door again and pounded on it with her fist. 'Logan! Let me out of here!'

She heard nothing. Callie began pacing back and forth angrily, her mind spinning with fury and a huge sense of betrayal. Before they had even cleared the channel markers at the basin entrance, she had worked herself into quite a frenzy. Only when they were a good distance up the river did she hear the lock click again. Logan pushed the door open, and Callie flew at him in a rage.

'You bastard!' She slapped her hand across his face, leaving a dark red imprint. 'What do you think you're doing? How dare you trick me into coming here?'

'Callie, calm down.' Logan grabbed her arm as she drew back, ready to let another blow fly towards him. His fingers tightened around her wrist. 'You've refused to come home, and I've been finding your behaviour very tiresome.'

'So you decide to kidnap me?' Callie shouted. 'What kind of bastard are you?'

'This is clearly the only way I could get you to come to your senses.'

'*I'm* not the one who's lost their senses! You think this is going to make me want to come back to you? Well, fuck you, Mr Dictator. I want a divorce!'

His expression hardened. 'You're not getting one.'

'The hell I'm not! I'm calling the police and charging you with kidnapping and lying and entrapment and . . . and false imprisonment!'

To her shock, Logan's mouth actually quirked at the corners. Now he was laughing at her? She bunched her fingers into a fist and slammed it into his stomach. The bastard didn't flinch, which only served to make Callie all the angrier. How could she have thought that she might actually love him?

She tried to push past him, hoping that she could get hold of the radio to call the coastguard, but Logan suddenly gripped her arms.

'Let go of me!'

Logan shook his head. 'I can't have you causing a scene on deck.'

Callie gaped at him in outrage. 'Causing a scene! Don't you think I have every right to cause a scene?'

'Once you've calmed down, we'll talk about this.' He pushed her back against the bed and reached into a drawer of the bedside table.

Callie was shocked when she watched him remove two pairs of handcuffs. Handcuffs! A sudden rush of fear went through her, stirring her adrenaline. She yanked herself out of his grasp and darted towards the door. Just as her hand closed around the doorknob, Logan's arm grabbed her around the waist and hauled her back towards the bed.

'Let go! I swear, Logan, I am throwing you in prison for this.' Callie kicked him in a fury, feeling a grim

227

satisfaction when her shoe made contact with his kneecap.

'Callie, calm down.' Logan clamped one of the cuffs around her wrist and attached the other to a bedpost.

'I will not calm down!' Callie railed. 'How could you do this to me? How could you trick your own wife into getting on this stupid boat? You know, *this* is exactly the problem! You can't just run around thinking you're a goddamn sheikh expecting everyone to follow your orders and kidnapping women to take to your . . . your tent in the desert!'

'I am well aware that I'm not a sheikh,' Logan replied dryly. 'Moreover, I don't even own a tent. Or a desert, for that matter.'

His total control infuriated Callie all the more. She gave him another furious kick, aiming directly for his groin. Unfortunately, he moved aside just in time.

'Ow!' Pain radiated up Callie's shin as her toe slammed against the table. The pain shocked her into submission and she sank down on to the bed, panting heavily. She slipped off her shoe and glowered furiously at Logan. 'Now look what you did. My toe is broken.'

He approached her and reached down to examine her foot. Callie yanked her foot away from him.

'Don't touch me.' She peered down to look at her throbbing big toe. Before she could stop him, Logan grasped her ankle in his hand and took her toe between his thumb and forefinger.

'Does this hurt?' He wriggled her toe from side to side.

'A little,' Callie admitted grudgingly.

'I doubt it's broken. It's probably just bruised.' He left for a moment and returned with a roll of gauze.

'You'd better go back to the bridge or we're going to run aground,' Callie said.

'Don't worry. I dropped anchor.' Logan tore off a length of gauze and began wrapping her toe, giving her a mildly amused look. 'I suggest you refrain from kicking anything else with this foot. Particularly me.'

Callie scowled. 'Don't you dare laugh at me. I am so sick of you and your damn *loas.*'

He finished wrapping her toe. 'My what?'

'That's why voodoo isn't working on you,' Callie muttered. 'It's because you have too many protective *loas* around you. They keep diverting the power of my spells. I swear, Logan, I'm asking the mambos to put a black magic spell on you next.'

He lifted a quizzical eyebrow. 'What makes you think that will work any better?'

'It's worth a shot.' Callie slipped her shoe back on. The ache in her toe began to ebb a bit, but she still wished she could kick Logan from here to kingdom come. 'Now, would you please turn this boat around and drop me off on the shore? And what is with this handcuff?' She jiggled her wrist furiously. 'You unlock me right now, Logan Waterford, or I swear I'm filing for a divorce.'

Logan leant his hips against the back of a chair and shook his head. 'Sorry, calla lily. Not until we figure this out.'

'What is there to figure out?' Callie retorted. 'I had it all figured out that you were an overbearing, domineering ass, and now I have it further figured out that you're also a deranged kidnapper. See? All figured out. So take me back right now.'

He gave her a brooding look. 'Is there someone else? That fucking Goth?'

Callie latched on to the explanation as if it were a lifeline. She'd only seen Eldrich platonically since their night of weird poetry and candle wax, but Logan didn't have to know that. 'Yes. Eldrich and I are lovers. There. Adultery is grounds for divorce.'

Logan's mouth twisted. 'Eldrich?'

'He's very romantic.'

'Uh huh.'

Callie glared at him. 'You don't believe me? You can ask Tess.'

'Yes, she seems like a very reliable source of information.'

'See? There you go with the contempt again! Tess happens to be one of my closest friends.'

'And I suppose you'll be dying your hair green next,' Logan replied coldly. 'Was she the one who introduced you to voodoo, or was it your punk lover?'

'Wouldn't you like to know?' Callie taunted. Her hands clenched into fists at her sides. 'And wouldn't you especially like to know that Eldrich was a much better lover than you ever were?'

Logan's lips thinned as he came towards her. Callie recoiled slightly, remembering all too clearly what had happened the last time she criticised his sexuality. She swallowed hard at the memory.

'Is that right?' Logan asked in a voice that was deceptively soft. 'And did you nearly milk his prick dry the way you did mine last Saturday?'

Callie flushed hotly. 'You bastard.'

'Did you?'

'None of your goddamn business,' Callie flung back. 'Why? Have you been with another woman? Would it assuage your guilt if you found out the truth about me and Eldrich?'

She knew quite well that she was pushing him too far again, but she'd had enough. As a matter of fact, he should be worried about pushing *her* too far this time, dammit.

'We're not talking about me,' Logan replied.

'No, of course not! We never talk about you, do we? Everything is my fault.'

'Now you're channelling the Queen of Melodrama again.'

Callie struggled against another urge to hit him. 'It's not melodrama!' she shouted. 'You refused to listen to me or even to try to discuss our marriage, so why should I bother explaining anything to you?'

'Because you're my wife.'

'And you're an arrogant bastard.' Callie lashed out at him with her free hand, managing to give him another hard slap across the jaw.

Logan's expression darkened. 'Not a good move, Callie.'

He reached for her free hand and the second set of handcuffs. Callie yelped in outrage and tried to scramble back on the bed, but Logan came after her. Hindered with one wrist already cuffed to the bed, Callie kicked at him with both feet and tried to rake her fingernails over his face. Unfortunately, the battle was short lived.

'Callie, stop it,' Logan snapped. He grabbed her flailing wrist and forced it down on to the bed. Callie thrust her knee upwards, catching him close to the groin. Logan swore and pushed her down, then straddled her waist and held her free wrist over her head.

'Get off!' Callie shouted. She twisted and tried to shove him off, but it was like trying to move a freighter. Tears of frustration filled her eyes. 'I hate you.'

'I'm beginning to discover that.' Logan clamped her wrist to a bedpost and looked down at her, his expression hard.

Panting, Callie glowered right back at him. 'This is really good, Logan. This is exactly the way to make me want to come back to you. You must be a fucking Einstein.' She twisted furiously, never before having felt so helpless in her entire life. Her heart nearly stopped when her hips bucked upwards accidentally right against the hard bulge in Logan's shorts. Oh, Christ. She stilled suddenly.

'Don't worry,' Logan said. 'I'm not about to use you as my personal sex slave.' His mouth twisted. 'That is, not unless you want me to.'

'Hah,' Callie retorted. 'Believe me, if I wanted to be someone's sex slave, I wouldn't pick you as my master.'

231

'Yeah? Who would you pick then? Your Goth friend?' He didn't move from his position, his grip still tight on her arms even though she was clamped to the bedposts.

'As if I'd tell you,' Callie snapped.

Something appeared in his expression that Callie had never seen before. He released her arms and put his hands on either side of her head, lowering his head slightly so that their faces were closer together.

'In other words,' he murmured, 'the idea of being a sex slave isn't entirely abhorrent to you.'

Callie stared at him. How did the man manage to twist her words around like that? Good God, his cock felt like steel against her abdomen. She closed her eyes and tried not to think about it.

'What are you talking about?' she said tightly. 'I don't want to be a slave. And certainly not to you!'

'No? Funny, I almost expected you to beg me to punish you again.'

Callie's eyes flew open. 'Beg you? I never begged you! You're such a belligerent ass that you just grabbed me as if I were a sack of flour and then –'

'A sack of flour?' Logan chuckled and shook his head. 'Funny, you didn't feel much like a sack of flour to me. If anything, you felt like warm, sweet honey.'

Callie swallowed hard. How had they even started this conversation? She remembered how, that night several weeks ago when Logan had spanked her, the heat had flowed into her blood and fired her arousal. She took a breath and reminded herself that Logan had kidnapped her. This whole situation wasn't turning her on. At all.

'Go on, admit it,' Logan murmured. 'Don't you remember trying to fuck my fingers after I spanked you?'

A hot flush rose to colour Callie's cheeks. You wanted this, she reminded herself. Well, maybe not *this* exactly, but oh, she had wanted him to show her evidence that he was actually human. A month ago, she would have given anything for Logan to respond to her the way he was doing now. She had so wanted to see him look at her with hot eyes, his breathing rough against her skin, his discipline hovering on the edge. Of course, she hadn't expected to be handcuffed to a bed at the time, but a woman couldn't have everything. Yes, she had also hoped that he would look at her with tenderness, but at least he was finally reacting. Maybe he just had to be confronted with events that were beyond his control.

'You liked it too,' she reminded him hoarsely. 'Was it the control, Logan? Did you like having that kind of physical control over me? Or was it because for once in your rigid life you finally lost control of yourself?'

His jaw clenched. A flutter of triumph rose in Callie as she realised she'd hit a weak spot. She suspected that he disliked being reminded of his own behaviour. He might have her physically restrained, but that didn't mean she couldn't strike out at him with her words.

'Which one was it, Logan?' she continued. 'Look at you now. A struggle with your wife, you handcuff me to the bed, and you're already turned on. I've always known that you relish your self-discipline, but doesn't it feel good to lose it just a little?'

She knew she was provoking him more than was wise. His mouth tightened as he glared down at her. His erection pressed against her belly with increasing insistence. Callie's heart thrummed wildly like a vibrating guitar string as she realised she was completely at his mercy. For an insane instant, she remembered the Tarot card reading she had done for herself. It seemed like ages ago when she had explained to Eldrich that her future might consist of a dark, male force and captivity. If only she had known then how true her prediction would turn out to be.

'Is that what you wanted, then?' Logan asked, his voice edged with harshness. 'You wanted to push me over the edge by leaving me?'

'I didn't even know you had an edge, let alone whether or not I could push you over it.'

'Bullshit,' Logan retorted bluntly. 'That's why you came on to those men at the dinner party, wasn't it? You wanted to irritate me.'

'All right, yes, I did!' Callie snapped. 'I know I succeeded in irritating you, but I was hoping you'd snap. When you didn't, I realised you were a fucking oak tree. So damn solid you'd never snap.' She paused and took a breath. 'If I'd realised that leaving you would finally push you over the edge, I would have left much sooner.'

His weight was beginning to feel overwhelming. Callie tried to squirm underneath him, but he didn't budge.

'You know, you have quite a variety of reasons for leaving me,' Logan said. His grip tightened on her arms. 'First, I get the idea that you wanted a real fuck, then you wanted me out of your life, and now it's because you wanted to goad me.'

He bent his head towards her. His breath brushed her hair like a hot whisper. Callie's blood grew thick, her entire body oppressed by his weight and the anger emanating from him. Her arms began to ache from their constrained position above her head.

'Which one is it, Callie?' Logan asked, his voice hard.

'All of them,' Callie retorted. 'And they all worked.'

Logan's mouth tightened. 'Did they? You'll never get me out of your life. You can bet on that.'

His words were spoken with such determination that Callie's breath caught in the middle of her chest. She had never even considered the idea of what might happen if he refused to let her go.

'What then?' she snapped. 'You're going to keep me chained to your bed for the rest of our lives? Interesting way to maintain control.'

'No. Although I'm beginning to suspect that you might like it.'

Callie gasped. 'God, you are unbelievable! You kidnapped me! Last I heard, that's illegal, not to mention incredibly archaic.'

He continued looking down at her, his eyes darkened to a deep brown. Callie could feel the tension in every line of his body.

'You do get off on this kind of edgy behaviour, don't you?' he said roughly. 'Making men want to fuck you, dancing at voodoo ceremonies, getting spanked . . .'

His voice trailed off into a husky whisper. Callie stared at him as his words sank into her skin. God, he was right. She did love that sensation of doing something beyond the ordinary, something that society decreed should be forbidden. It stimulated her nerves, firing parts of herself that she hadn't known existed. She squeezed her legs together as her sex quivered.

'You like me that way,' she said, trying to stop her voice from trembling. 'You've treated me completely differently since I left you.'

'Then does this excite you, too?' His mouth curved into a slight smile. He released her arms and placed his hands on either side of her head. 'Knowing I could do anything I want to you and that you'd be helpless to stop me?'

Callie's body quickened at the idea. She was beginning to wonder if Logan didn't know her better than she once thought.

'I know you wouldn't,' she said hoarsely, only realising as she said the words that they were true.

His eyebrows lifted. 'And how do you know that?'

Callie didn't reply. She squirmed and tried to push him off. 'Logan, get off me.' When he didn't move, she glowered at him. 'Don't deny this arouses you, too,' she snapped.

'I'm denying nothing of the kind.' He eased back a bit and lowered his lips to her forehead. His gentle kiss was a surprising contrast to the rock-hard erection throbbing against her belly. Callie strained against the handcuffs.

'Logan –'

'I'm not letting you go.'

Callie wondered if he meant in this particular situation or *ever*. A wave of confusion and growing need rose in her chest. Logan's hand skimmed down her chest, undoing the buttons of her dress. With a quick motion of his wrist, he unsnapped the front clasp of her bra and bared her breasts. Callie closed her eyes as a flush painted her skin a rosy pink. She had never felt so totally exposed and defenceless. Sensations swirled in her belly as the slightest hint of fear edged her confusion. She had never feared Logan before, but then he'd never physically restrained her. Logan placed his palm flat against her pussy. Callie flushed, even as her hips pushed slightly upwards. Logan's mouth touched hers.

'What do you want me to do to you?' he murmured.

She opened her eyes. 'Unlock me and I'll tell you.'

'No deal. I guess I'll just have to figure it out for myself, then.' He slipped his fingers into the waistband of her knickers and down to her pussy. Callie drew in a sharp breath when his forefinger eased into her slick folds. God, his fingers worked magic on her. Her clit pulsed. She stared at her husband and wondered what kind of person he was becoming. Or had he always been this way? Was he just now letting some innate need break free? Something that had been dormant for too long?

She watched as he worked the buttons on his shorts. A waterfall of want spilled through her as she decided she could continue yelling at him later. At least, after he'd pumped her full of that gorgeous cock. Her arms ached, but somehow the pain began to mesh with the other feelings that twined through her body. She squirmed, painfully aware of how she must look, splayed out on the bed like a captive slave. Bewilderment gripped her as she wondered how she could be so aroused by this situation when he had tricked her into this, but suddenly that no longer mattered. Her skin was hot with sweat, her pussy throbbing with moisture, and all she wanted right now was to feel the weight of Logan's body on hers. And the power of his body in hers.

He didn't fuck her immediately. Instead, he pushed her moist thighs apart and delved his tongue into her slick folds. Callie's body went rigid with pleasure, her back arching as she thrust her pelvis towards him. His tongue plunged into her juicy slit, licking up pearls of moisture as if he had done this hundreds of times before. His lips and tongue moved with delicate precision, swirling around her aching clit as he pushed a finger into her. Callie gasped, her arms straining against the handcuffs as he continued working at her. In the three years that she'd lived with Logan, he had never exhibited such passion towards her, such want. She'd felt more desired by him in the past month than she had in the past three years.

Logan came up over her then, shoving her damp thighs apart as he thrust into her. His mouth descended on hers, the salty taste of her juices stimulating Callie's every nerve. She gave a muffled cry and wrapped her legs around his back, her entire body reacting to the sensation of his cock pumping inside her. His breath rasped against her breasts as he took her nipples between his lips and sucked. Pleasure travelled along every nerve. Thoughts flitted through Callie's mind: memories of the restrained, dispassionate husband she'd lived with for so long. Now, he'd been replaced by this driving, potent man who electrified her with his unpredictable behaviour and the passionate lust that inevitably followed.

'Wider.' The rough command broke through Callie's haze. She writhed underneath him as he hooked her legs over his shoulders, spreading her fully open.

'Oh, God.' Callie closed her eyes and gripped the chains of her handcuffs, thrusting her hips upwards to impale herself on his oiled shaft. She moaned and worked herself into an increasing frenzy, feeling her bones begin to weaken as pleasure swelled. Just as she was about to explode, Logan pulled out of her. Callie's eyes flew open.

'What –?'

'Turn around.'

The chains of the handcuffs were long enough to allow her to turn. Logan stripped off her dress and bra, leaving her naked. A new wave of excitement began to spread in her belly as she felt Logan's hands grip her hips and pull them upwards. He shoved a pillow underneath her pelvis, making her arse jut towards him. Callie buried her face in the bedcovers and trembled as she felt his finger probe gently at her arsehole. Her muscles clenched around him, quivers travelling up her spine. She felt the flexing muscles of his chest on her back as he lowered himself over her. His warm lips touched the back of her neck.

'OK?' he whispered.

Callie nodded. Oddly enough, she felt as if her restrained position had liberated her in some manner to give herself to him in ways she never had before. And she suspected that he knew it. His hand spread her buttocks apart, his fingers forcing her tight muscles to relax. Sweat broke out on Callie's forehead when she felt the knob of his penis pushing at the closed aperture, lubricating it with his own fluids. She gasped, suddenly uncertain that she could do this, but Logan stopped and waited for her to get used to the pressure. His other hand slipped underneath her to caress her breasts, his fingers toying deliciously with her nipples.

Callie bit down on a corner of a pillow as her body reacted to the simultaneous sensation. She spread her legs further apart as she felt Logan begin to ease into her. She could feel the tension in his body, and it occurred to her fogged mind that they were both battling two different forms of restraint. The thought created an intense wave of feeling and arousal, even as Logan's cock pressed painfully against her hole.

Alongside the pain, however, came shudders of pleasure that spread outwards from the juncture of their union and through Callie's entire body. She moaned into the pillow and thrust her bottom up towards him, wanting him to fill her completely. Logan drew in a sharp breath at her movement, then thrust into her like a cork into a bottle. Callie gasped with a mixture of pleasure and pain, realising she had never felt so wholly possessed by her husband. Or by anyone.

'Oh, fuck, Callie.' Logan's voice was tight with restraint. His pelvis pressed against her moist buttocks, his hands gripping her hips tightly. 'Are you OK?'

'Y-yes.' Callie's thoughts swam in such an ocean of sensation that she could barely get the word out.

She shifted her hips to signal that she was all right, and then Logan's hand slipped underneath to her soaked pussy. Relieved, Callie felt him start to manipulate her clit as he began easing his cock back and forth gently. His breath rasped hotly against her back. He didn't try and force himself into her beyond what she could take, but the stimulation evoked by the movement of his cock in her tight channel had Callie moaning and writhing underneath him. Every nerve reacted to the erotic friction as Logan rubbed her slippery clit with increasing force. The double pressure was unbelievable, thrilling Callie on multiple levels. She squirmed against Logan's hand as the tension built.

'Come on, baby,' Logan whispered huskily in her ear. His forefinger thrust into her wet pussy as his thumb continued working at her clit. 'Come for me. All over my hand.'

His words were her undoing. With a cry, Callie came with a violent force that caused her entire body to shudder and clench around his fingers and his cock. Logan made a guttural noise in the back of his throat before he pushed into her with a final movement, pulling her against him as he shot deep inside her.

For a moment, they didn't move. Logan slipped out

of her, his hand stroking her bottom as he eased away. The sound of panting filled the air. Callie twisted around and opened her eyes to look at Logan, stunned by the expression in his eyes. He reached out and brushed his forefinger against her lips before pulling himself away from her. Callie watched him dress, aware of a throbbing, but rather delicious, ache in her arse. She tugged futilely at the cuffs again.

'Logan, unlock me.'

He looked at her for a long moment. Then, to her complete surprise, he picked up the key and unlocked the cuffs. Callie groaned as her muscles loosened. She rubbed her wrists and reached for her clothing.

'I don't want you to call the coastguard,' Logan said.

She shot him a glare. 'Was that why you fucked me? To keep me quiet?'

His expression darkened. 'You figure that one out.'

He left the room, closing the door behind him. Callie waited to hear the click of the lock, but it didn't come. She felt completely ravished and taken, her body both sore and sated.

After a moment, she went cautiously to the door and turned the knob. She stepped outside and climbed the stairs to the navigation room. Logan wasn't there. Callie eyed the radio. She could easily call for help now, but she couldn't help wondering what good that would do. Would it solve her and Logan's problems? Hardly. In fact, it would probably create more of them. And she was suddenly in no mood to deal with anyone other than her husband right now.

Logan stood at the railing of the boat and stared at the Savannah skyline. He knew he was a bastard for abducting Callie, but he'd become desperate. Still, he supposed it would serve him right when she called the police. His need to talk to her alone would be a flimsy defence. He turned when he heard her footsteps on the deck.

Callie came towards him, her hair still tousled and her

skin flushed with lingering heat. Logan's body tightened. She had been right when she said that they'd never reacted to each other the way they had during their estrangement.

'Don't worry,' Callie said. 'I didn't call anyone. Not yet, anyway,' she added.

Logan leant his hips against the railing and looked at her. Now, more than ever, he didn't want to let her go. 'So, what's it going to take, Callie? I made you come here because I want to have this out once and for all. Alone, for a change.'

'And kidnapping me was the way to do that?' Callie shook her head in disbelief. 'You know, Logan, if you'd ever given me one smidgen of an idea that you understood why I left you, then maybe we might have had a chance. But you are so bull-headed and dictatorial that you couldn't even fathom that you might be at fault.'

Logan tensed. 'And leaving me in the middle of the night without a word or explanation keeps you in the clear?'

'OK, I admit that maybe I should have said something,' Callie conceded. 'But, dammit, you know very well I tried to talk to you about our problems! I wear a short dress and you tell me I look sluttish, I visit my sister and you tell me to avoid her, I ask you why you married me and you tell me I'm being silly. Do you have any idea how frustrating it is to be on the receiving end of all your disapproval?'

Logan considered her words. He remembered saying those things to her, of course, but only because she'd pushed him.

Callie stared at him for a minute, her hand gripping the railing. When she spoke again, her voice was lower.

'Do you get it, Logan? Are you actually thinking about what I said? And don't tell me I didn't try and discuss this with you, because I did.'

'All right,' Logan finally said. 'Maybe I've been too disapproving, but you know very well that you deliberately provoked me.'

'Only because I wanted to get some kind of response from you. You acted like such a statue that sometimes I wondered if you even had emotions.'

'Despite that, I recall you telling me you weren't unhappy.'

'Well, do you think I would have left you if I wasn't?' Callie replied.

Logan frowned. 'I gave you everything you wanted.'

'You did not.' Callie sagged against the railing, looking suddenly defeated. 'You never gave me yourself.'

Wasn't marriage enough? he thought. 'I don't even know what you mean by that.'

'Of course you don't. That's the point.' She looked at the tense lines of his features and the way the slight breeze brushed through his hair. 'Remember the night of the voodoo ceremony?'

'Yes.'

'That was the only time in the three years of our marriage that I actually felt connected to you.'

'Don't tell me you were invaded by a spirit.'

Callie sighed. 'No, Logan. And don't criticise voodoo because you'll sound like a hypocrite. Abiona told me you went to see her, too.'

Logan's fists clenched as he thought of the voodoo priestess. He turned away from Callie and went back to the cabin. 'I don't want to discuss this.'

Callie followed him on to the bridge. 'Logan? Why did you go to see her?'

He shot her a glare, unwilling to tell her about his experience with Abiona. 'We're not talking about me. We're talking about you and why you left me.'

'I left because we *never* talked about you!' Callie cried. 'Jesus, Logan, I don't even know what your childhood was like. I don't know what kind of relationship you had with your father. In fact, I barely know anything about your past.'

'There's nothing to know,' Logan replied. 'Just bad memories.'

'Then why don't you tell me about them?'

He didn't respond. How in the love of God could he tell her? He would surely lose her for ever, even though he was dangerously close to that already.

Callie let out her breath in a long sigh and turned towards the cabin. 'Forget it, Logan. This is a totally pointless venture. If you wanted to convince me to come back to you by kidnapping me, then you're a fool.'

She went into the cabin. Logan remained on the bridge and looked out at the water, his hands gripping the wheel. He felt like he was in the middle of a huge maze, meeting one dead end after another no matter which way he turned. He'd been losing Callie slowly but surely over the past month, and he realised now that the only chance he had left was a gamble. Telling Callie the truth could easily disgust her so much that she'd walk away without looking back. At the same time, she might very well do that if he didn't tell her. That was obviously one of the things she'd been trying to tell him all along.

Logan went back on to the deck and sat down. The sun was beginning to set, painting the sky with ribbons of red and orange. He had the sudden thought that he didn't want to leave the boat. He wished he could stay here with Callie for ever, isolated from the rest of the world where nothing could touch them.

He heard Callie's footsteps approach and glanced up. She carried two bowls of tortellini and held one out to him. 'I thought you might be hungry.'

He gave her a surprised look. 'You brought me dinner?'

'I'm a nice person.'

Logan smiled. If there was anything he knew about his wife, it was that she was a nice person.

'That much I did know,' he said.

'Well, don't get the wrong idea,' Callie muttered. 'I'm still mad at you.'

She settled into a chair next to him and winced slightly.

'Are you all right?' Logan asked.

'Yes. Just a little sore.'

Shame prodded at Logan as he realised that he'd hurt her. 'Hell, I'm sorry. I didn't want to hurt you.'

'You didn't really,' Callie said. 'And I wanted it. And you know, Logan, if you'd been willing to experiment earlier in our marriage, we might never have ended up in this situation.'

'I never knew how you'd respond if I did.'

Callie threw him a derisive look. 'You could have found out if you'd bothered to try.'

The way Logan saw it, there were a number of things he could have done differently. They ate in silence, watching as the horizon swallowed up the last bit of glossy sun.

'So, tell me one thing,' Logan finally said.

'What's that?'

'What in the love of God is Tess trying to say with her performance art?'

Callie chuckled. 'If I knew the answer to that, I might even join her performances myself. As it stands, I have no idea.'

'So why do you bother going?'

'Because she's my friend. Sometime you have to do things for people because you like them. That's the way it is with Tess.'

'The officials are going to shut that show down if they find out what she's doing. Probably arrest them all, too.'

Callie shrugged. 'So, she'll come up with something else. She's resilient.' She gave him a wary look. 'You're not going to turn her in, are you?'

'No.'

'What about Adam?'

'What about him?'

'Did you have to fire him?'

Logan was irritated. 'Of course. What if one of our clients discovered what he was doing in his spare time?

I don't have the time to start dodging bullets.' He glanced at her. 'He told me he talked to you.'

'He's a good kid. Odd, but good.'

'Odd is right,' Logan muttered. 'Depraved thing to do, getting sodomised in front of a crowd.'

'You know, Logan, simply because people aren't like you doesn't mean they're depraved,' Callie said. 'Besides, other people might think that it was perverted of *us* to do what we did at a voodoo ritual.'

'That was entirely different.'

'Yes, it's always different when you're the one doing it, isn't it?'

Logan frowned at her, even though he knew she was right. He put down his bowl and walked to the railing. 'So, what is it you want from me, Callie? If you suddenly want me to become one of those New Age, sensitive fools, it's not going to happen.'

'I don't except you to become an entirely different person,' Callie protested. 'I didn't marry you so that I could shape you according to some other standard of what I was looking for in a husband. Believe me, I knew from the outset that you weren't the changeable type.'

'Sure as hell sounds like that's what you're trying to do now.'

'No, I'm not, and please stop putting all the blame on me. Besides, didn't you spend three years trying to change me?'

He gave her a startled look. 'What does that mean?'

'You were always commenting on how I behaved,' Callie replied. 'How we had some fictitious image to maintain. How I was supposed to act according to your standards rather than my own. And when I didn't, you blamed it on my upbringing.'

Shit. He really had done that, hadn't he? Logan dragged a hand through his hair and sighed. 'I realise I've been uptight about our image,' he admitted. 'I have my reasons, but I don't want you to change, Callie.'

'Well, I'm asking that of you,' she said. 'I don't mean

entirely. I'm simply asking you to give both me and yourself some room to breathe. Admit it, Logan. Even you find it difficult to adhere to all your standards. As for our image, well, who cares what other people think?'

Logan didn't respond, turning again to look out over the river. A sudden image of his father sprang to mind. The man had presented a distinguished persona to the world that was wholly different from who he really was.

'Yeah, well, propriety can be a bitch,' he muttered. 'You have to have standards.'

'That's fine, but they shouldn't rule your life.' Callie approached him almost cautiously. 'Where did they come from?' she asked quietly. 'Your father?'

He gave her a surprised look. She'd always been more perceptive than he had ever given her credit for. 'Partly.'

'And where else?'

'You don't want to know.' Logan's hands clenched on the wooden railing so tightly that a splinter jabbed into his palm. He ignored the mild pain and tried to convince himself that telling Callie everything would clear the air between them. At the very least, it might make her trust him again.

'Yes, I do,' Callie said.

Logan turned away from her, unable to look into those brown eyes of hers. He forced the bitter words out of his mouth. 'I'm being blackmailed.'

Callie went silent with shock for a moment. 'Blackmailed?' she repeated. 'By whom?'

'A woman I used to know.'

'Is she a client?'

'No.' Logan picked up their bowls and went back to the cabin, still unable to look at her. Callie followed him.

'Then who?' she asked.

'Her name is Elenore Lawrence. She's an evil, manipulative bitch.'

'Well, what does she want?'

'Money, and lots of it. She's renovating a nineteenth-century riverboat because she wants to turn it into a hotel and gambling casino. She has an apartment, but the last I heard, she was staying on the boat.'

'Doesn't she already have investors?'

'Yes, but she needs more.'

'Namely you.'

'Namely me.'

Callie paused in the doorway of the kitchen and watched as he scrubbed the dishes. Logan knew where this was all heading. The very idea made him sick, but he risked a glance at his wife. She was watching him with both wariness and curiosity.

'So, is it a bad investment?' she asked.

'Any dealing with Elenore Lawrence is a bad investment. She and her husband became experts at money laundering and trading on the black market.'

'She must be rich if she had the money to buy a riverboat.'

'She claims she's lost a great deal of her fortune,' Logan replied. 'Her husband died five years ago and left her with sizeable debts.'

'If she wants money, then what is she blackmailing you with?'

Logan's blood went cold. He couldn't tell her this. He'd locked it all away for so many years that he could barely even think about it himself. Callie frowned at the look on his face. She approached him and reached out to put her hand on his arm. 'Logan?'

'Never mind, Callie.' He brushed away her touch as if it were a pesky mosquito and headed for the bridge.

'No!' The word, edged with anger, broke from Callie's throat as she followed him. 'You're not pushing me away again, Logan. You brought this up, not me. Who is this woman and what does she want?'

Logan's jaw clenched so tightly that it hurt. He knew Callie wouldn't let up until he told her the truth.

'Logan, what is it? Don't tell me you murdered someone years ago.' She smiled faintly.

Logan didn't react to her weak attempt at humour. He

wrapped his hands around the wheel so tightly that his knuckles turned white.

'She just knows some things about me, Callie, that's all.'

'What things?' Callie persisted. 'And how ironic is it that this stranger seems to know more about you than I do?'

He threw her an exasperated look. Maybe she'd give up if he shut her out. 'It was a long time ago. Years before we even met.'

'*What* was a long time ago? Would you talk to me, please? You can't just tell me you're being blackmailed without giving me the details.'

Logan yanked the engine into gear as he headed back to the marina.

'Was this the reason you went to see Abiona?' Callie asked.

He shot her a glare. 'How did you know about that?'

'She told me, but don't worry. She wouldn't give me any details.' Callie leant her shoulder against the bulkhead and continued looking at him curiously. 'I admit I was surprised that you'd even think about going to see a voodoo priestess.'

'Well, it was a foolish thing to do,' Logan muttered. 'I wasn't thinking, obviously.'

'Nevertheless, it must be quite serious for you to go to such lengths,' Callie replied. 'What on earth is going on? What does this Elenore woman know about you that I don't?'

'Things you're better off not knowing at all.'

'I'm not better off when I don't know my own husband,' Callie retorted. 'Haven't you realised that yet? You know nearly everything about my past, yet I know nothing about yours.'

'Believe me. You don't want to know this.'

'Does this have something to do with the bad memories you mentioned?' Callie asked.

Logan looked at her. She was watching him with such

concern that it went straight to his heart. He didn't know how she would react, but he realised that he owed it to her at least to try to explain. God knew he'd kept enough from her. He took a breath, his gaze focused on the undulating movement of the river.

'After I graduated from university, I went to work with my father at the law firm,' he said. 'My father was a right bastard, to put it mildly. He was an abusive alcoholic and gambler who managed to win cases by intimidation and bribery. It took me about three months to realise that he was sinking the firm into bankruptcy. He'd gambled away most of our personal savings and he was starting on the firm's. Two of his partners discovered the mess and told me that they'd turn him in unless we found a way to repay them within a year. I knew we could never recoup the money through court cases alone, so I took another job.'

A hint of dread suddenly flashed in Callie's eyes, as if she knew that his next words would be nothing good. She edged closer to him. 'What job was that?' Callie whispered.

'Elenore Lawrence was one of my father's clients,' Logan said, fighting to keep his voice from wavering. 'She heard about our financial troubles and knew of a way I could make a lot of money fast. She suggested that I moonlight as an escort.'

'An escort?'

'Nice way of saying a male prostitute,' Logan explained. If she was going to know the truth, then she'd better know all the ugliness of it. 'I fucked for money.'

Callie stared at him in shock. 'Wh . . . how l-long did this go on?' she stammered.

'Over a year. I started with an agency, and then Elenore and her husband paid me to come to live with them.'

'And you did?'

'They offered me more than enough money to get my

father and the firm out of the hole. I could never have made that much in another job.'

Callie still looked stunned, but she began to appear vaguely intrigued in spite of herself. 'What did they want you to do?'

He shot her a wary look, steeling himself against the look in her eyes. 'You name it, I did it. I fucked them both, I let them fuck me, I played all their games. Elenore had a thing for rough sex. She loved being tied up and whipped. Her husband often got off on watching, but he was also a sadist. One of his favourite games was to tie her to a saddle horse and whip her until she nearly bled. Then he'd make her frig herself against the saddle.'

Callie gasped. 'And she agreed to that?'

'Agreed? She loved it. After that, it was usually my turn.' An ugly sensation twisted in Logan's gut as the unbidden and unwanted images started appearing. A tall, grey-haired man with a set mouth and a penchant for humiliation, sinking to his knees in front of a rigid prick, Elenore lashed to the wall like a sacrificial lamb, Logan tied to a rack while Gerald toyed with them both to the edge.

'You mean they whipped you?' Callie asked.

'Like I said, Gerald Lawrence was a sadist. That was the reason he kept me around. He liked trying to break me because he knew that I could satisfy his wife, which made him jealous.'

'And he tried to break you by whipping you?'

Logan gave her a faint smile. She didn't know the half of it. He realised then that part of the reason he'd shut her out was because he had wanted to protect her innocence. So much for that idea.

'Believe me, calla lily. There was a lot more involved than whipping. I wasn't allowed to wear clothes for that whole year unless they were for role-playing games. The old bastard buggered and gagged me or he'd make me do the same thing to him. He'd tie me up anywhere he could. His masochistic tendencies came out when his wife wasn't around. He liked to be impaled on the prick of a statue of the Greek god Priapus, then he'd want me to lash him. Or sometimes he'd want me to be on the receiving end. And then there were times when other people were involved.'

'But why didn't you leave?'

Logan shrugged. How many times had he asked himself the same question? 'I'd signed a contract, and I needed the money desperately. If I couldn't pay off my father's debts, the firm would go under and the partners would sue my father for everything he had. The worst part is, he knew what I was doing.'

Callie drew in a breath. 'Your father knew?'

'He didn't know the details, but he knew I was fucking for money. You'd think that would have changed him.'

'It didn't?'

'No.' A familiar streak of resentment coursed through Logan.

'Logan, I'm so sorry. That must have been horrible for you.'

Logan glanced at her. She was watching him with a mixture of sadness and pain, but he saw none of the disgust he'd expected.

'I consented to it,' he admitted. 'But that doesn't mean I enjoyed it.'

Callie eyed him curiously. 'Not any of it?'

Logan shrugged, unwilling to tell her just how deeply he'd become involved in the whole drama. There had been times when he'd actually begged for a lashing. 'There was sexual satisfaction. Actually, that was usually part of the deal. I had to get off, too, because then they could say that I was enjoying what they were doing. It was a way for them to remind me that they were controlling me.'

'Why didn't you ever tell me this?' Callie asked.

She sounded so hurt that he couldn't help feeling guilty. Logan approached her almost warily, as if afraid she might break. She didn't back away, only looked at him with a hundred questions in her eyes.

'Oh, Callie.' Logan shook his head and sighed. 'It's such an ugly episode of my life. It's obviously not something I'm proud of.'

'Did you think I wouldn't understand?'

Logan reached out to brush a lock of hair away from Callie's neck as an excuse to touch her. 'I didn't know,' he admitted. 'Hell, I don't even understand it myself.'

'So this is what Elenore is threatening you with?' Callie asked.

Logan nodded. 'She knows it could ruin me.'

A flash of anger appeared in Callie's eyes. 'She can't do that. There has to be something we can do.'

'We?'

'Well, we're still married,' Callie reminded him. 'I want to help you if I can.'

Logan shook his head, unable to believe that this incredible woman was his wife. After all he'd done, she still wanted to help him. 'There's nothing you can do. This is my problem.'

'Your problems are also mine,' Callie said. 'Can't you just give her the money?'

'No. I'm not giving in to her again. And I'm not risking my financial situation or my reputation for this.'

Logan turned back to look at the river. He realised then with startling clarity why he'd married Callie. After over ten years of dealing with coiffured, calculating society women, he'd recognised something honest and genuine in Callie. He may not have consciously married her for that reason, but he knew now that he'd wanted someone good in his life for a change. And then he'd proceeded to stifle her with his uptight need to retain a certain image – and for what? To impress the very people he disliked? To try to pretend that he'd always lived an untainted, moral life?

He looked at Callie. Now, more than ever, he didn't want to let her go. At the same time, he knew he had to.

He couldn't force her into doing what she didn't want to do, nor make her into a person that she wasn't. And he didn't want her to be anyone else.

'I'm sorry,' he said.

'Well, I'm glad you finally told me,' Callie replied. 'I'm shocked, of course, but if you'd told me three years ago, it wouldn't have made me change my mind about marrying you.'

'So what changed your mind about staying married to me?'

'The fact that you've kept so much from me,' Callie said. 'Are there any other secrets that I should know about?'

'None of that magnitude.' Logan guided the boat back to the marina entrance and through the lighted buoys that marked the layout of the basin. The wake slapped against the breakwater almost inaudibly, the sound of the water like a whisper. 'I'm leaving you on land. I want to stay out here for a while.'

'So what happens to us now?' Callie asked.

'You know I want you back at home,' Logan said, taking the bowline and fastening it over a cleat on the dock. 'But I don't want this shit with Elenore to hurt you.'

Callie turned towards the cabin. 'I need some time to think about this. I'm not willing to give up on us so easily, Logan, but I want to know that you understand why I left you.'

'I'm beginning to.' For the first time, a faint hope rose in him.

Callie placed her hand on his arm and nodded. 'I'm beginning to understand you, too. And that was all I ever wanted.'

Chapter Sixteen

'Callie, did you ever return that batch of seaweed soap?' Tess called from the loft. 'The stuff that smelled like rotten potatoes soaked in iodine?'

Callie looked up from her book and scratched her head. 'I think so.'

Tess peered over the railing. 'You know, you have been acting very strangely today. Are you feeling all right?'

'I'm fine. I just have a bit of headache.'

'Kava root is good for headaches,' Adam remarked. He finished cleaning the front of the jewellery cabinet and came around the counter. 'Hey, Tess, we should start selling herbs.'

'Not a bad idea, handsome.'

Callie had to smile at the pleased look on Adam's face. Tess had hired him to work at Nebula Arcana after he'd been fired from the law firm, and Callie thought that Adam seemed much happier in jeans and T-shirts rather than business suits, anyway. He was even sporting a pierced ear and a pierced lip, thanks to Tess's body-modification expertise.

'So, have you heard from Logan lately?' Adam asked.

Callie shook her head. She was reluctant to talk about

what had occurred between her and Logan but, at the same time, she had no idea what to do about it. If Logan with all his resources and courage couldn't even figure out how to banish Elenore Lawrence from his life, then what could Callie do? She'd been unable to stop thinking of Logan and what had happened to him. She couldn't imagine her upstanding husband lowering himself to such depths.

At the same time, she was also beginning to understand more about Logan's personality than she ever had before. If he'd been in a humiliating situation for an entire year and forced into degrading sexual acts, then it was no wonder he'd shut down emotionally. One would have to in order to survive. But once Logan shut down, he'd been unable to open up again. At least, not until the other day on the boat.

'Yes, we've talked,' Callie finally admitted to Adam. 'But things are still pretty complicated.'

'So, um, how is he?'

Callie remembered Tess telling her about Adam's crush on Logan. She smiled again. 'He's fine. Arrogant, of course, but fine.'

'Yes, he was always arrogant,' Adam said wistfully.

The telephone next to the cash register rang. Callie picked the receiver.

'Nebula Arcana. Callie speaking.'

'Callie, it's Gloria. I just got your message that you wanted to talk to me.'

'Gloria.' Callie closed her eyes and wondered if she was about to make a huge mistake. At the same time, she knew of no one else who could help her right now. 'Yes, I really need to talk to you. Can we meet for lunch somewhere?'

'Sure, sugar. I'll meet you in an hour at that café near your shop.'

'Great. Thanks.' Callie hung up the phone and pressed her fingers against her temples. She was still trying to sort out everything that had happened over the past two days. She'd considered going to see Abiona again, but she knew that spells and rituals weren't the route to take any longer. They needed something a great deal more concrete at this point.

After an hour, Callie walked to the café next door to meet Gloria. Her sister was already waiting, seated at a table by the window with a glass of iced tea in front of her. Callie eyed Gloria carefully as she approached, relieved to see that her sister was clear-eyed and sober. For now, at least.

Gloria wriggled her fingers at Callie. 'Hi, sugar. Have you moved back in with Logan yet?'

Callie shook her head and sat down. 'No, but please don't lecture me. We have a problem.'

Gloria's plucked eyebrows rose as she leaned forward slightly. 'What kind of problem?'

'I can't give you the details, but suffice it to say that Logan is being blackmailed,' Callie explained.

'Blackmailed? Logan?' Gloria reached for her tea.

'Yes. This woman wants money from him, and he's not willing to give it to her. She's threatened to ruin him if he doesn't.'

'How on earth can anyone ruin Logan?'

'Well, she knows some things about him,' Callie said carefully.

Interest sparked in Gloria's eyes. 'Really? You mean Logan has secrets?'

'Apparently so,' Callie muttered. 'I don't know what to do, Gloria. He only told me about this yesterday, but it's been going on for the past week. He knew this woman fifteen years ago, and now she's come back to town.'

'Who is she?'

'Her name is Elenore Lawrence.' Callie felt another rush of fury towards this woman she didn't even know. And, alongside that, a surprising streak of jealousy that Elenore Lawrence had known all about such a cryptic part of Logan while she, Callie, had known nothing.

256

'She apparently married a wealthy husband who left her with a number of debts after he died. Now she wants Logan's money.'

Gloria pursed her lips and reached for a breadstick. 'Hmm. And he can't do anything about this?'

'I don't think so. He has someone investigating her, but it looks like she holds all the cards.'

'How fascinating. This must be the first time in that man's life that he lacks control.'

Callie let that remark pass without comment. 'I need your help, Gloria, but I don't want Logan to know about it. If he knows I came to you, he'd be furious. You know how he is about dealing with his own problems. Even getting him to tell me about this was like pulling teeth.'

'How much money does this woman want?'

'Two million dollars.'

Gloria's eyebrows shot up again. 'Good God. What on earth for?'

'She's refurbishing a riverboat to turn it into a hotel and casino. I guess she wants authentic furnishings or something.'

'Does she have collateral?'

'I don't know. She blackmailed Logan, so I don't think collateral was really an issue.'

'Why doesn't he just give her the money?'

'I asked him the same thing. He said that doing that could ruin him just as easily because the Lawrences are into money laundering. Plus, I think he also has some innate block against giving in to blackmail.'

'Hmm.'

Callie could almost hear the wheels turning in her sister's head as a waiter came up to take their orders. Callie ordered a salad, suddenly too nervous to eat anything more substantial. If Gloria was unwilling to help her, then she was at a complete loss over what to do next.

Gloria sipped her tea and placed her napkin over her lap. 'I don't know, Callie. That's a great deal of money.'

'I know.'

'Do you know where this woman lives?'

'Logan said she's staying temporarily on the riverboat.'

'I want to speak with her before I make any decisions about this.'

Callie nodded, relieved that Gloria hadn't immediately said no. 'I'll go with you. I want to see this woman for myself.'

'However, Callie, if I agree to help you and Logan, I must tell you that I have a condition of my own.'

'A condition?'

Gloria nodded. 'I want you to return to Logan.'

Callie stared at her sister. 'You're kidding.'

'No. I've had enough of your nonsense, and I know Logan has as well.'

'Great. Now you're blackmailing me? Jesus, Gloria, what kind of sister are you?'

Gloria frowned. 'I am not blackmailing you, Callie. I am simply tired of your behaviour, so I'm imposing a condition. And you know very well that I've been a good sister to you.'

'I've been one to you, too!' Callie reminded her. Her thoughts jumbled up in her head like puzzle pieces that she couldn't fit together. Yes, she wanted to help Logan because she hated seeing him on the verge of defeat, but what would it be like if she went back to him?

'I know you have,' Gloria said. 'And I don't like seeing you so torn up about what to do with your life. You belong with Logan, sugar. You married him, and it's about time you worked out your problems. You can't do that unless you go back to him.'

'I tried working things out, Gloria.' Callie glanced around to make certain that none of the other patrons were within earshot and lowered her voice. 'He responded by kidnapping me,' she hissed.

Gloria's blue eyes widened. 'Kidnapping you?'

'Yes. He tricked me into going on the boat, and then he handcuffed me to a bed. Can you believe it?'

Gloria stared at her for a moment before she burst into laughter.

'Gloria!'

'I'm sorry, sugar but, quite frankly, I think that's extraordinary. Half the women in Savannah would give their firstborn to be kidnapped, if that's the definition you're using.'

'That's not saying much for the women of Savannah,' Callie muttered.

Gloria's eyes gleamed. 'And handcuffing you to a bed, no less. That must have been absolutely delicious.'

'No, it wasn't.' But even as she denied it, a quiver of excitement went through Callie's body. She remembered certain sensations with a strikingly sharp clarity. Forbidden sensations.

'Oh, come on. Don't tell me you're not the slightest bit flattered that he would do such a thing.'

Callie glowered at her. 'No. I'm still angry with him about that. Who does he think I am, his property?'

'Well, if you're so furious with him, why do you want to help him?' Gloria asked. 'You can stand back and watch him sink if you're so hostile.'

'Well, I don't want to do that,' Callie muttered. 'He's still my husband, after all. I never wanted to see him hurt.'

'Exactly. He's still your husband. And if I agree to help you, then you'll go back to him. Do we have an understanding?'

Callie rubbed at a scratch on the table and tried to understand what she was feeling deep down inside. She was surprised to discover that, above anything, she wanted Logan to be free from the shackles of his past. She didn't want him to be tormented any longer, and she would do whatever she could to prevent that from happening.

Logan enraged and infuriated her almost beyond

imagining, but these past few weeks had given her glimpses of his character that she hadn't known existed. And with those glimpses came a sense of being connected to him in ways that went far beyond a marriage certificate. She could only hope that he wouldn't retreat back into his shell again.

She nodded. 'All right, Gloria. We have an understanding.'

Gloria smiled with delight. 'Great, sugar. We'll go and see this blackmailing bitch and deal with her together. And stop looking as if you've been sentenced to prison. Logan is a good man, and you know it.'

'I know,' Callie replied. 'I'm just confused. I mean, I left him because I couldn't even relate to him, but I've learned more about him in the last month that I have in three years. And I guess I'm just surprised at how much I want to protect him from harm.'

'I'll bet everything I own that he feels the same way about you.'

Callie looked at her sister. 'You think so?'

Gloria nodded. 'I know so.'

'Sometimes I still doubt he feels anything for me,' Callie admitted. 'Or I think he wants me back only for his ego and not for any other reason.'

Gloria eyed her speculatively. 'I suspect he wouldn't have told you about the blackmail if he was trying to salvage his ego.'

'True.' Callie sighed and put her head in her hands. She groaned. 'I don't know, Gloria. I admit that he seems to understand both himself and me better now. And even on the boat, I felt like I was actually talking *to* him and that he was even listening. I've never felt like that before. But it's all so confusing.'

'Sure it is, sugar. Love is always confusing.'

Callie gave her startled look. 'Love? Whoever said anything about love?'

'Oh, please. If you're not in love with him, then I'm

not a sex goddess.' Gloria smiled pertly. 'And we both know that Aphrodite herself envies me.'

Gloria powdered her nose and reapplied some lipstick before grabbing her handbag and hurrying downstairs. 'Ted?'

'In here, darlin'.'

Gloria paused in the study, where Ted was busy watching a football game and drinking beer. He glanced up at her and gave a low whistle.

'Well, look at you.'

Gloria smiled and twirled around so that he could admire her new violet suit with matching high-heeled shoes and handbag. The suit hugged her figure and exposed just enough of her cleavage to be enticing.

'I declare, you look good enough to eat,' Ted said. 'Why don't you come on over here so I can do just that?'

With a giggle, Gloria approached him. She bent to kiss him, letting her fingers drift down to caress his prick. 'I'd love you to, sugar, but I have an appointment.'

'Doing what?'

'I have to rescue my sister and her husband,' Gloria replied. 'Honestly, those two manage to get themselves into the stickiest situations.'

'So what do you have to do?' Ted asked.

Gloria kissed him again, drawing his lower lip between her teeth. 'We'll talk about that later, OK? I'll be back later this evening. Perhaps we can watch *Octopussy* and I'll take you up on that offer of yours.' She smiled as she felt his prick harden. 'So, you just hold that thought.'

She hurried to the hall when the doorbell rang. Callie stood dressed in a dark suit on the doorstep. She looked slightly nervous.

'Gloria, maybe this isn't the best idea,' she said. 'I mean, what if –'

'Now, don't have second thoughts,' Gloria replied. She took her sister's arm and marched her to the car.

'You can't let people treat you and your husband like this. Really, if some bitch was doing this to Ted, do you think I'd just sit back and take it?'

'Ted isn't exactly Logan,' Callie reminded her.

'Don't I know it,' Gloria muttered. 'Now, don't you worry about a thing, sugar. I'm going to take care of everything. She knows we're coming, I hope.'

'Yes, I call her last night. She didn't sound very pleasant.'

Gloria chuckled. 'Sugar, she doesn't even know the meaning of unpleasant. But I reckon she will after we get through with her.'

She drove to Wilmington Island and into a car park near the marina. The docks were lined with smaller boats and luxury yachts, but Elenore Lawrence's riverboat, *The Over Easy*, was an attraction in itself. Four decks high, the brilliant white vessel must have been at least three hundred feet in length with a huge, red paddle wheel at the rear and two large smokestacks. Gingerbread trim lined the decks, giving it an air of elegance and beauty.

Callie shook her head. 'Jesus. No wonder she needs all that money.'

They approached the gangplank that connected the riverboat to the shore. A burly man stood guard with his arms crossed. He nodded when they told him their names and ushered them inside.

'Mrs Lawrence is waiting for you in the officer's quarters,' he said.

Callie and Gloria stepped on to the boat and were led inside the forecastle. The renovations were still in progress, but it appeared as if this area had been designated a sitting room and bar with crystal chandeliers and mahogany furnishings.

Before Gloria and Callie could complete their survey of the decor, a pair of carved wooden doors opened at the other end of the room. A woman stepped out, dressed in a long, blue chiffon gown with a strand of pearls around her neck. Her dark hair was swept back from her forehead, and she carried herself with a great deal of poise.

'Hello.' She moved towards them and extended her hand. 'I am Elenore Lawrence.'

'And I am Gloria Harper,' Gloria replied sweetly, rather intrigued by the other woman's aura of self-possession. 'This is my sister Callie.'

Elenore's dark gaze turned to Callie. 'Ah. So you're Logan's wife.'

Callie nodded. 'That's correct.'

'Isn't that nice?' Elenore murmured, her eyes scanning Callie from head to toe in quick but thorough assessment. 'Do come inside. Please forgive the mess but, as you know, we're still working. Luckily, the officer's quarters have been finished.'

The quarters were decorated in plush green and rust with antique furniture, paintings and models of historical riverboats, velvet curtains and a mahogany bar manned by a handsome barman. Elenore gestured towards two cushioned chairs in front of the marble fireplace.

'Please, sit. May I offer you a drink or coffee?'

'I'd love a martini, please,' Gloria replied, giving the barman a smile. She glanced at Callie, sensing that her sister was more than a little uncomfortable about this entire situation. It was hardly a wonder. Elenore Lawrence and her magnificent riverboat were a bit out of Callie's league.

'Nothing for me,' Callie said.

'Your boat is beautiful,' Gloria remarked. She scanned the other woman quickly, noting the curves of her body and the weight of her breasts. Not bad for a woman who had at least twenty years over Gloria herself.

'Thank you.' Elenore settled into a leather, wing-backed chair. 'I'm quite excited about it. We've just purchased a steam-powered organ for entertainment, and we're working out the tour packages. We're going to have close to a hundred staterooms, and I want to offer the finest in riverboat travel. We also plan to offer one of the largest riverboat casinos on the promenade deck.'

'How fascinating,' Gloria drawled. 'Are you going to live here?'

'No, I have a home in Hilton Head. I'm going to sell my Savannah penthouse soon.'

'And is that how do you intend to finance this venture?'

Elenore's expression hardened slightly. She looked from Gloria to Callie. 'Correct me if I'm mistaken, but I believe you know that already.'

Callie nodded, her eyes flashing with hatred. 'I think what you're doing to my husband is abhorrent.'

Gloria cringed. Elenore laughed.

'Do you, now?' Elenore asked. 'I'm terribly sorry about that.'

'Would you excuse us for a moment, please?' Gloria put down her martini and grasped Callie's elbow. She tugged her sister outside and closed the doors.

'Callie, you can't talk like that to this woman,' she hissed.

'Why not?' Callie retorted. 'I hate her.'

'I know, but you have to play the game,' Gloria whispered in annoyance. She herded Callie back to the gangplank. 'Now, listen. I want you to go home and wait for me there. I'm going to deal with this woman alone.'

'But, I want –'

'You want to scratch her eyes out, I know that,' Gloria replied. 'But if you want me to handle this, then you'll stay out of it. Believe me, Callie, I know how to deal with women like her.'

'I don't want to leave you alone with her,' Callie said.

'I'm going to be fine.' Gloria shoved her sister gently on to the gangplank and back to land. 'Now go, all right? I'll call you as soon as I return.'

She waited until Callie walked back to the car before smoothing down her skirt and returning to the officer's quarters. Elenore was still waiting, a glass of scotch in her hand. She raised her eyebrows when Gloria returned.

'I'm so sorry about that,' Gloria said sweetly as she settled back into her seat. 'My sister sometimes says things without thinking.'

Elenore shrugged. 'I dare say she was merely speaking her mind.'

'That, too,' Gloria allowed. 'Nevertheless, she was very rude.'

'I thought she'd left Logan.'

'That was only temporary.' Gloria waved her hand in the air dismissingly. 'They're very much together. Logan is quite devoted to Callie.'

She watched with satisfaction as something ugly flashed in Elenore Lawrence's eyes. Hah. So the other woman didn't like the idea of Logan being attached to his wife, did she?

'I'm surprised to hear that,' Elenore said, recovering her composure quickly. 'Callie doesn't seem like Logan's type.'

The air thickened slightly with acrimony. Gloria sipped her martini and crossed her legs. 'You, of course, know exactly what his type is.'

'I like to think so.'

'Then you'd be wrong, wouldn't you?' Gloria asked. 'And speaking of Logan, I believe you know that he's the reason I'm here. As Callie rather bluntly put it, she's not happy with what you're doing to her husband.'

'Funny. I've been quite happy with what he's done to me.'

Gloria's eyes narrowed. 'Before we go any farther with this, why don't you tell me exactly what happened between you and Logan? From what I understand, you're blackmailing him, but I have no idea what you're blackmailing him with.'

Elenore chuckled. 'I imagine even little Callie doesn't know that.'

'On the contrary. I believe she does.'

'Really? What does she know?'

Gloria shrugged, unwilling to admit that Callie hadn't even told her. 'Why don't you give me your version of the story?'

Elenore stood and moved over to the bar. She looked at the barman and waved her hand towards the door. He poured her another scotch and left the room, closing the door behind him. Elenore turned back to Gloria.

'My version is also his version,' she said. 'Since we're being blunt, I'll simply tell you that he was a gigolo.'

Gloria didn't even try to hide her shock. She stared at Elenore and reached for her martini. 'Logan?'

Elenore's lips curved as she nodded. 'Shocking, isn't it? Such a reputable man. Such a sterling character. So righteous and moral. And yet he used to make a living doing something as base as selling his cock for money.'

'You're not serious.'

'I most certainly am. And I can do so much damage to him now because my husband and I paid him to live with us for a year. Of course, we paid him for services well rendered.' She paused, a dreamy look in her eyes. 'Very well rendered, I might add.'

Gloria shook her head. If it had been anyone else in the world, and if her sister hadn't been involved, she would have found the whole story utterly fascinating. As it was, she couldn't help feeling a mild admiration for Elenore Lawrence. Here was a woman who certainly knew how to get what she wanted.

'My God,' Gloria muttered. She could have easily believed Logan's involvement in illegal financing or any number of white-collar crimes, but a gigolo? And did Callie know all the details about this? An image of Logan's body entwined with Elenore's appeared so swiftly in her head that she drew in a breath. Her pussy contracted in response. God, what a sight those two must be in action.

'As I'm sure you realise, I have Logan ... shall we say, between a rock and a hard place.' Elenore chuckled.

'I have to admit I rather admire you for that,' Gloria said, trying to compose herself. 'I suspect you're the first person to have Logan in that position.'

'I imagine I am.' Her gaze slid over Gloria's figure. 'So, what is your role in this entire venture?'

'I'm standing in for Logan. I'll give you the money you want on the condition that you leave both him and my sister alone.'

Suspicion sparked in Elenore's eyes as she considered Gloria's statement. 'And what's in it for you?'

'I have my reasons.'

'Quite a noble thing to do, sacrificing yourself for your brother-in-law.'

Gloria shrugged. 'You're welcome to think of me as noble if you like, but I'm hardly a sacrificial lamb.'

'What makes you think I'd be willing to give up the control I have over Logan?' Elenore asked.

'Because you want the money more,' Gloria replied. She gave the other woman a sly look. 'I know women like you, Elenore. And you know that if you fuck with Logan now, he'll spend the rest of his days seeking out ways to get back at you. Are you certain you want to live with that for the rest of your life?'

For the first time, a hint of trepidation appeared in Elenore's expression. Then she drew herself up and took another swallow of scotch. 'You know, Logan and I had another little condition to our agreement.'

Gloria had no doubt as to what that condition was. 'And what might that be?'

'He fucked me when I wanted him to.' Elenore levelled her dark gaze on Gloria. 'What do you intend to do about that part of the agreement?'

'What do you want me to do?' Gloria watched as Elenore's eyes went to the exposed skin of her cleavage.

Her heartbeat quickened. She'd been with women before, but none with the kind of determined hardness that Elenore Lawrence possessed. 'I don't have a prick to fuck you with.'

Elenore's eyes gleamed as she pulled open the drawer of a side-table. 'No. But perhaps we can remedy that.'

Gloria stared as Elenore removed a double-sided dildo – two rubber penises attached by the balls – from the drawer. Her mouth went dry. Elenore tossed it in Gloria's direction with a challenging look.

'Well? You seem like a woman of substance. Just how far are you willing to go?'

'As far as it takes.' Arousal skipped over Gloria's nerves. Her lips curved into a smile as she bent to pick up the dildo, tracing her fingers over the plastic ribbing on the shaft. Power had always been a heady aphrodisiac for her. And Elenore Lawrence had power. She radiated it. Gloria lifted her gaze as she caressed the two phalluses. 'I want our agreement in writing first.'

Something resembling respect appeared in Elenore's eyes. 'Smart woman.' She walked to a desk and removed a sheet of paper. After writing the conditions down, she signed the paper and handed it to Gloria. 'It's not notarised, but I hope this will do.'

'We'll work out the legal aspect tomorrow,' Gloria assured her.

'Then come here.' Elenore stood there with her hands on her hips, every inch the woman who expected everyone around her to do her bidding.

Gloria made a mental note to try to cultivate Elenore's regal behaviour. Such an attitude could prove to be very beneficial. She rose and approached her, aware of a slight trembling in her hands and the rapid beating of her heart. Gloria was so often the one in command of her sexual situations that this encounter had a wholly different feel to it. She was startled when Elenore reached out to rip the buttons from her suit, tugging them off to expose the globes of her breasts covered by a flimsy lace bra.

'Nice,' Elenore murmured approvingly. She pinched one of Gloria's nipples between her long fingers, causing a spark of pain.

Gloria winced, even as her cunt responded with a swell of moisture. She didn't move when Elenore walked around her, tugging off her jacket and unzipping her skirt. She knew instinctively that the other woman wanted to control this situation, and Gloria was more than willing to let her. The edge of animosity in the air only served to increase her desire. Within seconds, she was standing there in only her bra and knickers, while Elenore scrutinised her fleshy curves.

'You have a body that was made for fucking,' Elenore remarked, giving Gloria a slap on the arse. 'I suspect you know that, don't you?'

'I've been told,' Gloria agreed.

She watched with hungry eyes as Elenore returned to stand in front of her. She unbuttoned her diaphanous gown and let it fall to the floor. She wore nothing underneath it, and the sight of her breasts and peaked nipples made Gloria's mouth fairly water. She looked lower at Elenore's mons, her blood surging as the sight of the delectable, shorn apex that concealed nothing.

Elenore smiled and sat down on the leather couch, spreading her legs apart. 'Go on, then, you shameless whore. Do what you're best at.'

Gloria approached her and knelt as if she were worshipping a queen. She parted Elenore's legs and thrust her tongue eagerly inside, licking her way around the perimeter as she sank two fingers into the wetness of Elenore's slit. Her fluids tasted tangy and slightly sweet. Gloria dug in deeper with her tongue, suddenly wanting to prove to this woman that she could provide infinite amounts of pleasure. She clutched Elenore's thighs, feeling the heat of her skin burning into her palms.

Elenore's hand stroked through Gloria's hair. Her

body tensed with growing need as Gloria continued working at her cunt. Gloria reached up to cup Elenore's breasts in her hands, plucking at her gorgeous, hard nipples. She loved the sensation of Elenore writhing and panting, knowing that she had the other woman's pleasure entirely in her hands. And in her mouth. She captured Elenore's swollen clitoris gently between her lips and sucked at it lightly, drawing sensations from her until Elenore bucked underneath her. Her body jerked violently as she shrieked out her ecstasy. Gloria soothed Elenore with her tongue, drinking up the final rush of moisture as Elenore's body shuddered through her climax. Elenore sucked in a breath of air and gazed down at Gloria.

'And now I want you to turn around.'

Ropes of tension constricted in Gloria's lower body. Her pussy fairly ached with need for her own release, but she obeyed Elenore's command. Excitement licking at her nerves, Gloria turned around, bracing her hands on the plush carpet as she presented her rounded buttocks and spread vulva to the other woman. Her body quivered when she felt Elenore's hands skimming over her arse and exploring the dark crevice between them. Then Elenore moved around to stand in front of her. She held the dildo in her hand, and with a swift movement, she inserted one of the phalluses into her cunt. Gloria stared at her in utter rapture, captivated by the sight of a woman with a cock.

'Do you want me to fuck you?' Elenore asked huskily.

'God, yes.'

Elenore pointed to a mirror across the room. 'Watch yourself in that.'

Gloria stared at the mirror in fascination, loving the sight of herself on her hands and knees, her juicy breasts topped by hard nipples. Elenore smiled and moved behind Gloria again. She was all womanly curves and breasts but, then, after what seemed like an eternity, Gloria felt the head of the phallus teasing the wet folds of her pussy. She drew in a sharp breath of pleasure as Elenore turned the dildo to a low vibration and began to push the second penis into her.

Gloria gave an unmistakable groan of delight as the dildo filled her. The vibrations beat heavily against her inner walls, evoking such intense delight that Gloria had the sudden thought that men might not be terribly necessary after all. Her lips parted on another moan as Elenore began working the phallus back and forth slowly. The glorious friction made Gloria's clitoris throb with the need for release, and she couldn't stop herself from sliding her fingers down to her sex.

'No!' Elenore's sharp voice stopped Gloria's movement.

With a mutter of frustration, Gloria leant on her elbows, closing her eyes against the intensity of sensations created by the dildo. The vibrations seemed to ricochet through her entire body, inflaming her ache to an extreme level. Her fingers clutched tightly at the carpet as she fought to retain control. She was unable to prevent herself from thrusting her hips backwards in an attempt to impale herself on the phallus.

Elenore gave a husky laugh. 'You little slut.'

She began working the phallus faster, her fingers digging into Gloria's arse as she drove herself towards another climax. Gloria stared at the incredible sight of Elenore in the mirror. Her breasts swayed as her hips thrust back and forth like a man's, working herself on one phallus while pleasuring Gloria with the other. Her eyes were half closed, her skin damp with sweat as her thrusting increased. Urgency built in Gloria's body with all the power of a freight train. And then she could stand it no longer; her body couldn't take any more of this delicious assault, and her climax burst over her in waves of rapture so intense that her world became subsumed in pure feeling. She heard Elenore's cry of pleasure as the other woman continued pumping the dildo until she was fully satisfied.

Gloria fought to regain her breath as she turned stunned eyes on Elenore. Elenore smiled and let the dildo fall to the floor. She spread herself out on the couch again, stretching her body like a cat.

'Gloria, that was incredible. I must say, this might not be a bad trade-off after all.'

Gloria stood up and went to make herself another martini. Her entire body continued to pulse with sensation. What a delicious way to combine woman and man. She sipped her martini and gave Elenore a pointed look.

'I should tell you that I'm not willing to be at your beck and call,' she said. 'I don't care what kind of arrangement you had with Logan. Although I'll be more than delighted to indulge myself with you, I have no intentions of letting you take advantage of me.'

To her surprise, Elenore laughed. 'Oh, Gloria, I would hardly expect that of you. You're very much your own woman. Believe me, I know your kind. I happen to be one myself.'

Gloria smiled. She poured Elenore another scotch and joined her on the couch. She discovered that she rather liked the other woman, manipulation and all. A few thoughts began to turn in Gloria's brain. 'By the way, I'm having a dinner party this Friday if you'd like to come.'

Elenore's eyebrows lifted. 'You're inviting me to a dinner party?'

'Don't look so surprised,' Gloria replied. 'And I'm not inviting you out of the goodness of my heart. I intend to recoup my investment, and there will be some people there who might help you with your business. The more successful it is, the better it will be for me.'

Elenore gazed at her for a moment before her lips curved. 'I like you, Gloria. You're a bitch, but I like you.'

Chapter Seventeen

*L*ogan pressed the button to open the gate. As he pulled into the driveway, his gaze went to the car parked near the garage. He frowned. What was Callie doing here? He went inside and left his briefcase near the front door.

'Callie?' Logan went into the kitchen and found it empty. He shrugged and went into the sitting room, his gaze going to the French windows that opened on to the terrace. The doors were wide open, allowing a breeze to ruffle the curtains.

Logan stepped on to the terrace and found his wife in the garden. She was kneeling next to the flowerbed, pulling clumps of weeds from around the pansy plants. She wore a dirt-covered pair of jeans and one of his old shirts. Logan thought that she had never looked better.

'Callie.'

She looked up, brushing her hair out of her eyes with the back of her hand. 'Logan, you might have at least weeded the flowerbeds while I was gone.'

'While you *were* gone?'

Callie dumped another handful of weeds into a bucket and stood up. She brushed off her jeans and watched him approach.

'I'm back,' she admitted.

'For good?' He couldn't quite believe it. 'What brought about this change of heart?'

'I knew you were going to ask me that question,' Callie said. 'And I've spent a lot of time thinking about how to answer it. I admit that I thought about lying to you, but that would be a pretty lousy start to a reconciliation.'

'True enough,' Logan allowed. He reached out to brush a speck of dirt off her chin. 'So what's the real reason?'

'Gloria.' She looked at him, her eyebrows drawing together slightly with concern. 'I told her about Elenore Lawrence. I didn't give her any details, but I did explain that you were being blackmailed. She agreed to help.'

A rush of irritation tightened Logan's muscles. 'You told your sister?'

'Don't get angry with me. Even you have to admit that you were at a loss about what to do. I knew that Gloria could at least try to help.'

'What the hell did she do?'

'She went to talk to Elenore. I don't know exactly what happened since she made me leave, but they worked out a deal. Gloria promised to give Elenore the money as long as she agreed to leave us alone.'

Logan stared at her in shock. 'And Elenore agreed to this?'

'From what Gloria said, yes, she did.' Callie eyed him cautiously. 'I'm sorry I didn't let you know I was going to tell her. I knew you wouldn't approve, but I couldn't think of any other way to help you.'

Logan sat down on one of the terrace steps and tried to understand what Callie was telling him. 'I can't believe this.'

'It's true. Gloria called me last night and told me that she and Elenore were working things out with their lawyers.'

'Why in the love of God would Elenore let me go that

274

easily?' He'd thought that Elenore would keep him dangling on a string for as long as she pleased.

'Maybe she realised that getting the money wasn't a sure thing with you,' Callie suggested. 'But she knew it would be with Gloria.'

'And why did you do this?'

'I wanted to help you. I've been angry with you, but I never wanted to see you ruined. Despite everything, you're still my husband. I care about what happens to you.'

Logan shook his head, still too stunned to believe this was actually happening. 'This is unbelievable.'

'It's the truth.' Callie approached him and sat down next to him. 'But Gloria had a condition for agreeing to help us. She wanted me to come back to you.'

'You mean you're here because she forced you?'

'Partly,' Callie admitted. 'But I suspect that she would have helped even if I was adamant about not coming back.'

'So why weren't you?'

Callie shrugged. 'Our relationship is far from perfect, Logan, but I'm not willing to give up yet.' She glanced at him and added, 'Although I'm still mad at you for kidnapping me.'

'Point taken,' Logan muttered. 'I just ... I wanted to talk to you. Every time we saw each other, we either argued or got interrupted. But I didn't mean that you should come back under duress.'

'It certainly seemed like it sometimes,' Callie replied. 'I left you partly because you were too controlling. I don't want to leave you again for the same reason.'

'I know.' Logan let out his breath in a long sigh. He pinched the bridge of his nose between his fingers and closed his eyes. The slightest spark of hope rose in him, but he refused to let himself believe this was all true.

'Logan.' Callie put her hand on his thigh. 'Gloria is having a dinner party tonight. She wants us both to attend.'

'I really don't –'

'It's the only decent thing to do,' Callie reminded him. 'We owe her a lot, but she did say that Elenore would be there. I think you need to talk to her.'

'I have nothing to say to that woman.'

'I know, but if you want her out of our lives for good, then you have to end it.'

Logan couldn't help noticing Callie's use of the phrase 'our lives.' He opened his eyes and looked at her for a long moment. She was watching him with concern, her brown eyes filled with an emotion that he couldn't identify.

'I'm sorry,' he finally said. 'I went ballistic when I realised that you'd left. I hated living in this house without you. I hated being without you.'

Callie's fingers twined through his. 'Logan, I'm going to ask you a question.'

'All right.'

Callie hesitated. Her hand tightened on his. 'Why did you marry me?'

Logan no longer had to think about that question. He looked at his wife. He could have gazed into those eyes for ever. 'I married you because you were the one good person who ever came into my life and there was no way I was going to let you go. I'm only sorry it took me so long to realise that I love you.'

'Hello, sugars!' A slightly tipsy Gloria opened the door and gave Logan and Callie a big smile. 'Come on in. Logan, do I get a kiss for saving your arse?'

Logan bent to kiss her cheek.

Callie gave him a wry smile. 'You realise, of course, that we're going to be paying for this for the rest of our lives,' she said.

Gloria giggled. 'Don't worry, darlings, I don't expect anything except that you both live a long and happy life together. The key word is *together*.'

She led them into the sitting room, where a group of

276

about ten people sat around drinking and munching on hors d'oeuvres. Logan's gaze went immediately to Elenore Lawrence, who sat perched on a chair near the window. By her side, a silver-haired man gazed at her with a rather rapt expression. Elenore looked away from her admirer and met Logan's eyes.

Callie squeezed Logan's arm. 'I'm going to talk to Ted,' she whispered. 'Find me when you're finished, OK?'

Logan nodded. He walked across the room towards Elenore. For the first time, he didn't experience a wave of disgust at the thought of an encounter with her.

'Elenore.'

She held out her hand as if expecting him to kiss it. 'Logan, hello. This is my new friend, Daniel Franklin.'

Logan shook hands with the other man before turning back to Elenore. 'I need to speak with you.'

'Of course,' she replied smoothly. 'Daniel, will you excuse us for a moment, please?'

He nodded and went towards the bar, giving Logan a slightly hostile look. Logan sat down and levelled a gaze on Elenore.

'Is he one of the new flies caught in your trap?'

She laughed. 'Hardly. However, he certainly wants to be in my trap. So to speak.'

'I hear you've found your investor elsewhere.'

Elenore glanced across the room at Gloria. 'Yes. Callie and her sister are rather extraordinarily different, aren't they?'

'They're half-sisters,' Logan explained. 'And they have very different backgrounds.'

'I admit that I enjoy Gloria,' Elenore said. 'I didn't have a chance to get to know Callie, but she seems sweet. Not the kind of woman I'd have picked as your wife, but sweet nonetheless.'

'What kind of woman did you expect to be my wife?' Logan asked. 'Someone like you?'

'Possibly.'

Logan laughed. 'That would have been one of the universe's biggest jokes.'

'Really, Logan, don't you think you might have married Callie because she was the opposite of the type of women you'd experienced in the past? The refined, well-bred type?'

'That might have been the reason I was attracted to her in the first place,' Logan allowed. 'But it's not the reason I married her. And as it turned out, she's a great deal more refined and well bred than any woman I've known. Women like you only wish you could be like Callie.'

Elenore's eyebrows rose. 'Goodness, Logan. There is no need to slight me. I didn't have to accept Gloria's offer, you know.'

Logan gave her a guarded look. 'Does that mean that you did?'

'Our lawyers have already drawn up contracts,' Elenore replied. 'As Gloria so aptly put it, I knew I had a better chance of getting the money from her rather than you. You can be terribly stubborn.'

'And does that mean that you weren't just out to ruin me?'

'Logan, I have no grudge against you,' Elenore replied. 'I never have had. You provided both me and my husband with enormous amounts of pleasure. Of course, I was quite upset when you decided to leave, but I haven't spent the last fifteen years cultivating ways to enact revenge.'

'Then you have a way with blackmail,' Logan said. 'I assumed you had some vendetta against me.'

'I wanted your money.' Elenore sipped her drink and shrugged. 'I knew you weren't going to give it to me willingly, so I had to think of other ways. Frankly, I didn't know who else to turn to.'

'And you thought that dragging my past into the present would get you two million dollars?'

'Logan, why do you persist in being so hostile about

your past?' Elenore asked. 'You did what you had to do. There's nothing to be ashamed of, for heaven's sake.'

Logan struggled against a sudden rush of images of himself locked in all manner of sexual positions with Elenore and Gerald. He tried not to cringe. That whole episode of his life had been so degrading that he wished he could banish it from his memory.

'Logan?' Elenore gave him a quizzical look. 'You're not ashamed, are you? Because there's no reason to be.'

'What does that mean?'

'Selling sex is just another form of commerce. You were well paid for what you did.' She smiled. 'And, if I recall, you rather enjoyed much if it yourself. Is that what's bothering you?'

'Nothing is bothering me, Elenore. It's just part of my past I'd rather forget about. I don't appreciate your coming back into town and threatening me with it.'

'We all do what we have to do,' she reminded him. 'And you can't forget about your past, dear heart. It's part of who you are now.'

Logan looked across the room at Callie. As much as he still disliked Elenore, he couldn't help wondering if she was right, at least in part. He'd hated his year with the Lawrences and hated himself for letting them use him. When it was over, he'd been determined never to let anyone degrade him again. As a result, he'd kept such tight control on himself that there had never been room for anyone else. Not even his wife.

Elenore reached out and put her hand on his leg. Her expression was oddly compassionate. 'Think about it this way. If you let your past decisions haunt you now, then you'll never be free.'

'Thanks for the psychoanalysis, Elenore.'

She smiled. 'And keep in mind that I love the way you fuck. I'd hate to think you lost that edge.'

Logan thought that the only thing he'd been in danger of losing was his wife. And maybe his sanity. It occurred to him that if Elenore hadn't come back in his life, it might have taken him a hell of a lot longer to come to terms with his relationship with Callie. As it was, Elenore's threats had forced him to confront himself and his feelings for his wife.

'I'll be leaving for Hilton Head next week,' Elenore said. 'I don't suppose you'd be interested in another rendezvous before I leave.'

Logan shook his head. 'No way. We're finished, Elenore. If you come near me or Callie again, I swear you'll regret it.'

Elenore's lips curved. 'This determined attitude of yours is quite attractive. You don't have to worry. Gloria and I have an understanding.'

'Good. And now you and I have one, too. Goodbye, Elenore.' Logan stood up and began walking back to Callie. Daniel Franklin passed him on his way back to Elenore.

'Logan, what did she say to you?' Gloria grasped Logan's arm in passing and pulled him to a halt.

'Nothing important, Gloria. And I know I owe you my eternal gratitude. I promise I'll pay you back.'

Gloria smiled and glanced towards Daniel Franklin and Elenore. 'As much as I'd love having your gratitude, sugar, I might play less of a part in this little drama than I initially thought.'

'What does that mean?'

'Daniel Franklin. He's a shipping magnate. Worth at least half a billion dollars, and he seems to be very taken with Elenore. With my help, he might be persuaded to do a little investing in her venture. That way, I keep my money and she's still out of your life.'

'Gloria, I think I'm actually beginning to respect you.'

She gave a delighted giggle. 'Not so loud! I don't want you ruining my reputation. I'll keep you posted, sugar.'

Logan kissed her cheek again and went to find Callie. She smiled as she saw him approach, but her expression was concerned.

'How did it go?' she asked.

'It went,' Logan replied. 'I don't think she'll bother us again. She's leaving for Hilton Head next week.'

'Are you all right?'

Logan slipped his arm around Callie's waist and pulled her against him. He couldn't imagine ever losing her again. And he would never forget how perilously close he'd come to that. He pressed a kiss against her forehead. 'I'm fine,' he said. 'How about we get out of here?'

Callie nodded. They went back out to the car and drove home. As they walked up the steps to their front door, Callie glanced at Logan.

'So, what did Elenore say?'

'Nothing much, calla lily.' Logan unlocked the door. 'She tried to convince me that I shouldn't be ashamed of my past.'

'Maybe she's right.'

Logan shrugged as they went upstairs to the bedroom. He was cautiously relieved to see that Callie had already unpacked her belongings, although he was bothered by the fact that she'd been coerced into coming home. He stripped off his jacket and shoes, then tugged at the knot of his tie.

'Your sister told me she was hoping something would happen between Elenore and Daniel Franklin,' he remarked.

Callie chuckled. 'She's always been a matchmaker. I have little doubt that she's right, too. Gloria knows how to manage things to her own advantage.'

She gave him a smile as she slipped out of her navy, silk dress, leaving herself clad in a black slip and a pair of navy heels. Logan watched her approach him. Her hair was done up in a twist, her silver jewellery glittering against her pale skin, her nipples pressing against the thin fabric of her slip. Logan's prick hardened with lightening speed. He'd always thought Callie was a lovely woman, but he had never fully appreciated her sensual beauty until recently.

Callie reached up to press her lips against his. Her breath was as warm and sweet as wine. Desire flared inside him. His wife. She was home. Logan slipped his hands over Callie's small breasts, then down to the curve of her hips and around to her firm bottom. With a quick movement, he tugged her against him. Callie drew in a breath as she felt his erection nudging her abdomen. She smiled against his mouth and cupped the hard bulge in her hand.

'I love this instant response,' she murmured. 'But this time, I don't want you to do anything. Promise?'

Logan felt a mixture of aversion and a desire to please her. He no longer wanted to be trapped by his past, but years of self-restraint weren't easily allayed. He reached up to take the pins out of Callie's hair, watching it fall into shimmering waves to her shoulders.

He nodded. 'Promise.'

She squeezed his prick and parted her lips underneath his. Her tongue played with slow insistence over his teeth as she began to unfasten the buttons of his shirt. Her warm hands slipped between the folds to stroke his skin and fondle his flat nipples. Logan's apprehension quickly disappeared as he watched her, loving the growing flush on her skin and the way she touched him with such tender yet aggressive designs. He realised he'd had no reason to fear old memories, because they had nothing to do with Callie. Nothing could taint his relationship with her as long as he didn't allow it to.

He watched as Callie pushed his shirt off and painted a path over his chest with her moist tongue. Excitement quickened his blood. Her breath was hot on his skin. Callie's hands went to the fly of his trousers, which she unzipped with rapid motions. After she had rid him of the trousers and briefs, she went down on her knees in front of him and grasped his cock in her hand. Logan tensed. He was highly aroused by the sight of her kneeling in front of him, her eyes dark with hunger as she eyed his stiff prick, but something ugly pushed at the back of his mind. How many times had he been forced to let Gerald or Elenore do this?

Callie's tongue darted out to lick her lips as she glanced up at him. 'I know you never wanted me to do this, Logan. I think I understand why, but I'm not them.'

Logan threaded his hands through her hair. His cock throbbed. He wanted this, wanted his wife to take him in the hot cavern of her mouth and suck him dry. He nodded. 'I know.'

Callie's lips curved before she grasped his shaft and drew him towards her mouth. Warm, wet heat enclosed Logan as Callie eased his cock into her mouth, her tongue stroking the sensitive underside as she took him in. Logan's hands tightened on her hair as heat scorched him. He'd never realised that she knew how to do this with such tender finesse. Her hand came up to cup his balls, caressing them gently as she sucked him in deeper, so deep that he felt wholly surrounded by her. No, this was nothing like the sick feeling he'd had with the Lawrences. This was all want and need. Callie's movements felt almost loving as she pulled back and licked the knob of his cock before she took him in again. She repeated the movement, fucking him with her mouth as her hands came around to clutch his buttocks. Logan groaned. Pressure built. His hands gripped her head.

'Callie, wait,' he gasped.

She looked up at him, her breathing rapid. 'Isn't it good?'

'Oh Christ, baby, you're amazing. But I don't –'

Callie interrupted him with a shake of her head. 'You're not supposed to do anything, Logan. Don't forget.'

Her eyes gleamed as she leaned forward to take his cock in again. Logan almost winced as the sensation of her tongue drove him closer and closer to the edge. An ache began at the base of his penis, building like the force of a volcano. With a groan, his hips thrust forward as his entire body craved the enclosure of Callie's mouth.

Her lips began sliding faster and faster over his shaft. Logan's fingers tightened on her hair as he pushed forwards and let himself fall over the edge. He shot powerfully into her mouth, his hips working as he thrust into her. Callie didn't flinch; she only pulled him closer and greedily drank every drop. Then she pulled away, stroking her tongue lightly over the engorged tip of his prick before giving him a sultry smile.

'Nice,' she murmured. 'I like it when you let me do what I want.'

Logan drew in a shaky breath and sank down on to the bed. Sensations continued to pulse through him. 'I could get used to that, too.'

Callie stretched out next to him and ran her hand lazily through his chest hair. She had a contented look on her face that reminded him of a sated cat. He rolled on to his side and propped his head on his hand. He cupped her silk-covered breast in his other palm, flicking his thumb over her rigid nipple. He wasn't surprised when his prick stirred again.

'Uh uh,' Callie scolded gently. 'You're not supposed to do anything.'

'You mean you're not finished?'

'Not by a long shot.' She tugged her slip over her hips and pulled down her dark blue knickers.

Logan put his hand on her thigh, hoping she'd decide to forget her dictate, but Callie swatted his hand away. She moved her shoulder slightly so that one of the thin straps slipped down her arm and exposed the gentle swell of her breast. She closed her eyes, slowly sliding her fingers underneath the crevices of her breasts and up to her nipples. As she circled the tight buds with languid movements, Logan watched her with an increasing wave of lust. Callie's hands moved down to her pussy, spreading her legs as she stroked her forefinger into the damp folds. Logan was unable to take his eyes off her, captivated by the slow movements of her fingers and the way her body arched to meet the caress of her fingers. His hand moved to his groin, rubbing the thickening stalk of his penis.

Callie opened her eyes to look at him, smiling at the sight of his erection. 'You planning on doing something with that?'

'I was hoping you would.'

Callie got to her knees and pushed him back on the bed, straddling his hips as she lowered herself slowly. His penis bulged up towards her. Callie shifted her hips slightly to rub herself against him. The heat of her pussy nearly undid him. Callie splayed her palms over his chest, stroking his muscles and rubbing his nipples. Logan curled the straps of her slip around his fingers and drew them down to expose her breasts. Desire filled him as he palmed her breasts, massaging and squeezing them. Callie leant forwards to give him better access.

'Go on,' she whispered. 'You know what to do.'

Logan closed his lips around her right nipple. Callie drew in a sharp breath as his tongue flicked over the tip. She braced one hand next to his head on the pillow, closing her eyes as she enjoyed what he was doing to her. His hips bucked upward, his cock pressing more insistently into her pussy. Logan's heart throbbed as Callie moved back on to his thighs, grasping his shaft as she positioned herself above him.

Slowly, she eased herself down on to him and leaned forwards with a little whimper, bracing her hands on his chest as she began to pump her hips up and down. Wet silk enclosed Logan's cock like a glove. God, he loved this sensation of being totally buried inside her. He grasped her hips to hold her in place as she rode out her pleasure, loving the sight of her over him, her breasts swaying and her face contorted with pleasure.

Sweat broke out on Callie's skin as she worked herself with increasing frenzy on his cock, harder and faster until she cried out, digging her fingernails into Logan's chest. The feeling of her pussy clenching around him drove Logan to the edge. He thrust his hips urgently upwards as he propelled himself towards another explosive release.

Callie splayed her body over his, her chest heaving as her mouth descended on his for a deep kiss. Logan stroked her back.

Callie lifted her head to gaze down at him. 'See? It can be nice to let someone else do the work sometimes.'

'Amen to that,' Logan murmured. He brushed his finger against her moist lips. 'So does all this mean you're back for good?'

'Did you mean it when you said you loved me?'

Logan nodded. 'I meant it, even though I've been lousy about expressing it. But I'm not thrilled that you're back because Gloria forced you into it.'

Callie rolled off him and on to her back. She stared up at the ceiling for a long moment. 'I never wanted to give up on you, Logan. Leaving you just finally seemed like the only way I could get you to hear me.'

'Do you think it worked?'

'Do you?' she retorted.

'Yes,' Logan admitted. 'I'm bull-headed, stubborn, dictatorial and a pompous ass. I heard all that quite clearly.'

Callie smiled. 'And does that mean you understand why I left?'

'I know I can be a bastard, calla lily. But I meant it when I said I don't want to lose you.'

'And I don't want to be lost, but that's what was starting to happen. So I had to leave.'

'I know. I'm sorry I forced you.'

Callie propped herself up to look at him, stroking her hand over his chest. 'Well, sometimes you have to leave in order to find your way home again.'

Chapter Eighteen

A breeze of fresh, salt-scented air wafted in from the ocean as Callie slipped out of her shoes and dug her feet into the sand. The sea stretched out alongside the beach like a mirror of the black, star-dotted sky. Voices drifted from the peristyle, where people were busy setting up for the ceremony.

'It didn't exactly happen the way I'd expected it to,' Callie said. She polished off a piece of sweet potato pie and looked at Abiona. 'And I'm still trying to come to terms with what he told me. I sometimes wonder if I ever will.'

The voodoo priestess smiled. She looked radiant in a pure white gown and turban that made her dark skin glow. 'You will, child. You are stronger than you know. I believe that is why your husband needs you so badly.'

Logan needed her? Callie had never thought of it that way. She shrugged. 'I know it won't be easy. He's been so withdrawn for so many years that the shield might go up again any minute. I've never seen him the way he's been during our estrangement, but now that I'm back . . .' Her voice trailed off.

'Callie, I do not think that Logan would risk losing

you again,' Abiona said. 'Quite frankly, he wouldn't want to go through the hell of it a second time.'

'Neither would I,' Callie replied. Well, she might be willing to go through certain parts of it again. A shiver raced up her spine.

'Hey, Callie, did you bring the incense?' Adam came stumbling over the sand, nearly tripping over his loafers. 'I wanted to show it to Kadja.'

'Yes, it's in my bag.' Callie pulled out the package and handed it to him.

'So, you and Logan are really back together again?' Adam sounded both pleased and slightly forlorn.

Callie nodded. 'We really are.'

'Are you leaving the shop?'

'No, of course not. I'm still going to work there.'

'If you're back with Logan, that must mean you figured out whether or not you love him,' Adam said.

A sudden warmth towards her husband filled Callie's heart. 'Yes. I figured that out.'

Adam glanced around and shuffled his feet. 'Is Logan here with you?'

'Yes, he's around.' Callie couldn't help smiling at the young man's attempt to hide his eagerness. 'I'm sure he'd like to see you.'

'Really? You think so?'

Callie spotted her husband standing near the peristyle, talking to one of the drummers. 'Logan,' she called. 'Could you come here, please?'

He glanced up and approached her, his gait slow and easy. His gaze went to Adam. Callie waited as Logan took in Adam's pierced ears, eyebrows, nose and lip. To her relief, he didn't comment.

'Hello, Adam.'

'Logan ... uh, sir.' Adam flushed and held out his hand. Logan shook it.

'I kind of wanted to apologise for being in the show and all,' Adam went on.

Logan shrugged. 'No need to apologise. You have a right to do what you want with your own time.'

Adam fairly gaped at him. 'You mean you're not mad at me?'

'Well, I doubt I'll be attending another one of your performances, but I'm not mad at you, no.'

'Good,' Adam said, looking quite relieved. 'Because I'm really sorry I didn't tell you. I know it could have hurt the firm.'

'It's a pity you're not going to be a lawyer,' Logan said. 'You would have made a good one.'

Adam beamed with pleasure. 'Really? Thanks, but I'm pretty happy working at the shop and stuff. Tess is great.'

'I imagine she is.' Logan glanced towards Tess, who was busy doling out portions of casserole. 'Is she still slightly unhinged?'

'Logan,' Callie admonished.

'Oh, yes, sir,' Adam replied happily. 'That's why I love her.'

Callie chuckled. A smile even moved Logan's lips. He reached out and gave Adam a squeeze on the shoulder.

'Good luck to you, Adam. You and Tess will have to come for dinner one night.'

Adam glowed. 'Thank you, sir. That would be exquisite.'

He trotted off towards Tess with a distinct spring in his step. Logan looked at Callie.

'Exquisite?' he repeated.

Callie grinned. 'Adam thinks very highly of you, in case you couldn't tell.'

The ritual drums began to pound out a simple rhythm as the crowd began to move towards the peristyle. Abiona rose and held out her hand to Logan.

'I am so pleased to see you have worked out your troubles,' she said.

Logan glanced at Callie. 'I am, too. Thank you for your help.'

Abiona smiled and kissed his cheek before drifting off towards the peristyle. Callie watched her go, then looked at Logan.

'You know, you never told me why you went to see her.'

Logan shrugged. 'Desperation, I guess. I thought maybe she could help with the whole Elenore debacle.'

'And did she?'

'She certainly tried.'

Callie suspected there was something he wasn't telling her, but she didn't press him. They certainly couldn't reveal all their secrets at once. She stood and brushed sand off her skirt before she and Logan began walking towards the peristyle. As the drumbeat began rising in volume and complexity, chanted prayers emerged into the night as if from the very earth itself. The air began to vibrate with primitive music.

Logan pulled Callie against his body and pressed his lips against her hair. 'Will you dance for me?' he murmured.

She smiled. 'Yes. I'm so glad you decided to come with me tonight.'

'This is infinitely more interesting than the dinner party we were supposed to attend,' Logan admitted.

'Most things are,' Callie replied dryly.

Logan chuckled. 'True enough.' His hands moved down to her hips as he tugged her closer. He bent his head to brush his lips against hers. 'I love you.'

Callie smiled again. He had been telling her that often lately, as if he were making up for years past. Callie slipped her arms around Logan's waist and hugged him. She was beyond grateful that he was easing into a new relationship with her, one based on love and trust. She knew they still had to work on their relationship, but he had been more open, honest and receptive to both her and himself than he'd ever been before.

And Callie realised that this Logan, the one who was

finally emerging, was the man she knew she had married all along. She leant her head against her husband's chest and listened as the heady sound of the drums began to merge with the beating of his heart.

Epilogue

*A*biona lit the third candle and knelt in front of the altar. She had always felt the spirits strongly, even as a child years before her initiation. A small, wooden idol of Ghede looked back at her. The *loa* exuded an aura of mischief and carnality. In front of him lay a dish of nuts, a package of cigarettes, a small bottle of gin and two cloth dolls bound together face-to-face with a silk thread. Abiona picked up the two dolls and smiled. She sprinkled them with orange-flower water and murmured a prayer.

Logan and Callie's path wouldn't always be easy, but Abiona knew that they would work out their troubles together. The *loas* would continue to watch over the couple with all their emotions, secrets and stubbornness. After all, the *loas* had once been humans themselves. They knew well the difficulties involved. Abiona placed the two dolls in front of the altar, blessed them and gave their fates to the spirits.

BLACK LACE NEW BOOKS

Published in April

SAUCE FOR THE GOOSE
Mary Rose Maxwell
£5.99

Sauce for the Goose is a riotous and sometimes humorous celebration of the rich variety of human sexuality. Imaginative and colourful, each story explores a different theme or fantasy, and the result is a fabulously bawdy mélange of cheeky sensuality and hot thrills. A lively array of characters display an uninhibited and lusty energy for boundary-breaking pleasure. This is a decidedly X-rated collection of stories designed to be enjoyed and indulged in.

ISBN 0 352 33492 4

HARD CORPS
Claire Thompson
£5.99

Remy Harris, a bright young army cadet at a prestigious military college, hopes to become an officer. She understands that she will have to endure all the usual trials of military life, including boot-camp discipline and rigorous exercise. She's ready for the challenge – that is until she meets Jacob, who recognises her true sexuality and initiates her into the Hard Corps – a secret society within the barracks.

ISBN 0 352 33491 6

Published in May

INTENSE BLUE
Lyn Wood
£5.99

When Nan and Megan attend a residential art course as a 40th birthday present to themselves, they are plunged into a claustrophobic world of bizarre events and eccentric characters. There is a strong sexual undercurrent to the place, and it seems that many of the tutors are having affairs with their students – and each other. Nan gets caught up in a mystery she has to solve, but playing amateur detective only leads her into increasingly strange and sexual situations in this sometimes hilarious story of two women on a mission to discover what they really want in their lives.

ISBN 0 352 33496 7

THE NAKED TRUTH
Natasha Rostova
£5.99

Callie feels trapped living among the 'old money' socialites of the Savannah district. Her husband Logan is remote, cold and repressed – even if he does have an endless supply of money. One day she leaves him. Determined to change her life she hides out at her sister's place. Meanwhile Logan has hired a detective and is determined to get his wife back. But she is now treading a path of self-expression, and even getting into the ancient art of Voodoo. Will he want her back when he finds her? And what will she do when she learns the naked truth about Logan's shady past?

ISBN 0 352 33497 5

To be published in June

ANIMAL PASSIONS
Martine Marquand
£5.99

Nineteen-year-old Jo runs away from the strict household where she's been brought up, and is initiated into a New Age pagan cult located in a rural farming community in England. Michael, the charismatic shaman leader, invites Jo to join him in a celebration of unbridled passion. As the summer heat intensifies, preparations are made for the midsummer festival, and Jo is keen to play a central role in the cult's bizarre rites. Will she ever want to return to normal society?

ISBN 0 352 33499 1

IN THE FLESH
Emma Holly
£5.99

Topless dancer Chloe is better at being bad than anyone David Imakita knows. To keep her, this Japanese American businessman risks everything he owns: his career, his friends, his integrity. But will this unrepentant temptress overturn her wild ways and accept an opportunity to change her life, or will the secrets of her past resurface and destroy them both?

ISBN 0 352 33498 3

NO LADY
Saskia Hope
£5.99

30-year-old Kate walks out of her job, dumps her boyfriend and goes in search of adventure. And she finds it. Held captive in the Pyrenees by a bunch of outlaws involved in smuggling art treasures, she finds the lovemaking is as rough as the landscape. Only a sense of danger can satisfy her ravenous passions, but she also has some plans of her own. A Black Lace special reprint.

ISBN 0 352 32857 6

If you would like a complete list of plot summaries of Black Lace titles, or would like to receive information on other publications available, please send a stamped addressed envelope to:

Black Lace, Thames Wharf Studios,
Rainville Road, London W6 9HA

BLACK LACE BOOKLIST

All books are priced £5.99 unless another price is given.

Black Lace books with a contemporary setting

RIVER OF SECRETS £4.99	Saskia Hope & Georgia Angelis ISBN 0 352 32925 4	☐
THE NAME OF AN ANGEL £6.99	Laura Thornton ISBN 0 352 33205 0	☐
BONDED £4.99	Fleur Reynolds ISBN 0 352 33192 5	☐
CONTEST OF WILLS	Louisa Francis ISBN 0 352 33223 9	☐
FEMININE WILES £7.99	Karina Moore ISBN 0 352 33235 2	☐
DARK OBSESSION £7.99	Fredrica Alleyn ISBN 0 352 33281 6	☐
COOKING UP A STORM £7.99	Emma Holly ISBN 0 352 33258 1	☐
THE TOP OF HER GAME	Emma Holly ISBN 0 352 33337 5	☐
VILLAGE OF SECRETS	Mercedes Kelly ISBN 0 352 33344 8	☐
PACKING HEAT	Karina Moore ISBN 0 352 33356 1	☐
TAKING LIBERTIES	Susie Raymond ISBN 0 352 33357 X	☐
LIKE MOTHER, LIKE DAUGHTER	Georgina Brown ISBN 0 352 33422 3	☐
ASKING FOR TROUBLE	Kristina Lloyd ISBN 0 352 33362 6	☐
A DANGEROUS GAME	Lucinda Carrington ISBN 0 352 33432 0	☐
THE TIES THAT BIND	Tesni Morgan ISBN 0 352 33438 X	☐
IN THE DARK	Zoe le Verdier ISBN 0 352 33439 8	☐
BOUND BY CONTRACT	Helena Ravenscroft ISBN 0 352 33447 9	☐

VELVET GLOVE	Emma Holly ISBN 0 352 33448 7	☐
STRIPPED TO THE BONE	Jasmine Stone ISBN 0 352 33463 0	☐
DOCTOR'S ORDERS	Deanna Ashford ISBN 0 352 33453 3	☐
SHAMELESS	Stella Black ISBN 0 352 33485 1	☐
TONGUE IN CHEEK	Tabitha Flyte ISBN 0 352 33484 3	☐
FIRE AND ICE	Laura Hamilton ISBN 0 352 33486 X	☐
SAUCE FOR THE GOOSE	Mary Rose Maxwell ISBN 0 352 33492 4	☐
HARD CORPS	Claire Thompson ISBN 0 352 33491 6	☐

Black Lace books with an historical setting

THE INTIMATE EYE £4.99	Georgia Angelis ISBN 0 352 33004 X	☐
GOLD FEVER £4.99	Louisa Francis ISBN 0 352 33043 0	☐
FORBIDDEN CRUSADE £4.99	Juliet Hastings ISBN 0 352 33079 1	☐
A VOLCANIC AFFAIR £4.99	Xanthia Rhodes ISBN 0 352 33184 4	☐
SAVAGE SURRENDER	Deanna Ashford ISBN 0 352 33253 0	☐
INVITATION TO SIN £6.99	Charlotte Royal ISBN 0 352 33217 4	☐
A FEAST FOR THE SENSES	Martine Marquand ISBN 0 352 33310 3	☐

Black Lace anthologies

PANDORA'S BOX	ISBN 0 352 33074 0	☐
PANDORA'S BOX 3	ISBN 0 352 33274 3	☐
WICKED WORDS	Various ISBN 0 352 33363 4	☐
SUGAR AND SPICE £7.99	Various ISBN 0 352 33227 1	☐
THE BEST OF BLACK LACE	Various ISBN 0 352 33452 5	☐
CRUEL ENCHANTMENT Erotic Fairy Stories	Janine Ashbless ISBN 0 352 33483 5	☐
WICKED WORDS 2	Various ISBN 0 352 33487 8	☐

Black Lace non-fiction

THE BLACK LACE BOOK OF
   WOMEN'S SEXUAL
   FANTASIES

Ed. Kerri Sharp

ISBN 0 352 33346 4

☐

--------✂--------------------

Please send me the books I have ticked above.

Name ....

Address ....

....

....

.... Post Code ....

Send to: **Cash Sales, Black Lace Books, Thames Wharf Studios, Rainville Road, London W6 9HA.**

US customers: for prices and details of how to order books for delivery by mail, call 1-800-805-1083.

Please enclose a cheque or postal order, made payable to **Virgin Publishing Ltd**, to the value of the books you have ordered plus postage and packing costs as follows:

UK and BFPO – £1.00 for the first book, 50p for each subsequent book.

Overseas (including Republic of Ireland) – £2.00 for the first book, £1.00 for each subsequent book.

If you would prefer to pay by VISA, ACCESS/MASTER-CARD, DINERS CLUB, AMEX or SWITCH, please write your card number and expiry date here:

....

Please allow up to 28 days for delivery.

Signature ....

--------✂--------------------